THE VAULT

THE VAULT

SERAPHINE'S CHOSEN
BOOK TWO

CARA NOX

STELLA CHARTA PRESS

THE VAULT

For more information on the publisher, including upcoming releases, preorder bonuses, giveaways, and more, visit stellachartapress.com.
For more details on the author and their works, visit caranox.com.

For those who keep going, no matter how bleak.

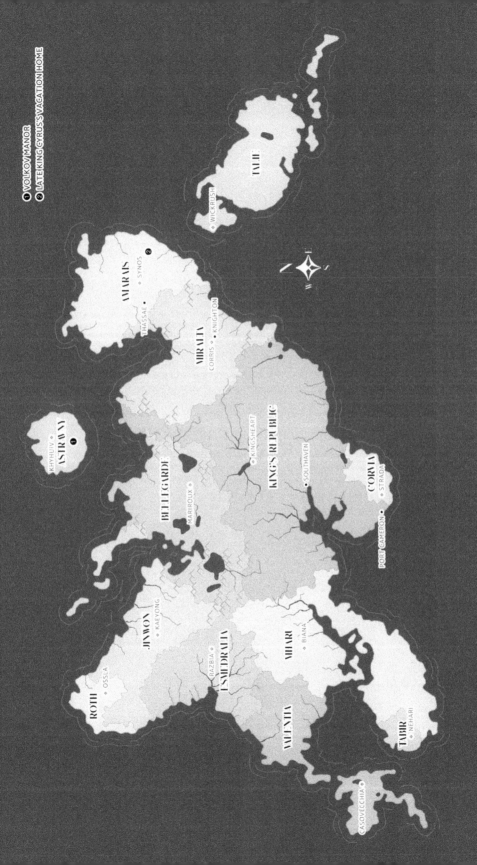

VOLKOV MANOR

LATE KING CYRUS'S VACATION HOME

ASTRANA

KHYHUIV

ROTH

OSSLA

JINWON

KAEYONG

BELLEGARDE

MARROUX

AMARUS

SYNOS

THASSAE

MIRVELA

CORRIS

KNIGHTON

KING'S REPUBLIC

KINGSHEART

SOUTHAVEN

CORVIA

STRADA

PORT CAMERON

TAEJI

WICKRUSH

ESMELDRAEH

RAZBIA

VALENTIA

MIHARI

BIANA

TABIR

NEHARI

CASOVECCHIA

CONTENT WARNINGS

I've attempted to compile a list of prominent warning keywords to the best of my ability. However, since I'm only human, it's very possible I've glossed over something that could be sensitive to you. Please use your own discretion when reading and only continue if you feel safe to do so.

This story contains: alcohol, anxiety, blood, childhood trauma, death, depression, discrimination, mention of drug use, emotional abuse, gore, grief, loss, manipulation, murder, parental neglect, physical abuse, suicidal thoughts, violence, and mention of vomiting.

THE VAULT

1

TALIE ✦ 2704-12-17

GLACIER

The comforting warmth of the fireplace woke Glacier like a hug—a deceptive welcome to the disarray that greeted him. Dull portraits watched him rise to his feet, dust stirred in his wake, and dread followed him into the hall, where his reflection stared back at him from the blackened glass. An eerie stillness stretched beyond the house to the untouched snow outside, barely visible past the bright lights of the corridor.

He started toward the office, shivering with every creak of the floor. "Kat?" he asked, swallowing the last of her name. Too loud.

"I'm right here."

Glacier jolted, spinning around to where she stood behind him, her arms folded over her chest.

"It seems you still haven't fixed anything yet."

"Where were you?" he asked. "Did you really send my dad here?"

"Yes. I thought it would help. Clearly, it didn't."

"I thought you were mad at me for ignoring you—"

"Oh, please, let's not act like you weren't."

"I wasn't—"

"Then why isn't this damn house fixed yet, Glacier?"

He threw up his hands, letting them fall with a sigh as his collapsed against the wall.

Useless, aren't you?

Kat's face softened into pity, her own arms untangling in her reach for him. "Glacier..." She squeezed his shoulder. "Gods... I feel like it's so obvious, and you're trying to explain it all away. I wish I could give you all the answers, but I can't. You have to seek them out—"

He scoffed, shoving her hand away. "What do you think I've been trying to do?" It didn't sound nearly as angry as he'd hoped, instead hitting a sad note that reverberated through him, begging for escape. So, he turned to the office doors.

"Glacier, wait—"

Glacier threw his body into the doors, catching himself as they flung open to light hurtling around the room. He froze, staring up at the pendant lamp, mesmerized by the way it violently spun. Shadows ungulated in the corners, creeping forward and back like lapping waves threatening to pool against the furniture. Cool air tickled his skin.

"*Shit!*" Kat darted past him, throwing the window shut.

"Wh- why was the window open?"

She twisted around and pointed at the desk while half-fumbling with the latch. "Check the drawer. Make sure all of the keys are still there—the locked one too, don't forget it."

His body finally moved then, but each action turned shaky. He slid the first drawer free. *Eleven, twelve, thirteen...* He dropped to his knees and tugged on the bottom handle. It blinked red. "They're all here, and the bottom drawer's still locked. What's going on?"

"Something got inside, but we caught it before it could get all the way into the rest of the house," she said, sounding breathless as she ran her fingers over one of the bookshelves, muttering numbers and titles. "Glacier, this is why I was worried. Things are falling apart, which means that it won't be long before *that*—or something like that—will find another place to break in."

He watched her continue down the line, checking piece after piece while he rose to his feet. His sights remained locked on the window, filled with desire to glimpse what had crawled past his childhood safe haven— over a cushioned bench once cluttered with toys. Swallowing, he crept over to it, cupping his hands around his eyes to peer out into the dark, snowy void.

Nothing.

No signs of footprints or disturbances around the house. Whatever it was, it was long gone, leaving without a trace.

"I don't see anything out there," he whispered, his breath obscuring the glass.

That is, until he found two, shining pinpricks cutting through the night. Like eyes staring back at him.

Glacier shot up in bed, gasping for air and trying to tamp down the sudden panic of it being *too dark.*

"Wha- What's going on?" Cecilia popped up from her pillow, sounding groggy.

"N-nothing. Just a nightmare," he whispered, forcing the wobble from his voice. "Everything's fine."

She sank back into the mattress and gently patted his forearm with a yawn. "Go back to sleep."

The bed complained as he laid back down. Cecilia's breathing grew steady, but he stared up at the ceiling. All the vague talk of grimoires and daemons had gotten under his skin and slithered into his dreams. Thinking about the keys didn't help either, not when they were all connected. Strung together in the perfect tapestry depicting the apocalypse. It might as well have matched the one hanging out in the apartment's living room—the lighthouse a disturbing representation of Noa in Lazarus's visions—whatever they'd been.

He turned his head to the door, staring at the faint blue outline of the natural light cutting through from the hallway. His legs swung over the side of the bed, and he padded out into the quiet stillness of the early morning.

Glacier rubbed his arms as he passed the arch windows, spotted with pattering rain, and stopped at the threshold to the living room. Noa sat in the middle of the sofa, her face bleached to a deathly hue from the light of the tablet in her hands. She looked up and scooted over—a silent invitation he took and settled into the cushion beside hers.

"Do... do you think Nyx is right?" he whispered.

"No, because I don't want her to be right."

He sank further down into the couch. "There was... something wrong with Adam."

"Clearly."

"No, I mean—" He tilted his head back. "Maybe it was a trick of the light or something, but I swore that I saw something wrong with his eyes."

"Maybe it was just your imagination? I didn't notice anything weird, outside of his orders in Astravnian."

"Speaking of... You're Astravnian, aren't you?"

She let out a short, quiet laugh. "I'm not."

"You're lying."

"Why? Because I'm Volkov? And the Volkov clearly must live in Astravny because it's an Astravnian word? Try again."

"No. You're Astravnian because you match the build. You also said that you came from a poor family who could barely survive. That, and while you were able to pull off a Bellegardian accent back in Miralta for that guy at the border, it still wasn't anywhere *close* to how easily you slipped into Astravnian like that. Don't lie to me and tell me you aren't. You're either from King's, and your parents were Astravnian, or you're actually from Astravny."

Her eyes widened, finally letting out a nervous chuckle. "Okay. You caught me. I'm Astravnian. Happy?"

"Are the Volkov located in Astravny too?"

"Now *that* is a little too much information," she said, frowning. "Not only do you not need to know where the Volkov live, but it's a rather bold assumption to say that they're in Astravny with no evidence."

He looked away, quietly admitting defeat. She was right. It was still an assumption, considering the others weren't necessarily from Astravny either. "You... mentioned that Kole is Amaraian, right? Where are the others from?"

"Do you mean where they're *from*, or where they *appear* to be from?"

"Appearance. I think I'd rather know about what they look like, so I know who to look for."

"Not so you can make another hypothesis?" Her mouth ticking up at the corner with amusement, dampened by his serious look. She sighed. "Fine. Ezra was Astravnian like me and two others—they're blood siblings, Kole's Amaraian, and the youngest is Jinwonese. Myron... looks like a mix of something... Talican with a couple other places mixed in that blend a little too finely together."

"Fantastic..."

"I would mainly keep an eye out for Kole. We'll have bigger problems if the rest start showing up."

His shoulders slumped. "How typical that the Amaraian wants me dead," he mumbled.

CECILIA

Cecilia cracked open her door, swallowing when she saw Noa prowling down the hall. "Noa—" she hissed, watching her spin around. "I need help with the back of my dress."

"Let me guess," Noa mumbled, tugging on the fabric of her own and rolling her eyes, "it's another subtle, black thing. Honestly, I'm over it."

Grimacing, Cecilia pulled the door the rest of the way open and blushed when Noa's mouth hung open. "Oh, damn."

"Would you hurry up and get in here?" she begged, she shot a quick glance up and down the hall.

Noa shut the door behind her, and Cecilia hunched in on herself, noting how she wasn't looking her in the face anymore. Admittedly, the sapphire blue princess gown was now the prettiest thing she'd ever worn. It'd stopped her heart when she'd pulled it from its cover and felt the silky fabric between her fingertips. Each gem sewn into it glittered like the twinkling garden lights she'd glimpsed in the days leading up to the last party in the palace.

Her face heated. "Stop it," she said, her voice wavering in her attempt to sound irritated. "I should've just asked you to get Nyx or Glacier."

Noa's straighter, immediately shaking her head. "No, no—just turn around."

"What? So you can enjoy the view?"

"No!" she protested a little *too* quickly. "I mean... maybe a *little*." Noa tossed her clutch onto the bed. "Come on. Turn around."

Cecilia hiked up the skirt of her dress and spun around. Noa helped her hair over her shoulder and started running her fingers over the clasps.

"It doesn't even have a damn zipper... Rune is going to be pissed once he realized he won't be able to rip this off you."

"*Noa!*"

"What? If I'm thinking it, then I know he'll be. *Damn* does he have good taste..."

Cecilia buried her head in her hands.

"The dress is gorgeous, by the way. The color brings out your eyes." The snap of the final clasp came with a gentle pat on the back. "See? I can be nice."

When she half-turned to gauge Noa's expression, she found one of pride, rather than sincerity, like she should be rewarded for keeping her hands to herself. Cecilia slapped her arm.

"*Ow—*" Noa's recoiled. "Bitch, here I am helping you and giving you compliments, and you have the *audacity*—No. No, you know what, *fine*. I've changed my mind. I don't want you anymore. Maybe I'll go back to Rune."

"I hear his brother is free," Cecilia said, fidgeting with her gloves.

Noa gagged as she reclaimed her things and opened the door. "Come on, killer. Let's save the catfight for later so you can get to your escort, and I can join my... well... *escort* if you catch my drift."

Noa led the way down the hall, leaving Cecilia on her heels. Her footsteps tapped softly in comparison to Noa's strides—how she entered the living room with her head held high. But every eye moved from her to Cecilia, even when she hovered in the doorway.

Noa hooked her arm through Crow's. "Close your mouth, you'll catch flies."

He staggered behind her, tripping and cursing on their way out the door until three souls remained. Nyx and Glacier ducked their heads, returning to their work with hushed mutterings. Then there was one.

Rune in his simple black suit—a perfect match to Crow's, though she preferred how he carried himself in it. He stood regal yet relaxed, a member of the royal council plucked straight from home, even if his Bellegardian coloring didn't match the part.

You're above your station tonight. Step into the shoes of the person you want to be.

Her white gloves dug into the fabric as she started forward. Blonde hair fell over her shoulder in a cascading waterfall, obscuring her vision when she passed him, but the way his dark eyes followed her with awe stayed seared in her mind.

"Gods help me," he whispered, sending heat flooding her cheeks before he moved to get the door for her.

NOA

"Did you see—" Crow started, staring back behind them like he might catch another glimpse of Cecilia.

"How hot she was?" Noa finished. "Yes. Now shut up and keep walking." She gripped his arm a little tighter, nearly dragging him down the street.

"I can't believe that Rune gets to have her on his arm while I just get—"

"You shouldn't finish that thought," she said through gritted teeth. "Though, I at least got the satisfaction of helping her into her dress." She let a sly smile creep onto her face.

"That's not fair." He scowled.

"Life's not fair. Get used to it. But while we're on that topic... Glacier's off-limits, and if I catch you even *looking* at him like that again, Rune will be an only child."

"Noted," he mumbled.

"Back to business, then. Play this like Corvia. We just need to make our way into the museum while avoiding patrols and cameras. No tours to work around this time."

"Sounds like a walk in the park." He flashed her a grin.

"Just what I would expect from you," she said, patting his arm. "Now at least try to act like you like me, okay?"

He pulled his arm from her grip and wrapped it around her waist—an act that Noa wasn't a huge fan of, but he was technically doing as he was instructed. She leaned into him and slowed her steps to match the beat of the instrumental melodies pouring out of public spaces for the event. They wove through small crowds of would-be fireworks watchers and parade attendees dressed in everything from jackets and jeans to suits and dresses, much like them. But all walked under the twinkling overhead lights strung from lampposts, as dazzling and bright as the prospect of a new year.

CECILIA

The hum of excitement in the main hall set off fluttering in Cecilia's stomach. Every grouping of guests tapping their glasses to one another's in an early toast or retelling some animated story set her at ease. The suffocating atmosphere she'd stepped into during the event back in Corvia was replaced with something a little more hopeful—whether that was due to her past nerves or the fact that her arm was now looped through her *boyfriend's*, she wasn't sure. For all she knew, it could've been the sparkling rose gold-framed mirrors breaking up the wall tapestries depicting ruins, ships, and sheep scattered through fields.

Rune gave her hand a squeeze, anchoring her again. She soaked in the room while they walked, watching each group, each waiter, each unsettling shift of a guard along the walls. Cecilia pulled down on his arm, lifting herself up to whisper in his ear. "I think the woman at the entrance has a panic button."

He flagged down one of the waitstaff for drinks before braving a glance back to what she'd seen: a woman with red hair pulled back in a severe bun holding a tablet. Her blouse didn't quite hide the cheap bead chain around her neck.

"I think you're right," he mumbled into his glass. "Control panel on your right." Rune maneuvered them for a better view of one of the tapestries: a crumbling monument under a dark sky with the faded image of a woman woven out of the specks of stars. Two guards stood in front of the roped-off archway next to it, leading into the depths of the museum, where the security panel glowed a faint blue just inside the entrance.

The lights dimmed, and silence rolled over the room, calling everyone's attention to the upper-level balcony at the end, drenched in spotlight.

"Welcome, my dearest friends, patrons, and saints!" boomed the man at its center, his coppery hair slicked back and brushing his crisp, white dress shirt collar. "Let us say our farewells to the past year and ring in the new year of 2705!"

The crowd erupted into applause and cheers, nearly drowning out Nyx's signal for Noa and Crow to make their way inside.

CROW

Crow basked in the noise echoing through the courtyard, tumbling through the open glass doors every several minutes. Applause, cheers, laughter—they all might as well have been for his brother like when they were kids putting on street performances and Crow bumped up against the audience members, scanning ID after ID, none ever the wiser.

The one major downside to this job was the damn maze of rooms he and Noa had to navigate through. And while he'd studied the map, seeing it in person turned into a whole other animal with how many doors were locked or blocked off. He now understood why Nyx had given him an electronic lockpick before Noa had dragged him outside. The doors were on their own little network.

He pressed it against one of the remaining set of double doors standing between them and their key, sending it springing to life. A blue outer ring began to lurch forward and pause as it tried to override the lock. Well, until Noa threw herself in front of it, grabbed his tie, and yanked him *way* too close.

"What the hell are you trying to do?" he hissed. "Stop making passes at m—"

"Oh, you *wish*. If a guard turns that corner, they'll assume we're just making out."

"I thought you were just going to kill them if we got caught."

"No, you idiot! Then it'll look *super* suspicious."

"Well, I'm more of the grab it and don't get caught type. Not so much the distraction type, let alone the espionage type—"

"Oh, the irony," she mumbled, her head jerking down to the blinking light muffled behind her. She pried it off the door and tossed it to him before slipping inside.

"Well," Crow began, shutting the door behind him with a soft thump against the frame, "I suppose when you kill people for a living, you're forced to consider how best to not get caught in the act." He placed a hand to his chest. "I, on the other hand, have someone to take care of that issue for me."

He strode towards the case displayed along the far wall. The Song of Talie sat tucked inside, resting on a silk cushion. The emblem made him think of a ripple disturbing a still pond, its rose gold metal rings spanning outward, crashing into pearls to make shallow waves of their own. Then again, he supposed they could've been placed like music notes, spiraling in infinite song.

"Well…" he said, "looks like no grimoires this time."

"I'd rather not think about those right now anyway," Noa muttered, wasting no time prepping the case and putting a hand up to her earpiece. "In position."

CECILIA

"Pride and Gluttony, hold. Greed and Envy, stay alert," Nyx said. "I'm timing the security to drop when the fireworks start in a moment."

Cecilia rocked back, bumping her shoulder against Rune while half the room spilled onto the steps leading out into the garden for a better view.

"I've... never actually seen fireworks in person before," she said quietly.

"Then we'll have to step outside once everyone gets settled, won't we?" Rune said, a smile on his face brightened by the first of the lights shooting up with a scream, bursting into dazzling sparks ripping apart the night sky.

CROW

Crow popped the glass off the case, and Noa dropped the fake over the original, tugging out the latter. He dropped the lid back into place and began removing the demagnetizers with a grin.

Noa's voice came over the comms, "Clear. We're on our way out."

"Man, if only every job went this smoothly," he mumbled, bouncing his collected tools in one hand with a short series of clicks.

"Maybe you should give Sloth a little more credit," she whispered, half turning to him on their way to the door. "There's a reason why your brother and I ask, 'how high' when she says 'jump'." She snapped her clutch shut, tucking the key's new case under her arm.

He rolled his eyes. "Gods, you sound like my mother. 'Listen to your coordinator.'"

"Sounds like she knew what the hell she was doing."

RUNE

Rune wrapped an arm around Cecilia's waist at the all-clear, ushering her toward the glass garden doors. They stopped on the steps and tilted their heads to the sky. She jumped, bumping into him when another firework hurtled upward, and a laugh bubbled up from his throat.

"They're beautiful," she whispered in awe.

"Maybe next year we could go to Valentia for New Year's?" he suggested, pushing a lock of hair out of her face. He hated how his mind tacked on the caveat of if they managed to live that long, but she still gave him a warm smile.

"I'd love that."

The smile didn't reach her eyes though—there was a distinct lack of hope there, telling him she feared it too.

2

TALIE ✧ 2704-12-18

GLACIER

"Get your things," Nyx said, keeping her eyes on the cameras, "and grab my bag while you're at it, please. I can handle them until they have a decent opportunity to leave."

He stood and stretched. "Will do."

The walk down the hall to collect their bags left him feeling unsteady—a feeling he shook off when he turned into his room. It persisted, sending bumps trailing down his arms even after he scooped up Nyx's bag. He slowed during his return to the hall, turning his head to stare out the windows.

A shadowed figure hovered in the alleyway across the street. Glacier tightened his grip on the bag straps, his heart kicking up a notch at the soft, faint glint of red in the silhouette's eyes. The low thrum in his core impressed an urgent warning in his mind. A couple walked by, falling into each other—all laughs and songs, and the red rings disappeared. The blackened spot vanished, but Glacier's dread remained.

Maybe it wasn't Adam.

He forced out a breath on his way back to the couch, dropping the bags the moment the front door flung open. His stomach dropped, fear shooting through him until he saw Noa and Crow.

"Let's get the hell out of here," Crow said, pulling his tie up over his head. "I'm ready to grab a few drinks in the lounge on the way back to Miralta."

Nyx shook her head slightly, moving her hand to her comm piece. "Clear?" she asked, pausing for a couple of seconds. "We'll be ready when you get here. Hurry back."

Crow's dress shoes echoed down the hall, along with quiet jabs back and forth between him and Noa, silenced by the shutting of doors. Glacier melted into the couch, drawing his hoodie zipper up and down while Nyx began closing out all her commands and windows. His vision fell out of focus, and the image of Adam consumed his thoughts.

The seat next to him dipped down, jolting him from his mind to find Noa there. Metal clinked against metal, all strung through that cord—seven in all. Just over halfway.

"That's probably going to get heavy," he said as she slid it back over her head.

"Well, I don't exactly want them somewhere where they can get stolen," she said, dropping them under her shirt again and zipping up her jacket like a layer of armor. "I can deal with it." Her confidence pierced through her voice, but there was a completely different story told through her eyes, where a flicker of uncertainty stared back at him.

Her eyes tore away when the door opened again, Rune and Cecilia spilling inside with conspiratorial smiles before Cecilia reddened and ducked her head on her way back to her room. Rune lagged behind, his sights set on her while he tugged off his suit jacket, lost in a dream of his own.

Nyx caught Glacier's attention again in the midst of shoving her computer mat into its case, and she started saying something to Noa that sounded muffled. Everything twisted and shifted, blurring as he followed Noa down the steps from the apartment, each clang ringing out too loud down the alleyway.

They brushed past the glowing windows of bars and the occasional brightened apartment. He huddled in his jacket, checking the eyes of each person they passed, but most were a varying hue of hazels or grays.

Until they hit the port.

Under the lampposts and through the yellow blankets of light pouring from the nearby convenience stores outlined a few late shoppers, workers, and a single figure standing still in the middle of them all, red peeking out from under his hood.

Glacier had to refrain from lurching forward and grabbing onto Noa's arm, pushing down that urgency to run in favor of blending in. *Head down. Walk with Noa. Head down. Walk with Noa...*

The chant looped on their way down the dock, through the deck, past the lobby, and when Nyx dropped a key into his hand.

"Rest up," she said, vanishing into the room next door.

The keycard shook in his hand, taking a couple of times for the door to read it before he stumbled inside. Safe. He was safe. He dropped his bag on the floor and turned to engage the secondary lock, biting back a scream at the dark outline of a person blocking his path.

"You scared the shit out of me," he said breathlessly, collapsing onto the edge of the bed.

Noa plucked at her bag strap. "Sorry, I..."

Quiet stretched between them, compounding every creeping thought into a single moment: she'd sought him out. Every mention of letting her know he was awake to her running to him for peace he'd written off as one thing or another, allowing him to write the narrative of obligation—obligation of her needing him for the Soul of Amarais and obligation of him needing her to live. But at some point, that obligation had blurred into *want.* *Wanting* to get up and watch the sun rise with her, *wanting* to start opening up about himself because she didn't judge, *wanting* to feel her hand in hers without a glamour. Selfish little ideas he'd stamped out like sparks before they could catch ablaze.

That didn't mean they hadn't left their marks.

Her teases had always sobered him—sending him diving back down to reality, where he'd ask himself why she'd somehow be the exception to the rule. Why she'd managed to find as much to like in him as he did in her. But maybe...

"Well, um..." he started, pinning his hands between his knees. "At least we won't be traveling over water anymore." He couldn't even work up the nerve to ask her to stay.

"I'll just be glad when we get back shore," she mumbled, her eyes falling on the window. "But Nyx mentioned we were heading down south, so she's sort of dragging out this last nightmare."

He turned, stretching over the bed and wrapping his knuckles against the glass to obstruct her view. "Better?"

"Thank you." Her bag fell to the floor, and she tugged off her boots.

"Um..." He felt a flush crawl up his neck, making him grateful for the dark.

Noa balled up her jacket and tossed it on top of her things. "I just want to go to sleep and wake up in Miralta." She rubbed her arms.

Glacier stared, taking far too long to realize she was still standing there. *Waiting.* He jumped to rip off his boots and jacket before shimmying to the opposite side of the bed. Their shoulders bumped as he fell onto his back next to the window, and she laid on her stomach along the edge. His fingers brushed against hers until she shifted, sending pinpricks up his arm when she pressed against him.

He was glad to be lying down with how his head spun, fueled by emotions best kept in check—so uncontrollable now. All he could do was wait for them to leave port, and the lapping of waves lulled him to sleep.

The quiet crackling of the fireplace greeted Glacier, casting the room in a harsh light—all hard edges and eerie shadows. He stood, searching the recesses of the dark like silvery dots might shine through.

Mage.

He spun around, his vision dipping into a momentary black in trying to find the source of that rasping whisper. But he *wasn't* a Mage. That wasn't true. Because if it was—

The suffocating heat forced him out into the hall, checking up and down the corridor for Kat. Too scared to call out her name. Too uncertain of what to do next. Too—

Glacier caught movement on the opposite side of the window and froze. A hooded figure stood in the shallow snow, irises rimmed in a faint, glowing red. He stumbled backward, ramming his back into the doorframe as Kat screamed his name.

NOA

Noa shot up at the quick brush of skin against her arm and the sheets snapping against her legs. Glacier's breaths came out ragged and shallow. Panicked.

Oh shit. Oh gods.

"W-what?" she forced out, feeding off the fresh pulse of adrenaline. "What's happening?"

"S-sorry—" His body shook as he reached for his face, obscuring it from view. "It-it was just a nightmare."

He sounded so small and afraid it might as well have been a knife through her heart.

"Was it... something to do with Amarais?" she asked quietly, barely catching a slight shake of his head. "Or Adam?" He didn't move, so she sat up and gently pulled his hands away to look him in the eyes. "It's okay. You can tell me."

"I..." His pulled his sleeves over his hands, wrapping his arms around himself. "I-I don't know."

Her fingers dug into the sheets, hating how helpless she felt. She didn't know what to say to put his mind at ease, let alone how to reassure herself with the weight of the keys around her neck. So instead, she nudged him back down to the mattress and draped the blanket over them, enveloping them both in the comfortable weight of the darkness.

CECILIA

Cecilia turned her mug around slowly, letting the heat graze her fingertips as it scuffed against the ship's café tabletop. Crow didn't even react to the vibration of it with the side of his head flat against the table. His eyes were closed after lamenting about the glint of the shiny decorations strung along the ceiling lights.

"Maybe you should consider *not* drinking for a while," she mumbled.

A tray slid between them, the plates on it loaded with bacon, eggs, and large croissants that Rune divvied out between the three of them, along with the silverware.

"Thanks for grabbing the drinks," Rune said, dropping a medicine packet in front of Crow and giving him a light pat on the cheek. He groaned, and Rune rolled his eyes. "Did you happen to see anyone else this morning?"

"Only Nyx," Cecilia said, unrolling her utensils. "I passed her in the hall earlier, and she said that she might meet us for breakfast once she was done working on some things. I guess Noa and Glacier are sleeping in?"

Crow crinkled the medicine packet, slicking the sweat off his water glass. "Maybe they're having sex without me."

Cecilia's shook her head. "I'm pretty sure they're *not*. Stop getting wild ideas." She huffed and blew some of the steam off her coffee, but that little nagging voice in the back of her head conjured up all the times Glacier had chosen Noa over everyone else here. The mornings she'd run into them in the observation car or finishing up in the dining car. How he'd stuck with her on the ferry to Valentia, and Rune's mention of them training together in the mornings during their stops. And finally, the way he'd watched her when Nyx had pulled Noa aside.

She gripped her mug tighter. It'd been something she'd written off until their arrival in Talie because she'd built up the idea that he'd been testing out the idea of another friendship—finding common ground because they needed each other anyway. But the way he'd looked at Noa... Cecilia couldn't recall catching him ever staring at someone like *that*—like the way she'd caught Rune staring at *her*.

But once Noa had the Soul of Amarais, she wouldn't need him anymore. What would stop her from taking all her keys and leaving them all behind in search the Vault?

"Is something wrong?" Rune asked. "You haven't touched your breakfast..."

"I... was just thinking about... if Noa gets the last key, and things down work out in Amarais... We're taking Glacier and finding my parents. I want to take them to King's or... I don't know—literally anywhere else."

His eyes widened. "What? Of course. Did you think we wouldn't?"

"No, but... do... do you think that Noa will try to leave us after she gets the last key?"

"No."

Relief washed over her.

"No, I... think that she's attached to us, whether she's willing to admit it or not," Rune said, pushing around his eggs. "She might act tough, but she cares, deep down. I could imagine her trying to ditch us *after* we leave Amarais, but she wouldn't leave us stranded there."

She took a sip of her coffee, swallowing back her fears with it. At least he was certain they'd make it out if they weren't wanted in Amarais, but that would still leave her to deal with the aftermath of Noa ripping Glacier's heart into pieces once discarded.

RUNE

Rune tapped the room key against his fingertips on his way down the hall, counting down the room numbers until he reached the one Nyx mentioned was Glacier's. After he'd opened Noa's to check on her, per Nyx's request since she also hadn't seen either of them, he'd flipped on the lights to find... *nothing*. Crisp white sheets lay neatly tucked and folded against the mattress and no luggage in sight.

He stopped in front of Glacier's room, his hand poised to knock while his eyes narrowed on the door handle. His arm dropped, and he tapped the key to the pad instead, sending light pouring over two bags, two jackets, two sets of boots, and two forms intertwined in the bed. Noa's arm wrapped around Glacier, and her face was nuzzled in his hair. Neither stirred.

Rune rubbed his cheek, contemplating waking them before he decided against it. Their exhaustion had been evident during the majority of the trip between Glacier's drooping and Noa's occasional hidden yawns. They needed the rest, though he couldn't help but imagine that Noa might be trying to hide her attachment to someone Rune considered to be her polar opposite.

A smirk tugged at the corner of his mouth as he started back down the hall. Maybe Cecilia's worrying for Glacier was all for nothing after all. He jogged up the steps to the café's deck, weaving through the tables to drop the keys in front of Nyx.

"They're dead asleep," he said, reclaiming his chair.

"Figures," Nyx mumbled, tearing apart her croissant. "I doubt that either of them slept much in Talie anyway."

"There's a fix for that if you drink enough," Crow offered, sipping his water.

Cecilia sighed. "Says the one with a hangover. Why can't you just enjoy what's around you? You could take a walk or get some fresh air…"

"But it's easier to meet people when I'm blasted."

"Then maybe you shouldn't be meeting people. Maybe you'll find someone good for you if you stop trying to pick people up while you're absolutely trashed."

"And where's the fun in that?"

Her head fell into her hands, and Rune stifled a laugh. "Crow," he started. "What would your ex say if she was sitting here right now?"

"Probably something along the lines of 'stop being a whore, you stupid bitch'."

Nyx raised an eyebrow with a morsel of her croissant partway to her mouth. "Can we trade Crow for his ex?"

"Seriously?" Crow asked, pounding his fist against the table.

"She *is* a good thief," Rune said.

"And Noa said that you confirmed she's hot, right?"

"She is, in fact, easy on the eyes," he said, glancing at Cecilia. "Though, she's not really my type."

Nyx chewed thoughtfully, starting to nod. "Deal."

"*Wow*."

3

KING'S REPUBLIC ✧ 2704-12-18

ARRINGTON

Wilton Arrington leaned back in his office chair and closed his eyes. Too many damn meetings over the course of the morning had left him agitated to the point he considered canceling his next appointment with one Shane Delacroix. At least he didn't have to put on a show for him like how he'd been going through the numbing motions of pretending to give a shit about anything and everything going on in the Intelligence Agency.

His mind was wholly elsewhere, his focus on the pressing matter of luring out the thieves he'd taken a calculated risk on. So, now he'd hoped their former accomplice would be enough to remedy his error. Weather Blackburn would have to be the key to trapping them again, and this time he wouldn't try to flip them to his side in the name of greed.

Arrington tapped his finger to his cheek with a low hum, recalling Jinko's original warning that they should ship the twins off to prison and be done with it. But she'd been new to their operation—he'd discounted her foresight. He heeded her advice now whenever Shane mentioned bringing Alyvia into their circle—a *costly* choice, considering the issues he and Shane had run into with his former technical supervisor.

Shane slipped inside, the sound of the door shutting behind him alerting Arrington to his presence. "Any updates?" he asked, earning a shake of Shane's head.

"Unfortunately, no... but I don't think that there's much we can really do until the new year anyway. What with transportation coming to a halt soon, and all..."

Arrington rolled his stylus into his palm and tapped it against the desk. "And most of the building will be on holiday soon... I suppose we'll have to continue to our search the best we can in the meantime—"

The door burst open, and Shane muffled a surprised curse as Arrington narrowed his eyes on the woman darkening his doorway. Ice blonde hair, stormy gray-blue eyes, and a permanent scowl. He suppressed a cringe in favor of intertwining his fingers on the desktop during her march across the room.

"We need to talk," she said, straightening her suit jacket as she came to a stop.

"Director Bristol..." Arrington replied.

Shane's eyes darted between them in the slow rise from his seat. "I'll... come back later."

"Shut the door," came Bristol's order, not bothering to spare him a glance on his way out.

They locked eyes like two debate opponents before a match—an activity that he'd used to coast on during his time in academia and well into his career here. The problem was that she had the potential to outmatch him. Fortunately, she was likely the *only* one due to her experience.

He reclined, feigning amusement. "What can I help you with?"

The slight tick of her jaw cued her irritation, which, in turn, meant she'd be put at a disadvantage somewhere.

"There's been a rumor going around that you've received an anonymous tip that involves my department, and *you've* neglected to share it with me."

Fontaine's tip. He shook his head, trying to play dumb. "I'm not sure what you m—"

"Cut the shit, Arrington. You know that it's my job as the Director of

Art and Culture Preservation to know about anything related to prospective museum thefts."

"Well..." he said coyly, "you know, don't you?"

"Which means that this is under *my* jurisdiction, not *yours*," she snapped. "This has no bearing on the Intelligence Agency, outside of the fact that someone had given you intelligence. From here forward, you will comply by handing over *all* the information you receive in relation to this potential theft. *My* agents will be the ones on-site during the New Year's Gala to patrol."

He paused, a quiet, disbelieving laugh escaping him. "Understood."

The slight uptick at the corner of her mouth made him grit his teeth. "Good. Then we can either work together on this with my department in charge, or I can take it from here."

"I will do whatever I can to help, then."

"Glad we could come to an agreement." And with that, she turned to leave, bumping into Shane on her way out the door. "I'm finished with him. You may resume." She waved a hand and vanished down the hall.

Shane stood slack-jawed, watching her go. Arrington's fists tightened, taking everything in him not to pound them against the desk. He shoved himself up out of his seat and began to pace. Another plan mutilated. At this rate, he might not have a choice but to resort to his original method of disposal.

"What did she—" Shane started, pulling the door shut again.

"She's screwing us. She heard about our anonymous tip, and she's taking over since it's technically under the Art and Culture Preservation department."

"What? But—She can't—"

"She *can*, and she just *did*." He ran his thumb along his chin, his hum bordering on a growl.

"Then how are we supposed t—"

"*Quiet.* I'll figure something out to fix this mess. I'll have to before the damn gala. We just need to have access to that thief once they apprehend her."

Shane grabbed onto the back of the chair, watching Arrington's trail along the windows. "What do you want me to do?"

Sighing, he slowed to a stop behind the desk. "Continue working with Watson. Try to locate them. If we can somehow find an alternative, then it could work in our favor. Outside of that, leave it to me."

ALYVIA

Alyvia stared at her monitor, her brows knitting together as her eyes flicked back to the other window. No results. But *how?* She pressed the refresh button. Still no results. Something *must* be broken.

She tapped her fingers against the keys in contemplation before hammering in the name of one of the twins again. There he was—image and blacked-out information with a big, red 'Restricted Access' warning underneath and a mark that voided the entire profile from basic viewing access to the general public.

A quick click of a random person in the still frame of the Southaven crowd pulled up a similar profile, but this one was fully populated with all their data. So it wasn't her access... She selected the woman again.

Nothing.

How did she *not* exist in the databases? Even if she lived outside of the Republic, her data would've been shared the second she entered the country from her homeland. Why the hell wasn't she logged?

"Any luck?"

She jolted, whipping her head around to take in Shane gripping the back of her seat.

"Oh, I—" She swallowed. "No, I was just reexamining those frames that you told me to take another look at, but I think I found a glitch in our system because this woman just... doesn't exist for some reason?" She laughed nervously, eyeing his reaction.

He leaned in closer to the monitor, and she stiffened, trying to lean out of his way. "Weird..." he mumbled, squinting at the small face. "She's not showing up anywhere? Not in another supplementary database?" He pulled away, tilting his head with a frown.

"Yeah, I can't seem to find her anywhere..." Her mouth almost snapped shut as a cold wave of horror spread through her. This woman could very well be *Nyx*.

"Keep looking into it. I'll make a note on my copy of the stills you sent over. Don't spend more than another hour, though. If you can't find anything, just return to the missing agents." He patted the back of her chair and started back toward his office

The door swung into the frame, bouncing slightly off it before she fished out her phone and opened Nyx's encrypted app.

> Is this you?

She sent the message with an attached a zoomed-in still from her screen. A plain-looking woman half-turned in the crowd near the twins—far enough away she might not be with them, but close enough it could be considered suspicious.

> No.

Her head spun with relief as Nyx's three little message dots pulsed with a follow-up.

> But I'm going to need you to ignore her too.

> Wait, what? Why?

A flicker out of the corner of her eye made her jerk up to take in entry after entry populating the screen with an image similar enough to the woman on the camera—about a hundred different false-positive results marked in orange and red. At least she would be able to tell Shane that it just hadn't loaded properly.

> Because I need her too.

She flipped to the next still frame, cursing when she saw the same woman talking to one of the agents.

> Well, bad news.

> I may have accidentally pointed her out to my boss, but that doesn't matter now because I apparently have footage of her talking to them.

> She's about to become a person of interest if he hadn't deemed her one already.

Alyvia's knees bounced against her phone while she debated hurling her phone at Jinko's office. If she hadn't talked down to her every chance she'd gotten, maybe Alyvia wouldn't have resorted to this madness in the first place.

> Well, shit.

That wasn't a phrase she'd ever wanted to read from Nyx.

> Backup plan then: do what you have to for now but start ignoring her too.

> I'll try my best to keep her profile looking normal for the time being to cover your ass.

> I'll see what I can do.

> Thanks for letting me know.

Alyvia shoved her phone back into her pocket as she got up and headed for Shane's door. She gave it a slight push and wrapped her knuckles on the frame. "Hey, so I think it was a glitch in the system..." she said with a sheepish grin.

"Figures," he said, chuckling in his shuffling of synthetic papers. "Isn't that usually what happens when your boss is looking over your shoulder? But I did notice her talking to them in one of the other stills." He flipped his monitor around, showing her the image she'd encountered moments ago.

"Um, yeah, I just noticed that too. I'll try to narrow down the correct profile since she's getting a ton of false positives for matches."

"Of course. You do good work, Alyvia. Keep it up." He grinned, approval radiating off of him like a beam of sunshine in the middle of summer. Sweat began beading on her back, making her squirm a little in her jacket after her mumbled thanks and her retreat back to her desk.

Maybe she *should* turn them in, despite that creeping feeling of wrongness to it all. Shane had been her sole champion during the time she'd started working under him while Arrington and Jinko treated her like every other tech—there to do their bidding and scurry out of sight. That wasn't something she could afford to do when she had such high goals. High goals that she was now sacrificing for answers since she fell further and further from the former anyway.

Sorry, Shane.

Nyx was her priority now, which meant she'd do whatever she had to in order to delay their progress in finding their rogue agents and their new friend.

4

MIRALTA ✧ 2704-12-18

NOA

Soft chimes and announcements bounced off the walls, rippling through the station like the nearby waves. Noa welcomed the trade of blues from the boat for the greens of the projected Miraltan hillsides emulated along the wide corridors. Sparkling gold fringe garland trailed in their wake, sprinkling in the New Year's cheer through the bouncing children holding their parents' hands on their way to see their grandparents, aunts and uncles, cousins. All the people none of their crew could go home to, dropping them into a quiet, somber mood before most of their party split off to freshen up or restock. Only Rune had stayed with her in their bench cubby, *staring* at her.

She narrowed her eyes at his lazy smirk, like he had a secret taunt her with. "What the hell are you looking at?"

"Just a sleep-deprived psychopath."

"Is there a reason why you're suddenly acting friendly with me now? I thought you made it clear you're with Cecilia..."

"I know you weren't in your cabin last night."

Her eyes widened. "Excuse me?" She glanced around, checking for any of the others before leaning in and dropping her voice to a whisper. "I'm sorry, did you just imply that you snuck into my room?"

"I volunteered to check on you and Glacier since no one had seen either of you since we boarded, and strangely enough, I discovered *you* wrapped around a certain prince," he whispered back, adding to her mounting horror until his amusement fell away with a sigh. "Look, Noa, I won't tell anyone, but—"

"Stop right there," she said sharply. "First off, it's not even *close* to what it looks like—"

"So you didn't tell my brother that Glacier's off-limits, and you're somehow not monopolizing all of his free time?"

She sputtered. "It's not like that."

"You were literally in each other's arms, Noa."

"That doesn't mean that I *like* him like that—" she hissed, her stomach turning at the flash of Lazarus's blood on her hands. "Let's just be honest with ourselves for a moment."

"Please, I would love nothing more," he said, folding his arms over his chest with a smugness that made her want to shoot up from her seat and slap him.

"Hypothetically speaking," she ground out, "if I *was* interested in Glacier like that, and *any* member of the Volkov were to find out about it, they would wield that information against me, just like they did with Lazarus. That's what got him killed, in case you forgot. It'd come back to bite me in the ass. So, let's just drop it."

He closed his eyes and shook his head, radiating disapproval. "Fine. Make as many excuses and rationales as you'd like, but I'm not sure which is worse: having you lie to yourself and everyone around you about how you really feel, or that you're outright denying yourself happiness when there's a strong possibility that we don't have much time left." A flash of pity consumed his features. "Stop fake-flirting with everyone when you can have the real thing."

He stood and walked away, leaving her staring at the dark-painted brick behind where he'd been. The air felt like it'd been pushed from her lungs until her hands curled into fists. How *easy* it was for him to say something like that when Rune didn't have an entire group of killers specifically hunting both him and Cecilia down. The Volkov were after *her*. They were after *Glacier*. They wouldn't show either of them mercy, but she'd already decided that she'd have to stand in the way to save him—to save *all* of them.

Giving in to that selfish want to curl up next to him again like she had *twice*—mere days apart—or lose herself in the deep blue and green hues of his eyes was setting herself up for failure. Not only that, but maybe *he* didn't even want that after all the times she'd bullied him. He was a kind, gentle soul that couldn't say no to putting up with her, so slapping a larger target on his back was the very last thing she wanted to do.

He was born and bred for a kingdom. That's where he belonged at the end of this—that's where she promised to return him. Whether or not she was the successor to the King didn't matter in all this, so long as she played her part to see her promises through. Her happiness was irrelevant now because the risk wasn't worth the reward. If anyone deserved to die, it would be her.

"You okay?"

Noa's head snapped up to Glacier hovering next to the bench, his face clouded with concern.

Don't give in to those feelings, Noa.

"I'm fine," she said, pushing herself to stand. "Rune and I were just talking, and it... just led me down some uncomfortable 'what-ifs.' That's all they are though." She started past him, swallowing back her discomfort in his lag behind. It stung more than she'd hoped.

She stopped next to Nyx on the opposite side of the terminal, tucking her hands into her pockets as Glacier stepped up next to her with those gemstone eyes pinned on her. Her heart squeezed.

"So, slight issue," Nyx mumbled, flicking off her phone screen.

"What now?" Noa breathed.

"One of my associates informed me that you're now a person of interest in King's."

"I'm sorry, *what?*" Her mind immediately jumped to Ezra and his demise in Southaven.

Nyx nodded over to Rune and Crow, standing in another queue with

Cecilia further down the platform. "You were caught talking to those two on a station camera in King's."

Well, at least she wasn't wanted for murder.

"They were spotted on those recordings about a week after we arrived, and they've been trying to figure out where they went. You just happened to be talking to them in their lead material, so now they want to know how you're connected."

"Wait..." Glacier said with a frown. "Who's wanting to know?"

"I'll explain on the train," she mumbled with a brief glance around as their train signaled to board. She pushed through the line, leading the way to their compartment. Noa trudged over the emerald-green carpeting and scolded herself for thinking about Glacier's green eye.

Nyx wrapped her knuckles on the window as Noa pulled the door shut behind them.

"Now that we have a little more soundproofing, here's the deal: Rune and Crow were Republican spies.

Glacier's eyes went wide. "W-what? I thought that they were thieves—"

"They *were* thieves," Noa answered.

"By the time they contacted me," Nyx continued, "they were spies under the Republic's Intelligence Agency. The short of it was that they were caught during a job that was considered to be under the agency's jurisdiction. When they were brought in, they were given a choice. They could either go to prison and the agency would hunt down the rest of their associates involved in the heist, or they could work for them in exchange for no prison time and their associates would be forgotten."

"So..." he mumbled, rubbing at his arm.

Noa's shoulders fell. "They took the deal. They chose to save the other dumbasses with them. They fell on the sword to make sure the others got away clean."

"But they're not spies," Nyx said with a short, bitter laugh. "Rune is probably the closest thing to a spy, but even then, I can't picture him being someone that would forcibly extract information from people."

"Then why bother?" Glacier asked, looking between them. "Why offer that if they weren't going to do that great of a job?"

Noa sighed and fell into her seat. "It could be for a number of reasons. For starters, they're disposable, so that's probably the greatest part, considering how it might not be worth sending top-tier operatives into something they might not come back with. It's probably the most compelling argument I can come up with."

"But that doesn't make them *effective*." Glacier said, almost in argument against that point. "Yes, sure, they can be disposable, but that's like sending Rune to do Crow's work or vice-versa. They *can*, but they're more likely to screw it up or come back with nothing."

"I never said that these people made sense, okay?"

Nyx took a seat across from Noa. "All that matters now is that they know they went to Bellegarde, never showed up at their *rendezvous* point or communicated with their contact, and then vanished for months, only to appear in Southaven a few weeks ago. All because they swapped trains to get on one—"

"With me on it instead," Noa finished. "From there, Rune found me and said that he knew Nyx, despite never meeting her in person. She'd told him that he and his brother could be useful allies if they wanted out of the spy game for one last-ditch effort at freedom."

The cabin fell silent, Noa's eyes fixed on Glacier to gauge his reaction. Slowly but surely, everything appeared to sink in, evident but the way he sank down into the seat next to her. "So... did either of them know that you were Volkov when you met?"

"No. I didn't tell them until after we met with Nyx. Honestly, I was pissed that she had dragged more people into this mess since I was planning to go it alone. Clearly, she had other plans."

"Yeah," Nyx said. "It's called strategy, and it worked in our favor. They clearly thought that whole Volkov bit had been a joke until she and Rune got into a fight on the way back from finishing the first job."

Noa chuckled. "The look on his face after he realized I'd taken out three of the thugs that jumped us in the time he'd managed to take down one was absolutely priceless. I overheard him talking to Crow about it and how big of a mistake this whole deal was back at the hotel once he finally realized what they had signed up for."

"We also hadn't told them why we were stealing the emblems either," Nyx said. "Not until they'd calmed down after the heist that night. After that, Rune looked like his soul had left his body, and Crow was on the edge of hysterics, saying something along the lines of 'fuck it, why not?' before shoving an entire mini-fridge of booze into his bag."

"Okay…" Glacier said quietly, his sights set on the floral pattern running along the floor. "So… now the King's Republic government understands that you three are connected. But… what about the rest of us?" Panic lit his gaze as he turned to Noa. "Do they know about *me?*"

Nyx shook her head, pulling his attention away. "I've instructed my associate to pass all the information through me if it involves anyone else. Even though you and Cecilia are on the Southaven footage, she hasn't noticed, and if she does, she'll overlook it. Not to mention that it'll be a huge pain in the ass to figure out which identity of yours is real. The problem with Noa is that she wasn't even in the system because of the Volkov. They were systematically erased through the use of a *really* good hacker or puppet master who assisted in getting rid of them so they could move undetected. They don't get picked up for facial recognition or anything since it eliminates automatic detection. Only a manual process would be able to pinpoint that there's something wrong, but once it gets to that point…"

"You typically eliminate the loose end," Noa said, watching Glacier pale.

"Please don't say that you plan on killing her."

"What—No! No one's killing Nyx's associate for finding me. Myron definitely doesn't give a shit if I get caught right now, but it might help him find me faster. Trust me, she's safe unless we die, only then will he consider cleaning up any possible trails. She's *helping* us, so of course I'm not going to *kill her.*"

"If Myron catches onto her, she'll be treated just like every other client anyway," Nyx said. "We'll find the best place to relocate her where she can be situated in a new community and a job that can continue benefiting us. I give all our clients generous monthly stipends to get them started too. I've got a good handle on the customer service aspect of this mess. Speaking of which..." Her focus shifted to Noa. "You're *sure* that you don't want to join me in collecting the rest of the replica keys?"

Noa vehemently shook her head. "Nope. Not going. Especially after hearing about being picked up on camera in King's, then that seals the deal for me. It's far too close to the border for comfort. Plus, I don't enjoy the panic that ensues with me showing up."

Nyx rolled her eyes. "I can just have her lock him in his room again, so he doesn't see you and start screaming."

"Like that'll help much. He'll still know that I'm there. The man has a screw loose—he thinks I'm going to run up and stab him."

"Fine," Nyx said, relenting with a smirk. "You don't have to go."

"Thank *gods*."

"But I was considering taking Glacier along if you don't mind. Seeing how he's my assistant, I think he might benefit from the trip."

Noa hesitated, digging her fingernails into the sleeves of her jacket. Part of why she'd not wanted to go was to keep an eye on Glacier just in case. "I don't know if that's a good idea..."

"Because you think that the Volkov will be waiting for an opportunity to strike?" Nyx sighed. "Noa, I'm pretty sure that they—minus a single Amaraian among them—will be far more inclined to deal with you before Glacier. A little separation won't hurt, especially for three hours, at most."

Noa held her tongue, a bitter taste filling her mouth from the mere thought that Glacier could be more at risk of dying by being with her than without.

Nyx raised an eyebrow when she didn't immediately reply. "Any objections?"

Noa's thoughts held onto what Rune had said back in the station, twisting her stomach into knots. She needed to push him aside. "No. He's all yours."

GLACIER

A silence settled over the cabin before Noa left with the excuse to sweep the cars. No invitation for him to walk with her, though Glacier had hoped she would turn around at the door. He slid his hands along his jeans, pushing away that feeling of being brushed off when he'd found her in the station. It was like trying to rub off the phantom imprint of his bag's woven strap from how hard he'd been gripping it, but it lingered anyway.

"So..." he started, the sound too elongated and awkward with how it filled the void, "how long are we going to be staying in Miralta?"

"Until next year," Nyx said. "We'll jump towns at least once to be safe, but it's best to lay low for the time being."

He absently picked at his fingers, staring at the back of her tablet's black pleather cover. "Is there anything you want me to do?"

Say yes. Please say yes.

Her eyes flicked up, where they roamed his face—long enough to give her pause. His heart sank before the first syllable left her mouth. "Glacier, did you sleep much last night? You look exhausted."

His head dropped, and a hand went to the back of his neck, hoping to conceal any trace of the heat climbing up it. "Sort of..." The memory of waking up in the middle of the night with Noa's breath tickling his scalp left him dizzy, dropping him somewhere on the outskirts of a peaceful dream that'd evaporated the second he'd opened his eyes. She'd been in it—wherever it'd taken him—but the rest had been lost to whatever consumed the instances that didn't involve Kat or his father's home. He sighed, letting his shoulders fall. "I'm having trouble staying asleep recently. Not that I haven't been having problems sleeping in general... ever since we left Amarais."

Regret lanced through him at the shake of her head before she said, "Trying to keep up with Noa probably isn't doing you any favors."

Glacier's head popped back up. The judgment he'd been so afraid of wasn't there. Instead, sympathy filled her gaze, broken up by her pushing her glasses up the bridge of her nose.

"It's a big change... Going from existing in such a small sliver of the world with a handful of people to being dumped out into the hands of a bunch of crazy strangers. I'd be stressed too if I were you. I can't say I wouldn't be having trouble sleeping."

"I think... I think what makes it worse is that I can't stop dreaming about Kat. It's like her ghost is following me around most nights, trying to tell me something I don't understand or can't remember." He ran a hand through his hair, tugging at the short locks. "I think it started blending together with all the paranoia I've been feeling after our encounter with Adam." Hearing it come straight from his own mouth made him want to reach out into the air and somehow take it all back. "Gods... I must sound insane..."

"You don't," Nyx said quietly, resting the tablet on her legs. "You're overwhelmed. We each deal with stress differently, and right now we have some time. You should use it to try to relax. Don't push yourself."

"And what if I want to help? I'd prefer staying busy..."

She hesitated, glancing down at her lap. "Well, if you're insistent on helping somehow, I think you might be able to look around Daxton's missing acquaintances. Maybe there's another connection we're missing that has nothing to do with Noa's quest and an encroaching apocalypse..."

Glacier winced, as she retrieved a second tablet from her bag and handed it off to him.

"I'll try my best." He tried to pull it from her hand, but his arm jerked forward with it, forcing him to meet her stern, unyielding gaze.

"Just don't overdo it, okay?"

"Okay."

NYX

Nyx leaned back in her seat, rubbing at her eyes after Glacier left to stretch his legs. The reprieve gave her a moment to wrangle the creature tickling the back of her brain, trying to piece together the thing from his confession that hadn't sat well with her.

Her phone buzzed, shattering that thought, and she groaned. Her hands fell away to reach for her phone.

> Was thinking of you. How are things?

She smirked as her glove trailed the message's metal frame.

> A little crazy right now.

> Will you be in town again soon?

Her gaze drifted towards the window where lines of bright, lush trees cut up the gray-blue sky, never ceasing its threat of rain.

> I'm hoping soon, assuming you haven't found someone else to spend your time with while I've been gone.

> Please, Nyx. You know me better than that.

She could practically picture the eyeroll and bit her lip while she waited for the next message. The three little signal dots jittered.

> How's my dad?

> He's good. Could be better, but I've been keeping up with him recently.

> He misses you.

> I miss him too. Send him my love, would you?

> Of course.

> And be safe. Take care of yourself.

Nyx's heart twisted at the sight of those words, wishing she was somewhere else.

> I always do.

> You're a terrible liar. I'll see you soon.

The status indicator switched from green to gray, leaving a wave of sadness in its wake. The phone softly clicked against the tablet screen as her hands fell into her lap. Her vision blurred at the mere thought of a comforting voice in her ear

Eyes on the prize.

She tossed the phone next to her on the bench, blinking back the unshed tears. There was only one way to get through this, and that was to press forward, not look back. She tilted the tablet and paused, immediately sucked into a new message from V.

> Consider this your trustworthiness test. I need some tools and quick.

> I'm meeting with the rest of the rebels soon. I have a shopping list I'll send over momentarily.

One minute turned into two, but a list appeared like she'd said, though it was one that made her eyes bulge slightly.

> This is quite a lot. How short of a turnaround are we talking?

> I need if before the tenth. I know it's a lot to ask for in a short period of time, but I promised that I'd be there by then with as much as I could manage to bring.

> I can't go any later than that.

And here she thought she'd ask for it in a week.

> Consider it done.

Nyx didn't even hesitate to type it in. Despite being a lot, it was doable with her contacts in Bellegarde, Miralta, and King's. She could get it all organized before the New Year's shutdowns and have it shipped on the third.

> Wow. Alright. I guess we'll see just how good you are.

Nyx split up the list and divvied it up to send off to her contacts one by one, earning a handful of estimated shipping dates while the sun crept closer to the tree line.

> Would the fifth be okay? If that's too early, I can hold them for a few days.

Hell, if you can do the fifth, then do it.

I'll let you know if I have an issue getting to the drop-off point. I was planning on making a detour anyway, so I'll be glad to have the extra time.

> Just let me know. I'll work around your needs.

If you get everything to me on the fifth, I'll get you the highest recommendation possible.

That was exactly what she had hoped to hear. Potential enemy or not, at least Nyx had leveraged V to walk her way straight into the rebels' new system, and just in time for the new year.

NOA

Noa suppressed a cringe when Nyx shoved open the door to their apartment—another Miraltan-style, cookie-cutter unit with a step-down living space that might as well have been ripped straight out of Knighton. The only real difference was the dining room where Cecilia and Glacier's room had once been, now likely transferred to a spot down the much longer hallway. She wondered if tumblers matching the ones she'd plucked from the cabinets before she had Glacier recite *The Origin of Magic* would be there if she popped one of the doors open above the sink.

"Welcome home," Nyx said with a dry, sarcastic flourish of her arm showcasing the earthy tones seared into Noa's brain.

"I need a drink," Crow muttered, probably making the same connection as Noa. She was more inclined to think he was remembering his slow-building frustration while she was stuck on that distance between her and Glacier—or, rather, the lack thereof now.

He started down the hall, tossing his bag inside one of the doors to claim it, and began to pass her on the way back. She held out an arm to stop him. "Give me a second," she mumbled. "I'm joining you."

Crow raised an eyebrow—something that normally would've pried a laugh from her, but the weight on her chest kept it bottled up to match her somber mood.

Since you can't have Glacier, you can allow yourself a few drinks. Just this once.

She threw her bag in the first room and hurried shoulder-to-shoulder with him back out the door, circumventing the others in their plans for a later dinner. Rune eyed her on the way out, further fueling her need to escape.

The jog down the steps and out onto the weathered brick path ended in a chilly, welcoming embrace of the evening air.

"Finally deciding to loosen up?" Crow elbowed her with a teasing grin.

"Shut the hell up, dude." She gave him a shove, light enough for him to bounce back from after stumbling into the street. "I've just had a rough couple of days, and I want to pretend like I'm someone else and somewhere else entirely."

He threw an arm over her shoulder. "Then let's go get wasted and see if I can find a new playmate for tonight."

"You better not be talking about me."

"*Hell* no."

Noa decided to let Crow's chumminess slide in favor of a peaceful night out, despite how her heart sank at the mere thought that his arm felt wrong around her.

GLACIER

Glacier stretched on his way into his room, letting his arms drop at the sight of Cecilia rummaging through her bag on the bed. She turned around with a loose sleepshirt in hand and combed her fingers through the end of her hair.

"Oh, um... would it be okay if I switched rooms for the night?" she asked.

"Sure? I guess?"

"Don't worry—You won't be with anyone else or anything. Rune's just kicking Crow out because he's doubting that he'll even be back tonight, so..."

"Oh."

"Look, I understand if it would make you feel uncomfortable about me staying in his room, but we're not going to do anything—" Her eyes went wide, quickly shaking her head once she realized how it all looked. "I'm not —I mean—"

"No, no, it's okay, Cecilia," he said, holding back a laugh.

"I mean, I'm nowhere *near* ready for that yet—"

"That's fine. I understand that you'd rather be sleeping next to your boyfriend than me."

She hesitated, her mouth dipping into a frown.

"It's okay, *really*." He put on his best, practiced smile. His heart wasn't in it, not after the ups and downs he'd struggled with talking himself out of the idea of Noa liking him, especially after she ditched them for dinner. "I'm glad that you found someone that looks at you like you're his everything."

"You... you think he does?"

"I've seen other guys look at you over the years when you weren't paying them any attention, and I've never seen any of them look at you the way he does. He thinks that you're special, and he's right."

Her shoulders dropped, and she stepped forward to pull him into a hug. "I really like him."

"I know, Cecilia. I know." He hugged her back, trying to force open that trapped box of happiness crammed in the corner of his head. "I'm so glad that you're happy."

"But I want you to be happy too..."

It almost stole the air from his lungs, but he forced out another one of his lies to cover it up: "Don't worry about me. I'll be fine."

She pulled away, staring into his eyes. "We'll find someone that makes you just as happy, okay?"

"Cecilia—"

"I'm serious." Her hands squeezed his, gentle but commanding. "You deserve joy too."

The flickering images of Noa reaching out for his arm, curling up next to him, holding his hand consumed his thoughts before Cecilia let go.

"Try to get some rest, okay?"

"Yeah," he said with more confidence than he felt. "I will."

The door pulled shut behind her, and he sighed, rubbing at his temple. Sadness wrapped around him like a warm blanket as he changed and crawled into bed, tucking himself in to watch the sliver of moonlight creep along the comforter with each passing minute. It transported him back home, to the stillness of his bedroom—a place where he'd occasionally whisper into the darkness with the hope his father heard him from wherever he was.

His eyelids started to droop right as the door creaked open, sending light cutting over his head and spilling onto the wall for a brief moment. He guessed it must've been Cecilia slipping back in to collect something she'd forgotten until the side of the bed dipped. His head lifted, and he tried to prop himself up to see who it was.

Glacier collapsed back into the mattress again at the gentle shove of his head back into the pillow.

"Crow's asleep on the couch, it's *fine*."

Noa.

Her slurred words made him blink, puzzling out that she must've thought he was Rune.

"Noa, I'm not—"

"*Shhhhh*—" She wobbled, her hand catching on the headboard. "I just want to go to sleep." She fell into the bed, draping her arm over him and nuzzling into the back of his neck.

His whole body tensed. *Keep calm. She's drunk. She thinks you're Rune. Just breathe.* A bitter taste formed in his mouth at the idea that she wasn't there for *him*, but he managed to relax, holding fast to the calm that she'd brought with her. And then he descended into whatever dreams awaited him.

5

MIRALTA ✧ 2704-12-19

NOA

Noa woke to a slight pounding in her head and a bit of a euphoric smile. Being cuddled up against someone who wasn't trying to shove her off the bed was a welcomed surprise, especially since she'd tried it with Nyx—*twice* —and ended up eating the floor at least once. She stretched, pushing herself up with a cat-like grin.

"So, was that as good for you as it was for m—" She froze, swearing her heart stopped when she took in the profile of her sleeping partner.

Oh no.

She carefully slid backward, each painstaking movement making her body scream until her feet landed softly against the floor. Noa retraced her steps, starting from the end of her night by popping open the bedroom door, and paused, recalling which room Crow had stopped at—the *far* one.

Biting down on her tongue, she crept along the hall and nudged the final door open to take in the blonde waterfall of hair cascading down the pillow. Cecilia's small frame lay neatly tucked into Rune's embrace.

Shit.

The taste of blood told Noa to walk away, making her warpath toward Crow's limp form half-falling off of the couch. Facedown. Snoring. Pinning the blame on him would be so easy: Crow, you should have gone to your room. Crow, you shouldn't have gone out drinking. Crow, you shouldn't have—

Noa jumped at the sound of a door opening and spun around to catch Nyx adjusting her glasses, frowning as she took Noa in—yesterday's clothes and all. "Funny," Nyx mumbled. "I wasn't sure that you made it back last night."

Noa swallowed, leaning against the back of the couch as she passed. She threw on that carefree smile and tried to mask her nerves with a chuckle. "Yeah, well..." She chuckled. "I almost didn't." Her eyes fell on Crow again, her fingers twitching with the need to roll him off the couch while Nyx rummaged through the kitchen for silverware.

Another door creaked open, and she jolted again, her whole body whipping around to face the kitchen instead of *Glacier*.

Don't panic. Maybe he doesn't know.

Nyx flipped the switch on the coffee maker. "So, where did you end up sleeping last night?"

"The armchair," she said smoothly as she strode over to the kitchen island, about a step ahead of Glacier until he stopped next to her. His jaw went slack before he mouthed the word 'liar,' sending her blood running cold. She made a cutting motion across her throat, and he doubled down with a 'do it.' Her energy of wanting to roll Crow off the couch was suddenly transferred to the urge to shove Glacier into the pantry.

Unfortunately, Nyx turned around before she had the chance to commit, her dark eyes sliding between them with a raised, calculating brow. Glacier's bright smile didn't appear to help quell her suspicion at all from how her pupils narrowed. "Uh-huh... Stop smiling and get dressed. We're leaving after we eat."

His shoulders fell, accompanied by a slight eyeroll on his jog back to his room.

He knows. I want to die.

Embarrassment crashed into her, shattering her on impact with how likely it was he wouldn't let her live it down—a harmless tease to him that would rip her apart stitch by stitch until she was completely unraveled. 'Just stop thinking about him,' appeared to be easier said than done, especially in close quarters.

Look at you, Noa. Do you really *believe prince—a potential* king *has any interest in* you?

A mousy, plain-faced killer who was far from *nice*. Noa had considered that maybe she could be an acquired taste, but in reality, she'd be lucky if he considered her a friend. He'd be the most powerful friend she'd ever had, even after taking one of his most priceless heirlooms. And, at the end of the day, that's exactly what would happen: she'd take her key, and they'd part ways. No more reasons for them to stick together, to get along, to keep each other moving forward each day for the promise of facing whatever tomorrow brought.

She gritted her teeth and shook her fists when Nyx turned back to open a loaf of bread.

Stupid. Stupid. Stupid.

The toaster clicked into place, and Nyx faced her again. Noa dropped her hands to the counter, acting as if nothing happened.

"Is there anything else I should get while we're gone?" Nyx asked.

Noa hummed, too absorbed in her own self-indulgent thoughts to actually process the things they had, let alone things they needed. "No, I think we're fine for now."

Glacier draped his jacket over the back of one of the bar chairs on his way to the bread bag, recoiling at the pop of the toaster. "Um, so..." He cleared his throat with the hint of a laugh to brush it off. "Where, are we going, exactly?"

"That's confidential," Nyx said. "Only Noa and I know the exact location, and we don't discuss it. After I take you there, I expect the same from you. Don't mention it to anyone. Not even the couch dweller." She nodded her head in the direction of Crow as she dropped her toast on a plate.

"I... don't think you'll have to worry about him," Glacier said slowly. "Are we sure he's not dead?"

Noa shrugged, cupping her chin in her hands. "Eh, I'm sure he's fine." She didn't even bother checking. Instead, she was insistent on repeatedly breaking her rule of ignoring Glacier by *watching* him—watching him complete mundane actions like shoving bread in the toaster and pouring coffee so Nyx wouldn't tell him to hurry.

"Is it easy to get to?" he asked between bites, the crumbs falling from his hands finally breaking whatever trance she'd fallen into.

Pull yourself together. Holy shit.

"No, which is why we're borrowing a car," Nyx said.

"Oh. Then maybe it's a good thing that Noa's not going."

Noa's eyes went wide, taking in the smug smirk he tried to hide behind his coffee. "*Excuse me?*"

"Do you *not* remember how you were driving back in Amarais? Because *I* do."

"How *dare*—"

"Sounds about right," Nyx mumbled.

Noa's hand went to her chest as she reared back in mocking devastation. "Of all the people to betray me, I never expected it to be *you*."

Nyx ignored her, brushing past to grab her jacket off the rack. "All right, let's get a move on, Glacier."

He wolfed down the last couple bites and put both their plates in the sink. When he scooped his jacket off the chair, he paused next to Noa, sending her heart into overdrive with what she swore was a glimmer of hope reflected in his gaze. "Are you really not coming along?"

Everything in her screamed to grab her jacket and follow them out the door, but the fleeting memory of Lazarus's hands closing around hers rooted her to the spot. "No," she forced out. "I need to take care of some things here anyway." She tried to soften it with a dismissive half-shrug.

"Okay." His mouth dipped a little at the corner—a nearly imperceivable reaction that formed knots in her stomach.

The compulsion to laugh it off and take it back turned into an uncontrollable monster, threatening to consume her as she followed them to the door and leaned against the back of the couch. It clawed at her mind, telling her she should take Rune's advice—to throw caution into the wind and let herself be happy. To damn them all, rather than just herself.

"We'll be back soon," Nyx said, pulling the door open.

Glacier stepped out behind her, glancing back before they fell out of view again, pummeling her with regret. She'd just let her plan-keeper and her key to the Soul of Amarais walk out on their own. Her eyes darted over to the clock mounted on the wall. They'd be back in three hours. She could do this. She could wait.

Noa bit her thumbnail, watching the display as the minute changed, and her inner monster demanded she grab her jacket.

A moan ripped her from her thoughts, accompanied by rustling against the couch. "Oh, gods *why...*" Crow half-pulled himself up along the back of the cushions, grabbing his head. "I think I'm dying."

"No," she said, not bothering to hide her irritation. "You're probably dehydrated." He reached for her like a man who was drowning, and she slapped his arm away. "Don't touch me and go drink a damn glass of water."

GLACIER

Glacier climbed into the rental SUV and sank into the soft, pleather seats. The seatbelt snapped from his hands a couple times his fixation on the apartment window, despite Noa being nowhere in sight.

He'd been wrong. Again.

Unsurprising, considering how he tended to paint things in a brighter, more hopeful light to keep himself going. Noa was just using him. Whether they were friends or not, he couldn't tell, but that was the best he could ask for. Why he'd built himself up to think anything more had to have been a naïve fantasy. There wasn't much to like about him anyway, right?

Nyx started the car, and he leaned back, letting the whipping of wind against the soft top take him somewhere else. He ran his fingertips along the door, nicking the cool glass. The distant memory of escaping the palace pushed into his mind, dusting each tree they passed with snow until he blinked it away.

He pushed himself up. "Should we be concerned about people noticing us driving around in this?"

"It's a lot of dirt roads through the woods," Nyx said, "so I'm not worried."

Glacier leaned forward, peering through the windshield as he rubbed his hands on his pants. The thought of the fluid pulsating through the engine matching the same blue liquid running through Nyx's arm kept him from falling into the despair in his head. "Out of curiosity," he said, "were you ever interested in cars? Because of your familiarity with..."

"Not really." She shrugged. "I did a little mechanical work when I was a teenager, but I got bored with it. I liked software more than hardware, and I think that my family was a little disappointed by that."

"That's... a little ironic, don't you think? You'd think someone from a wealthy family wouldn't be encouraged to get your hands dirty."

She chuckled. "True... But my dad helped design and create the prosthetics. That was his business."

"Oh... so... your family was disappointed when you didn't take to it?"

"Especially since I use one of his designs, yes—they weren't thrilled. I still learned all I could from him growing up, but it just wasn't my passion like it was his. He'd built it from the ground up before I was even born to come up with a solution for his heart. With the possibility that one of his kids would end up with the same problem, he decided that he couldn't afford to stop."

"Was that the case?"

"Fortunately, no. Just a kid with a missing arm. It's not nearly as detrimental, in my opinion, but I won't discredit his hard work. After he saw how he could make my life better, he realized how much of an impact he could make on the rest of the world. He was a good man, and it's a shame he didn't get the chance to help fight to prove what his and countless others making similar prosthetics could do for the better. So many people just look on companies like his with disdain now."

"You have the chance to, though," Glacier said, feeling as if he were channeling Kat.

You were born for this.

Nyx drummed her fingers on the steering wheel. "You're right. Some-day, I think that I might be able to break down that wall, but we'll need to finish this first." Her mouth lifted into a wistful smile with a spark of hope reaching her eyes. "One step at a time."

"I never thought I'd see you so optimistic," he said with a laugh.

"And yet you're not optimistic about breaking down the barrier in Amarais, are you?" She glanced over at him, hefting a focus onto him that left him feeling heavy. "Our situations aren't that much different. I'm modded. You're half-Miraltan. We're both part of a supposed problem, and we both have some influence to change that if we put ourselves up to it."

He started to shake his head. "You can hide it though. You can convince someone without them knowing that you're different. People see me and know I'm not full-blooded Amaraian. Hell, most people assume that I'm not from Amarais because there's no way I'd survive looking the way I do."

"But you have the rebels behind you."

"They were behind Kat, not *me*. I'm not like her. I'm not like my father. They'll take one look at me and realize I'm not worth rallying behind."

"I don't think you give yourself enough credit. You're smart, Glacier. You see things differently, and I believe that they'd look past your hair and eyes to find that too. You ask the right questions when you have the right information."

I need you to start asking the right questions.

Kat's words rang out in the back of his mind, posing a particularly rele-vant question to his current curse. If Nyx was right about him, then what information was he missing?

His head snapped back to the windshield as the SUV slowed, rolling into a small clearing with an old, rustic cabin. Overgrown flowers covered the base in rioting pinks, blues, yellows, and greens, spreading outward with mismatched stone pavers cutting through to the door. Various tools cluttered the covered porch railing, resting under painted wind chimes and etched glass shards. Wood planks leaned against the side of the house, leading the way to a small shed at the back, attached to a laundry line obscuring a small garden. A self-sustaining environment.

He jumped at the slam of the driver's door.

"Are you going to gawk all day, or...?" Nyx asked, leaning over the door.

Glacier wrestled with the seatbelt and hopped out, jogging to catch up with her as she rounded the hood. "Is... this a client?"

"Yes," she mumbled. "Just... don't say too much. And try not to mention Noa around the guy. He's... a strange one."

He nodded, only half paying attention as his eyes fell over a canvas propped up under one of the windows. A red boat sitting on a still lake, surrounded by trees. To think that something like this was sitting out here in the middle of nowhere with only the creator to appreciate it made his heart sink, drawing him a little closer as Nyx knocked. The raised globs of paint still shimmered slightly in the reflections of the porch decorations sending the sunlight spinning in all directions. He tried to imagine how much his uncle would've offered to pay for a piece like this.

Glacier hoped that it would end up in a museum or gallery, rather than a stuffy rich person's home, but it was much like the value of a physical book—a commodity usually snapped up by the highest bidder because of its uniqueness or artistic value. Something to claim because it either spoke to them, or they simply had the money to burn and didn't want anyone else to have it.

The door opened, and Glacier stepped back to Nyx's side, hovering a little behind her like a shadow. The woman standing in the frame looked to be in her mid-forties with paint smudged along her pale fingers and staining strands of her coal-black hair. His eyes went wide when he took hers in, stuck on the periwinkle blue.

"Nyx! Hello!" she said with a warm smile. "I was wondering when you'd stop by for the rest—" She cut herself off the moment her head turned to Glacier.

"This is my assistant," Nyx said. "He's been with me for a few weeks now. Anything you would say to me, you can say in front of him."

Her smile didn't waver. "I believe he and I have something in common anyway." She pulled her hand from the door frame to touch a finger under her right eye, leaving a smudge of green in its wake.

And this was why Nyx had wanted him to come along. To meet a half-

Miraltan, half-Amaraian just like him. The only difference is that they were raised on different sides of the border, one of them accepted, despite her abnormalities while the other was rejected and isolated. Even though he'd always been mistaken as a half-Bellegardian by everyone that didn't know, it didn't make him any less of an outsider in the end.

"I'm Lyris," she said, offering a hand before seeing the paint on it and pulling it back with an apologetic giggle. "I'm sorry, I tend to forget about the mess. What's your name?"

"Morgan."

He kept close to Nyx as Lyris invited them inside and shut the door.

"Just give me one moment to clean up before I take you to the goods," Lyris called as she vanished behind a divider. "It would be rather irritating to have to fix them after how much time I spent."

Nyx checked her phone as Glacier scanned the walls, overwhelmed by the mismatched frames and canvases of art in various sides. Portraits, landscapes, abstract, realistic... All different styles, making him feel like he'd been dropped straight into a museum.

"Who's down there?" came a booming, outraged man's voice.

Glacier tensed, snapping his head up to the balcony, where a man overlooked the entry. His wild, green eyes were obscured by the reflection in his glasses, and his shaggy black hair stuck up at odd angles.

The kitchen tap shut off before Lyris reappeared with a towel in her hands. "It's just Nyx, you old fool," she shouted. "No one else bothers coming out here. We're fortunate that she brought her assistant with her."

"*Assistant?*"

The word lingered like a curse in the air, sending Glacier shrinking away with how he leaned a little further over the railing. The silver streaks in the man's hair and his wrinkles stood out starkly in the harsh light, giving Glacier the inkling that he was likely close to fifty.

His eyes went wide before he pointed at Glacier. "Who is—"

"His name is Morgan," Lyris said with a fondness to her tone as if she were referring to a nephew.

"I was expecting that she-devil."

Nyx smirked as she tilted her head up. "I decided to keep her in her cage. You're safe for now."

His hands relaxed their grip on the railing, but Lyris sighed and shook her head. "Please ignore Niklaus. He's... got some quirks." She gave Glacier a sheepish, apologetic smile before turning to Nyx with a finger pointed in the air. "To the workshop!"

She skipped a couple steps down the hall, waving for them to follow. The steps down into the basement complained under their weight. Cement sounded under Lyris's house shoes at the bottom, where her humming echoed off the metal cabinets and drawers lining the walls with little blinking keypads. A few bore painted decorations of lilies, ivy, and roses. Jars cluttered the countertops next to the sink along the wall, most capped and labeled, some of their former contents staining the drop cloths covering swaths of the floor.

Glacier hovered at the bottom of the stairwell, watching as Lyris retrieved a box from her worktable shelf and popped it open for Nyx with a key from her apron. The shine of the metal and gems against Nyx's black gloves awakened a strange sensation deep within him he couldn't explain, outside of feeling entranced. The corner of his mouth dipped down at the light tug at his core, instructing him to head back upstairs—a pull like the one that had led him to the Vision of Valentia back in Casovecchia.

He hesitated, but it persisted, coaxing him as if he'd gone the wrong way and missed something he should've seen before trailing down here. Biting his lip, he crept up the steps, eyeing Lyris and Nyx with each creak threatening to expose his escape. If they'd noticed, they didn't show it.

Glacier followed the pull through the first floor, backtracking down the threadbare rug in the hallway, and stopping at the base of the second-floor stairs. He paused, squinting up at the darkness leading up to where he'd seen Niklaus towering over them before. As much as he didn't care to run into him again, Glacier swallowed and began climbing up the steps.

It brought him past the collages of art to a closed door with a gold plate and crystal knob. The old-fashioned keyhole held its key in what Glacier hoped was simply for decoration. He twisted it, and it gave way to a trickle of light from a far window. He slipped inside, pressing the door shut behind him, and let his eyes roam over every centimeter of the room in search of whatever had demanded his attention.

The room was little more than a nook. Dust motes stirred in his wake as he started for the shelves lined with books on the top rows—the rest held storage boxes he assumed her all filled with old hard drives, based on the one he peeked in. He ran his hand along the edge of the desk, reading snippets of notes jotted down on stacks of synthetic papers.

He looked up to the far wall by the door and paused, tilting his head at the mural there. A dark, starry sky with a crescent moon tipped on its side set the backdrop for a tall, dark Miraltan woman with the Shield of Miralta cupped in her hands. Glacier took a few steps forward, standing face-to-face with the Messenger, taking in every detail of her form—the long black hair spilling from her hood, cascading over her ethereal white cloak. Even the backs of her hands were marked with that crescent moon and cradled star.

He scowled, trying to find what his gut told him he wasn't seeing, but there wasn't anything that stood out. No hidden maps. No secret words written among the dotted specks of white. His fingers itched to touch the paint and peel it away to whatever lie beneath—to whatever felt both so horribly familiar yet strange.

The sound of a voice downstairs snapped him free of his thoughts, and he popped open the door to check for any signs of movement nearby. Fortunately, all was quiet, except for Lyris's chatter. He pulled the door shut behind him and hurried back down, freezing on the bottom step as they came into view.

Lyris's eyes went wide with surprise, and Nyx frowned, forcing him to put on an apologetic smile. "Sorry," he said, rubbing the back of his neck. "I followed some of the paintings upstairs. It's like a museum in here."

Her eyes lit up. "You like them?"

"Yeah—" He hesitated, glancing at some of the frames lining the walls again. "Did... did you make *all* of them?" At first, he had pinned her for being a collector and enthusiast, mixing in her own pieces or using all of these for inspiration, but between what he had seen in the basement and the understanding that she was a professional forger...

"Yes! Oh—But you should see my favorite piece." She motioned for them to follow her back upstairs, leading the charge straight to the office door. Glacier had to tell himself over and over again to act surprised as she reached for the knob.

"*Hey—*" Niklaus rounded the upstairs corner. "That's *my* office! You can't just—"

"Oh, shut up, old man," Lyris said, waving him off.

"But the *salt!*" he wailed, pulling at his hair.

Glacier looked down to where he was staring in dismay, finding a broken trail of salt with Lyris's shoe cutting through it. He clutched a handful of his shirt at his side, relieved that she'd taken them back up here since he'd likely disturbed it in the first place. Apparently, Niklaus was paranoid enough about intruders that he'd resorted to old-fashioned security methods.

"In here," Lyris said, ushering them inside anyway.

"I was trying to keep that daemon woman out of my office..." Niklaus lamented.

Glacier ducked his head to stifle a laugh. Or maybe he wasn't paranoid about intruders after all. He'd created a makeshift trail of light to ward off Noa.

Even Nyx smirked at that. "Perhaps chalk might work better?"

He huffed as he started inside and began tidying his desk.

Lyris rounded on him. "Would you be *quiet?*" She made a short, frustrated noise as she shut the door, finally displaying the mural.

Tranquility settled over Glacier at the renewed sight of the piece. The details and deliberate brush strokes, the rune-like marks scratched out in a circle creeping outward and upward from the Messenger's cupped hands...

"It took me a while to finish," Lyris said. "I had a Seer friend describe a vision she had before we parted ways."

"And this was from her vision?" Glacier hadn't even realized that he was the one who asked at first until Niklaus glanced over at him, slowly tapping a stack of papers against the desktop.

"Yes."

The longer he stared at it, the brighter the runes appeared, making him wish Cecilia was standing next to him to tell him what she thought each one might've stood for.

"It's very lovely," came Nyx's voice, sounding muffled.

Color leached from the furniture and walls, sending everything around him into a white abyss like the untextured model homes his uncle had rendered for the mansion he drew up plans for months ago. His breath caught as the runes lifted off the wall and the Messenger began to lift her head, pinning her bright green eyes on him.

"Morgan."

He blinked, the illusion shattering in his shift in attention to Nyx, whose brows knitted together in concern.

"Yeah?"

She eyed him, hesitating before she turned to Lyris. "We should probably be going. I have somewhere to be later, and I'd hate to overstay our welcome."

"Oh, not at all!" Lyris said. "And I'm glad you came, Morgan. It's always nice to have someone new enjoy my work. Gods only know it's been a while since anyone has." She pulled the door back open and trailed through the salt again, sending Niklaus's papers falling from his hands in horror.

Nyx took a wide step over the threshold, and Glacier started to do the same until he felt something grab his arm, tugging him back. Niklaus's wild eyes stared back at him.

"Wait—just—wait *here*. Don't move." There was some hesitation before he let go like he was afraid Glacier might make a run for it.

But, he waited, even as Niklaus rummaged through his desk and retrieved a key from the same drawer that held all the keys in his dreams. Glacier shivered, rubbing his arms while Niklaus crouched down and unlocked the drawer under it. The plunging, icy scene from the palace never came, but he couldn't shake the feeling that someone was about to creep up behind him and slit his throat.

Niklaus pulled out a box and dumped it out onto the desk, sending its contents clattering against the mess of papers. He pushed a few things around and scooped something into his grasp. Niklaus turned back and seized Glacier's wrist, pressing something into his palm.

"What are you—" Glacier flinched.

"*She* chose you," Niklaus whispered, his eyes grazing the mural.

Glacier shrank back. "It's... just a paint—"

"No, no, you don't understand—" He vehemently shook his head, his green eyes hardening. "She chose *you*."

The sound of footsteps clamoring back up the stairs accompanied Lyris's voice. "*Nik*, leave that boy alone."

Niklaus let go at her command, stepping back with a glance between her and Glacier. Glacier took an uncertain step backward, afraid to turn his back on him until he remembered he still had something in his hand. He held it out to Niklaus, trying to have him take it back, but he shook his head.

"No. Take it." He motioned for him to go.

So, he did. Glacier hurried past Lyris and jogged down the steps to Nyx, who appeared a little baffled as to why he'd taken so long.

"Thank you again, Lyris," Nyx said as Lyris's footfalls sounded on the steps behind him.

"Of course. I love nothing more than to have my work in a museum. And Morgan, I'm sorry if Nik bothered you at all. I'm glad that you came."

"Thank you, Lyris," he said, the words feeling automatic. Whatever Niklaus had given him bit into his palm as his grip tightened on it. It took everything in him not to hurl it at the floor as Lyris opened the door for them to leave.

"Safe travels," Lyris said, waving as they stepped onto the porch and headed for the SUV.

His head spun with each step through the grass, his breath stolen away by the darkened skies and distant rumble of thunder.

"Are you okay?" Nyx asked, stopping him short of the vehicle.

"Y-yeah, I'm—" He struggled to get the words out with how erratically his heart slammed against his ribs.

She frowned, looking down at his closed fist. "I heard him rambling upstairs. Did he give you something?"

"I- I don't—" His hand shook as his fingers unfurled to reveal a necklace—a miniature Shield of Miralta. A small replica of the one held in the Messenger's hands. He felt the blood drain from his face. "Why would he..."

Nyx plucked it out of his hand, turning it over to reveal a small rune carved into the back. "I think it's a warding charm," she said, shrugging with a slight smirk when she dropped it back into his palm.

"What's so funny?"

"It's to protect from daemons. I think he's trying to protect you from Noa." She chuckled, starting for the driver's door.

Glacier didn't laugh. Instead, he shuddered at the thought of Adam's red-ringed eyes.

She chose you.

Chose him for *what?*

NOA

Noa tapped a finger against the coffee table, shifting her weight against the carpet while Crow took his sweet old time deliberating over his digital playing cards on his phone. She forced out a slow, controlled breath and set her sights on the clock in the corner of the tablet laying between them, alerting her it'd been two hours and forty-two minutes since they'd left.

She told herself that they probably made a couple stops on the way back, and she was worrying over nothing. Her thumb pressed harder against the phone screen, forcing a popup she had to dismiss for the second time.

Two hours and *forty-three* minutes.

"I fold," Crow finally said, placing his phone face down on the table.

Noa groaned and fell back against the floor with a thud, glimpsing Cecilia padding out from the hallway as Crow nursed his water. A light, melodic hum filled the kitchen in her rustling through the cabinets.

Crow muttered something to himself in a bitter tone before pipping up with, "Sleep well?"

The humming stopped, and Cecilia's voice turned a little sour. "Clearly you didn't."

Rune interrupted with a stretch and a yawn, surveying the room before his arms hit his sides. "I'm shocked you two were up before us."

"I may be up," Crow grumbled, setting his glass back down, "but I'm not *alive*."

"Well, maybe you should consider retiring from drinking yourself to death."

Crow shot him a glare as he rounded the couch and dropped into the armchair. Rune's gaze shifted from his brother to fixate on Noa.

She supposed that lingering embarrassment from drunkenly climbing into bed with Glacier, despite the idea that he could somehow read her mind.

"Please tell me you didn't drink as much as he did."

She rolled her head away.

"*Noa.*"

Crow chuckled darkly. "Oh, she kept up with me, all right."

She propped herself up on her elbows, narrowing her eyes at him. "At least I can hold my liquor better than you."

His grin immediately vanished.

The release of the apartment door's lock pulled everyone's attention away from the subject of drunken mistakes and onto whatever news Nyx had to offer, but more importantly, she and Glacier were back. Boots squeaked against the entry tiles, perking Noa's ears until she caught Rune staring at her, so she twisted to catch sight of the window behind her instead. She grimaced at the sight of rain falling past in sheets.

Crow shifted to sit sideways on the couch. "You two look awful."

"You're one to talk," Nyx replied, dropping her boots against the wall.

The volley continued, muffled to Noa's ears while she watched Glacier tug off his boots and start toward his room. She traced his hunched figure with her eyes until Rune blocked her view, so she snapped back to Nyx, pressing down the urge to ask if he was okay.

"We have the rest of the replicas now," Nyx said, dropping her bag on the couch, "which means we're set for the final half of this suicide gauntlet. And yes, they're flawless, just like the first set."

Noa fully sat up, trying to act casual about her next question. "And did everything go okay? No issues at all? Well, outside of the rain, I mean."

"I think so... Other than our rental car's soft-top cover being a little jammed, everything was fine. I got it fixed, so it was a non-issue."

It wasn't exactly the answer she'd hoped for, but she quieted as the discussion evolved into their plans for the New Year. Noa tuned it all out, playing with the cuff of her pant leg as her thoughts fell into childish daydreams of watching the fireworks next to him.

6

MIRALTA ✧ 2704-12-21

NOA

Noa stared up at the ceiling's plaster circles from her chair, hating that she'd been locked out of her room again so Nyx could work on her little research projects in peace—her words, definitely not Noa's. Every time she'd wandered down the hall to cry to Nyx, she contemplated knocking on Glacier's door. She hadn't seen him in over a day now, and her only assurance that he was alive was Cecilia saying he didn't feel well.

She wished Rune wasn't hanging all over her so Noa could pester her more about what might be bothering him, but every time she opened her mouth, she smacked straight into Rune's raised eyebrow. Rune's casual smirk. Rune's smug body language that made her want to hoist him out the window and down two floors to the street.

"I'm worried about Glacier," Cecilia finally said after *far* too much idle chatter.

Thank gods someone said it.

"Why?" Noa asked, keeping her tone neutral.

"I don't know... he just seems... overly exhausted? Maybe depressed?"

Noa's jaw tightened, refusing to make eye contact with Rune. She already knew what she'd find there, but she was too busy focusing on walking that fine line of acting friendly but not *overly* friendly.

Crow's muffled voice sounded from his facedown position on the couch. "Maybe it's because he just needs to get laid."

Noa leaned forward, grabbed a fistful of his hair, and yanked up, earning a yelp.

"*Shit!* What the hell?" He scrambled to sit up with wide eyes.

"Erase that thought from your mind right now," Noa snapped. "It isn't going to happen."

Rune cut her a sharp, knowing look that sent her sinking back into her seat like if anyone was going to make a pass at him, it'd be *her*. She bit down on her tongue and folded her arms over her chest. Too bad he was wrong.

Cecilia brought her knees up to her chest. "I'm just concerned. He said that he didn't feel well when I checked on him earlier, and we haven't really talked much recently. I think he was stressed about how close we were to Amarais a couple days ago. I can't really blame him though. I'd like to go up and find my parents, but…"

"And we'll go back for them," Rune said, tucking a lock of her hair behind her ear. A quick kiss on her forehead sent a ripple of jealously through Noa. Her nails bit into her palms.

"Maybe he just needs some space," Cecilia said, "since he doesn't seem to want to talk."

"Maybe." Rune turned his face toward the window. "How about we take a walk. It'll be good to get some fresh air. You should invite Glacier. Maybe it'll cheer him up some."

"Good," Crow grumbled, snuggling back into the couch. "Everybody get the hell out."

"You're coming too."

Noa's fixed her sights on Cecilia as she got up and jogged down the hall to push his door open, drowning out the petty argument between Rune and Crow until she returned. She shook her head, looking disappointed before Rune glanced over to Noa.

"Do you want to get some fresh air too?"

A trick question. An option. A *trap*—one that allowed her to stay here, practically *alone* with Glacier. Neither answer would allow her to win in his eyes, but she intended to pretend like it didn't matter.

"I'm exhausted," she said. "Since Nyx locked me out, I'd like to borrow someone else's room while you guys are gone."

He rolled his eyes and motioned for Crow to stand. "All right. Let's go then."

Crow complained and tossed a decorative cushion on the floor on his way out while Cecilia gave her a quick wave goodbye. The door shut, and Noa rubbed at her temples. After staring at the clock for a few minutes, she pushed herself up out of the chair and made her way to Cecilia and Rune's room, collapsing into the bed and falling asleep the moment her head hit the pillow.

Noa woke to the peaceful silence of the apartment, minus the neighbors' muffled noise. She stretched and retraced her steps to the living room to discover a black-clad form taking over the couch again.

A breathy chuckle escaped her as she opened the kitchen cabinet to peruse their snacks. "So, you managed to escape, huh?"

"No."

Noa paused, her head whipping around to check the body again. It wasn't Crow. She swallowed, creeping over to take in his face, where only his green eye was visible in his absent stare out the window.

"I thought you left with them," Glacier said quietly, his gaze only flicking up to her for a brief moment.

The hollowness of his voice made her drop into the armchair, immediately locked in. "I decided not to. I was too worn out from not sleeping all that well last night, so I took a nap."

Silence.

"What's wrong?"

He bit his lip like he was about to tell a lie to make her leave—a lie she knew with every fiber of her being would result in the opposite.

"I..." he started, his voice wavering ever so slightly, "I don't think that I'm going to live through our return to Amarais."

The words manifested as a punch to the gut, forcing the air from her lungs. Anger welled up inside her, but it wasn't like that anger that had been directed at him back in Knighton—this time it was rage directed at anyone who'd consider ripping him away from her. She wouldn't let that happen. Not after all the shit they had been through. Not unless they took her first.

She got up, moving to sit on the edge of the coffee table to block his view. "You are *not* going to die in Amarais." Her words were firm, though she tried to lace them with a kindness that she wasn't sure she could convey. "Why the hell would you even think that?"

"I... used to think... that maybe fate was something we could change. But now I'm starting to believe that the most we can do is just delay the inevitable. My dad... Kat... they died trying so damn hard to do what I'm supposed to do now. I'm not even close to measuring up to either of them. I barely even made it out alive, even when they didn't."

He sat up, not bothering to try to fix his hair in the way it stuck up at odd angles. "It's not like I can't *try* though, not unless I want to make all their efforts be for nothing. I just feel like I'm running with stolen time because I should've died back in the palace—just like them."

"Are you saying that you somehow deserve to die? Because of what— your green eye and black hair? Because you're half-Miraltan and didn't get a choice in that?" Her throat constricted at the mere mention of it, wanting nothing more than to pull him into a hug and tell him that he was worth so much more. She wanted so badly for the Volkov to simply disappear. For Amarais to fix itself. For everything else like the damn keys and the Vault to just cease to exist. Noa didn't want to face any of the consequences that came with that show of affection.

"I feel like there's something else wrong with me," he whispered, his voice wavering as his face dropped into his hands, "and I don't know what it is or how to fix it. I just want it to stop."

There's nothing wrong with you, she wanted to say, but the words wouldn't come out.

"Glacier," she said sternly.

He lifted his head to meet her gaze.

"There isn't a single person among us that would leave you to die in Amarais, not unless it took the rest of us too. We're in this together, so we're either going to survive together or die together. Understood?" She waited for his response, narrowing her eyes at him.

There was a brief moment of pause before he began to nod.

She pushed herself up, wiping her hands on the sides of her pants. "Good. Now, since we're behind on your training, and we've suddenly run into a plethora of unscheduled time, you and I will be continuing with our agreement. No excuses. You'll get some sleep, you'll eat, and you'll occupy yourself appropriately to keep your mind off of this nonsense that you're just going to die. Because you're not. You're going to live."

His face remained blank. "Forgive me for not being all that optimistic about becoming king of a country that hates half of who I am."

"It could be worse."

He tilted his head, his brows furrowing.

"You could be someone completely ill-equipped to run a country, let alone potentially an entire realm of existence through the course of a suicide mission. In other words, you could be me."

7

KING'S REPUBLIC ✧ 2704-12-25

ARRINGTON

"What can I do for you, Director Arrington?"

Director Bristol's office was a museum compared to his own, decked out with wall-to-wall shelving units mounted around periodic articles of framed art. They were all forged pieces she'd picked up during her career, much like how one might keep hunting trophies. He recognized the styles or pieces they were modeled after from every large case she'd sent straight to headlines.

Arrington eyed one of the modular chairs in front of her desk until he decided it would be better to stand, just in case his plan backfired and he needed to leave immediately. Desperate times and all that.

"I need you to give me back control of the case." He gave himself a pat on the back for not flying into a rage like he'd wanted to, controlling his voice, softening his letters in all the right ways to emphasize what was required. It turned into less of a demand and more of a command, though it didn't taste the same as when it left his lips to get what he wanted from someone he'd never see again.

A quiet scoff sounded from Bristol. "And why would I bother doing that?"

"Because there's a possibility that this case involves three criminals that my department has been following for the past few months. They're related to another case that occurred about a year ago when two of them attempted to collect and distribute sensitive information in relation to a very prestigious organization—one I'm not at liberty to discuss. However, they have a new accomplice that was spotted with them recently, so if you play this too aggressively, you'll scare them off."

It was a well-crafted lie, one that would only stay between them since he knew how Bristol worked. She wouldn't tell a soul unless they needed to know, and with the Monettes' data restricted in the system, he could give any sort of reasoning he wanted. After all, it was a large building. It was unlikely that she had run into either of them before, let alone the possibility of running into either of the twins later anyway. He just had to pretend that they might show up, even when he was only banking on them making a later appearance.

"And what makes you so sure that they'll show?" She folded her arms over the desktop, her forehead beginning to wrinkle.

"Because I received another tip that one of their former accomplices could be potentially carrying out the theft. The problem is that I have no idea *who* since we never caught any of the others, but if there's still any loyalty, then it'll at least lure them out."

She sighed, pressing her fingers to a temple. "And how did you lose the other two in the first place, Arrington?"

"They escaped during transport." Close enough. "It's not exactly something that I'm proud of, but my department messed up and they got away."

"Arrington... Look, I understand that you want the case back, but the issue is that is still lies in my jurisdiction. It doesn't matter if your shit has somehow gotten mixed into it—"

"No, I don't think *you* understand—" His eyes darkened as that desperate need for control took over, conjuring up that poisoned magic thrumming somewhere in his core. It tangled with his words, bending the influence of each sound—whether it made it more pleasing or urgent, he didn't know, but he also didn't care, so long as it got him what he wanted.

"This is also still under my jurisdiction as well since this individual could tie back to the data breach. We should at least work *together* on this."

Her face went blank, like a child learning something new. She blinked rapidly a couple of times after that, regaining her composure, along with a slightly begrudging nod. "Seeing as how this information specifically pertains to my department. I will still oversee the handling of this. However, since you're cooperating, and you bring up a good point, I think we can work something out."

Arrington held back a smirk, opting to tug his suit jacket instead. Risk, meet reward.

"Give me their profiles, and I'll keep an eye out for them," Bristol said, "I'll hand-deliver them to you myself if they happen to show up. If not—" She shrugged. "I suppose it's on your department to clean up your own mess, isn't it?"

He reasoned that it was likely the best he could ask for. So, he retrieved a disc from his pocket and placed in on the desktop, where three profiles popped up with minimized information. His two rogue agents and the mystery woman.

"We're still pinning down who the woman is, exactly," he said, "but we know that if she shows up, she can lead us to them." The fact that he still didn't know who she really was further agitated him, but once he got his hands on her, he'd make sure to pull out every word he was looking for.

Director Bristol waved a hand over her desk, dismissing the holographic images. "Thank you. I'll do what I can."

He supposed that was all he could do for now, which was enough to work with, despite wanting more control. On the plus side, this was still time to pull a few more of her strings with the power he had at his disposal.

ALYVIA

The rumble of cleaning carts skipping over the tiles in the hall called for Alyvia to stand. She stretched, welcoming the relief that came with knowing she'd made it through her last day of work before a long holiday off, along with the rest of the office. Her sole problem now became whether or not she should catch the last train back home to her parents' house—a decision that they'd probably frown at after pulling her into a hug. Her mother would tell her that she should've stayed and hung out with friends, and her father would've teased her for coming back to 'babysit' them.

"Are you heading out?" Shane pulled the door to his office shut, holding a jacket over his arm and a bag hanging off his shoulder. He looked about as exhausted as she felt, taking in his rumpled, rolled-up sleeves and disheveled hair.

"Yeah," she said, grabbing her bag.

"Let's walk out together. Just give me a second to lock up."

She nodded, waiting as he fumbled for his key to tap it to the panel. Alyvia's eyes drifted over to Jinko's door, where a thin strip of light was visible through the bottom crack.

"Maybe we should see if she wants to talk out with us?" Alyvia asked with a half-hearted point to her office. As much as she didn't really care to, it was the holidays, after all. Being a little nice wouldn't kill her.

Shane grimaced as he stopped next to her, starting to shake his head. "I don't think she'd want to be disturbed right now. I think she's trying to wrap up on some proofing before she gets out of here for the break."

"Oh, um—"

Before she could offer to stay and help to offset her recent sabotage, Shane held out an arm toward the exit like a gentleman opening a door. "Shall we?"

His cheerful, warm smile indicated that he couldn't care less about Jinko's problems, which disturbingly put her at ease. The strange feeling of solidarity forced her to nod. They started their journey to the elevators, passing the dwindling staff, cleaning carts, and through the final wall of badge scanners. Just like that, they were on the street, free for a week's worth of time to rest and relax.

Puddles glowed and flickered in neon reds, blues, and pinks while advertisements flashed, absorbed by the clamor of people making their way through. Local bars had lines out to the patterned pavers along the promenade and restaurants began turning customers away.

"Are you heading out to see your family for New Year's?" Shane asked.

"I'm actually not sure yet..." she admitted with a nervous, tired laugh as she picked at her coat sleeves.

"Well," he said, stuffing his hands into his jacket pockets, "if you *do* decide to stick around, there are a few of us from work and a couple extra friends of mine that are meeting up the night before. You should join us."

She chewed on the inside of her lip. "That... might be nice. My parents typically encourage me to spend time with others this time of year anyway. I've just been feeling a little homesick, so... It's been a rough couple of weeks."

"I think you should stay," he said.

"I—Thank you."

"I'm... honestly a little surprised that there's no one else that you'd rather spend your New Year's with." He rubbed the back of his neck, loosing a nervous chuckle. "I sort of assumed that you were dating someone."

"Oh, no—" She forced out an awkward laugh. "I've been spending my time just... working."

Their pace slowed, coming to a stop on the commuter platform.

"Just, um... Let me know if you decide to stick around," he said as the hurtling cry of the next train began breaking in front of them and the passengers shoved their way off.

"I will. Thanks." She gave him a quick smile and wave before she merged into the traffic climbing onto the train.

She grabbed onto a handle and turned to the window to find him waving back—a fleeting image that she hung onto as the doors shut, whisking her away to the next stop. Her smile fell, taking that warm, fuzzy feeling of acceptance with it. Guilt took its place, telling her that she was undermining all his work for the selfishness of recovering lost, fragmented memories of her aunt. The woman wasn't even alive, not with how long she had been gone, so it was ridiculous to try to convince herself of that lie. But at least she and her family might have closure in the end.

That was the primary reminder that kept her from buckling under the weight of Shane's kindness—that, and the condemning words and actions from Arrington and Jinko.

8

MIRALTA ✧ 2704-12-26

GLACIER

Mist clung to the windshield of the soft-top SUV in the early hours of dawn. Glacier shivered as he dumped his bag in the trunk and climbed inside, bumping shoulders and elbows with Cecilia before pressing up against the door. All he could do was watch the apartment building fade away in the rearview mirror and wait.

There was a numbness to it all he couldn't explain, eased by the comfort of a newfound routine of training with Noa in the early hours of the morning until breakfast, then going out with Cecilia and Rune to roam the town until lunch. Each stop at a park to sit and take in the calming trickle of the stream that cut through it or a jog inside a store advertising hand-crafted trinkets always got Cecilia curious looks. They'd either overlook Glacier altogether or greet him with kind smiles.

In the afternoons, Nyx would hand him small projects to work on until dinner. After that, she'd take whatever tools she'd given him away, and he was left to his own devices until bed. That time always turned into more research—research about anything and everything related to whatever Nyx had given him most of the time. Anything but what was happening around him.

The worst part was that Noa's absence after their morning sessions had begun to leave a sort of void. When he'd wake before her, he'd somehow know before he'd crept out into the living room. When she'd slip out at night, his mind forced him to stay awake, waiting for a sign of her return. When they'd practice, and he turned his back on her, he always knew where she was. All he had to do was close his eyes, and he'd find that small spark wherever it went.

That anchor—tether—whatever he could call it—brought him an unnatural sense of peace or dread, depending on how far it stretched. More often than not, he'd been stuck with the latter. Not that he could blame her.

To Noa, Glacier was *Glacier*—the pathetic prince. Her final key. Nothing more. He'd been foolish to ever consider that she might see him differently, let alone allow himself to fall for someone so wrapped up in her own inevitable self-destruction masquerading as invincibility.

His head lulled against the window during the drive, watching the trees part to brick buildings every dozen-or-so kilometers. The distance between him and civilization became an ever-changing mark with a couple breaks to stretch their legs and eat. Finally, Rune slowed the car as the pavement turned to rumbling pavers, passing spindling iron fences under drooping willows until he turned into a side alley nestled between two homes.

Glacier nearly slipped on the wet leaves in the driveway, too preoccupied with staring up at the cheerful, soft-yellow shutters framing circular windows at the peak. Much of the house was locked in its own battle against the dreary ivy weaving down the trellises. They clamored up onto the porch, where two doors greeted them. A duplex.

Nyx opened the door to a smaller living room tucked next to the stairs. It blocked the closet of a kitchen at the back of the unit, but the good news was that there were four bedrooms on the second level for both he and Crow to have their own individual rooms.

The need to immediately occupy himself sent him straight to Nyx's room across the hall, hesitating at the sight of Noa further inside. Cecilia grabbed his arm, ripping him from the darkening corners of his mind and dragging him downstairs to join her and Rune on their first excursion into town. Not having much of a choice, he went with them.

He tucked his hands into his pockets, wobbling each time Cecilia nudged him to point out something that made her eyes light up. Hand-crafted jewelry, hand-painted pottery, and hand-sewn scarves became reasons for them to stop into each store, where it smelled of warm apple and cinnamon, lavender, and eucalyptus. Their final stop's cashier tilted her register screen toward them, excitedly advertising the small evening concert in their town square.

Home. Dinner. Bed, at least for almost everyone else.

Glacier remained downstairs, curled up on the couch with a tablet filled edge-to-edge with news articles about Amarais and anything potentially related to their fake emblems being noticed. All of it resulted in the same as it had a week ago: radio silence.

The front door opened, and Glacier clutched the tablet to his chest, freezing Noa to the spot. She glanced at the clock and narrowed her eyes at him. "Shouldn't you be going to bed?"

He clenched his teeth and dropped the tablet onto the couch as he stood. "Are you avoiding me?"

Her eyes went wide. "W-what?"

"You... you know that you can tell me if I said or did something, right? I'd rather that than—"

"No, it's not—"

"At least do me the favor of not lying to me, okay? I understand that I'm not exactly pleasant to be around—"

"That's not it," she said sharply. Her hand went to her hair, her fingers knotting in whatever they could while she stared down at the floor. "*When the Volkov catch up to us, they're going to go after you and me first. Us acting friendly with each other—doing so much together—just increases the odds that they'll go after you first. I'd rather them go straight for me so the rest of you might have the chance to run.*"

His shoulders fell. "I... I thought you told me that we're in this together."

"Yes, except for *this*. They don't give a shit about the rest of you when it comes to me unless it'll hurt me. I'm the one that chose this—"

"Noa, you didn't *choose* to be Volkov—"

Her voice rose, immediately quieting him. "Glacier, I had the chance to walk away and *didn't*. They thought I was dead three years ago. I didn't leave because godsdamned Lazarus told me not to, and he'd still be alive if I had just done it anyway."

The pain in her voice made his heart drop. "But... if you had... wouldn't Nyx be dead right now?"

She scrubbed at her forehead.

"And... Rune and Crow would still be trying to find a way out of the Republic, right? I mean, Cecilia and I would be dead too... We're all here because of *you*. The choice you made gave us more time that we wouldn't have had, and maybe Lazarus knew that you needed that."

Her wrist slid down her face like she'd wiped away a stray tear. "Do you really think that your twisted notion of delaying the inevitable is right?" she asked evenly. "Because I really hope you're wrong."

"I guess we're going to find out, whether we like it or not."

She wrapped her arms around herself, pinning her eyes on the floor again. The two of them locked in place with uncertainty of what to do next.

"You should..." Noa started, her voice climbing from a whisper once she cleared her throat. "You should go to bed."

Glacier hovered for a moment before he collected the tablet and started up the steps, stretching that invisible bond between them as it ebbed back into focus. She was still in the entry by the time he'd made it to his room. He kicked the door shut behind him and pushed the tablet onto the nightstand as he crawled into bed. He counted the seconds until Noa moved again, making her way upstairs and into her room before sleep pulled him into its welcoming embrace.

9

MIRALTA ✧ 2704-12-30

NYX

Nyx roused to a soft light emanating from the nightstand. Grumbling, she clicked off the tablet's display and twisted to check on Noa's prone form— a rare, but welcomed treat at 4:00AM, though rather inconvenient this time. She slid out from the covers and scooped the device into her arms before tiptoeing out into the hall.

Light washed over her face, triggering a wince until she read the message consuming the screen: *unlocked.*

Her eyebrows rose. There it was: the decryption key prompt. The final hurdle to get Alyvia her answers and secure a much-needed ally. She tapped on the little question mark for a potential hint, and her excitement quickly faded to irritation.

You bitch.

Three logged entries. Two key updates. Whatever it'd been when Juniper had left, it wasn't anymore. Releasing a quiet, low hum, she composed a message to Alyvia.

> Good news: it's unlocked.

Bad news: I sure as hell hope that you know what she might've changed her key to, because she did it twice.

She attached a copy of the journal, fearing this might be the bottleneck she might not be able to complete on her own. At least, not before the Volkov decided to finish them off. The best-case scenario is that it would scramble the journal data with the wrong key. The worst, it would delete it entirety and send a beacon out to wipe all other copies with it.

She flipped back to the log to re-examine her clues, doing a double-take when her eyes caught on the entry dates. According to the data she'd accumulated, the final change had been just over a *year* since she had left for Amarais. She'd been alive during all that time and hadn't told her family about it—but *why?*

Perhaps she was still alive after all. Maybe she was hiding out in the far reaches of the country somewhere, moving from family to family like a damn saint to teach their kids magic or something. Nyx sighed and clicked off the tablet again. Regardless, Alyvia likely wasn't awake yet, and there would be plenty of time to craft theories later in the day. She opened the door, ready to return to bed and sleep on the fact that Juniper had been alive much longer than they both had originally thought.

10

KING'S REPUBLIC ✧ 2704-12-31

ALYVIA

Alyvia scrolled through her phone during her commuter train ride, not really paying attention to anything on the screen. Her mind remained stuck on Nyx's progress with the journal—specifically the key to it. Each clue had seared into her thoughts while she'd brushed her teeth yesterday morning, and every guess she had, she'd typed into a notepad until she ran out of steam after half-interrogating her father over text.

Her obsession tethered on insanity with the hope that her aunt was still alive, and she forced herself to let it go in favor of enjoying her New Year's Eve. She squeezed her phone, blacking out the screen as she gripped the pole and stared out into the sea of strung lights crisscrossing over streets. The intercom called her stop, and she pulled herself to her feet, hopping onto the platform the second the doors opened.

Sharp, cool air filled her lungs and gnawed at the tip of her nose. She dipped her chin into her scarf as she moved past patron after patron on their bar crawls. Some burst into off-key songs and others giggled at their sweaters, decorated with tacky, glowing decorations and numbers representing the new year. Special holiday tents with cheery blue and purple flashing signs took over every free nook and alleyway, bursting at the seams with everyone from teenagers to older couples holding hands and pointing up at the twinkling displays overhead.

Alyvia pushed through to the pub, stepping inside to find a sea of strangers mingling around her, holding up glasses and talking animatedly in the corners. She gripped her bag strap and scanned the crowd until she caught sight of a figure waving at her.

Shane half-stood, grinning from his seat along the far wall. She weaved through, apologizing when she bumped shoulders with some of the people standing along the bar.

"I'm glad you made it," he said, moving over along the bench to give her a spot to sit.

"Sorry it took me so long," she replied, hesitating as she settled in next to him and began tugging off her gloves.

No Jinko. She eyed each of the people at the table, not recognizing any of them from the office, Shane confirming her suspicions with his quick introductions. Every name was lost to the raucous laughter and cheers from a nearby group absorbed in a table game. The guy across from Shane started an order for a second round of drinks right before they launched into stories from earlier on in the year.

Alyvia slid down in her seat, feeling a pang of regret at her decision to join. Everyone else here appeared to know each other with their claps on the backs and inside jokes she tried to follow. An outsider.

"You okay?"

She whipped her head towards Shane, whose brows knitted together in concern.

"Oh, yeah—I'm good, just... tired." She turned her glass around, scratching it against the tabletop.

"Still upset about work?"

She shrugged. "A little."

"Trust me, I get it," he said with a bitter laugh. "You're doing the best you can though, which is far better than the rest of those dumbasses. I wish I could just fire them all and start over." He tipped his drink back, and her eyes went wide, surprised he'd actually said that.

She forced out a nervous laugh. "Y-you don't actually mean that."

"No, I do. Most of them are useless. They just clock in to fill a seat. It's ridiculous that you don't get the recognition you deserve."

"I'm honestly kind of used to it by now."

"What? Why?"

She shook her head, trying to hold back a bitter, knowing smile. "Shane, I'm not exactly what people picture when they talk about a technical officer or expert." She pointed to her green eyes.

A guffaw escaped him. "But you're *Republican*."

"With dual citizenship until I turned twenty. That on its own made a lot of potential employers hesitant. After all, why would a Miraltan be specializing in a field not related to magic."

"You realize that you outmatch everyone in that office, right? If I had it my way, I'd see you promoted to report to Arrington. You're wasting your talent doing all this grunt work."

"Well, I'm not so sure that Arrington likes me very much."

"Don't take that personally, Alyvia," he said with a smirk. "He doesn't like anyone very much. You deserve a promotion, and that's what I'm trying to get you."

"Shane..."

"No—I won't hear it," he said jokingly, holding up his hands in mock defense. "We're within the last five minutes, so there are no more arguments allowed for the year."

Guilt trickled through her again, hating that he was so hell-bent on helping her. The shushing by the other patrons pushed it away in the final count as some people got up in search of friends or lovers to hug or kiss at midnight, including one of Shane's acquaintances that stopped another guy along the wall. The rest pulled out their phones for the timer.

Shane held up his glass to her with a smirk. "To the new year."

At the sound of 'ten' being chanted throughout the room, she lifted her glass in turn. They clinked at five and drank as the room erupted into cheers.

11

KING'S REPUBLIC ✧ 2705-01-03

GLACIER

The grogginess that'd gripped Glacier that morning held fast as they hurtled past quaint countryside and densely wooded havens. The lingering warnings and reminders from the others the night before had left him feeling uneasy, but the biggest feeder of doubt had been the discomforting glances at one another. This job would be different: higher security, room for fewer mistakes, and a city that became the perfect landscape for the Volkov to hide in.

Noa had told him not to leave wherever they were staying without her escorting him, despite the consensus he'd need to at least glamour his blue eye. Without that identifier and the distinct lack of identifying images of him, he'd assumed that he should be okay, but the way Noa's fingertips had dug into his arm told another story.

Between that and her whispered explanation of more officers per square kilometer than their past destinations, he'd told her that they'd just have to plan like everything could go wrong. He'd spend every waking hour making sure he didn't miss anything that might send them spiraling into another disaster like Amarais.

Cecilia grabbed his chin and turned his head toward her. "You can stop staring out the window for a second to look at me," she said, biting her lip as she uncapped her eyeliner pen.

He focused on the new faces of his cabinmates—an Astravnian with a face scrunched up in irritation, masked by shaggy brown hair and matching dull eyes, and a Corvian with darker, wavier hair with vivid violet eyes set on the ID in front of him, exuding that mask of calm. The pressure of the pen fell away, and Cecilia smirked. "See? Quick."

Her grin slipped into obscurity as she leaned to the side, staring past him and the deep blue curtains framing the train cabin window to the upward climb of buildings upon their entry to the city. Sprawling neighborhoods of single-story homes turned into two-story, then apartments, high-rises, and skyscrapers. Clean, precise Corvian designs of glass and steel mingled among whimsical Bellegardian façades. Jinwonese elegant, circular archways countering embellished, curtained tiers of Esmedralian ones.

The whole of Avaria cobbled together into a single spot.

"Does it feel weird?" Glacier asked, barely above a whisper as he tore his eyes from the window to a Corvian-glamoured Rune.

Rune frowned, tilting his head.

"Returning home like this. Does it feel weird?"

He huffed a breathy laugh. "Yeah... yeah, it does." He turned his face to the city outside, his violet eyes reflecting that weighty sadness that Glacier had felt back in Miralta. That unspoken feeling of knowing there'd be no one welcoming them home.

"When I made you promise not to go anywhere without me, I meant it."

Glacier spun around, grabbing the hand clamped onto his arm in the corridor of the train. He redirected to clap a hand over his mouth the moment his took in Noa—scowl and all.

"Did Nyx really do it to you *again?*" he asked through coughs of laughter.

"Shut the hell up," she hissed. "Of course she did. She couldn't pass up another damn opportunity to humiliate me. I'm sick and tired of being a Bellegardian. Just look at me," —she held out her arms from her sides— "it's like Crow and I swapped places."

"I'd say you look more like Rune than Crow with the darker eyes..."

"They're basically *black*, Gl—" Noa snapped her mouth shut, cutting herself off with a grimace before swapping to a tight smile. "*Morgan*. At least you got it easy with a pretty green eye to match the other."

"I don't know... I think darker eyes look nicer," he said, hesitating the moment it slipped out. She reared back a little in surprise, and he tried to shove away the image of her fawn-brown irises lurking beneath her glamour.

Then her face hardened again, and she slugged him in the arm.

"*Ow*—holy shit—"

"Alright you two, break it up," Rune said, pushing past with Cecilia and steering Glacier back around.

His bag bounced against the car wall, matching the sound of Noa's footsteps stalking behind him. He rubbed his arm, glancing back at her with a scowl as she pulled out her phone. Back to ignoring him. Again.

Glacier's shoulders fell in their trek to disembark, where they all collided and became another strangely mismatched crew. Nyx shoved him next to Bellegardian Noa and Cecilia next to Astravnian Crow, partnering everyone off before she signaled for Corvian Rune to walk off next to her first.

When the doors opened, Glacier froze up and squeezed his bag strap at the sheer number of people lining the walls, the queues, the platform. Passengers waited shoulder-to-shoulder, checking their phones and hovering near their travel mates with bags at their feet. Noa yanked him onto the yellow rumble strip and pulled him through the sea of blurred faces. Blinking markers and illuminated pathways glowed from resin-coated monitor-panel floors. They followed them under brick archways leading from platform to timetable listings to the exit for local lines.

It dumped them out onto a local platform crammed with just as many people per square meter, which Noa forced them to merge in with.

Volkov. Volkov. Volkov.

He took a deep breath, reminding himself that Noa was right next to him and keeping an eye out at every turn, despite his thumping of his heart drowning out all sound. He swallowed, leaning into her. "Do you know where we're going?"

"Nope." Her head snapped over to a couple giggling next to them, her body tensing briefly before the next local train screamed to a halt.

Passengers filed off or reshuffled from poles and handholds into seats lining the windows. Glacier was dragged on board, tensing at every person brushing up against him to fill up the remaining space. He hooked an arm around a pole and pressed a knuckle to his chest where the miniature Shield of Miralta rested, flooding him with a reassuring safety.

The doors slid shut, and his eyes followed the turn of Cecilia's head, taking in the wall of windows facing away from the station. A blend of designs coming together through the crammed strips of shops across the street.

Cecilia grinned, turning back to him with a giddy, child-like enthusiasm. "This is so cool!" she said, a slight squeal to her voice that made him lift the back of his hand to his mouth, trying to hide his amusement. It was quickly diminished by the other passengers glancing up from their phones with slight frowns or confused looks, finding an Amaraian and a Miraltan sharing some sort of joke. Self-conscious, his face fell again, though it didn't stop Cecilia from gawking at each street they passed.

Several stops flew by before Nyx elbowed glamoured Rune again in a signal that the next stop would be their exit. They stepped off into a district paved with larger sidewalks lined with small cages at the bases of short, thin trees. Luxury and rental cars parked under some, dotted with leaves or petals. Minimalistic buildings touting large glass panes framed by black or white sleek marble-looking square beams took over each block in view.

"Damn," Crow said with a whistle. "You got us the nice side of town."

"I did my research," Nyx said, undaunted by the residents passing by in business suits, pencil skirts, and well-fitting dresses. "I didn't exactly want us to be hassled in the bad part of town."

Rune let out a low hum, mumbling, "I'm pretty sure the people that live in the bad part of town don't want to deal with the hassle of residing in the bad part of town."

"Fair, but the upside is that this is equidistant from both the museum and the station we'll be leaving from, so it's a linear getaway to swing by the hotel before we head out."

She turned into a set of wide, shallow steps leading up to a series of double and revolving doors. The sight made Glacier recoil, taking in a merged amalgamation of their hotel in Corvia with the Amaraian palace. He was guided upward anyway, straight into the grand entrance, boasting more of Amarais than he'd seen since they'd left.

Large, white-marbled slabs covered every surface, disrupted by an enormous compass-like design in the middle of the floor. Valentian bronzed fixtures like the near-black piece at the far end of the lobby dropping sheets of water down to the indent in the floor over a cursive name he couldn't read.

"Wait here," Nyx instructed, motioning only for Rune to follow her to the counter.

Glacier bit his lip and tugged on Noa's sleeve, causing her head to whip around. "You, um... you didn't see anyone you know out there, did you?"

"No."

His chance to ask more was disrupted by Nyx's wave for them to proceed to the elevator bank, sending them up a dozen floors to a black-and-white hallway. Occasional dots of blue, purple, and green popped out from the monochromatic modern paintings hung along the walls as Nyx led them to the end.

She pressed her key to the lock, and pushed it open to their new, temporary residence. Crow's face lit up as he pushed past them and dropped his bag to the floor. "Now *this* is what I'm talking about." His voice echoed through the two-story lofted unit.

Glacier spun around to the walkway above them leading to the bedrooms. It had to have been at least twice the size of any of the apartments they'd been living in over the past couple weeks—maybe even the one they'd rented back in Talie. A piano was tucked into the far corner by a games table that sat in front of a wide, electric fireplace where digital blue flames licked at black rocks. Crow placed a hand against the two-story-tall floor-to-ceiling windows framing a picturesque view of the sprawling city

"Now," Nyx said, calling everyone's attention, "the first rule is that no one leaves without express permission from either Noa or I once we're finished with prep work. The four of you need to leave in pairs and scout out the museum before it closes." She fished out a device from her bag and tossed it to Noa. "I just need you to get that inside the museum for about thirty seconds. It'll cut through any interference. Once that's done, I'll let you know, and you can move back outside if you'd like."

"So," Noa started, turning it over in her hands, "you want Crow and I to go inside first?"

"Correct. Cecilia will also need to re-glamour all of you before you leave. We can't exactly afford to burn the ones you all are wearing right now." She turned, snapping to regain Crow's gaze from the windows. "Call the shades once, please."

Frowning, he complied and turned back with a giddy, surprised expression when it had only minorly deterred from the view. "Oh, hell *yes*. Privacy shades?"

"Yes, I know," Nyx waved a hand. "I pull out all the stops, so you don't have to stay glamoured in here. Now hurry up. You'll have tonight and all day tomorrow to enjoy the view." She set her sights on Glacier and started for the couch. "Now let's get set up."

SHANE

Shane paced in front of Arrington's desk, tugging at his hair, eyeing the door—*waiting* for him to return to his office. Torture was certainly one word for what he was feeling now, but he still wasn't sure how to describe that *thing* that lay still in the city. He'd been sitting at his desk, tapping a stylus against his desk one minute, and the next, fighting back a rustling climbing up his spine, itching for him to *move*.

It'd rolled in like a slow-creeping fog, both everywhere and nowhere all at once, leaving it spread so far it became nearly impossible to pinpoint the source. Well, except for becoming the source of his newfound agitation.

He stiffened and spun around at the catch of the door in the frame. Arrington strode inside, leaving the shades tinting the interior hall windows. "Sit," he instructed.

"You know what it is, don't you?" Shane whispered, dropping into a seat.

"I'm fairly certain that it's a Seer," Arrington said, slowing at the window like he was surveying where their quarry could be hidden among the glass, steel, and brick jungle.

"We could split it." Shane tried to swallow back the plea, but the gluttonous impulse had gotten the better of him.

"No. Not for a Seer," he said, causing Shane's shoulders to drop. "Perhaps for an Elementalist or a type of magic that deals in physical manifestation. If we ended up splitting a power like this one, then we'd risk too much of its integrity. You split that, and you don't get nearly the full potential out of it." He hummed, tracing a finger along his jaw as he lowered himself into his office chair. "Seeing how we're all a unit, I'd like for you to have it."

Shane sat up a little straighter. "Y-you're serious?"

"Yes," he said, his voice hitting a sharp note with the rest of his conditions, "However, considering their power, I would imagine they'd be able to sense our presence as well..."

Shane cringed, hating how he personified it. These were wells of power, not *people*—vessels wasting their potential that Shane intended to reap.

"You should be careful if you decide to pursue them on your own. Don't make a scene, and certainly don't let your reckless minions cause any problems if you send them in your stead."

Shane stood, unable to suppress a crooked smile. "Naturally. I don't suppose you'd mind if I ducked out early for an appointment, then?"

Arrington waved a hand. "Go. Let Jinko know you're stepping out for business."

CROW

Crow scanned the street, eyeing every nook and camera he passed with Noa hanging on his arm. He reached up and brushed the red hair out of his eyes and frowned down at Noa's phone. Whatever notes she had up were too small for him to read with her own reflection of coppery hair taking up the majority of the screen. Frustrated he couldn't free his arm and focus on his own work without toting her around, he huffed.

"Deal with it," Noa mumbled, sliding her phone back into her pocket.

"Do you think the other two are somewhere behind us?" he asked, glancing over his shoulder. "Or do you think they ditched to get a hotel room down the street?"

"As much as I hope they wouldn't do that, I'd honestly just say good for them."

Crow's eye widened. "What the hell is that kind of double-standard?"

"Please tell me the last time you've seen your brother get any action. Because the last time I checked, you've disappeared nearly every night since this whole mess started while he's been sitting around like a good boy."

He grumbled, setting his sights toward the museum again.

"That's what I thought. At least you and Cecilia seem to finally be getting along."

"She's *fine*, I guess," he said, though that was a lie. Cecilia was growing on him, especially since she was finally starting to hold her own in their small challenges. "She's a little *too* nice, but I think I'm starting to wear on her."

"I'm just waiting for the day when she snaps and kills you in your sleep," she mumbled.

"That would require me to actually be sleeping and not—"

"And we're done talking," Noa said with a tight smile, squeezing his arm a little harder in warning as they jogged the shallow concrete steps leading into the museum.

"Can't I at least know why *Morgan* is off-limits?" he asked out of the corner of his mouth.

"It's because I said so. Now shut up." Her hand went up to her ear, like she was brushing back a wisp of hair when she touched her comm piece. A quiet call came through to his ears, alerting Nyx that they were entering the lobby.

Crow immediately picked out the cameras from when he'd visited with

Rune and Corrine. Every single one a familiar and welcomed sight that he didn't overlook before noting the security panels and sensors—new and old —set into the walls. It was like reentering a childhood home with all the furniture rearranged. But *this* was his element, and his memory was his strongest weapon.

He refrained from running his fingers along the damask patterned blue walls as they passed into the main hall, where marble busts sat illuminated in recesses. Noa slowed near the first plaque, and Crow frowned at the glimpse of a nearby guard passing through, then *another*. The further he and Noa went, the more guards he found milling about—at least double from what he remembered last.

Finally, they stood in front of the large, thick glass window separating them from the case within. Blue velvet ropes quartered it off from any special visitors allowed into the room, mainly academics, who occasionally requested a closer look at The Heart of the King for research. He recalled seeing the windows tinted several times for what he assumed must've been cleaning.

The silver of the key glinted under the skylights, becoming him before catching sight of the four posted guards at the edges of the outer room. He bit down on his tongue, reminding himself there was a gala they were preparing for. A black-clad form in the corner of his vision made his head whip around, swearing it'd been an employee in a suit until he found another guard behind them. Crow shook the phantom image from his mind on their way back to the hotel.

WEATHER

"Son of a *bitch*—" Weather hurled a one of her high heels across the studio apartment. "Brigitte, do *this*, and Brigitte, do *that*," she said in a mocking, nasally voice. "That damn bitchy coordinator is going to get what's coming to her. I'm not some damn college student looking to help decorate for this godsdamned party."

She flopped back onto the bed with a groan, her dress shirt half-untucked. How people could stand making an honest living like this when it was far easier to take from those who wouldn't miss it was beyond her. Even worse when she'd been under the assumption that she'd be working immediately under the museum director after submitting the fancy letter of recommendation she'd gotten from Giovanni. Instead, *Brigitte Wagner* had somehow ended up turning into an assistant to a Ms. Giselle Ziegler: her new mortal enemy.

Her original plan had been to assist with handling some of the museum pieces, rather than the party, to give her a leg up in learning the security system. Granted, she had still managed to learn most of it in her free time, but now it was more of the principle of the matter.

Weather pulled a pillow over her head and groaned. She just needed to survive two more days. After that, she'd be ready to bolt across town, scrape up some more credits, and figure out where to go next. She wouldn't be able to stay here. Not anymore.

But that was a normality for Weather, a drifter—a nobody. A soul lost in a sea of souls with no one left to lift her chin up when the world pushed her down. She pulled the pillow down over her chest and stared up at the ceiling, a weary sigh escaping her. She wished on a sky that she couldn't see that her life would stop being such a horrible mess, only to change her mind. The mess was actually fine, so long as she didn't have to go it alone anymore.

12

KING'S REPUBLIC ✧ 2705-01-04

GLACIER

Glacier laid in his bed, staring up at the ceiling around 3:30AM while fidgeting with the Shield of Miralta still hanging around his neck. Dread pressed in, keeping him from sleep like something out there searching for him. It felt different than when Adam had stalked them out to the ship, which left him wondering if the little charm had something to do with it. Then again, he thought he might be tricking himself into thinking he was being hunted.

He pushed back the heavy white comforter and swung his feet to the plush carpeting. The sharp white corners of every piece of furniture made him move with caution to the door, where he took in the faint blue light emanating from the downstairs sofa. He tucked the charm under his shirt and padded down the steps until he stood at the edge of the living room.

Noa ran her thumb over the edge of the tablet, her brows furrowing until she glanced up with a gasp and a hand over her heart. "*Shit*—What the hell do you think you're doing?" she hissed, snapping her fingers and pointing back upstairs. "Go back to sleep."

Feeling more confidence than he probably should have, he stood up straight, folding his arms over his chest. "Make me."

She released a low, frustrated growl and pinned her eyes on the tablet again. The sudden switch didn't have any friendliness to it, but discomfort, like she genuinely didn't want him there. It was just enough to twist that part of his heart that had invested in this lie he still refused to let go of. So, instead of leaving, he motioned to her legs. "Move over," he whispered.

Surprisingly, she did, bringing her knees to her chest. Glacier sank down into the cushions. "What are you reading?"

Noa paused, her eyes seemingly stuck on her work in contemplation. "It's... just some information on one of Daxton's friends. Nyx gave it to me last night because she wants to check on him today. He's been acting paranoid I guess."

"Like *Adam* paranoid, or...?"

"Like someone's following him. Daxton thinks he's been distancing himself because someone isn't thrilled with what he's doing. I guess someone broke into his house and left a note on the screen of his refrigerator. They also moved a couple of things to prove it wasn't a hacker. He told Daxton he's being watched but didn't really specify *why* he thought that or by *who*."

"Um, so when you say, 'we're going', do you mean—"

"Just me and Nyx. You're staying here."

"But Nyx still has quite a bit more prep work to do that I can't," he said cautiously. "I think she's going to need the extra time if we're worried about gala. Not to mention that wouldn't it technically be safer if I was with you anyway?"

"I mean, *technically* yes, but—"

"Then wouldn't it make more sense if I went in her stead?" he asked. "I could even go with you to pick up your dress after we're done."

Her lips pressed into a thin line as her fingers drummed against the tablet. "Fine."

Glacier shoved his hands into his pants pockets after he and Noa stepped off the platform, a little surprised and hurt when she didn't grab onto his arm for assurance that she wouldn't lose him in the crowd with their glamours—his minimal Miraltan one and her Bellegardian one. Though, he supposed he looked pretty much the same, so maybe there wasn't too much to worry about, despite his memories of her keeping him within her grasp back in Valentia.

The feel of soft, microfiber gloves tickled his fingertips with Nyx's reminder to take them just in case they planned on going inside.

"It might be a little cold out anyway," she'd said, "but I'd like it if you took a page from my book since you're, well... dead. I also don't know how involved the authorities might get with whatever's going on either."

Glacier worried his lip, contemplating that maybe he should've stayed behind and tried his best in Nyx's stead. He wasn't given much time to think on it at Noa slowed outside the iron fence of an apartment building and turned up the uneven brick steps to the door. Tendrils of ivy framed windows, looping through the short mimicries of bowing princess-balconies.

Noa touched the pad near the door, selecting 'H. ROUSSEAU' from the list and pressed the call button. A minute ticked by before he stole a glance at her, taking in her deepening frown.

"Is he home right now?" Glacier asked.

"He's *supposed* to be..." she mumbled, retrieving her phone. "He works from home during the day." Her eyes flicked back up to the touchpad, pulling up the unit next to his. She sucked in a breath. "Of course we're in the damn Bellegardian district."

A woman's voice came over the comm the second she pushed the button, her thick accent highlighting that she wasn't a King's Republic native. Noa slipped into a slight smile and began sweet-talking her in a flurry of words Glacier couldn't understand. The most he could make out was sympathy from the resident until the lock clicked to grant them entry. Noa gave the woman a quick '*merci*', and the door shut behind them with a thud.

"What did you tell her?" he whispered as they started past menu panels and groupings of off-bronze mailboxes.

"I said we're friends of Hugo's," she said, dropping her voice with glances at each door breaking up the lavender-colored walls peeking above dark gray wainscoting, "and that he's been acting unwell lately. That's not exactly all that far off from the truth, seeing how we're friends of a friend and he has been acting odd."

She rapidly tapped the elevator button at the end of the hall, finally dropping her hand when the display began counting down the floors. It opened with a chime that rang out in the empty hallway. He tugged on his gloves as they rode the elevator car up to the top floor, eyeing Noa's bare hands.

You're being paranoid again.

He tucked his hands in his jacket pockets, and the doors slid open to a hallway slightly narrower than the one on the ground floor with fleur-de-lis woven in lighter patches along the dark carpet, pointing them to the round window at the other end. Light classical music slipped under one of the doors, its slow, lilting, Bellegardian tune both eerie and comforting.

Noa stopped in front of a door and wrapped her knuckles against it, mumbling something under her breath when there was no response. Out came the gloves as she stole a glance down the hall. She fished a square key from her pocket and pressed it to the door, triggering the small hidden light above the handle to pulse yellow a couple of times before flashing green.

It swung open, and the two of them hurried inside. The click that sounded behind them rang out louder than the music next door, like they'd been dropped into Lyris's middle-of-nowhere cabin. Considering the décor —rather, Hugo's collection—they might as well have been there.

Shelves were crammed with trinkets and digital photo frames—a section for each country that included books and drives plastered with vinyl stickers from tourist traps found in Casovecchia, Razbia, Biana, Corris, Mariroux... The short glass display case under the window held the rest of his tome collection, except these boasted gold and silver ink on the spines, both types containing the word 'magic' in their titles. It appeared to be the sole ordered piece of furniture in the chaos, considering the nearby worn, wooden chair with its flat, flannel-printed padding and the flaking pleather couch overtop of a fraying, wheel-patterned rug looking plucked straight out of Tabir.

Glacier shifted, wincing at how the floor complained slightly under his weight, and Noa took a couple more steps inside to peer around the immediate corners.

"Check the front room," Noa mumbled, motioning to the right. "I'll check the back."

He nodded and started for the door on his right, lined up with the hallway Noa trailed down before she vanished into the first room. Glacier nudged it, and it creaked open to a spartan bedroom. The bed was made up with powder-blue sheets and a throw at the foot of it. An antique travel trunk sat at the end, across from a wardrobe and mirror reflecting a couple of cheap, copied paintings. He tugged the wardrobe open to hanging flannel, polos, and button-up shirts with slacks folded underneath. Frowning, he slowly shut it and got on his knees by the bed, turning on his phone flashlight to illuminate a couple pairs of worn dress shoes.

Glacier sat back up on his knees, searching around for something out of the ordinary, but came up blank. He pushed himself to his feet and headed back into the living room, starting for the hall.

Noa burst through the door at the opposite end with a hard look in her eyes as she strode toward him. "We need to get the hell out of here. *Now.*"

"What? Why? Oh, gods... don't tell me he's—"

"No, it's much worse," she said through gritted teeth and spun him around. "Now *move.*" She ripped the door open and shoved him into the common hall, hurrying him into the elevator, her face a mask of undaunted calm.

The second they jogged down the steps and hit the street, she grabbed his elbow and steered him forward. "I said *move.*" Her head turned to glance over her shoulder.

"Is—Was it Vol—"

She shook her head. "It's—I'm not—The office window was all the way open, his office was in ruins, and the desk lamp was still on. He must have been working in the dark this morning because the document he had up auto saved at 5:46AM, *mid-word*."

A chill went through him.

"There wasn't a body, but there was sure a shit-ton of *blood*," she hissed, letting go of his arm in favor of getting out her phone. "Since it's 8:11AM, I'm assuming that someone is coming back any second now to clean that up before someone finds it. The last thing we need is to get caught up in whatever the hell just happened."

"But what if he's still alive?" Glacier asked. "What if—"

"He's *not* alive. Not with how much blood there was and how violently that *thing* got inside. The fucking windowpane was cracked clean in *half*."

Glacier hesitated, his mind snapping back to Nyx's words in Talie. "You don't think it was—"

"We are *not* discussing this *here*. Whatever the hell that was, it's loose. That's all we need to know. We don't have time to stop and deal with this when we're currently dealing with our own problems. If we somehow manage to live through this entire ordeal, *then* we'll circle back to it."

"How can you even *think* that when there's something out there dismantling people?"

"In case you forgot, *I* used to be something that did that, yet here we are. We are not at all equipped to deal with *that*." She gestured back toward the apartment. "If that really is what we're afraid it is, we're as good as dead if we try to fight it now."

"Okay," he replied shakily. "Okay..."

"Let's just get the hell back as quick as possible," Noa breathed. "Then we'll let Nyx know so maybe she can cover our tracks if someone notices that we were there."

ALYVIA

Alyvia checked her phone as she exited the Bellegardian coffee shop, afraid that she might be running late to catch the next commuter train after the long line. A quick scroll through her messages turned into enough of a distraction that she knocked into someone along the sidewalk.

She stumbled, but righted herself with hands hovering over her shoulders, ready to catch her. Her eyes snapped to that of another Miraltan's—a rare sight in this part of town. "I'm *so* sorry." he said, breathless as his hands dropped to his sides. "Are you okay?"

Alyvia hesitated, finding something unnervingly familiar about him, almost as if she had seen him before. "Y-yeah. Sorry," she said, putting on a bright, carefree smile like she'd throw on for Shane if he had asked the same thing.

He paused before giving her a reluctant smile of his own, and the two of them turned to part ways.

"Wait—"

Alyvia spun back around, and the boy grabbed her hand, pushing something into her palm.

"You dropped this," he said, a well-meaning glint of warmth in his gaze that finally helped her match that feeling of familiarity. But before she could thank him for whatever he'd returned, he ran—jogging past a few people towards a Bellegardian woman. Her eyes were wide and panicked until they caught on him. Then she seized his arm with a scowl and dragged him around the corner..

Alyvia stood in the midst of the morning foot traffic; her thoughts pinned on how the young man had reminded her of a younger version of her father. She smirked and unfurled her hand, blinking when she took in the small Shield of Miralta there. Her thumb ran along its edge, flipping it over to find a rune carved into the back. The world around her slowed, grinding to a halt. She knew that mark.

Her head snapped back up to where the boy had been mere moment before and forced herself to breathe. She'd just been handed a daemon-warding charm from a Seer.

GLACIER

One paranoid dress pickup later, Glacier and Noa had returned to the hotel. His arm hurt from her death-grip after he'd run into that Miraltan girl during their escape from Hugo's apartment. That experience alone had left him baffled, leaving him trying to figure out why the hell he'd given her the charm. His only explanation was panic. Panic that whatever had gotten Hugo would strike again, and that he should at least give *someone* in Kingsheart the change to possibly survive it.

Pulling in a long, deep breath, he snapped back to Noa's pacing across the living room. He'd sunk further into the couch, the soles of his shoes digging into the edge of the coffee table while Nyx continued sitting up straighter with each explanation of what they'd found.

"Well, shit," Nyx mumbled.

"You *think?*" Noa asked, stopping to face her. "Who the hell would be doing this? It's not godsdamned Volkov, that's for sure. I'm pretty strong, but not *that* strong."

"Unless the Volkov are toying with something much darker, I highly doubt it's them either... Did anyone *see* either of you go into his place?"

"Outside of pedestrians witnessing us go into the complex, no. No one in the building saw us enter or leave his unit. The neighbor didn't pop out to ask questions either, but seeing all the shit he kept in there, people will likely assume he took a trip. Who the hell knows when they'll report him missing—"

Nyx shifted to casually lean back in her seat. "Well, I hate to say, 'I told you so,' but—"

"Then *don't.*" Noa's hands went to her scalp, tugging on hair she'd pulled back minutes earlier. "No one can deal with any of this shit right now, let alone *us*. As much as I'd like to stop these people from dying, we can't fight back. We don't have a decent discipline of magic or any training in how to properly wield a rune weapon. Oh, and it might help if all of those weren't locked up in museums. We aren't godsdamned daemon hunters."

Glacier's mind flashed back to Adam's red-ringed irises again, this time in combination with a blood-soaked office. He shuddered, thinking about how Hugo wasn't even a Mage. Was it possible that there had been a mistake? Maybe there was a false assumption involved much like how Adam had claimed that Glacier had been one.

The sound of the door opening, accompanied by a bubbly laugh, cut through their heated discussion. He pushed himself up to peer over the couch. Cecilia and Rune were locked in animated conversation, complete with Crow dropping in his occasional snarky remark before kicking the door shut and rubbing the glamour rune off his face.

"Gods, I'm getting sick of this," Crow grumbled, giving Rune a light, backhanded slap on his bicep as he passed. "Take that damned thing off already."

Rune sent him a tired sideways glance, but Cecilia stood on her toes and gently rubbed her thumb over his cheek. He gave her a kiss on the forehead in thanks.

Crow's frown deepened. "Cut the cute shit."

Rune made a point of ignoring him by moving to hang their formalwear bags in the entry closet, his smile faltering when he took in the rest of the room. "Is something wrong?"

"Just a little stressed about tomorrow night," Noa answered, a slight tick of her jaw indicating otherwise from Glacier's perspective.

"Oh, please," Crow said, dropping into a chair. "This is my home turf. We got this."

Rune towered over his seat, his features darkening. "That's the kind of attitude that gets us caught."

"You're forgetting that I've actually been able to walk around that damn museum several times now," Crow said, irritation intermingling with confidence. "I know the layout. I can tell you all the ins-and-outs. If something goes wrong, it won't be on my end, and that's the part everyone's so concerned about, right?"

Nyx stood, her neutrality masking her leaning on one way the another. "Confidence won't get us caught, but cockiness will. Though, if Crow is comfortable with the layout and the security, then we should focus our efforts on the additional factors that could negatively impact the situation. Noa getting caught is one of them."

"Cecilia and I will be able to cover for her," Rune said, pushing away from his brother. "We can help her lose anyone she might pick up and use the back alleys to our advantage."

"But..." Glacier started, his voice sounding too quiet, even to his own ears. "What if someone notices Crow while he's in the process of the theft?"

"There's a connected sewer system I can escape into," Crow said, half-heartedly shrugging. "I know it pretty well, but for anyone that's unfamiliar, it's easy to get lost in. Worst case, I'll make it out on the other side and Cecilia can disguise me."

Rune folded his arms over his chest. "I suppose that we do have a bit of an advantage in this. As nervous as I am that Crow won't be glamoured, we have managed to get around without that sort of luxury for a long time before this."

"And that's just an additional precaution," Nyx said. "If things happen to go to hell, then the plan is to escape and sit tight to avoid detection until someone can get to you."

"See?" Crow said, a confident grin tugging at the corner of his mouth. "It'll be fine. Just you wait, it'll go just as smoothly as the others, and you'll have worried about it for nothing."

SHANE

The power had been so incredibly distorted that Shane had walked in circles for half of yesterday afternoon, unable to find the trail. Tonight, however, that distortion was gone, calling him toward the western portion of the city.

By the time he'd arrived on the opposite end of Kingsheart, he'd pulled his umbrella out from under his arm to shield him from the pattering of rain while he weaved through a couple of upper-class neighborhoods. He kept his head down, slipping into the role of a tired businessman trekking home after a long day of work, despite only leaving the office a couple hours prior.

Then it hit him. A suffocating wall of overwhelming energy halted him dead in his tracks. He lifted his head to take in the hotel across the street—sleek white marble and the upward climb of glass. He pulled out his phone to check where he was on the map, marking it since there wasn't much he could do tonight. But he'd found it.

Irritation welled up within him as he stared at the rooms. Lights on, lights off—it didn't matter, but he guessed some wealthy old bastard or young brat lurked inside, probably taunting him. A hotel meant that he was on a timer, but Shane at least knew where to hunt now. He'd be back tomorrow, and he wouldn't be alone.

13
KING'S REPUBLIC ✧ 2705-01-05

NOA

Noa jerked awake, gasping after emerging from that horrible sensation of drowning in a deep, dark abyss. The living room was dim in the twilight beginning to filter through the window shades, lightly skimming Glacier's curled up form in the armchair at the end of the couch.

Dead asleep.

She wondered how long he'd been down here, but the immediate peace she found from him being nearby helped slow the panicked fluttering in her chest. It fell in time with the soft pattering of rain.

Noa pushed herself up and scrubbed at her face as she started for the window. The empty street below reminded her of the long nighttime walks she used to enjoy in her past jobs as a member of the Volkov with all the time in the world. It was another life now—an eternity away from her current one. The confinement of the hotel made her appreciate that freedom now.

She looked over her shoulder to Glacier again, reminded of where she'd found him at the beginning of this journey. Her hand went to the back of her neck with a sigh, telling herself she could suffer a few days. It was nothing in comparison to what Glacier had lived. And hopefully it was another step to freedom for him—and everyone else—as well.

They could very well run out of Kingsheart tonight with all but five keys. A strange hope welled up within her at the thought of making it to the Vault before anyone could catch them—to manage to upend the world overnight. The six of them could be cut free of their pasts with that kind of power. Noa held onto that small kernel of light for their futures, refusing to let anything slow them down.

GLACIER

Glacier stiffened at the pop of the toaster in the kitchen, twitching with Noa's eyes narrowed on him. The jumpiness he'd felt in Talie had returned last night, brought on by his body's refusal to sleep. He'd tried, but that horrible feeling that something was lurking nearby had kept him alert and awake. Eventually, that feeling had led him downstairs, where he'd found Noa sleeping. Then that feeling had led him to the window.

That'd been a mistake. He'd known it the second he'd taken in the form of a businessman shadowed by an umbrella—something he normally would've written off as someone spying on his lover in the act of an affair or the like. The red ring around his irises told him otherwise, setting off every alarm bell in his head.

He shouldn't have given away that charm.

"Is there something wrong?" Noa whispered, rounding the kitchen counter to stand next to him, avoiding the others crowding the kitchen.

"You said we weren't followed back from Hugo's, right?"

Noa frowned slightly. "We weren't. Why?"

He hesitated, reasoning that it must be his paranoia again. His face heated as he tucked his hands into his sleeves, embarrassed by his overreactions. "Sorry, I'm just overthinking things." That glint could've been a trick of the light—that was it.

She hovered next to him for a little longer, her face contorting like she wanted to press further before she left. A breath slipped out once he was alone again, glad they'd be gone after tonight—far away from whatever the hell had gotten Hugo. Though the thought stuck in the back of his mind that there could be another just like Adam lurking somewhere else, and he tried to shake that from his mind too.

CECILIA

After finishing up with Noa's makeup and glamour, Cecilia hurried back to her room, where she walked in on Rune looping a tie around his neck.

"Hey," she said shyly, placing her makeup kit on the vanity. "Do you need help?"

"I got it," he said with a smirk, folding his collar back down. "You ready to fix me up?"

She snickered, shaking her head as he took a seat on the end of the bed. He held out his ID, and her thumbs pressed into the plastic while she stared down. Every facet and feature of the face she took in wasn't Rune, despite how much she wanted it to be by the time she uncapped her eyeliner pen and pressed it to his cheek.

When she took a step back, an Amaraian stared back at her. Blue eyes boring into her own. He glanced over to the mirror and stood, grabbing her hand and turning her around so they stood side-by-side.

"We look like a set," he said with a chuckle.

Cecilia reddened. "I- I think I prefer you the way you are without a glamour."

He wrapped an arm around her, pulling her in and letting his lips graze the top of her head. "I don't mind it because it reminds me of you."

She playfully pushed him away, heating with embarrassment. "I- I need to hurry up and change."

He smirked. "I'll be waiting for you downstairs then."

She rubbed her hands on her pants once the door clicked behind him and began unzipping the dress bag lying on the bed. Cecilia paused, holding the bodice in her hands like she was cupping a silvery waterfall, draped in layers upon layers of sheer fabric. She pulled herself from her trance and slipped it on to examine herself in front of the mirror.

She could've mistaken herself for an Amaraian princess if she didn't recognize her own face in the mirror. The near-platinum fabric and geometric cuts reminded her of something Kat might've worn.

Kat.

Cecilia's eyes stung at the thought of Kat standing next to her, elbowing her teasingly in the ribs. All this time she'd tried to hold herself together for the sake of Glacier before diving into the arms of anyone who'd keep her distracted from it all.

She swiped at her eyes and picked up the eyeliner pen again. This was for Kat. This was another step to finish what she'd started, and Cecilia would do whatever she could to see it through.

RUNE

Blue, gossamer curtains were draped over the walls, pouring onto hexagonal dark blue, white, and black tiles. Rectangular partition formations marked the corners of the party hall, where patrons revolved in slow-moving circles or clamored together in clusters near the bar.

"Clear," Rune whispered into his comm, feeling Cecilia's fingertips dig into his arm. His head swung over to the white-haired Rothian woman at his side. "Calm down," he said. "You look stunning."

"That's the problem," she said mumbled. "I already found a couple of people staring at me."

"If it weren't for the job, I'd probably only be staring at you too."

Her head whipped around, revealing her mask of horror. Rune bit back a laugh.

"Greed," Noa's voice echoed over comms. "I don't know what you said to her, but I would stop."

His glanced around the room, landing on a woman that looked to be maybe late-thirties, early-forties with severe features in a long, somber black dress with a champagne glass to her lips—giving him a stern look like she was his mother.

"Oh, shut up, you old bat," Crow's voice chimed in.

"I can and *will* kick your ass once this is over," she growled.

"Clear comms," Nyx said, "or I'll leave all of you for dead."

Rune put on a tight, pleasant smile, returning his attention to Cecilia. "Let's enjoy some art, shall we?"

NOA

Noa had waited for Crow to announce his position on the roof before escaping to the restrooms. Arriving early to the event had afforded her enough time to pick out all of the undercover officers thanks to Nyx IDing them through the cameras, but other than that, she'd been left rather bored. Well, that is until Nyx mentioned that once Director Paisley Bristol was in attendance—the head of governmental Art and Culture Preservation.

No pressure, she thought, staring into the wall of mirrors. Every faux wood-paneled stall door was propped open, so she locked herself in one and rubbed the rune off her wrist. She unzipped the side of her dress, slipped out of it, and reversed it into her new disguise. When she reemerged, she stepped up to the mirrors again to find a whole new person staring back at her: the Noa she'd always wanted.

A metaphorical goddess dripping in red. Her lips quirked up at one side and tapped a finger to her comm. "Ready when you are."

WEATHER

Weather straightened her blazer jacket on her way from the security room, taking hall after hall until she found the next staff-only door—her ticket to freedom. That is, until it all came crashing to a halt with a single, familiar voice behind her.

"Brigitte! There you are!"

She cringed and quickly slapped on a smile before spinning around to face Giselle in her royal blue blouse, pencil skirt, and high heels. Her deep purple eyes twinkled with something akin to what most people would mistake as joy, but Weather knew to be suppressed malice. Anyone that worked a job like hers and stayed this perky either hated everyone around them or themselves, Weather couldn't be convinced otherwise.

"I need you to do me a favor—" Giselle began, coming to a stop.

"Oh, I am so, *so* sorry, but—" Weather winced. "Director Quinn actually told me that there's an urgent matter he needed me for."

Of course, this woman was surprised, like the museum director would actually dane to give *the intern* the time of day. "O-oh..." Her expression faltered, giving an awkward, unconvincing smile. "Then just come find me once you're done, all right?"

"Will do."

She turned back to her destination again, listening to Giselle's heels click off in the opposite direction. *It'll all be over soon*, she thought. She shoved her hand into her pocket and pressed the button on the device there before she pushed the door open. The small red lights by each of the cameras flickered, telling her that her manual override was successful: they were looped on an empty hall. She was invisible. A one-man army.

Weather cinched her jacket over her top, forcing out a breath as her clothes tightened against skin. She smirked at she tied her hair back, and pulled on her mask, knowing the end was finally in sight.

CROW

Crow tugged on the cable again, shaking out his anxiety with the quiet clink of the hook locked into place. That and his fingertips grazing his mask became a comfort. With as many jokes he'd made, he refused to be the one screwing this up. He wanted this to be proof that he was, in fact, the best thief to have ever lived. This wouldn't best him.

He sucked in a breath and pressed the suctioned handholds to the window pane, waiting for the command. "Ready," he whispered, almost more to the blackness of the rooftop than the people in his ear.

"On your mark, Sloth," came Noa's voice.

"Window alarm disabled," Nyx said. "Go."

He pulled up, dumping all his trust into the words. A resounding click signaled it was free, allowing him to drag it off to the side. A third check of the cable, and he began his decent with a rapid, high-pitched zipping crying from the attached cable at his belt.

"I- The-" Nyx's stammer caused him to grab the line again, jerking him to a stop about a meter from the floor. "The security for the room is disabled…"

Frowning at her hesitation, he dropped the rest of the way and ducked under the view of the window to check for patrols. The windows were already tinted. His brows furrowed, and he stood, reading himself in position until his heart stalled. The case was *empty*.

Crow whipped around, feeling his chest tighten with panic. Something about the room was *off*, but he wasn't sure *what*—at least, not until the cable at his waist snapped taut. He panned back up to the skylight, where a shadow loomed over the murky city lights—lights that glinted off the silvery object in the silhouette's hand.

"Sorry," came a woman's voice. "Finders, keepers and all that…"

The Heart of the King.

NOA

Noa's eyes flicked over to Cecilia and Rune in their brief escape while dabbing at Cecilia's dress. A slow, cat-like smile tugged at her lips as she began channeling someone else. Nearly every eye fell on *her*, including every single undercover officer. The red, silky fabric of her dress became a bright, shining beacon. A thrill surged through her when Director Bristol's eyes widened. The woman's jaw set as she shoved her champagne glass into the hand of some poor soul standing next to her.

And *that* was Noa's cue to head for the exit.

"*Stop—*"

Noa bolted for the back door, shoving it open and slamming in in the director's face. "Need a lock," Noa mumbled into the comm, earning a *click* in answer.

"Done, but I think we have a problem," Nyx said. "Gluttony's not responding."

"Shit," she grumbled, ripping up the cords of her dress to hike up the skirt in favor of her black leggings.

"Envy and I are outside," came Rune's sharp tone. "Pride, ping your location and keep your comm on. Gluttony, respond *now*."

"Son of a *bitch*," Crow finally answered.

"What the hell is going on?" she demanded, ducking into the alley. She picked up speed in time with the beeping echoing from her comm's tracker, her sole indication that she was headed straight for Rune and Cecilia. Her ears perked at a heavy door smacking against brick, and she pushed herself to go faster.

She stifled a yelp as she started past a corner, caught off-balance as someone grabbed her arm and pulled her against the wall. Noa stood face-to-face with an unglamoured Rune. He shoved her head down as Cecilia boxed her in and their clothing warped into ripped-up jeans, baggier pants, hoodies and long-sleeved shirts. Once a group of well-dressed adults, now a group of ratty Bellegardian and Corvian teenagers.

Heavy footfalls came to a stop when two guards stumbled upon them, immediately spinning Cecilia around to take in her alarm. Noa instinctively shot forward, trying to put herself between them.

"Can we *help* you?" Noa said, sneering at her new opponent.

Hesitantly, they glanced at each other, taking a step back before the other's features hardened. "Did any of you see a woman in red pass through here?"

Noa put on her most baffled expression, and they all shrugged or shook their heads. The first guard cursed, pushing the demanding, larger one to keep moving through the alley. "Let's go. We don't have time for this," he growled in frustration. And they vanished around another corner.

The glamour dropped, and Cecilia released a shaky breath.

"*Greed*," came Crow's urgent plea over the comms. "I need you, *now*."

Rune hesitated, turning to Noa and Cecilia, setting his sights on the latter. "Do you need *me*, or Envy?"

"If I needed *Envy*, then I would be asking for Envy, you *dumbass*," he snapped, sounding a little winded. "Someone else beat us to it—"

"You want to run that by me again?" Nyx asked, cutting through the comms.

Rune emitted a frustrated growl, putting a finger to his comm. "Sloth, I'm going after Gluttony. I'll keep you updated." He looked to Noa, pushing Cecilia a little closer to her. "Take her back with you while I deal with this."

"Maybe *I* should—" Noa started.

"No, this is a thief, not an officer. I can handle it. Now take Cecilia and get ready for us to leave. We'll meet you back there with the Heart." He began to back up into the alley.

"If you get caught, I'll kick your ass," she said, trying to tamp down her concern that was further fueled by Cecilia's worried look in his direction.

"I won't get caught then," he said with a dashing smirk and a wink before he ran.

Noa's shoulders fell. "Son of a bitch."

CROW

Flipping on his tracker had been the last thing on Crow's mind during his chase. For *any* of them to get away with this, he'd quickly replaced The Heart of the King with the replica, cleaned up the other thief's mess around the display case, and then had to collect all of his break-in paraphernalia from the roof. He'd done it all while cursing under his breath, which he ended up saving once in pursuit of the key.

Crow slid down the fire escape and darted toward the river on her heels. The buildings were the perfect cover, but it was a twisting maze with only a couple of true exits—all of them running parallel to each other. So, when it dumped them out, he had managed to gain on her. She shot towards a vacant warehouse, and he sprinted inside after her, praying to every god that there wasn't an armed alarm.

The good news? There wasn't. The bad news? *She* was armed.

He ducked, cursing as a pipe grazed the top of his head, and hooked a foot behind her leg. She stumbled, grabbing for his arm to steady herself, and sending the pipe clanging against the cement. He snaked his arm around her to pull her closer, and aimed to grab the twinkle of metal at her side. He tore it free, and she smacked his arm down, sending it back into her hands.

Bitch.

She held it up, panting with a small, challenging giggle that only fueled his anger. Crow lunged, tackling her to the ground. The Heart of the King flew from her hand, skittering across the warehouse floor. Her fingers dug around his mask, tearing it free right as he went for hers. The second it was in his hand, his eyes went wide. That was his second mistake that night.

She jabbed him in the throat. He gagged, gasping while she shoved him off of her and hurtled towards her prize before her footsteps skidded to a stop. Swaying, he shoved himself off the floor.

Rune blocked her path, holding the relic up with his eyes narrowed. "Looking for this?"

WEATHER

Weather panted as she held out her hand. "Hand it over." She knew that she wasn't exactly in a position to make demands, but she was damn sure going to try. "It doesn't have to be because it's me, but I would hope that you'd at least give me a five-minute head start for old time's sake."

"No."

She barked out a laugh, her knees almost buckling in disbelief. "So, now what, Rune? Are you going to arrest me and haul me off to prison? Just give me a damn break—"

Her head whipped around at the raspy voice that followed. "We're not here to arrest you, dumbass," Crow said, rubbing at his throat.

"I wasn't talking to you, bitch."

"That's *enough*."

She snapped her jaw shut, cautiously turning her gaze back to Rune's.

"We're not working with any agency, Weather. We defected. We're rogue."

Her brows knitted together, confused but unwilling to rationalize what he was trying to say. "Then give me the damn Heart, and I'll be on my way." This felt like a trick—a trick she refused to fall for.

Rune grabbed her arm, and she gasped, attempting to wrench it away from him. "Absolutely not," he said, "I'm not giving you anything, especially not

until we have a talk about what the hell you were doing with it in the first place."
He roughly jerked her forward, keeping her at his side on their way out of the
warehouse. "Now, you need to listen to me or else we'll *all* be in deep shit."

Weather hesitated, letting her arm go limp when she decided to comply.
He loosened his grip, and she pulled up her hood, eyeing the Heart as Rune
handed it off to his brother. After the exchange, they made their way out
the alley door and into the street. Rune's hand dropped, sliding into hers—
a far more subtle way of keeping her from running, though she clicked her
tongue in disgust.

"How *romantic*," she said dryly, which was enough for him to cut her a
warning look. She faced forward again, basking in the silence held between
the three of them. It was a tense, yet familiar thing that almost broke her,
feeling both at home and unwelcomed at the same time. Just another piece
of her past there to haunt her.

From warehouses to the dimly lit streets of run-down apartments and
shops with flickering signs, they had made it to Rune's desired destination.
He guided her into a corner coffee shop with yellowing tiles and menu
screens-tinged purple in the corners, empty except for a couple of
customers tucked into a window booth. Rune brought her to the back,
giving her a small shove forward.

"Sit."

She shot him a glare before she slid into the booth, overwhelmed by
irritation when he blocked her in, and Crow took the bench across from
them.

"Now," Rune whispered, "I think it's time you explain why you were
stealing *that*." He pointed towards Crow, specifically towards his jacket
where she knew the Heart was tucked away.

"Because I was hired to," she said in a near-growl.

"By *whom*, Weather?"

She flinched, hating the seething anger that came with each word. It
had never been directed at her before, and it cut her deeper than she liked to
have admitted. There was also a sense of pride that she would lose in telling
him the truth, though she supposed that was long gone now. She had

already sold her soul to a tyrant, and a final plea might be the only way to get her out.

"Giovanni," she mumbled, her eyes shutting the moment she saw the disbelief on Crow's face. She *really* didn't want to see what Rune thought now.

"Are you *stupid?*" Rune hissed. "Have you lost your godsdamned mind?"

"Look—I fucked up, okay? I get that. I took a job for that psychopath after you two *traitors*—"

"Took the fall to cover *your* ass. We had a choice to either get locked up and let them hunt you and the others down or to sell our souls for them to let you go. *I* was the one that convinced Crow that we should do the latter."

Her eyes searched his, wide and starting to blur before that anger welled up inside her again. "And did you ever think about what *I* wanted, Rune?"

"No. No, I didn't. I didn't give a shit about what *you* wanted, Weather. I only cared that you were safe. That was the one thing that Crow and I agreed on, but you've managed to go and screw that up anyway, haven't you?"

"So, you want me to go back to Giovanni empty-handed? Then what, Rune? I won't be safe then because he's already threatened me—"

"And what do you honestly think he wants with The Heart of the King? Hm? Because I'm pretty sure the *only* reason he wanted you to get it for him was because someone we worked for put a target on your back to get to us. A plan for Giovanni to have you collect something big enough to get you caught since we've been evading arrest."

"Oh, please," she said, scoffing. "Don't be so self-absorbed. Not everything comes down to you and your damn brother."

"So, you don't think that Giovanni isn't just like his father? You think that he doesn't have government and civil authority connections? How the hell do you think he's managed to keep his business going? Tell me, where was the drop-off point, Weather?"

She hesitated, watching him fold his arms over her chest. He had her. Her eyes slid to some arbitrary point in the room, unfocused as she realized how much of a fool she had been. "The warehouse docks."

"Where any number of officers can hide. If he really wanted to do business, you would bring it back to his office."

She squeezed her eyes shut, willing back tears. Everything was ruined. "What the hell am I supposed to do?" she asked, hearing her own voice waiver. She couldn't look at him, and she *certainly* couldn't bring herself to look at Crow. So, instead, her head dropped into her hands, her elbows pressing against the fabric of her jacket on the edge of the cheap laminate table.

Weather jumped when Rune's hand gently fell on her shoulder. She lifted her head with surprise.

"Look," he said gently, that word alone nearly ripping her apart, "you have at least one fake ID left that you haven't burned, right?"

She nodded, afraid of hearing her voice crack.

"Give me your phone."

She did, her eyes following his hands as he typed something into it. Once he was done, he took her hand and gingerly placed it in her palm.

"This is my current number. When we leave, go home. Collect your things and meet us at the west station, just outside of downtown. I'll send you our departure details once I get them. I have someone that can help you disappear to wherever you'd like. Name it, and you'll be there by the end of the week."

He nodded to his brother, and the two of them slid out. She noticed how Crow refused to look at her, which she wasn't sure was better or worse than the pity found on Rune's face.

"And what are you two going to do with that?" she asked, giving a subtle nod towards Crow's jacket.

"That's not for me to tell," Rune said with some remorse. "If you want to know, then you can ask my boss when you meet us at the station." And with that, they left.

14

KING'S REPUBLIC ✧ 2705-01-06

WEATHER

Weather swayed in front of the cabin door, checking over her shoulder at the station platform sliding in the opposite direction. She rubbed her hands on her sleeves and checked her phone again to make sure the number was right.

Door will be unlocked. Let yourself in.

Her fingers curled into the recess of the handle, and she tugged it open to a set of stairs. She paused, letting the phone dim in her hand as a woman's voice rang out. There must've been a mistake. She tapped the screen again, triple-checking the number. Or not.

She followed the silvery trail of simple stars, flourishing swords, and embellished shields painted overtop the dark blue walls. Her hand curled around her bag's strap as the woman's sharp voice grew more tense and irritated.

"You can't go radio silent like that, Crow—"

Weather slowed her jog up the last steps, stopping on the landing. The woman whipped around, and Rune's arms uncrossed, his eyes brightening as he pushed off the cabin's far wall. Crow's hand went for his hair, and he turned his head to the side, staring down at the window seat cushion. Her eyes flicked to the Miraltan boy and Amaraian girl hovering around one of the far seats where a Jinwonese woman sat.

Weather cleared her throat. "Didn't mean to interrupt..."

Rune stepped up next to her, gesturing between Weather and the woman who'd been snapping at Crow—who rocked back on her heels with eyes narrowed at Weather.

"Noa," Rune said, "this is Weather, a friend and former associate. Weather, this is Noa, my boss."

"And here I thought I was your boss," the Jinwonese woman interjected dryly.

Noa half-turned. "You *wish.* Everyone clearly understands that I'm the one in charge except for this dumbass." She jerked a thumb at Crow, who shot her a glare.

"Well," the Jinwonese woman continued, "I suppose the only problem with having a last-minute guest is that we're short a bed. There are three rooms with two beds in each."

"She can have m—" the Miraltan boy started.

"She'll take mine," Noa said, her sights set on Weather again. "You can share a room with Nyx." She tiled her head towards the Jinwonese woman and smirked. "Worse case, Nyx and I can cuddle."

Nyx rolled her eyes.

"So..." Noa said. "I take it that you're Crow's ex, seeing how he's suddenly run out of inappropriate things to say, and Rune's clear concern for your well-being..." She hummed, looking her up and down with a tilt of her head. "Honestly, I'm completely surprised that Crow wasn't lying about you, but I'm even more baffled as to why you'd bother wasting your time on him."

"*Wow—*" Crow said defensively before she waved a hand to shut him up.

"Um..." Weather said hesitantly. "Thank you, I think?"

"Noa—" Rune said in warning.

Weather adjusted her bag, raising her voice over Rune, "So, um... I don't suppose that you would mind explaining why *you* want The Heart of the King, would you? Especially after these two took it from me to give to you?"

Noa sucked on her lip, playing with the collar of her jacket. "That's... something I'll only answer should you decide to tag along for," —she held her hands out to the rest of the cabin's occupants— "whatever the hell this is... But you should know that failure means more than prison cells." Her arms dropped to her sides.

Weather glanced to Rune, searching his face with a tentative, joking smile that fell away when he didn't mirror it.

"You have until we reach our stop in Bellegarde if you want that answer," Noa said with a shrug. "But there's no rush. In the meantime, get comfortable. Your room's on the end, the one on the right." She dismissed her by moving to drop onto the couch next to Nyx.

Weather shuffled to her room, ignoring the stray, curious looks from the Miraltan and Amaraian. The bunks she walked into were spartan with light gray sheets and royal blue fleece blankets. She dropped her bag onto a bed and sat next to it, running her hand over the fabric. Pressure built up at the backs of her eyes while she resisted the urge to wrap herself up in it and curl up in a ball. The only thing that'd be missing would be her dad stroking her hair until she fell asleep.

She jumped when the door snapped open again, and the Amaraian girl stood on the threshold.

"D-do you mind if I come in?" she asked, wringing her hands.

"Um..." Weather glanced to the bed across from her and flicked her wrist toward it. "No, go right ahead."

She closed the door behind her and took a seat, where she smoothed out her tunic-style powder blue shirt over her white leggings. "I'm Cecilia, by the way," she said somewhat apologetically.

"Weather," she replied hesitantly, scrutinizing her. "No offense, Cecilia, but... you don't exactly seem like the criminal type."

Her face turned pink, and she grabbed at the ponytail draped over her shoulder with a nervous laugh. "Well, um, you're right. I'm not."

"Then... why are you hanging out with all of *them?*" Weather pointed her thumb toward the door.

"Well, I... I'm an Illusionist."

Weather's eyes went wide. "What? No way—That's amazing."

The pink in her cheeks turned to red. "I—um—I honestly didn't want this to turn into a conversation about me. I actually wanted to check on you to see if you were okay. Crow mentioned you a couple of times... I can tell you mean a lot to him."

Weather gagged. "*Gods*... He's an idiot, Cecilia."

Cecilia clapped a hand over her mouth, stifling a laugh. "But you—" She jumped as the door pulled open again.

Rune ducked his head inside, fixed on Cecilia with a glimmer in his eyes Weather hadn't ever recalled seeing before. "I was wondering where you went," he said, that smooth, gentle cadence that sent a shiver through her—new as well. Not once could she recall him softening the edges of his seductive tones into something sweeter.

Weather shot up, standing nose-to-nose with him. "Rune, if you break this sweet girl's heart, I will snap you in half."

"W-what?" Cecilia asked, standing up behind her. "No-no! He wouldn't—"

"You don't have to defend him, Cecilia," she replied, keeping her eyes on Rune. "I know he's a charmer."

He sighed. "Well, Weather, I wasn't planning on that. I was actually looking for her so the two of us could collect some tea and liquor orders for everyone. Some of us would like to wind-down after a long night. Is there anything we can get *you?*"

Weather took a step back, glancing at Cecilia before falling to the bed again. "Just... get me the hardest thing they got." She didn't bother trying to hide the exhaustion seeping into her voice.

"Sure thing," he said, ushering Cecilia to join him.

She beamed, pausing to face Weather. "It was nice finally meeting you," she said, every syllable coated with sincerity. Her hand slipped into Rune's, and they left.

A bizarre sensation washed over her at the afterimage lingering in the doorway—a sight Weather wasn't sure she'd ever see after all the times she'd seen him avoid girl after girl when he realized he didn't enjoy their company. She'd sat on the apartment rooftops with him, listening to his mumblings about how he didn't know what he wanted, let alone who he wanted to be.

But he'd managed to find at least one of those things if it was worth risking everything for, according to Noa's ultimatum.

NOA

Noa rubbed her eyes with a groan, letting the tablet Nyx had given her fall into her lap. It might've been a mistake to pass on the alcohol and sleep, considering how she'd stolen looks at Glacier the entire night. The way he'd cupped his tea in his sleeve-covered palms unlocked something incredibly feral in her soul, especially with how quiet he'd stayed until he went to bed. Her jaw had clenched, hating how she itched to sneak off after him to bury her own arms into the depths of his sweatshirt and fall into the calming sound of his breathing. That drunken night in Miralta had royally screwed her up with how comforting that disaster had been.

She stiffened at the sound of a cabin door sliding free, her heart hammering in her chest with excitement—only to see Weather.

"Good morning," Noa mumbled, returning to the tablet. She tangled her fingertips in her hair and sank into the short-backed sofa.

The seat next to her dipped, and Noa swung her head toward Weather again.

"I have a question that doesn't pertain to The Heart of the King," Weather said. "So, may I ask why you have a very nice, gentle Illusionist girl from Amarais with you?"

Tone clearly meant everything here, so Noa decided to take the nonchalant approach. "Well," she replied, pulling the tablet to her chest with a mirthless smirk. "That's a bit of a funny story, seeing how we kidnapped her."

Weather drew back. "You *what?*" She shot up from her seat. "You-you did *not* kidnap that poor girl."

Almost on cue—*far* too late for Noa's liking—Glacier's door slid open, damn hoodie and all, rubbing the side of his face.

"Well, I mean, we kidnapped that one too." Noa said, half-heartedly pointing in his direction to fuel Weather's panic for her own amusement.

That satisfaction dissipated the second Weather started for him, and Noa squeezed the tablet.

Glacier took a step back. "Wait—what's going on?"

"Were you kidnapped?" Weather asked, angling her body like she was trying to shield him from Noa.

"I- I'm not sure I would quite put it like *that*," he said, tugging at the end of his sleeves.

She took a step closer, and Noa tensed, trying to make out her whisper —something along the lines of him being held against his will. Glacier shrank back before he broke into a smile and clapped a hand over his mouth. Weather reared back in surprise and spun to Noa again. "What is *wrong* with you people? Stealing The Heart of the King and kidnapping poor Miraltan boys—"

Crow emerged from his room, grimacing and rubbing his forehead. "Glacier's Amaraian, you idiot."

Noa mouth went dry as the heels of her palms pressed against the edges of the tablet, threatening to snap it in half. *Oh. My. Gods.*

"Shut the hell up, whore," Weather snapped. "He's clearly *not* Amaraian."

"Um..." Glacier winced.

Her hand moved from her side like she might point to his blue eye, stopping when Crow flipped her his middle finger with a triumphant smirk and collapsed onto the window bench.

"You look—Wait... did you say *Glacier?*"

Noa glared daggers at Crow, and his smug look fell into alarm. *Absolute dumbass.*

"Y-you're joking, right?" Weather asked, her voice on the edge of hysterics. "There's no way this is Prince Glacier Caelius—he's *dead*."

Crow partially hid his face and puffed out his cheek with his tongue. "He looks pretty alive to me..." he mumbled.

Noa bit back a growl and tossed the tablet onto the cushion. "All right, I'll admit that there was a *bit* of a mishap. I got a prince and an Illusionist instead of what I'd hoped to grab back in Amarais. At the time, it seemed like a questionable deal, but..." She shrugged, trying to play it off like this sort of thing happens all the time.

Weather just *stared* at her—her violet eyes unblinking long enough that Noa dared a glance over at Crow, who appeared to be *sweating*.

"So..." Weather started in a strangled voice as she turned back to Glacier, "the rumors... They're true? You're half-Miraltan..."

Noa's shoulders dipped at the careful, sympathetic way she'd delivered each word.

Glacier rubbed his arms, fixing his sights on the arm of the sofa like he was tracing the small navy splotches Noa had been stuck with most of the night. "It's..." he said. "It's not exactly something I care to admit to anyone, so I'd appreciated it if you didn't repeat that."

"And if any rumor starts circulating that he's alive," Noa said, razer sharp in contrast to Glacier's gentle request, "you should know that I have ways of dealing with those who go around saying stuff they shouldn't."

Weather put on a lopsided smile at first like Noa had tossed out a joke, but when she continued sitting stone-faced, watching for a sign of confirmation, Weather's mouth twitched back into something more serious. "U-understood."

"Good," Noa said. "Glad we've come to an understanding."

The upward climb of footsteps sounded behind the snap of the downstairs cabin door—two sets that gave way to Rune and Cecilia rounding the landing. Weather immediately pointed a finger at the former. "Did you *kidnap* that poor girl?"

Noa's hand went to her face.

Cecilia's stammering words worked their way into something almost coherent until Rune cut her off with, "*Technically*, yes—"

"Rune!"

Noa grimaced as Glacier piped up and reached to lower her arm—a gesture that curled Noa's fingers slightly. "We would have died if they had just left us there."

In the seconds that Weather turned to him again, something formed as a twinkle—or a maybe a tick—that she hadn't expected from her. It was like someone had flipped a switch from concern to opportunistic.

"Oh, *honey*," she said, her voice dripping with something sickeningly sweet as her arms wrapped him.

Glacier's body went completely rigid, stun-locked with his arms hovering at her sides like he wasn't sure if he should hug her back or not. Noa tasted blood while the little voice in her head screamed a chorus waffling between 'don't get up' and 'holy shit, end this'.

It took her almost entirely too long to notice Weather's smirk, let alone the way her eyes teasingly danced with amusement while they remained pinned on Crow. This was a game. A game that was making Crow's blood boil about as hot as Noa's, judging from the way his fingertips dug into his thigh.

"Weather," Rune said, interrupting her moment of igniting jealousy. "Why don't you join Cecilia and I for breakfast?"

"I thought that's where you two just came from..."

"We were in the observatory car this morning to take in the view first. Cecilia was actually asking if you might want to join us, but we're open to anyone else—"

"Glacier should join us," she said a little too excitedly. He froze like a wild animal on the train tracks.

"He can't—" Noa blurted before smoothing out the rest of her explanation. "Nyx needs him to help with some research we're doing, so he needs to stay up here just in case she needs him once she gets up."

"Research...?"

"He's good at analysis and tactics. He and Nyx are hacking a strategy for our jobs."

Weather's hand finally released his elbow. She shot Crow a glare before Rune led er out with an arm around her shoulder, clearly ignoring her faux pout.

Sighing, Glacier slumped down onto the couch next to Noa, making her head spin with the effort to remain glued to her seat.

So, to keep her mind off things, she decided to take aim at Crow. "Nice going, dumbass."

"Look, you act like she *wouldn't* have figure it out."

"I planned on telling her *only* if she decided to come along with us. Glacier has an alias for a reason. The more people that know—"

"Yes, I *know*."

Noa groaned and rubbed her temples. "So, I'm assuming that you still trust her, despite her hating your guts. If not, you're going to have to fess up to Nyx, and she's going to be *pissed*."

"I trust her." Lying or not, the words at least *sounded* genuine. "I... I know that we may not be getting along, but the three of us... We don't betray each other unless it's a sacrifice that would save another."

"And you're not opposed to me giving her the choice to join us, despite your issues?"

Crow glanced out the window, absently rubbing at the side of his face. "Well... I'd prefer if she didn't, but I can't exactly stop her. I don't want to see her get hurt, but I don't really have a say in that."

"She *could* be a valuable addition, especially with how she managed to out-maneuvered you back there. I'm not trying to belittle you, but having a second, *actual* thief couldn't hurt us."

His hand moved to trace the back of his neck. "She's... sort of a jack of all trades. Sure, she's gotten better at grifting and stealing, but she fills the gaps most of the time. I'd say she's speed, and I'm precision." Her breathed a mirthless chuckle. "Considering we're losing more of every day, and we're not sure when out time is up, that might not necessarily be a bad thing. But... if she knows what's good for her, she'll get off at Bellegarde. I don't really care if she never wants to see me again as long as she's safe."

Noa kept her eyes pinned on the window, watching Crow's reflection in the glass obscure the waking cityscape resting on the other side. His words lingered in the forefront of her mind—words that she'd felt all too well. It took everything in her not to look at Glacier.

ARRINGTON

"What do you mean she's *gone?*" Arrington demanded, slamming his fist into the desk. His palm throbbed from the way it'd hit the edge, but he'd barely felt it with how warped the office had become. He ripped off his glasses and sent them clattering along the faux-wood in favor of rubbing his temples with his free hand. The phone complained under the pressure of the other.

"She didn't show up like she said she would last night," Giovanni said. "So, I sent a couple of my men over to her place this morning. They broke in and found the place vacant. All her personal shit is gone—the bitch just up and left."

"This was supposed to be an easy job for you, Fontaine."

"And I held up my end of the bargain, *Wil*. Get the fuck off my back. I sent her in there, and *your* people didn't catch her. I had the meeting ready and played my part regardless, so don't you *dare* blame this on me."

Arrington pushed back a growl as his office door popped open. Shane shuffled in and fumbled with the sensor lock, muttering a curse. His head still hung like a sulking child by the time he slumped into a chair.

"I have to call you back," Arrington said, the words clipped, "I'm being pulled into a meeting. Keep an eye out for her and shake down her form associates if you have to. If *any* of them are involved, you inform me immediately, are we clear?"

"*So* clear," came Giovanni's bitter reply.

He hung up and dropped the phone back into the drawer.

"It's gone," Shane said, his voice sounding hollow. "I went to collect it last night, and it was gone."

Arrington's fists clenched and unclenched at his sides before he grabbed onto his chair. It turned into a renewed anchor to keep him from pacing again after more bad news. He ran a hand down his face and retrieved his glasses. "As *unfortunate* as that is, Director Bristol informed me that the woman Watson saw in Southaven was at the gala last night, so what *I* want to know is why we weren't even aware that she was within the city limits."

Shane's head jerked up. "Wh-what? But Alyvia would've said something if—"

"Well, they've either gotten better at hiding in plain sight, or Watson has been hiding them. There's no way that I'd buy the possibility that she just *happened* to miss them. She knows what she's doing."

"There's no way that she would—"

Arrington rammed his fist into the desk again. "Have her check," he ground out. "Watch her work. If they show up *anywhere* before that woman shows up in the museum, I'm having *you* deal with her after I fire her, understood?"

Shane's eyes went wide.

"*Understood?*" he asked again, gritting his teeth.

Shane started to nod and slowed. "But, what about—"

"Wait." Arrington held up finger as a though clicked into place. "You said that you went to collect last night, and the Seer was gone? *When* last night?"

Shane's mouth worked, his brows knitting together like he was trying to puzzle out what he was getting at. "Y-you don't think... It's not that woman, is it? I– it doesn't seem to move from the place it was hiding in the other night, but... *Maybe?* It would depend on when she appeared at the gala. I was on my way other there not too long after it started, maybe thirty or forty-five minutes?"

"Get Watson," Arrington said, pointing towards the door. "Scrub *all* of the surrounding museum footage with her. Don't let her have the opportunity to cover anything up from the gala. Find the time and see if it matches your timeline of last night. If it does, I believe we've found your Seer, and Watson's off the hook."

WEATHER

The rattle of dishes couldn't pull Weather's attention away from the Republic's western countryside. She sighed and cupped her chin in the palm of her hand, grasping onto fleeting memories of her face pressed against the warm glass of a small cabin with the ocean skimming the horizon.

But now she was heading north instead of south, with a handful of strangers and old friends instead of her father, as an adult instead of as a child. She certainly felt like a child again—scared and lonely, even among familiar faces.

"You okay?" Cecilia asked, twisting her cloth napkin on the opposite side of the booth.

"All things considered? Yeah, I'll be okay."

"Maybe... Maybe you'd feel a little better if you talked to Crow?"

Weather loosed a short, breathy laugh, trying to cover the pain and regret. "Cecilia..."

"He tries to hide it, but I can tell that he's miserable. He didn't even try to drink himself to death for once last night. He was just... unusually reserved."

Weather slid her gaze over to Rune, watching him sort their dishes into their respective bins. "You know... back when we were kids, I did just about everything to try to make Rune pay attention to me. He was the charismatic one—the smooth-talker that everyone liked when we were just hitting our stride. I thought that we'd make a good pair, but I think I was annoying the hell out of him, so he started to find ways to ditch me."

She huffed out a laugh and twisted a lock of dark brown hair around her finger. "I eventually got this stupid idea that maybe if I befriended his brother, I would earn some points with him, but... Crow didn't know what to do with me when we were alone. He was always the quiet one of the two —the awkward brother, but the nicer one at the time."

Cecilia crossed her arms on the crème-colored tabletop, tilting her head. Weather bit the inside of her cheek. "Rune tended to run off with their step-mother whenever she was busy with errands, so I stuck around with Crow. We started wandering around the neighborhood and just *talked*—about things we'd like to do, places we'd like to see, people we wanted to be... Turns out I liked him more than I thought I liked Rune. And Rune, being Rune got jealous once he found out we'd been spending more and more time together.

We'd gone from childhood friends to a complicated mess, and Rune was afraid I would take Crow away. We fought. I told him to grow up and stop being so selfish because his brother shouldn't always have to live in his shadow. We managed to find a new rhythm after that, but once their stepmom died..."

"He told me about Corrine," Cecilia said quietly.

Her heart twisted. "Then he must really think you're special. He... took it the hardest. He couldn't really talk about her much after that, let alone *do* much of anything for a while. Something in him died when she did, for better or worse. I never thought I'd see him be okay again—not until I saw him leave with you last night. I thought for sure he had just resigned to cutting himself off from anyone else entirely, outside of his relationships with me and Crow. As far as we were concerned, the three of us had this wild idea that we'd either live forever or go out in a blaze of glory together."

"So, you were upset when you found out they sacrificed themselves to save you?"

"Yeah," Weather replied, her voice clipped. "I was pretty pissed up until Rune told me what happened, but now..." She bit her lip, her eyes locking with Cecilia's again. "I'm really glad Rune found you. I always pictured some bitch I'd butt heads with, but I find you to be a pleasant surprise." Cecilia sputtered, and Weather laughed, reaching for her hands. "It's a compliment, trust me. I'm glad to have you as another member of my family."

Cecilia squeezed her hands as if in answer to Weather's offer.

"Please don't steal my girlfriend," Rune said, stopping at the end of the booth table.

"Do you think I'd seriously wait this long to do it?" Weather asked. "You act like that would be a challenge for someone like *me*."

Cecilia pulled a hand away, waving it in denial. "We were just talking about—"

"More about Cecilia's friend upstairs," Weather said. "You said Noa would kill me, but you didn't ever confirm if he was single..."

Rune narrowed her eyes at her. "You should highly consider dropping that idea."

"Why don't you talk to—" Cecilia started, patting her hands with a twinkle of hope in her eyes.

"All right, *all right*—I'm going already." Weather slid out of her seat, grumbling on her way back to the cabin.

Once the first door shut behind her, her feet started to drag. She rubbed her arms as she passed window after window, contemplating what she could possibly say to him. Her boots might as well have been filled with lead when she made it to the steps. The empty cabin that waited for her at the top left her lingering by the railing until she went for Crow's door and pried it open.

There he was. Hunched over his bag, pulling out a clean shirt. "I thought you were busy with Cecilia and—" He turned and the shirt slipped from his hands. His voice fell flat with his next word: "Weather."

"Cecilia's far too nice to you," she said, folding her arms over her chest. "Why do I feel like you've given her nothing but grief since she started seeing Rune?"

He pointed a finger at her. "I'd like to see *you* try acting all buddy-buddy with her when the first thing she does is blind the shit out of you—"

"Like you didn't deserve it."

His finger curled back into his fist.

Sighing, Weather dropped onto the bed across from him. "You didn't come back for me," she said quietly. "You could've when you and Rune decided to leave, but you didn't. I thought we were in this together."

He grumbled and shoved his bag to the side. "I agreed with Rune that we should keep you out of this—"

"So you two can go get yourselves *killed?* Crow, you two are all I have. I never knew my mom, and you were there when my dad finally ended up working himself to death. Corrine was the only other almost-parent I could lean on, and she's gone too. You two don't have the right to do this and just *leave* me—not when I never even got a say."

"You think I *wanted* to leave you?" he asked, hurt straining his voice. "Do you think that there hadn't been a single day since this whole mess started where I just wanted to talk to you—to *see* you, even if you couldn't see me? I honestly didn't give a shit if you'd yell at me or hit me—"

Weather lurched forward, grabbing him by the shirt collar and pressing her lips to his. He went rigid, relaxing just before she pulled back. "I'm going with you," she whispered.

Fear stared back at her—fear mixed with grief and a hint of resignation about his own fate. "No, you should—"

"Crow, I don't care about what you want me to do. I don't care if you think of this as *your* mess. I'm not willing to get off this train and sit around worrying about you all because you're afraid of losing *me*. I'm done being alone."

He closed his eyes and loosed a mirthless chortle. "You're going to think that Rune and I are the biggest fools in all of Avaria once you tell Noa you're coming with us."

"Oh, honey," she said, cupping his cheek. "I already know that."

NOA

"I'm sorry, I think I've completely misheard you," Weather said with a tight smile that bordered on manic from her seat on the couch.

"No," Noa said, her eyes briefly flicking over to Glacier's bench seat beside where she stood. "No, you did not."

Weather's head snapped between Crow and Rune on either side of her, her vivid, purple eyes wild. "Have you two lost your godsdamned minds?" she asked before leaning over to glimpse Cecilia on the other side of Rune. "Oh, please tell me that you don't actually believe this too."

Cecilia fidgeted with the hem of her shirt and chewed on her lip.

"Gods—let's just... back up for a moment," Weather mumbled, running her hands through her hair. "So, you believe that *you* are like... some sort of *champion* for Seraphine, or something right?"

"I wouldn't go *that* far—"

"And you're *Volkov?*"

"*Was* Volkov."

A hysterical giggle escaped her. "Yeah, sure, whatever—"

"She's not lying, Weather," Rune said. "Nyx and I have encountered those dealings and repercussions of the Volkov first-hand."

Her eyes went wide. "Do I *want* to know what the hell you've done?"

He hesitated, and Noa cut in again, "Look, all you need to understand is that this is exactly why you can't mention anything about Glacier being alive either. Right now, him being supposedly dead to the rest of the world is likely the only thing buying us more time before they decide to take another pass at eliminating him. Plus, if it gets back to Amarais, that puts Cecilia's family in danger."

"And if anyone else discovers that I'm half-Miraltan," Glacier said quietly, "it'd be the final nail in my *second* coffin."

Weather steepled her hands in front of her mouth. "So... you've somehow been tasked with saving the world... by a Seer."

"At least two Seers, but I'd rather not dwell on that," Noa mumbled, raising her voice again. "I'll be honest with you, I don't like where all of this is going, but I don't seem to really have many options. If I don't want to kill any more innocents and finish protecting the ones I've managed to save, then I'm sure as hell going to try to see this through if there's some small bit of hope that it's real."

Weather shook her head and rubbed her forehead as Crow leaned over to whisper something in her ear.

"I know it sounds insane," Rune said.

"That's..." Nyx started, pulling the attention of the room over to her. "That's not even the worst of it. Noa, Glacier, and I have been investigating some disappearances in Kingsheart. It was ones of the reasons why those two left a little early to get Noa's dress for the gala. They had gone to check on a research associate of a friend we met with back in Tabir."

"Are you talking about the person you met with at the casino?" Rune asked.

Crow's head whipped around. "There was a *casino?*"

Noa threw her arms out at her sides. "Well maybe you would've been able to go if you hadn't been wandering around to find someone to sleep with—"

"You did *what?*" Weather asked, her voice an invisible dagger at Crow's throat. "Did she just say that you were sleeping around *without* me?"

Noa's arms fell, and she furrowed her brows with a stolen look at Rune. His hand went to his face. "Good gods, not again," he mumbled.

"We weren't *together*—" Crow said.

Weather grabbed him by the collar. "If you're going to do it, you're going to take me along to make sure it's done *right*."

Rune made a sudden, rolling motion with his arm to indicate that they should move the conversation along.

"Anyway..." Nyx said, standing up and stopping next to Noa. "They discovered a distinct lack of a person, but quite a bit of evidence that he's likely no longer on this plane of existence."

"So what?" Weather asked, letting go of Crow's collar. "Someone must've just gotten fed up with the guy and offed him or something. It happens."

Noa let out a low hum. "I'm... not so sure that's completely the case, considering that he's one of several associates that have disappeared within the past few months. He's just the only one we have evidence that proves he's likely dead. The thing that bothers me the most is that they all have connections through magical studies or are Mages themselves."

"Not to mention our encounter with one of my now-former informants back in Talie," Nyx continued. "He turned on us when he thought Glacier was a Mage and tried to have his thugs grab him. Dumbasses got laid out by Noa."

"Wait—*what?*" Cecilia's face paled as she turned to Glacier.

The same sort of surprised, disturbed expressions crossed Crow, Rune, and Weather's face—the latter forcing out a nervous giggle. "You're not suggesting..."

"Noa," Rune said, "you and Nyx better be sure about this. That's a *very* serious accusation, and if you two believe that there's someone hunting Mages in Kingsheart—"

"*What?*" Cecilia squeaked.

Noa inwardly cringed, forcing her outward composure not to waver. "I think that there's a very strong possibility."

"And you didn't *say* anything?" Rune asked, hurt lacing his words.

Noa hesitated, guilt worming its way in. Nyx locked eyes with her, catching Noa's small cry for help. Nyx cleared her throat. "In Noa's defense, none of us were sure that it was the case back when we discovered it in Talie. We thought it could be something else. There was no real reason to jump to the conclusion that someone was actually hunting Mages."

"I'm sorry," Cecilia said, "but I don't understand... Why would someone hunt Mages? I mean, it would make sense for it to be happening in Amarais, but..." She glanced back at Glacier, her breath catching on her next question. "And why would someone think that Glacier's a Mage?"

"Knowing *why* isn't necessary right now," Nyx said. "Just know that there are some twisted individuals that do it. For whatever reason, it appears that those same type of people have also been hunting those associated with this special device's research, which is being developed to emulate the magical abilities of a Reader. So, eventually, it'll be able to trace magical signatures and auras—"

"Which would be both damning and useful to someone hunting said Mages," Rune mumbled, his hand moving to his mouth.

"Damning, *how?*" Glacier asked hesitantly.

"Let's drop it for now," Noa said. "In short, if all of this is seriously happening, then there's a good chance that what I've been tasked to do isn't some sort of cosmic joke after all—*unfortunately*."

Rune eyed Noa, his hurt bleeding through before he grabbed Cecilia's hand and began whispering something to her. Weather watched, her gaze going from sympathetic to steely before she faced Noa again.

"All right," Weather said, "I'm in. Just tell me what you want, and it's yours."

15
KING'S REPUBLIC ✧ 2705-01-07

NYX

Nyx stared at the journal decryption key box and contemplated everything she know about Juniper Everett. Huddling alone in her bunk with a tablet hadn't exactly been what she anticipated spending most of her trip to Esmedralia, but there she was: sitting in the dark and mulling over an answer that would solve so many of her problems.

At least, that's what she hoped.

Initial hint: my home.

> Ryland?

Alyvia had typed into one of their chat threads.

> I think Ryland would be the answer for the first one...

A person, not a place. That gave Nyx an idea of how to handle the next two hints.

First hint update: my heart.

So, if the first was her brother, could this be a lover? Nyx raised a brow, trying to think of how likely it could've been for Juniper to fall in love with a member of her Amaraian host family.

Final hint update: my world.

Nyx tapped her finger against the tablet, falling far into the depths of her memory—back to a time where she sat at workshop tables and inhaled the scents of green and black teas, depending on the day and her father's mood. She'd scratched out her homework onto a tablet in the midst of metal and plastic pieces scattered before her, catching her attention just as often as her hair did whenever it fell over her eyes. So—*often*.

Her old arm had set next to the new one, a sleeker, larger casing to match her growth spirt. He'd hummed while he worked, stopping every once in a while to rest and admire the wall of his children's achievements.

"Why do you keep all that junk?" Nyx had asked, jabbing her stylus toward a crude metal bracelet she'd made a couple years prior.

Her father chuckled. "Because all of you are my world."

Nyx checked the timestamps for the hints again, her eyes catching on the ten-month stretch between the second and the final changes. Enough time for a child to enter the picture. She turned over the dates in her mind, unable to let go the familiarity about them she couldn't quite place.

She closed her eyes, stuck on the second hint's update—a few days after King Cyrus's installation. Then the thoughts unspooled, connecting to one things after another and *another*... Juniper had likely felt safe enough to change her key to this lover once King Elias was gone, but no one had really known what Cyrus would do yet.

The thread snagged, realizing there was another potential connection she'd overlooked before. Nyx pulled up King Cyrus's profile and broke through that censored barrier to call up his travel logs. A list of registered places months before his takeover took over the screen, save a random address located not too far away from his father's vacation home. She pressed the address and got a name: *Valeria*.

So, *Prince* Cyrus had been meeting with his future advisor and his advisor's *Mage* sister, the two of them living out in the middle of nowhere by themselves. A place where it would be easy to hide a Mage tutor. A

Miraltan Mage tutor that had landed one of them in prison and sent the other on the run.

Nyx bit the inside of her cheek, knotting her threads together as she switched back to the journal's key entry screen once more. Her hands hovered over the keyboard, wanting to be wrong, but allowing herself this one wild guess. She wanted to be wrong because if she was somehow right, there wasn't any way she could tell Alyvia without some sort of explanation that wouldn't incriminate her.

Seven letters later, her finger held still over the button to lock in her answer. She exhaled and dropped it to the glass. The box pulsed green. Nyx's jaw hung slack as the entire journal compiled before her eyes, weaving an entire tapestry of words before her—answering the question that'd been nagging her ever since she'd discovered Alyvia's aunt had been alive for so long without sending any word home.

Juniper Everett didn't know how to explain that she had fallen for Cyrus Caelius, and the two of them were having a son.

16

BELLEGARDE ✧ 2705-01-08

NOA

"Ariadne Valeria," Nyx said, tapping the image of an outdated, younger image of a woman with ash-blond hair brushing her shoulders stared up at Noa from the tablet.

Noa frowned and shifted her position on Weather's bunk. "Okay... and she is?"

"A former *royal* tutor's assistant."

Noa lifted an eyebrow. "That's nice and all, but where are you going with this?"

"Well, for starters," Nyx said, rocking back on her bed, "I'm almost positive she's my newest Amaraian rebel contact. I wasn't completely sure if she was trustworthy until I managed to connect her to a few other people, but now I'm convinced that we can get her on our side. She'd fight for us the moment we step foot in Amarais again."

"Quite optimistic of you, considering we only have her past job to go off of... A lot of people work for someone they hate."

"Which is what I was taking into consideration, until..." —she leaned

forward again and swiped a finger across the screen to reveal another photo
— "I found that there are more dots to connect."

A new woman with familiar, honey-colored hair took Ariadne's place,
this one's name reading, 'Mariana Angelis'. "This is..."

"Cecilia's mother, the tutor Ariadne was assisting. Which brings me to
Ariadne's brother, North."

The screen changed again to a portrait of an older man with that same
ash-blond hair, cropped and slicked into place. But this one actually
matched his listed age in his forties.

"Cyrus's advisor..." Noa mumbled.

"Of course, you're undoubtably about to say that this doesn't mean
that either of them has any loyalty to the throne," she said flippantly, almost
trying to mimic Noa, "And I'd say that you're correct, aside from an interesting discovery that I stumbled upon while gathering what I thought was
unrelated data. North was arrested for harboring a Miraltan Mage, and
Ariadne was never caught."

They locked eyes while Noa's mind hovered on Glacier's mother.

"Naturally," Nyx continued, "I speculated why a man in his position of
power would have ever considered risking everything to potentially get
thrown in jail or *worse*—" Nya tapped the screen again, giving her a picture
of a Miraltan woman to stare at, the name 'Juniper Everett' listed underneath. "That is, until I realized that he took the fall to give his sister the
chance to run. North was harboring a Mage to teach his sister how to use
magic."

"Holy shit..." Noa whispered, staring down at those haunting, emerald
green eyes—as if Glacier was staring back at her. In a moment, the image
was replaced by another. Cyrus Caelius in all his regality took the spotlight,
casting Juniper back into the shadows.

"And then we have our king who did whatever the hell he wanted,"
Nyx continued, her eyes flicking up to Noa's face, "because how else do you
end up with a half-Miraltan prince out of this entire mess."

"You realize that this could all just be speculation, right?"

"No. Not when I have proof. I have Juniper Everett's journal. She
detailed everything that happened from the moment she stepped foot in

Amarais. Ariadne fell in love with her, but she rejected her since she was fifteen, regardless of whether or not she would have considered her if she was at least eighteen. However, Ariadne still stuck by her anyway, even when Juniper fell for Cyrus..."

"And now she's probably pissed that her friends are dead. And her brother is in prison..."

"Plus, she believes that the son of the woman she loved is dead too."

Noa grimaced, understanding that Ariadne probably thought that there was nothing left of them now. "Have you told her that Glacier's alive?"

"No. I'd rather not get her hopes up in case we get ambushed by the Volkov. I don't want to give her hope that might end up being meaningless. It's better that he stays dead, rather than potentially mourning him twice."

Noa bit down on her tongue, hating how it sounded. "But... does *Glacier* know about this? Did you talk to him about what you've found?"

Her hesitation caused Noa to stiffen, a little afraid of what Glacier might be riding on, in terms of hope. "No. I had considered asking him a couple of times, but after I found all of *this*..." She shook her head. "Noa, I found *more*. It's not directly related to Glacier, but it's stuff that you'll be interested in seeing. I... also don't know that you're going to like it."

Noa's grip tightened on the tablet, her eyes locked onto Nyx's hand as she pushed the screen's data aside to reveal an entire mapped tree of connections. Noa's eyes followed the branches to name after name until they snagged on what Nyx wanted her to see. Her breath caught. She'd been right—Noa didn't like it, but it was exactly what they needed.

17
ESMEDRALIA ✧ 2705-01-09

NOA

Noa leaned against Weather's doorframe, watching her sift through her bag. Weather stood up and spun around, slapping her hand over her heart with a gasp. "N-Noa," she said with an uneasy chuckle. "Can I help you?"

"Actually, *yes*," Noa said with a smirk. "First, I'd like to officially welcome you. However, you should be aware that there are some general ground rules. What I say, goes. Sure, Nyx will typically toss orders around, but she ultimately defers to me as well. Your boyfriend has had some difficulty coping with this in the past, so I want to make sure that there isn't any miscommunication with us but tackling this now. I would rather not have to remind you that I am very much not a thief, but a trained killer."

Weather's hesitant smile dropped.

"You should also be aware that I'm not here to keep you against your will. Should you decide that this is all too much, you can leave whenever, but it'll be at your own risk. There's only so much I can do if the Volkov realize you and I are connected, and they will eventually act on it, understood?"

Weather began to nod. "U-understood."

Noa clapped her hands together, brightening a little before striking the final blow. "Good. Now that we're squared away in terms of business, there's just one more rule: Glacier's off-limits."

Weather's brows raised, taken off-guard by the shift in topic, but she nodded. Granted, the action came with a glimmer of recognition in her eyes that Noa wasn't so sure she liked.

She decided to brush it off for now, putting on her most charming grin. "Welcome aboard, Lust."

Weather blinked before her mouth ticked up at the corner. Seeing that, Noa turned to leave, mentally patting herself on the back for dealing with the hardest task of her morning before the train stopped. She collected her bag by the window seat and slung it over her shoulder.

"What are you smiling about?" Glacier asked, adjusting his own bag as he stepped out from his room.

"Oh, nothing," she said in a sing-song tone that earned her a suspicious frown.

The view of Esmedralia's capital city of Razbia outside their hotel bay windows stretched into the mountainous backdrop separating them from Jinwon and Bellegarde. Pale-stoned historical and holy buildings with lines of tear-dropped archways gave way to crisscrossing triangular, multicolored banners shading the city streets in maroons, blush pinks, pale yellows, and golds. And right in the heart of it all sat their next key.

"It's in a *university* building?" Noa asked, holding back mild irritation at the image plastered on Nyx's rolled-out computer mat. The Blood of Esmedralia rested in a glass box atop a pedestal, where it spread across the silk pillow like a gold lotus sprinkled with rubies.

Weather waved her hand over the image with a scowl like she was personally offended by the archive's décor. "The lobby of this hotel looks more suited to display than *that*."

Noa had to agree, though she refrained from nodding as she slid a thumb across her jaw. Between the glossy pink quartz countertops at the reception desk and the coffered ceiling with its ornately carved floral patterns, it blew the drab, dark academia interior with its grays, navy blues, and bland white paneling out of the water.

"Regardless of how it looks," Nyx said, "it's still in the university archives building."

Noa grimaced. "So, it'll be *crawling* with students."

"Yes, but—"

"Please tell me that's a *good* 'but'."

Nyx folded her arms over her chest at the sudden interruption. "*But* we have a doctorate student who has quite a bit of influence when it comes to the head archivist. He's able to schedule a late-night reservation to use the building with his assistant for some uninterrupted research time. That means that the receptionists will be sent home, and only a single archivist will be around to tend to him. So—"

"The relic will be unattended?" Noa asked, her hope amplified by Nyx's smirk.

"Exactly. We'll just have to wait a couple of days since he could only manage to get it scheduled for the eleventh, at the earliest."

Noa's leaned back and stretched, pleased with the promise of non-traveling downtime. "We can work with that."

"So, the plan is for Crow and Weather to scope out the place tomorrow morning in disguise. Rune and Cecilia will act as overwatch with us." Nyx motioned between herself and Glacier. "As for *you*, I'd like you to meet with an associate of mine. He told me that he's concerned that the Volkov might be close to being called on him if they haven't been already. I'd like you to meet with him tomorrow morning to get a rundown of his schedule since he's trying to stick to it up until he leaves to avoid suspicion. And when our thieves collect the key, I'll need you to do an extraction from his teaching assistant office."

"Fine by me," Noa said with a shrug.

"Does…" Weather started nervously, ripping her gaze away from the mat. "Does that mean that the Volkov are *here*? Like, right now?"

"No," Noa said with a shake of her head. "Not necessarily. It depends on when this guy started messing around."

"He told me that it was two or three days ago," Nyx said.

"Then we should be fine. Usually, it can take about a week after a request, assuming that the timer started the second he was messing with something he shouldn't. So we probably still have a couple days at the earliest before they show up. After that, it would take them about a week to scope everything out and learn his schedule. Plus, considering that they're down two people, it could take them longer just to get to this point..."

"So we have time," Rune said, "but we still have to be quick, so we don't run the risk of overlapping the Volkov's schedule."

"Especially if Kole ends up here several days early," Noa said. "Because if he were to suddenly appear and realize Glacier was here..."

"He'd drop whatever the hell he's doing and go for him instead," Nyx mumbled, rubbing her forehead. Her hand dropped back to her lap with a sigh. "Let's be efficient about all of this, shall we?"

"So..." Weather started, a hint of a tentative smile, "does that mean we're free for tonight?"

Noa giving a slight, noncommittal shrug before Nyx returned to Weather's question. "Yes, you're free for the rest of the day."

Weather pushed herself up from the floor, rounding the couch for the door. "Crow, we're exploring the town!"

His eyes lit up, and he scrambled off the couch, tripping after her.

"Oh! Wait—" Cecilia said, her voice pitching with excitement. "Rune, we should go with—"

"Cecilia," Rune said with a wince. "I don't think you want to be a part of *their* exploration..."

"What? Why?"

"I mean," Weather said, half-turning with her hand on the door. "She's welcome to join us if she'd like—"

"*No*," Crow hissed.

Rune put on a tight smile "You and I can go have a look around with Glacier later, along with anyone else who'd like to join."

"Glacier can join u—" Weather started again. Noa's head whipped around as she squeezed the life out of the throw pillow. Weather's mouth snapped shut, and a wide-eyed Crow moved to shove her out the door.

"You just *had* to..." he grumbled before the door fell into its frame behind them.

"Ah, yes," Nyx said flatly, deadpanning back to Noa. "Another night of debauchery, except now there's *two* of them."

"Oh..." Cecilia mumbled.

Rune's hand went to his forehead with a sigh. "Well, now that they're gone, is there anyone who would like to join us for an *actual* city exploration that doesn't involve climbing into a stranger's bed?"

"Pass," Nyx said, standing up from her chair. "I have to meet a client tonight."

"What about you, Glacier?" Cecilia asked with a bright smile.

His eyes flicked to Noa, hesitating. "I—um—I'm actually pretty exhausted. I'm thinking I'll call it early and pass out in a couple of hours since I didn't sleep well on the train. Have fun without me though. Let me know if you see anything cool." He followed up with a weak smile.

Noa ran her tongue over her teeth, holding back her demand for him to leave with them and get some fresh air. "I should stay here, just in case," she added dryly.

But Cecilia slipped her arm through Rune's, and they left, leaving Nyx to finish up typing something on her phone.

"So," Noa said, "which client are you seeing?"

"Devi."

"Is there something wrong? Is she okay?"

"Yeah, she's fine. It's just to talk, that's all." She shrugged. "No Volkov, no weird information, secrets, or anything like that."

"Therapy. Got it," Noa mumbled, tracing a finger over the arm of the couch.

"Call it what you will. I'll be back in a couple hours. Call me if people start dying."

Noa turned to watch her leave, the scrape of the door against the carpet signaling that she was now officially alone with Glacier. He stood and started for Nyx's bag heaped on the opposite side of the couch, collecting a tablet before he reclaimed his seat.

"And what do you think you're doing?"

"Some reading before I go to sleep in *two* hours." He held up his fingers in a V.

"You should have gone with Rune and Cecilia."

"Noa, I'm fine, really. I just... didn't really feel like being dragged around everywhere tonight. I really am exhausted. That's it."

She didn't detect any lies rolling off his tongue—no hints of sadness in the depths of his eyes. Just exhaustion, mainly radiating out from the way he'd sank into the chair. Noa bit her lip and ran a hand through her long bangs. "Okay."

"Thank you."

NYX

Nyx leaned forward, gripping the seat of the garden bench. The diagonal path between the two L-shaped apartment buildings with its little ponds and walking paths among overgrown flowers and blossoming trees felt like a dream. She turned her face skyward to the garments hung out over glass-framed balconies and open windows whispering music or the latest news.

"I hope I didn't keep you waiting."

Nyx dropped her head to face a woman with her near-black hair tied back in a messy tail grazing the collar of her white, disheveled lab coat. Soft, dark eyes crinkled at the edges as she offered her a hand. Nyx took it, gold meeting bronze in a familiar embrace.

"Don't worry, I haven't been here for very long." She rose and bit down on her tongue when she still had to look up to see her face.

"Well, good," she said, grinning as she leaned down for a quick kiss. Nyx cleared her throat, rubbing at the side of her face as Devi broke into a melodic giggle and tugged her along to the building entrance. "Come on."

She tapped a badge to the door, the elevator, and then her apartment— a space where the only clutter came in the form of fresh-cut flowers on the kitchen bar top and succulents resting under the TV. Everything else was tucked away in a cabinet or a closet.

"Why do I feel like you inviting me up here is a trap?"

"Well, you're already here, aren't you?" she teased.

"Devi, I'm not sleeping with you."

"Well, of course you're not sleeping with *Devi*," she said, grabbing both of her hands. "Because you'd be sleeping with *Aiza*." She clicked her tongue in mock disapproval and tugged off her coat.

"You really shouldn't be saying that..." Nyx sighed.

"The neighbors can't hear anything through the walls, trust me," Aiza replied in a sing-song voice. "Sometimes I feel like I'm going mad with the silence. It's nothing like that apartment we shared or my house back in King's."

"And here I thought you'd just want to take a walk."

"We still could go for a walk. It just depends on how much time you have before Noa realizes you're missing."

"You know that if you kidnap me, she'll figure it out pretty quickly, right?"

"Oh, like you actually told her we're *together*, Nari." Aiza twirled a finger in a circle around Nyx's nose.

Nyx bit back a laugh, enjoying the way her real name sounded from her lips. It always sounded better coming from her.

"I also hope that Noa hasn't turned you into someone completely reckless either," Aiza said. "Because I'd prefer to have you back in one piece once this is over."

Nyx chuckled, shaking her head. "Don't you think it's already a little too late for that?"

Her face was blank for a moment before she frowned and playfully hit her right shoulder. "*Ha-ha*," she said mockingly. "You're missing an arm, very funny. I'm being serious, Nari. I don't want us hiding from the Volkov forever, just waiting for the day that you won't be able to message or call me back. I want our lives back. I want to start our future together."

The way Aiza brought her hands to her chest and the pleading in her voice seized Nyx's heart. Nyx grabbed her wrist and stepped forward. "I know you want this to be over. Trust me, I want this to be over too, but it's not that easy..."

To think she'd originally been intimidated by Aiza. Between her brains, looks, and charm, Nyx picked at everything that annoyed her when they first hid away from the Volkov along the coast of Esmedralia. It'd been an echoing rule of not to get emotionally involved with anyone she worked with ever since she shadowed her father at his company when she turned eighteen.

Every pretty face was a distraction, but now Nyx wanted nothing more than to be distracted. Distracted from her work. Distracted from the intimate relationships cropping up around her. Distracted from her potential demise—a fate she didn't wish to share with Aiza because Nyx considered herself a lost soul and a lost cause. Everything Aiza wasn't.

And Aiza was her reason why she'd see this through, even she was too much of a coward to tell anyone or confess all the details of Noa's half-baked plan to Aiza. Nyx closed her eyes and relived curling up on Aiza's couch in that shack of an apartment while she worked—sitting in bed with her tablet while Aiza pressed up against her at night. She had to believe that there would be more of those moments after their brief stay here.

"I just need you to trust me," Nyx breathed.

18

ESMEDRALIA ✧ 2705-01-10

NOA

Noa's head jerked up at the sound of the suite door opening around 3AM. She'd been so engrossed in her late-night reading on the couch that she'd missed the footsteps in the hallway—something that she cursed herself for until two silhouettes stumbled inside.

"Gods, you are *hot.*"

Crow.

Noa rolled her eyes and rubbed at her forehead while Weather's bubbly giggle bounced off the walls. The laugh faded right as her and Crow's eyes glinted in Noa's direction, their voices dropping to stage whispers.

"Maybe she doesn't see us..." Weather said from the corner of her mouth.

"Just... don't move."

They stood stock-still like Crow suggested until Noa panned back to her tablet, soaking in the eerie blue light. Then they fell over each other in the mad dash to their room and fumbled with the doorknob for an absurdly long time.

"*Move*," Weather hissed. "Let me do it, you dumb slut." She shoved him out of the way, and they tripped inside.

Noa sighed and shook her head, unraveling the red thread Nyx had left her with. She didn't even notice the sunlight creeping up her neck until a shadow fell over her. The tablet's display dimmed as she watched Glacier collapse onto the couch cushion at her feet, sinking into the scarlet flower print. Noa checked the time and forced out a breath—6AM. She slid the tablet onto the coffee table and swung her legs over the side.

"Ready to train?" she asked.

"I'm... not really feeling up to it today."

Her brows knit together. "You're not getting out of—"

"I'm twenty today," he said quietly, a faraway look in his eyes while he stared out at the mountains.

Noa's mouth worked to try to reply with something other than 'oh' before rubbing her hands on her pants. This was sort of a big deal—a right of passage. It was an end to that transition period from that awkward two-year stage of self-discovery as a functioning member of society. And here he was, spending his milestone birthday in a foreign city with a bunch of criminals.

He let out a short, bitter laugh. "I didn't think I'd actually make it this long."

Noa stood and started for the kitchen, feeling Glacier's eyes on her as she popped open the liquor cabinet and collected two short, glass tumblers. The question she'd asked he and Cecilia back in Miralta felt like years ago, rather than a month and a half, but the memory sat differently now. It sat like the sound of the tumblers scraping against the coffee table—familiar but new. She poured a finger's worth of amber liquid into each and handed one to him. The gentle way he took it from her was barely enough to distract her from the way their knees brushed together.

"I'll be honest," she said with a breathy laugh. "I'm not too sure what to toast to. I would suggest 'long live the king', but that doesn't really bode well with your family history."

He lifted his glass, with a somber expression exuding a level and serenity and confidence. "To all of the well-meaning, silenced kings before me."

A slow, pleased smirk tugged at the corner of her mouth, and she lifted her glass in agreement. They drank, but he tore his glass away with a grimace.

"What?" she asked, chuckling. "Didn't you ever snitch from the liquor cabinet at home?"

"*Yes*, but—" He gagged, shaking his head as he pushed it back onto the coffee table. "It tastes like the sort of stuff Kat drinks."

"A woman after my own heart."

"You can keep it." He nudged it towards her.

"Well, now you're just spitting in Death's face."

"Like you haven't."

"Oh, I *have*, but at least I have the skills to back it up."

He bit his lip, his eyes dancing with amusement. "So... what did you do when you turned twenty? Was it anything special?"

Noa hesitated with the glass partway to her lips, dropping it down to rest on her knees. "I became an official member of the Volkov. I took a test that I probably shouldn't have passed, but I did." She stared down at her drink, imagining the horrible stinging cold against her skin and the blur of her vision fading. "Do you know how the Volkov started?"

Glacier shook his head, transporting her back to Lazarus's workshop when she'd argued with him about going back. They'd sat face-to-face at the corner of his desk, and he'd began to spin his little yarn.

Noa smirked. "They were early wandering nomads who left Astravny to travel as craftsmen and entertainers."

Glacier chuckled. "They were a *circus?*"

"I mean..." she started, tilting a hand back in forth in a so-so motion, unable to hold back a smirk. "It was a *very* loose circus if that was the case. They were mainly merchants, but some of them had been hired to entertain royalty or high-ranking nobles. So, some of these wealthy folks decided that they could hire one of the assistants to kill someone in a rival house after inviting them because of a recommendation or jealousy because they wanted a lavish event. The day after the act, they would pack up and leave, and no one would be any wiser to the aristocratic warfare."

His eyes went wide. "You're... kidding, right?"

She knocked back the rest of her drink, shaking her head. "Nope. That's straight from one of those old history books people censor and bury."

"And do they just pass that kind of information down through the Volkov?"

"No," she said with a sigh. "Lazarus worked with books. He told me the story, and when I said he was messing with me, he pulled out the real thing —ink on paper."

"I never realized that you were such a well-educated killer," he replied with a teasing smirk.

"While strength and skill will help you survive, knowledge is the greatest weapon someone can wield. Knowing your enemy's strengths and weaknesses is just as important as knowing your own. Lazarus was just as vital to my survival as Myron, as much as I hate to acknowledge the latter. The difference was that Lazarus never tried to restrict my thoughts to make me a killing machine. He always encouraged me to look at how things were versus how they *could* be. I suppose that's why I slowly talked myself into trying to find an excuse to let someone slip away from a contract, and Nyx became that person."

"Maybe he was right to think you could open the Vault."

She turned to him with surprise, feeling torn over this bond they shared —whatever it was. Her hand went to the cord around her neck. "Glacier, if something goes wrong, and I die—"

He quickly sat up, shaking his head. "You're not going to d—"

"If I die, I want you to take the keys. Out of all the people here, I think you're the one that would be able to finish this if I can't."

Nyx made it clear to her that she didn't want to be a leader, and she had never intended to be one. Rune and Crow couldn't take it because she couldn't burden one without the other, and this weight seemed like too much for the both of them to carry. Cecilia *might* be able to manage, but she was still far too soft. And then there was Weather, who was still too new to this and far too reckless, from what Crow had explained.

However, Glacier had already taken everything that was thrown at him and had managed to keep going. There was determination to continue—to finish what his father and cousin had worked for. There was no one better to take the role of a king, let alone *the* King, than a prince, no matter how broken.

"Noa, I—" He bit back the rest of his words, the two of them peering into each other's souls. His gaze hardened, determination taking over. "You told me that if you're not dying, I'm not dying. That goes both ways."

"Glacier," she started, a breathy, humorless chuckle escaping her, "as much as we might plan, we're talking about the Volkov. If we somehow win, but they take me down with them, there will be no one left to stand in your way. I know you can finish it, just like how you plan to continue your father's legacy. So, promise me you'll do this if I can't."

He started to shake his head again, catching her eyes with a sad, resigned look once he seemed to realize that she wouldn't let this go. "Fine, I promise," he said reluctantly, "but you're not going to die."

She bit her lip, ducking her head to hide a smirk. "I suppose that's the best I'll get out of you."

"That's *all* you'll get out of me," he said, folding his arms over his chest.

His composure wavered when she met his gaze again, the two of them finally caving to how ridiculous it all sounded. There was something light-hearted and special about it all—about meeting someone she never would've imagined talking to about the Volkov, let alone discussing her past, her insecurities, and her worst nightmares. "Maybe one day we won't be a prince and a killer sitting on a couch trying to draw straws over who gets stuck with a cord of keys."

He laughed, tilting his head to rest against the back of the couch. "Assuming we make it, where do you think we'll be a year from now?"

"Well, you'll be the King of Amarais, and I'll be... I guess whatever sort of title I'll get." She leaned back, turning over the titles in her mind. *The Queen of Avaria?*

"Do you think we'll end up bitter rivals?" he asked with a grin.

"You make it sound like we'll be in one of those old cartoons where we'd perpetually mess with each other. Then one of us would screw up, accidently die, and the other would lose all meaning in life."

"Well, it's Amarais, Noa. If you're the hero, I'd be the villain."

"Oh, please—like *you* could be a villain. In case you forgot, *I* was the one to kidnap a prince. I don't think you can get more villainous than that."

CECILIA

Cecilia slipped out of her room with a small black box behind her back. The rounded, plastic corners slick in her palm as she wandered into the living room, slowing when she saw Noa, Glacier, and a bottle of alcohol. Her smile faded into a disapproving frown. "You're drinking already?"

Glacier shifted to face her, shaking his head with a grimace. "It was awful."

"*Hey*—" came Noa's protest. "That's the expensive shit. Don't say that."

Cecilia bit back a laugh. "I *suppose* that's okay now, and I doubt you'll go overboard." She pulled the box from behind her back and held it out in offering. "Happy birthday."

"Cecilia, you didn't have to—"

"I know, but I wanted to. I've never really been able to give you anything, and turning twenty isn't really a small thing, so... I wanted you to have something special."

"Thank you," he said, dropping his eyes down to the container as he popped up the lid.

Noa leaned a little toward the coffee table like she was trying to catch a glimpse of what he got before she tugged her phone from her pocket. Cecilia bit the inside of her cheek, eyeing her until Glacier held up a black ring with a smirk. "Did you give me Rune's box by mistake?"

Cecilia huffed and grabbed his hand. "It's not an engagement ring, you idiot," she mumbled, tilting it for him to see the inside of the band. His eyes fell to the engraving inside, and his face slowly changed from teasing to somber.

She'd gotten Katerina's name, birthdate, and death date written there. "I wanted you to be able to always keep a part of her with you. That way you're never alone."

She bit her lip as he stared down at it again, thinking she'd slipped up before he slid it onto his right hand's middle finger. "Thank you," he said. "It's perfect."

"I- I wanted to get her full name engraved, but—"

He shook his head as he stood and pulled her into a hug. "No, Cecilia. It's perfect. This means a lot."

She gripped the back of his shirt, willing back tears. Noa's head jerked away, finding another point in the room she suddenly found more interesting, but Cecilia could've sworn she'd caught a flicker of longing in her eyes.

RUNE

"Get up," Rune said, drawing back the decorative curtains and tapping the window shades. Crow and Weather hissed in a chorus of displeasure while shielding their eyes from the supposed safety of the bed.

"*Why?*" Crow said with a groan, trying to pull the covers from Weather's grip. She cocooned herself further into her awkward diagonal position over top of him, and he lightly smacked where Rune assumed her back was. "*Share*, dumbass!"

Rune sighed and picked up a couple stray articles of clothing, dropping them next to their bags. "You two need to go scout out the campus *early*, remember?"

"This isn't early," Crow grumbled, squinting over at the digital time display on the window and dramatically throwing his arm over his eyes. "This is torture."

Rune stalked over to the bed, emitting a low hum of frustration, and pulled the comforter free. Weather shrieked, and Crow chuckled darkly before she whipped around and started smacking him like they were locked in a cat fight.

"*Hey*," Rune said. "Cut it out. What time did you two even get back last night?"

Crow snorted while he shrank back from Weather's hand hovering above his face. "You think I actually paid attention to that?"

"I don't know..." Weather said with a shrug, glancing at Rune over her shoulder. "Maybe... three? I just remember waiting for that train forever..."

"*Oh*," Crow said with a grin, "that's not all *I* remember..."

Weather blinked, dropping her hand as a devious grin danced onto her face.

Rune rubbed his cheek. "Do I even *want* to know?"

"Since a certain prince is off-limits," Weather said. "We found our own." She held up a hand, and Crow high-fived it.

"You're got to be kidding me..."

"Rune, have you forgotten just how good I am at manipulation?"

"No, Weather. I'm pretty sure I remember. Especially since you have *this* dumbass under your spell again."

She draped herself over Crow. "Turns out Esmedralia's prince is pretty damn wild."

"Hell yeah he is." Crow stretched.

Rune stared up at the ceiling, waiting for a higher power strike them down. Or maybe they'd both burst into flames for coming into contact with the sun. Perhaps he'd never had a brother—maybe he'd only ever had an unholy shadow following him around his whole life.

"Also," Weather piped up, "why, exactly, is he off-limits?"

Rune shook his head and started for the door. "You two really are stupid," he mumbled before raising his voice in a command. "Get dressed. You have fifteen minutes."

"But—"

"You're being glamoured, Weather. You can worry about your makeup and everything else when you get back. Now get up." He pulled open the door. "Living room. Dressed. Fifteen minutes."

He pulled the door shut behind him, and a thump radiated out from the base. A pillow, most likely.

"Nice," Crow said, accompanied by a muffled giggle.

NOA

Noa basked in the shade under one of the large trees dotting the sprawling lawn of the campus. She'd become another student while she waited for Nyx's associate—blending in with the Bellegardian, Jinwonese, Valentian, and Mharuan students clustered together in mini study groups, waving around phones and tablets.

"Veronika?"

Noa's head lifted at the sound of her fake name, meeting the dark eyes of a thin young man with brown skin and mussed black hair. His wrinkled tee-shirt and skewed horn-rimmed glasses added to the exhaustion radiating off of him, but his nervous smile still had a sprinkle of enthusiasm in it.

"Indra?" she asked, pushing herself up to stand.

"That's me," he said with a breathy chuckle. "I was a little afraid that I might miss you with all the other foreign students that like to hang out on this lawn. Do you mind following me back to my private dorm to talk?"

"By all means. Lead the way."

She got him on the topic of hobbies, his studies, his dissertation, his consideration to travel abroad for school, and finally—simply because Noa couldn't help herself—the archives building. While she may have guided him into the final part of their discussion, he was the one to bring up the Blood of Esmedralia, though he didn't give her any new information.

Indra quieted as they pushed their way into one of the dorm buildings and up a flight of stairs. He unlocked a door and motioned for her to go in ahead of him. She stepped into a small, tidy space with a bed lofted above a desk and a mini-makeshift kitchen along the opposing wall. More surprising was the lack of a TV or dedicated game console.

She spun around as he shut the door, and he pulled out his phone—all anxious cheer gone. "Could I have your contact information? I'll send you my office location and a map. Nyx mentioned that you're leaving tomorrow night, and I've been staying late to grade some accelerated course work. That means I'll be there, not here..."

"Uh... sure..." Noa said cautiously, rattling off her number. Nyx likely already had all of the rest of the info he'd offered, but if it was for peace of mind, she guessed there was no harm in it.

"Thanks," Indra said, breathing a sigh of relief as he dropped his bag next to his bunk.

"So..." Noa folded her arms over her chest. "Nyx mentioned that you ended up finding something a few days ago, right?"

She wasn't a fan of the hesitation that followed. "Y-yeah, I—" He forced out a breath. "I was just digging around like I normally do when I'm doing research, and I checked out a book from the archives. It was from a section that's only available to higher-level students or faculty. There was a coded message, so I... well, I took it as a challenge."

Noa closed her eyes and rubbed her forehead. "You know that curiosity killed the cat, right?"

He sputtered as she reopened her eyes, his voice dropping to something more defensive. "Well, how was I supposed to know that it wasn't just some dumb upper-classmen joke or something?"

"So you figured out what it was?"

With a cringe, he nodded. "I... I'm pretty sure there's a cult on campus..."

Noa's eyebrows shot up and motioned for him to continue, fueled by her morbid interest.

He paused. "The... problem is that there's a highly-esteemed professor's name attached to this thing, so I *know* that he must be having people somehow overlook it."

"So you think this professor is trying to shut you up?"

"*Yes*," he said through gritted teeth, glancing towards his window like they were being watched.

She bit the inside of her cheek. Something wasn't adding up. "What was in the book?"

Instead of fear or panic, there was a flicker of annoyance in his reaction. "I- I don't remember the title. Just some book by Keaton Scott since I had been looking for one of his other books."

"And who's the professor?"

"Daniels," he replied without a beat of hesitation. "Professor Daniels."

That quick response held a small kernel of anger. His story was fabricated, but she wasn't sure of *which parts* were true or false. Usually, people told her or Nyx what was happening because they were confessing to a complete stranger—not admitting to their girlfriend that they'd cheated on her.

He checked his phone. "Look, I have to go," he said, ushering her back out the door. "If you have any more questions, text me, and I'll call you back when I get the chance."

"Yeah. Sure," she said casually, erasing suspicion from her tone before she stepped back out into the hall.

After that, he wasted no time locking up and giving a quick wave goodbye, leaving a sour taste in Noa's mouth that lingered during her trip back to the hotel.

GLACIER

Relief washed over Glacier when Noa returned, and he sank into the couch rubbing his thumb over the edge of the tablet Nyx had given him. The data on it had barely distracted him from the little makeup party Cecilia and Weather had been having on the floor after the latter complained about not having the time to do hers this morning. Noa patted Crow's boot hanging over the arm of the chair as she passed, earning a tired grumble. Rune smirked and locked eyes with her as she stared at the empty spot on the couch between him and Glacier.

Nyx stretched, her silhouette framed by the window as she rocked back along the plush, wine-colored rug. "So how's our friend?"

Noa huffed and finally took her seat on the couch, folding her arms over her chest. "I think he's lying about something."

"And what makes you think that?"

"His story seemed *off.*"

"Well, regardless, he's still coming with us. You can grill him on the train ride for your answers, but just worry about the extraction for now. In the meantime..." Nyx stood, brushing off her black jeans before she scooped up her phone. "I'm going to get some fresh air. If you need me, text me." She rounded the furniture.

Noa pushed herself up, twisting around with her mouth hanging partway open as the door shut behind her. "What the hell?" she mumbled, turning back around to Glacier.

He shrugged, shortly interrupted by Weather's sharp gasp.

"You're an artist..." Weather said, tilting the compact mirror around, shooting a ray of concentrated light around the ceiling. "You did *this* with just *that?*" She snapped the compact shut, pointing it at the small stash of travel-sized items Cecilia had been using for light party makeup and glamours.

Cecilia tugged on her hair, anxiously grabbing for her makeup bag. "Well, we don't really use it that much, so I don't have much, but—"

"This is a waste of your true potential. You need a *real* set of makeup, not—not *this.*"

Rune sat forward, tapping his brother's boot. "Crow..."

"What?" came Crow's muffled answer.

Weather pushed herself up. "An artist's talent is wasted without the proper tools. Get your ID, Cecilia. We're going to fix that."

Cecilia's eyes lit up. "You'll go makeup shopping with me?"

"Of course, I will," she said with a tinge of offense. "You've been around a bunch of unrefined men and uncaring women for far too long."

Noa's shook her head, rolling her eyes as Rune smacked Crow's boot this time.

"*Crow. Get up.*"

"Why?" Crow asked, finally cracking open an eye to shoot him a glare.

"Your girlfriend is causing *financial* problems. Do something before we have to get rid of her."

"Oh, please, you act like she'll actually *buy* the makeup—"

"Good gods, were you not paying attention?"

The back-and-forth continued as Weather took Cecilia's hand and led her towards the door.

Rune shot up, towering over him. "This is how it *starts*, Crow. First, she tests the waters with a makeup purchase, then it's clothes, and then—"

"*Shit*—" Crow scrambled out of the armchair. "Weather!"

"Oh, good!" Weather said he and Rune jogged after them. "See, Cecilia, now we have willing test subjects."

Another futile protest later, the four of them were out the door, leaving Noa and Glacier alone. Glacier turned back to her, finding Noa biting her lip as he cupped a hand over his own mouth. She broke first with a snort.

"I don't think I've ever seen Rune so panicked," she said through fits.

"I'm just imagining Cecilia coming back with a ton of makeup and clothes with the biggest smile."

Noa slid down into her seat with a grin, her eyes grazing the view before flicking back to him. "Why don't we go out for lunch? It would feel like a bit of a waste not to wander around somewhere that isn't dreary for a change."

NOA

Noa had decided she could make an exception for Glacier's birthday by treating him to lunch. She nudged him when they spotted an open-air restaurant, where they indulged in meat-filled dumplings with squash, topped with garlic sauce and a bowl of soup on the side. She'd regretted eating so much as she when they'd wandered past the strips of food carts and caught the scent of fresh-baked goods.

So, she steered them into material goods, secretly hoping to spot a place to purchase a present that might rival Cecilia's—a stretch, she knew—before considering how that might connect them. Arched, wide, double-doored shops lured in customers to tug clothing free from racks, examine home décor, or test electronic accessories. She stole glances at him, her heart filling with joy at each sign of wonder escaping in the form of bright eyes, a smile, or a breathy laugh.

They ducked into a sweets shop, and she purchased a small box of candy for them to try. She tucked it under her arm on their short walk to the plaza, relishing the misting spray of the illuminated fountain set on a timed loop as they nabbed a bench. Noa shoved the box in front of him to take the first piece, which he took before his face scrunched up. He shook his head, saying it was too sweet. She threw her head back and laughed, reveling in the sugar dissolving on her tongue.

After watching the water leap from side to side, she ushered him into the heart of downtown. Artisan, handmade works spilled out of every doorway, along with its patrons—all clamoring for prize swatches of cloth, sets of dishes, and metal figurines. They wove in and out of the crowds and lines, milling about until she turned back to check on Glacier.

She skidded to a dead stop. He was *gone.*

Noa spun around, her heart hammering in her chest with a million different horrible thoughts pouring in, trying to keep herself calm and composed until she caught sight of his plain, black long-sleeved shirt in a sea of color. She zig-zagged through bodies, excusing herself with her legs screaming to run for him.

Glacier stood in front of an old, mosaic-encrusted tranquility pool in the shape of a top-down lotus, softly bubbling at its center. Blue, shattered pieces of glass glinted in the base, climbing up the sides in a transition to pinks and then reds radiating out along the walkway, further and further apart. The epicenter of Razbia marked by a symbol in the shape of their national emblem.

Her boots crunched next to him while she glanced around at the few people resting nearby, whispering amongst themselves or enjoying the rays of sun pouring through the unshaded street hub. An older woman knelt down by the pool's edge and gently dropped a stamped coin into the water, letting it sink to the bottom where the small lotus-stamp lay face-up among its siblings.

Noa finally reached for his arm, her fingers lightly grazing the back of his hand. Glacier jumped, tensing up as his head swung toward her, and she reared back in surprise.

"Are you okay?" she asked. "You scared the hell out of me by vanishing like that."

"S-sorry," he said, rubbing his forehead. "I just saw this, and—well, I thought you were behind me..."

She bit her lip, hesitating before she gripped his shoulders and steered him away. "Come on," she said, resignation weighing on her. "Let's head back."

Noa's shoulders fell when they passed the plaza fountain's multicolored streams popping up against an orange-tinged sky.

It doesn't have to end here...

She shook away the thought, wrapping her arms around herself so she couldn't reach for his hand. Her eyes went to the rest of the people they passed instead—an older couple bickering over a set of plates, a girl offering another girl a drink, a boy winking at a girl who stepped up to his cart.

Then the world slowed. Noa's heart shot up into her throat, and she threw herself against Glacier, sending them stumbling into an alley.

"What are you do—"

"Quiet," she hissed, shoving him up against the wall and angling herself to obscure him before risking another glance.

There she was, just like how Noa had remembered her. Her dark eyes cold and hard, her bobbed hair swaying against lightly tanned skin. A viper waiting to strike at a moment's notice – an Astravnian wolf walking among Esmedralian sheep. Noa braced herself for Lexa to lock eyes with her, but instead, she continued striding straight into downtown, half-checking her phone like she was looking for a specific place. In a stretch of a few minutes that seemed like an eternity, she was gone, swallowed up by the crowd again.

"That lying son of a bitch," Noa whispered, seething as her thoughts pinned on Indra. "He lied about the *when*."

"What?" Glacier asked, alarm seeping into his voice.

"Volkov," she said in a breathy mumble. "We need to get the hell out of here because where there's one, there's bound to be another." Which left her with the problem of *which* 'other' was out here with her. As much as Noa wanted to bank on Lexa's older biological brother, Talon, there was nothing to solidify that now—not with how she had thrown everything into disarray.

She grabbed Glacier's arm, holding tight as she dragged him back to the local line. Noa peered over her shover every few steps, but Lexa hadn't turned around to follow.

"That dumbass," Nyx mumbled, a hand partially covering her mouth in her absent stare at a spot on the bedroom rug.

Noa suppressed urge to pace in the confines of her and Nyx's room, where she'd found Nyx sorting through her luggage.

"There's no way the Volkov could be here after a few days," Noa said heatedly. "Not with the four job-runners they have left at their disposal. Indra definitely lied about *when*, but why the hell would he bother lying about that unless he's trying to cover his ass for something else?"

Nyx's hand finally dropped. "Let's back up for a second and assess the situation. You said that you saw Lexa, right? And they normally work in pairs, so do you believe that Kole is nearby? Or someone else?"

"It's a one out of three chance. So, there's a possibility. Which means that this might get really bad, really fast."

"First thing's first," Nyx said, her eyes flicking between her and Glacier. "Glacier doesn't leave the hotel."

"No shit."

Glacier hugged himself, wearily glancing between them.

"Second," she continued, ignoring Noa's attitude, "we need to make sure that whatever Volkov are here don't happen to cross paths with Devi or Xasan—*especially* Xasan since he's our distraction to get the key. Lexa and her partner are likely watching that campus for Indra."

"Indra mentioned a cult," Noa breathed. "He told me that he found a coded message in one of the special-access archive books. He said he didn't remember the title, which feels even more like a lie now, but he said that the author was Keaton Scott. Could we look that up?"

Nyx reached for her tablet, and Noa's folded arms over her chest while rocking back and forth on her heels. She could feel Glacier's eyes pinned on her, hating every second of that attention earned at the exact *wrong* time. After a few more excruciating moments, a frown tugged at the corner of Nyx's mouth, and Noa bit down on her tongue.

"The archives here don't have any books by Keaton Scott listed," she said quietly, typing something else into the device.

"What do you mean there's not?"

Nyx mumbled something else that Noa could almost make out as a curse in Nyx's native dialect. She climbed onto the bed and tore the tablet from her hands.

"Noa, I don't think anyone would be sane enough to house a book by Keaton Scott unless they are highly specialized in handling sensitive informa—"

The words went muffled as Noa's skimmed the short summary of his works, detailing him as a scholar specializing in the handling and proper care of grimoires.

I had been looking for one of his other books.

"I'm going to kill him," Noa said flatly as Nyx ripped the tablet away. "I promise you that Indra likely started fooling around in something he shouldn't and dug himself a hole he couldn't escape. He likely pissed someone off in the process, and the Volkov were called to cover it up to make it look like it's unrelated."

"Or he decided to blackmail," Nyx said with a sigh. "His specialty is blackmail..."

Daniels. Shit. "Well, then there's a strong possibility he was blackmailing a well-respected professor who likely isn't willing to tarnish his reputation." A laugh spilled out, bordering on manic. "Now what? I don't want him coming with us. I certainly don't want him anywhere near Cecilia—"

"I can arrange a secondary cabin to lock him in for an interrogation. If it turns out we're better off dumping him, we'll dump him. Fair?"

Noa hesitated, still very much hating that answer. She wanted to leave him to deal with his own mess, not shove him in their back pocket to use later—not when he'd been dodgy to begin with. "Fine," she said, going against every fiber of her being.

"In the meantime, Glacier needs to stay in the common area where we can see him for the rest of today and tomorrow. Outside of that, he'll sleep in our room tonight."

"*What?*" came the clash of both Noa and Glacier's voices in unison, Noa's sounding a little too horrified than she'd care to admit.

Thinking that she had accidently slept next to him *once* was horrifying enough, but after spending a rather intimate day together that ended in nearly running into Lexa only made her stomach drop. The image of Kole breaking down the door to find them sleeping next to each other was her greatest nightmare now. Between that betrayal she'd inevitably see on Kole's face and the fear she'd find on Glacier's—

"Noa, the chair by the window is a pull-out," Nyx said, cutting through her thoughts. "We can move it in front of the door tonight to block ourselves in. If you're opposed to being in the same bed as him, you can take that spot, and I'll sleep next to him."

Noa started to shake her head, reminding herself this was just business. She just needed to turn off her emotional, irrational thoughts and treat it like what it was. "N-no, it's fine—"

"Just help me move the chair for later," she said with a sigh. "It's probably for the best anyway so you don't try to cop a feel on anyone."

"I- I wouldn't—"

"Oh, please, like you haven't tried to with just about everyone else here," Nyx grumbled, starting for the oversized chair. "I swear it's like I'm a godsdamned babysitter."

19
ESMEDRALIA ✧ 2705-01-11

NOA

Noa woke up sore and tired. Laying on her side all night in front of the door and constantly checking her phone to make sure no one was going in and out of the hotel rooms with Nyx's jury-rigged alarms had been a struggle. She should've slept the night before, rather than getting some winks in every hour or so. Her heart slammed in her chest whenever she roused from a nightmare of Kole looming over her.

When day broke, her slow-building rage had hit its limit: the Volkov had ruined Glacier's birthday.

Noa leaned against the kitchen island, staring at the edge of the white-marbled countertop beyond the emptied booze bottles, curiosity of Weather and Crow lamenting their demise from the start of the lockdown.

Rune stepped in front of her, sporting dark circles under his eyes and Cecilia leaned against him, stifling a yawn.

"So, we're stuck in here until tonight, right?" he asked.

"Preferably," Noa said. "I'll definitely need you two to act as overwatch for Nyx and Glacier while they work tonight, so if you two need to get a little extra rest, get it while you can."

"I might just have to..."

The three of them jumped at the sound of a fist pounding against the bathroom door, where Crow jiggled the handle. "Weather, open the damn door!"

"I'm almost done, you bitch. You can't rush perfection."

"Like *hell* I can't—"

Noa groaned. "Maybe we should've all had a drink to knock the edge off."

"I didn't miss this part of their relationship," Rune mumbled.

Weather threw open the door, and Noa's eyes went wide. Her hair was no longer that dark, chocolate brown, but a velvety black that curled into a royal, deep purple. Crow's jaw hung open, and Noa's face scrunched up when she thought she spotted drool.

"That's *so* pretty!" Cecilia said, clapping her hands together.

Rune scowled, his voice mixing concern and frustration. "Weather, don't you think that it would be more *subtle* to *not* dye your hair something noticeable before a heist?"

She waved a hand, pushing Crow away ever-so-slightly. "We have Cecilia, Rune. I can just magic over it." Noa imagined a silent 'duh' at the end, suppressing a gag as Crow wrapped his arms around her waist.

"Gods save us," Rune whispered. "She's going to distract my dumbass brother, and then this whole thing will go to shit."

CROW

Crow tapped Weather's shoulder and gestured toward the archives building from their spot in one of the nearby arched alcoves. The campus lights had flickered on in their walk here, turning into a nice early-night stroll—an activity enjoyed by at least a couple other people tonight.

A lighter-skinned woman with long black hair, a purple blouse, and a pencil skirt walked alongside a darker-skinned man with cropped, dark hair. Xasan and his assistant, judging by the tablet the woman tucked under her arm. They stopped in front of the glass double doors, chatting for a couple of minutes until a man appeared and let them in, vanishing somewhere deep within the building. The Blood of Esmedralia remained, framed by the soft, orange light beckoning them inside.

"That's our cue," Crow whispered, his voice clashing with Nyx's go-head over the comms. He started along the building, weaving under the awnings with Weather on his heels. Strangely, he felt transported back to Kingsheart, imagining the two of them in another place and time with Rune as their distraction—a comfort knowing he didn't have to watch his back.

When they reached the back door, he motioned for her to press up against the wall, and they waited for the door's lock to click free with Nyx's command. Once it did, they were inside, Crow leading the way with his eyes on every camera to make the slow crawl down the corridor while Nyx looped each one.

"Lobby clear," Nyx said. "Working on the case's alarm now."

He pushed off the wall, checking his corners before motioning for Weather. The two of them began pulling out the replica and demagnetizers in preparation. Weather's hands rested on the box, ready to lift it with a nervous smile.

"Don't act like this is your first time," he whispered teasingly.

"I'm just excited to work with you again," she replied, her smile turning sultry. His adrenaline kicked up a few notches and smirked as the replica dug into his hand.

"Now."

NOA

Noa forced herself to walk casually on the way to Indra's research building, fighting against the urge to run—or at least *jog*—to get the hell in and out. She pushed open the door to the lobby and tapped her fake student ID against the registration kiosk. The sole night guard didn't even bother to look up as she rounded the corner.

Her footsteps echoed down the hall, her boots squeaking on the tile as a door flew open. "Sorry—" Noa said, putting her hands up with a sheepish grin as the man skidded to a stop.

He looked to be in his late thirties or early forties with brown hair and eyes tinged a couple shades darker in the dim hall lighting. Her eyes flicked to the door's illuminated nameplate.

"No, I'm sorry," he said with a nervous chuckle. "I thought the hallways would be empty."

"Didn't mean to startle you, Professor Daniels," she said, starting past him before she could convince herself to launch into an impromptu interrogation. At the tapping of his dress shoes trailing off, she reminded herself that dealing with him right now wasn't an option. She'd come back for him later.

"There's a problem," came Glacier's voice over the comm. "The cameras are dead."

"Wait, wait?" Noa asked, her pace slowing slightly. Her eyes caught on one of the round domes in the hall. No blinking light.

"Lust and Gluttony," Nyx said sharply. "You need to finish up, *now*."

Noa launched into a jog, taking in each numbered plate of the teaching assistant offices until she found Indra's. She slowed, pulling in even breaths with the hope she wouldn't alarm him before she pushed the door open. Her stomach dropped as she stepped inside.

In the middle of the dark room, Indra was slumped over his desk with a small woman's silhouette in the moonlight, her inky black hair glinting blue. The snap of her metal case sent a jolt through Noa as she turned to face her.

Well, it wasn't Kole—for better or worse.

WEATHER

Weather slotted the glass case back onto the pedestal, her heart hammering as she helped Crow collect the demagnetizers. Then they locked eyes the second they heard the worst sound in the world: the sudden, whooping crescendo of the alarm.

Crow's hand flew up to his ear. "What the hell? I thought you said we wouldn't set anything off?" he hissed, glancing over his shoulder to the front doors—Weather's instinctual escape route.

"Hurry out the back," Nyx said in a rush. "This wasn't you two. Something else triggered it."

Weather bolted for the exit to try to regain those precious seconds, Crow chasing after her. Her body collided with the door right as the windows shuttered, and the two of them spilled out into the back alley. It smacked into its frame before shuttered as well, temporarily muffling the distant, shouted orders of security.

"Do *all* of your heists go like this?" she hissed as the two of them ran.

"Funny enough," he said, his breath catching as he yanked on her arm to pull her down another building cut-through, "things didn't start going sideways until *you* showed up."

They raced along the edge of the lawn as Weather glimpsed the shadow of a woman across the walkways. "Shit," she hissed, grabbing Crow's sleeve and pulling them into the recess of a nearby building. She grabbed his chin and pointed his face toward her new target.

It took him a second for his eyes to catch on her. "Pride," Crow's voice doubled through her comm. "I think Lexa's here."

"I know," came Noa's even tone. "I need a minute." It cut at the end, a distinct clip that caused Weather's stomach to drop.

"Son of a bitch," Nyx growled. "She turned off her damn comm. You two need to get back here *now,* and make sure you aren't followed."

"But what about—" Weather started, looking between Crow and the distance to the research building with wide eyes.

"I'm giving her two minutes. You two have the key. That has the priority. Now *move.*"

Weather hesitated, and Crow grabbed her arm, giving it a reassuring squeeze. "Noa can take *one* Volkov by herself," he whispered. "We need to go in case the second is going after Glacier."

She slid her arm free to hold his hand, and the two of them picked up their sprint towards the street again—all while Weather sent a silent thieves' prayer to no god in particular that Noa would be all right.

NOA

The memory of the final individual Myron had introduced to the rest of the would-be-Volkov had always held a special place in Noa's mind. A seemingly timid, quiet, twelve-year-old Jinwonese girl that he fondly named Alice. There was something about her that drew Noa in, like a genuine, sisterly kinship that she hadn't felt with Lexa, who had tried so hard to become her rival. Noa supposed that she had decided that it was her duty to protect her from the vicious influence of her sad excuse for competition, so a fourteen-year-old Noa had taken Alice under her wing.

Alice had held her hand and pressed against her side whenever they'd journeyed into town. She'd acted skittish whenever locals talked in Astravnian, tugging on Noa's sleeve for some sort of translation. At home, she'd followed Noa from room to room, even if Noa had told her that she'd be right back. Kole had even pulled Noa aside to voice his concerns that there was something wrong with her—a warning she'd brushed off.

However, a few weeks was all it took before Noa had seen the results of Alice's ghostly observations. Her silence had been shattered with a single mean-spirited comment from Ezra that Noa honestly couldn't recall now. She only remembered the blur of Alice hurling herself across the dinner table. The force of it had sent his chair tipping backwards and everyone else shooting up from their own. It had taken Myron, Kole, and Talon to pry her off of him, her arms and legs flailing with a manic grin on her face.

That sound of a fork clattering against the dining room floor after being pried from her hand had been the only thing to break Noa's stunned reaction. It turned out that Alice was a ticking time-bomb. She was mentally unstable and unhinged to the point that Noa had begun to see concern in *Myron* about her—like he might've actually made a mistake in bringing her here.

While Alice certainly lacked that finesse of Myron's other protégés, she certainly made up with it through brute force. You could stab her while she choked you, but she wouldn't let up because she would simply push through the pain to finish the job. As well as they were all trained to be swift and lethal, Alice could still take any of them head-on and manage to win.

After Ezra had retreated from the table with Alice restrained, Noa had seen terror in his eyes. It was terror that quickly hardened to arrogance like he was still ultimately invincible. So, he had taunted her, calling her, 'Malice'—a name that has caused her to throw her head back with a disturbed laugh. She had *reveled* in that name. And now, Noa would probably die to that little girl in this office, along with Indra.

Noa's heart raced as Malice turned to face her, a twisted, playful confidence lit in her features like she had encountered another toy. There was a pause, Malice's eyes widening with recognition, disbelief, *joy*.

"Noa," she said in a breathy whisper, her face softening.

Noa honestly wasn't sure what was worse, Malice hating her for leaving, or having to explain herself to a Malice that still had hope that she'd return before one of them would have to die.

"H-hey..."

"You're here," Malice said, her voice tinged with excitement. "We can go home—"

"I- I can't."

Her face fell. "But... you just have to kill that Miraltan—"

"It's not that easy, Mal,"

"Then *I'll* do it for you—"

"*No*—" The word ripped through her with such force that Malice took a half-step back. "No. I killed Ezra, and even if I hadn't, doing this task won't save me."

"But he said—"

Noa shook her head. "Myron won't welcome me back with open arms. I've defied him one too many times. No amount of groveling will prevent him from killing me the moment I step foot in that house. What's worse is that he won't just let me walk away. I'm nothing but a loose end for him now, and he won't stop coming after me until I'm gone." Noa pumped her fists, her fingers curling and uncurling to prepare herself for what was coming next. "I don't want to fight you Malice. I don't want to fight Kole. You two were the only people I considered to be my family."

"W-we can fix it."

"He was just using us, Malice," Noa whispered, releasing a quiet, bitter chuckle. "He's afraid of you, you know. He knew that you could sit at the top, but he never gave you the chance to challenge anyone because he thought that he'd have a better chance at controlling *me* than you."

Hurt fell over her face, nearing heartbreak. Noa couldn't tell if it was because Malice believed her or that she was upset that Noa would say something so horrible about the man that raised them. Either way, rage replaced it, and she lunged at Noa, sending her stumbling backward. She braced herself for a knife in the gut, but Malice's hands cupped her face instead.

"I'll kill Myron myself," she growled, catching Noa by surprise. "*No one hurts you without dealing with me.*"

Her hands slid away, leaving Noa stunned as Malice turned to collect her case. She tossed the strap over her head and stared up into Noa's eyes. It turned out that Myron had never had Malice's loyalty after all—*Noa* did.

So, Noa grabbed her arm, and they ran. "If you're being tracked by Lexa, ditch her."

Malice pulled her phone from her pocket and tossed it to her. Noa let go of her and powered it off, cramming it into her own pocket as she slammed into the side door, which smacked into a security guard. He hit the pavement, out cold, and Noa's shoulders sagged in relief. Well, until Malice flicked a blade out from her sleeve and poised herself to finish him off. Noa's eyes went wide and quickly seized her wrists, earning her a confused expression.

"*No*," Noa said sharply. "If you're coming with me, there's *no* killing unless I say otherwise." Despite her pout, the blade retracted into the hilt, and Noa let go. "Come on."

They kept to the shadows of the buildings, briskly walking past windows while Noa pressed her phone to her ear.

"Where the hell are you?" Nyx asked.

"Heading off campus now," she said, glancing at Malice striding next to her. Her head tilted in curiosity with her eyes on the phone. "I have good news and bad news."

"Oh gods, Noa..."

"The bad news is that we don't have to worry about Indra anymore, and I ran into one of the Volkov."

"Noa, is Indra *dead?*"

"Do you honestly need me to answer that?"

The question was met with muttering in her native Jinwonese dialect. "And the *good* news?"

"We're down a Volkov to deal with."

"Who? Lexa? Kole? Did you kill one of them?"

"No, Kole is still very much alive, but I... *may* have flipped a Volkov to our side."

A beat of silence.

"This..." Nyx began cautiously, "wouldn't happen to be the one you were initially worried about, would it?"

"Look, I just need you to swap that spare ticket to a different ID—" Noa made a hurried gesture to Malice, who scrambled to pull out her fake, placing it in Noa's hand. "I have the reference number."

"Noa, I sure as hell hope you know what you're doing. If you bring them on board and they go for Glacier, so help me—"

"Trust me, I'll fall on that sword if it comes down to it." It was enough to quiet her again before she asked for the number.

"Ticket transferred," Nyx said with no small hint of exhaustion in her voice. "Don't be late. We'll meet you there."

The beep of the call ending allowed Noa to whistle out a breath.

"Who was that?" Malice finally asked.

She looked over at her, seeing interest written all over her face. Noa could imagine how strange it might be to hear her talk to someone that wasn't Volkov like that—like someone you could trust. "A friend."

The train doors almost clipped Noa's jacket after she and Malice had taken the winding path to get to the station. Blood-red mandala window decals trailed behind them—an all-too-fitting color left in the wake of two killers.

Noa hooked her fingers into the luxury cabin door and turned to

Malice. "Do exactly what I say, got it? No one will hurt you as long as you don't hurt them."

Malice gave a reluctant nod, but it was too late to turn back now. So, Noa led the way into the stairwell.

Nyx's voice rang out above. "Lexa set off the alarm. It wasn't us, so relax."

Noa cringed at the poor timing, shrinking slightly as she stepped out of the stairwell to all eyes on her. Malice hovered next to her, scanning her confused audience, plus Nyx. The second her eyes set on Glacier, Malice snapped to her knife, and Noa grabbed her wrist. A brief squeeze, and she relaxed again—a final, unspoken acknowledgement that they weren't going to take the bait and try to go home to Myron.

"I thought Indra was a guy," Crow said suddenly, breaking the awkward silence.

"This isn't Indra, dumbass," Nyx said, scowling. "Does she *look* like an Indra to you?"

"I don't *know*."

"She's my sister," Noa said. Malice stood a little straighter, and one-by-one, that comment clicked.

Rune's brows shot up. "You brought a *Volkov* with you?"

"That's not really any different than me standing here, is it?" Noa snapped, watching the exchange of uneasy glances.

"So, um..." Weather said quietly, trying to break the ice with a welcoming smile. "What's your name?"

"Malice," she answered, a little *too* chipper than what Noa had expected.

Glacier's eyes went wide, and Noa immediately scrambled for damage control. "Alice—Her name is Alice, but she goes by Malice."

"Cute," Nyx said dryly.

"And I also really need to discuss a few things with her alone," Noa said, steering Malice into a bunk room near the end. Malice's stray look at Glacier on their way past made Noa's stomach clench, but the moment the door shut, she told herself the worst of it was over.

Now came the difficult explanation.

"They know we're Volkov," Malice said with a frown.

"Yes."

"Why?"

"Because they have a right to know, now take a seat." Noa dropped down onto one of the beds with a sudden realization that the only other bunk that would be available was in Glacier's room. She grimaced, deciding that perhaps it was for the best that she move Glacier in with Nyx after zero issues between the two of them the night before.

After shifting her footing, Malice finally sat, tucking her case behind her.

"They needed to be aware that if they came along with me that they might be killed. And if they want to leave, they're free to. I know they won't tell anyone else because I trust them, Malice. But... the reason *why* they're here is a little more complicated."

She wasn't quite sure if she should've expected some sort of interruption or a million questions after being separated for so long, but Malice remained silent. She patiently waited for Noa to continue, despite Noa already knowing how absolutely ridiculous it sounded.

"We're all here to pursue an opportunity to grant ourselves freedom, much like how I only want to be free of Myron."

"But don't we just have to kill him?"

"If it were only that easy, yes," she said with a breathy laugh. "But there's two of us and four of them. We're outnumbered because everyone here isn't trained like we are. However..."

Noa paused, rubbing at her forehead while she tried to think of the best way to say it. The only thing that surfaced to the front of her mind was a memory of the two of them huddled on her bed. Noa's hand had turned each page, waiting for Malice's indication she was done with the passage. Noa didn't *have* to read it again, not when she had known it by heart. Night after night of admiring it as her sole prized possession had ensured that she would recognize the feel of its cover if she was blindfolded.

"Do you remember the book I told you not to tell Kole about?"

"That magic book?"

Noa chuckled. "Yes, the magic book. And do you remember the end?

How there were thirteen new rulers and their emblems?"

Malice leaned forward, and Noa's hands felt slick with sweat. It had all started off as a bit of a joke—one that she hadn't *truly* expected to get this far with. That internal struggle against Lazarus's musings—his subtle clues and instructions had brought her here. Nothing about this was funny anymore, not after everything they had seen. Something gripped her soul, deep down, telling her that all of this was *real*.

"And how they're keys to a vault—*the* Vault. As... *impossible* as it sounds, I've been tasked with opening it."

Malice's eyes brightened with a child-like glee. "Does that mean I get badass powers?"

"I, uh—"

She grabbed Noa's hands. "Can I be the first one to get magic? *Please?*"

Noa cleared her throat, a little disturbed that Malice was requesting it without any questions along the lines of 'why you?' like all the others had.

"Um... sure?" She had no idea how this all worked, let alone if she would have a choice how it happened. However, she quickly saw how she could use this incentive to her own benefit. "Under *one* condition—" Noa quickly added, and Malice went from giddy to still. "There's only one person who can access the thirteenth key, and I need you to help me protect him. It's Glacier."

"The one Kole wants to kill?"

"Yes, and if Kole kills him, all of this will be for nothing. As much as I don't want you to kill anyone, you have my full permission to do whatever it takes to prevent someone from harming him."

A twinkle of excitement put Noa on edge, even though she knew that this was a good thing. She'd just bought Glacier's safety with a promise to one of the strongest people she knew. But there was still doubt and fear clawing at her insides, like she knew that their time was almost up after running so fast for so long.

She knew that this most recent act of betrayal against the Volkov would send Myron over the edge, but she just hoped that maybe she'd have one small, final opportunity to win over Kole before it was all said and done. Though she had a horrible feeling that would be sooner, rather than later.

20

MHARU ✦ 2705-01-12

GLACIER

Glacier rubbed his eyes, and when his hands fell back to the tablet on his lap, everyone but Nyx was gone from the living space. She tapped a gloved finger against her tablet and fidgeted with her phone. He sighed, twitching at the muffled shifting of metal under his shirt. At least he hadn't become the key's new permanent home.

His vision blurred, trying to focus on the work Nyx had left him with until a wisp of dark, inky-blue hair fell past his shoulder. He stiffened at the sight of another face reflected in the screen. "Holy *shit*—"

Malice climbed over the back of the couch, dropping down next to him with a smile. His entire body went rigid.

"Relax," came Noa's tired voice from behind. "She's not going to kill you." Fingers tugged at the cord resting against the back of his neck. Her light touch made his hair stand on end. The keys pulled free of his shirt collar, clinking softly as she pulled them out of view.

"How many do you have?" Malice asked, excitement lighting her gaze.

"Nine," Noa said as he shifted sideways to get a better look at her. "Four more to go."

"That leaves us with the Spear of Mharu," Nyx spoke up from her seat on the edge of the cluster, "the Mind of Jinwon, the Shield of Miralta, and the Soul of Amarais."

"The Shield of Miralta?" Malice asked. He found her pointing at him with her eyes fixed on Noa.

Noa shook her head. He tensed as she gently took his chin and tilted his face toward her. His pulse picked up up, trying to anticipate what she was doing before realizing she was showcasing his blue eye.

"The Soul of Amarais. He's a Caelius—the last *living* Caelius, which means we don't have a spare key to get our last."

She let go, and he awkwardly glanced away, rubbing the back of his neck. Malice leaned forward, and he sat back, eyeing her suspiciously.

"I like your eyes," she said softly.

It took him by surprise. The only other time he'd heard something similar was from Noa back in Kingsheart. He covered his mouth, slipping into laughter. Malice drew back in shock, and Noa's brows knit together in confusion.

"I- I'm sorry," he said. "That's not exactly something I expected you to say."

"Kole said you're an abomination."

"*Malice—*"

Malice shrank down.

"Now *that's* what I normally hear," he mumbled with a sigh. "It's fine, I'm used to it."

"No," Noa said, rounding the sofa. "It's not fine, and Kole has his head up his ass." She let out a deflated huff. "Glacier, would you please do me a favor and move your things to Nyx's cabin? I think you'd feel a little more comfortable sleeping in a room with her tonight."

"Who says he's not jumpy around me?" Nyx spoke up, making Noa roll her eyes.

Malice briefly glanced between him and Noa. "But I thought—"

"*Later.*"

"We'll be there early," Nyx said, dropping her tablet into her lap and stretching. "We should probably get some sleep now."

Glacier got up to collect his bag, shoving the tablet inside as he shuffled behind Nyx to her room. She yanked a bag down from the overhead compartment while he hovered on the threshold.

"It's all yours," she said, waving to the bunk. "I'll dump Noa's stuff outside."

"I hope you don't mean *literally*," Noa said. He jumped and bit down on his tongue. Not noticing her creep up behind him must've been from sleep deprivation—though, when he sought out that faint connection, it thrummed to life again. He ducked inside as Noa placed a hand on the door frame. "You... also wouldn't happen to have any extra clothes to donate for a now-homeless girl, would you?"

"Because I'm about her size?" Nyx asked. "Or because you're selfish?"

Noa gave a sheepish smile. "Maybe... a little of both?"

Nyx threw the bag into her arms. "Your sister. Your problem. Good-night, Noa." She hit the button to close the door.

Glacier snickered as he pulled off his hoodie, catching Nyx's stare. "Is something wrong?"

Her pensive look dissolved. "No, it's nothing. Just thinking, that's all... I think I just need to get some sleep."

NOA

Noa had forgotten how difficult Malice was to wake up in the morning. After resorting to literally *dragging* her out of bed and convincing her to wear one of Noa's spare changes of clothes, they made it to Malice's reward: breakfast.

A handful of their crew was already ravaging the dining car by the time they'd arrived, giving Noa pause as to whether or not she should snag some plates and return to their cabin to keep a little distance for now. But Weather had waved in an invitation to join her and Crow in their booth— an invitation she'd regretted accepting the second Glacier and Nyx arrived, taking their seats with Rune and Cecilia instead.

"Why is *he* here?" Malice asked when Crow returned to his seat. Noa bit her lip, holding back a chortle as she cut into her egg-filled dosa.

The corner of Weather's mouth tipped downward. "Unfortunately, he's my boyfriend."

"*Unfortunately?*" Crow demanded.

"He sort of just gives off bad vibes to everyone. It's an unlucky trait."

"If I'm so *unlucky*, then why am I with you?"

"Because you need good luck to offset the bad. It's a law of nature."

"And how are *you* lucky? Everything's gone sideways since we picked you up at the last stop—" Crow reached for one of the pastries Weather had set in the center of the table, and Malice lurched forward, skewering it with a butter knife. He jerked his hand back. "*Shi—*" He shoved the entire plate toward her. "Take it. I don't need it."

Weather watched in awe as Malice tugged the plate a little closer and slid one onto her plate with a melodic hum.

"Teach me how to do that."

"How to stab someone?" Malice asked through a mouthful of dosa.

"No, no—" she replied with a tinkling laugh before her velvety tone turned sinister. "How to strike fear into the hearts of men."

Crow's head swiveled toward her. "Excuse me?"

"Shut up. I'm not talking to you."

Noa chuckled, bringing her coffee mug to her lips. "She might trade you her secrets if you take her to get some new clothes. I have a feeling that she's not going to want to keep wearing mine for much longer."

She could've patted herself on the back for that brilliant play. Weather's eyes lit up at the mere mention of shopping, and Noa wouldn't have to be bothered to drag Malice through department stores just to find a couple outfits. Crow, already knowing that he would inevitably be sucked into the chore, shot her a glare.

"That sounds *perfect*. What's your preferred style?"

Malice paused her chewing, her eyes darting over to Noa like she might be able to translate for her. "Um..." Noa said, "I'm afraid she's not really accustomed to buying clothes for *fun*."

"Well, starting today, we'll figure out what you like," she said brightly. "We'll take Cecilia along too. The three of us can make a day of it."

GLACIER

Glacier eyed Noa through the gold-lattice divider between the kitchen and the living room of their new suite as he got a glass of water. She stared at the muted TV feeds for the Republic, sinking further into the geometric-patterned jade throw pillows while Nyx picked apart the instrument laying in Malice's metal case. Every little click and snap of pieces coming apart and reforming into lethal and mundane objects set him a little on edge, even if she was examining the engineering of it all.

"If she could concoct this deathtrap of a violin," Nyx muttered, pushing up her glasses as she turned to Noa, "think of what else we could smuggle in and out of places undetected."

Glacier made his way back to the couch as Noa snorted. "Assuming we even get a point where we could make shit like that. I think that damn thing took her months when she got pissed about not having certain tools at her disposal."

"Fair, but the same goes for infiltration equipment too... It's a dream." Nyx folded the case shut with a wistful sigh—an unusual sound that Glacier raised a brow at as he set his glass down. "I figure we can move on to discussing the Spear of Mharu now."

Noa frowned, tearing her gaze away from the TV. "Don't you want to wait until everyone else is back?"

"No need," Nyx said. "So, you like cathedrals?"

"Oh, *please* don't tell me we're stealing from a church."

"Then I won't tell you."

"Nyx! Good *gods*—Considering all the shit I've done, my odds of bursting into flames the second I step foot onto holy ground are astronomically high."

"And yet you've been chosen to collect all thirteen keys and save the world from destruction," Nyx countered, her tone even. "I think you'll be okay."

"We *cannot* steal from a church." Noa loosed a manic laugh.

"Would you like to hear the second option?"

She paused, dropping her voice to a whisper. "Did... did you forget to tell me that we pocketed a priest at some point?"

Nyx clapped a hand over her mouth, barely covering a snort. "No, you dumbass. I'm talking about Faraji Kamau."

"You lost me."

"He *owns* the cathedral. It counts as a yearly building donation, and he organizes keeping it maintained. Some sort of tax thing or something. I'm not sure on the specifics." —Nyx waved a hand— "But I finally got ahold of him a few days ago. You'll meet him tomorrow morning. Just bring the replica, and he'll take you to where it's housed to switch it out."

"So..." Noa started cautiously. "Does the relic belong to the church, or...?"

"Kamau has old blood. The relic ended up in his possession, so it's his. His family line can be traced all the way back to the original holder of the emblem, which is why no one disputes his claim. I guess he just leaves it on display for aesthetic. Whatever sort of sway he has, it's good enough that no museum or anything has managed to take it from him yet."

"Great," Noa mumbled. "Now I get to feel dirty about stealing from a man who generously donates to a church."

"And you don't feel guilty about *kidnapping* a prince?" Nyx held up her arms to showcase Glacier.

"Hey, that's *different*. He was going to die—"

"And the emblem is going to be wasted by just sitting there collecting dust. No one will know the difference between the real and the fake."

Noa pointed a finger at her like she was trying to come up with a counterargument.

"Well?" Nyx asked with a slight, victorious smirk.

"Godsdamnit, you're going to make me steal from a church."

21

KING'S REPUBLIC ✧ 2705-01-12

SHANE

Every still Arrington swiped through put Shane on edge. His throat bobbed as he stopped on a frame, and Shane's hand flew out to point at the timestamp.

"It's not her, but it was at the hotel until just after that woman vanished. She had enough time to get to the hotel and leave just before I got there. The only problem is that it hadn't moved until sometime after she appeared at the gala."

"So, you're implying that she's dragging a Seer around with her?" Arrington asked, a grumble to his voice that told Shane he wasn't buying it. "We haven't ever seen someone besides the twins with her."

"Maybe she's hiding it to make us believe that she's a Seer when she's not. She could be another con-woman after all. It could be feeding her information that she's manipulating it to get what she wants."

"That still doesn't explain where the other two are... Even if she does have a Seer that she's keeping hidden, there's still no sign of either Monette or a theft. I'm not stupid enough to believe that she simply appeared out of nowhere for absolutely no reason."

Shane gritted his teeth until Arrington's jaw dropped slightly. "Unless... they used the Seer and uncovered my trap. They used the woman as a distraction for Bristol after I told her to keep an eye out for them, and then they got away with one of their former crew members." He slammed a hand on the desk, and Shane jumped. "I think that it's possible that the three of them have been utilizing the Seer to manage to get a few steps ahead of us."

"So..." Shane swallowed. "Now what?"

"Continue collecting. We need to utilize whatever we can to our advantage. Odds are they'll be back to pull another trick if the Monettes are trying to get back at us, and when they return, their Seer will lead us right to them." Arrington leaned back in his chair, backdropped by the rapidly graying sky and the pattering of freezing rain.

ALYVIA

Alyvia kicked off her shoes in the tiny entryway of her studio apartment and yawned. Everything had come to a grinding halt. Again. Shane's insistence of her working in his office and the radio silence from Nyx had turned into the perfect storm.

My home. My heart. My world.

The words ran through her head over and over again as she changed, made a sandwich, and flipped through videos on her tablet. Then the journal key box sat in front of her again. She dropped the tablet onto the bed and fell back onto the comforter. Her fingers bumped against the stress ball on the nightstand and started tossing it in the air.

Up. Down.

Ryland had to be the first answer. He'd told Alyvia that he'd never really been attached to his hometown. Home was where your family was.

Up. Down.

So, who was her heart? She never recalled her father talking about his sister's host family or finding their names in his encrypted files. They were probably long gone by the time she'd looked through them anyway, even if she didn't want to believe he'd give up on her so easily and not try to match up all those reference numbers for himself.

Up. Down.

Maybe she had fallen in love with Amarais? No. It had to be a name. But then who else would be important enough for the third hint?

Up. Down.

Alyvia squeezed the ball, pausing and squinting at the ceiling as she remembered the dates. A smirk danced across her face as a name came to mind—one with so many rumors attached to it. It was a long shot, but she could allow herself a single, wild guess, couldn't she?

She sat up, tossing the ball to the side and collected the tablet. Dots filled the text box, and she drummed her fingers against the metal casing, biting her lip. *This is dumb.* But she pressed the button anyway.

And it unlocked.

The tablet fell from her hands, tumbling onto the blankets as the world bottomed out from under her. She stared at the decrypted page numbers climbing upward. She lunged for it, scrolling down further and further until she reached last dated entry page. Blank. Nearly a year after her final key change.

Two years. Her aunt had lived in Amarais for *two years*. She'd fallen in love. She'd had a son. And Alyvia had a cousin she'd never get to meet now —a cousin that could've been a king.

She reached for her phone, having to backspace every other letter from how badly her hands shook. Her thumb pressed the send button once she'd composed her message to Nyx that she'd solved it, and that was it. There wasn't anything else she could do—no one else she could tell. If she let her father know, it would give him closure, but knowing he'd had a nephew that might've never really known love... it would crush him.

So, this would be a secret she'd have to keep now, but she had her answers if there was ever a right time to share them. Alyvia squeezed her eyes shut, the small Shield of Miralta around her neck pressing into her palm. She conjured up a silent prayer that everyone who had been lost was now at rest, and that perhaps she might finally be at peace after a long few days.

22

MHARU ✧ 2705-01-13

NOA

"Forgive me, Mother, for I have sinned," Noa mumbled under her breath in front of the hulking cathedral, its tall, gray-stoned frame with white molding and inset windows looking like angry eyes peering at her. Imagining the semi-circle awning's pillars as teeth didn't help since she came to the conclusion that one of them could very well fall and crush her.

The thought that she should start praying to Seraphine in earnest before stepping foot into one of her holy spaces had crossed her mind until Glacier snickered. Her fingers curled into her fist.

Do not *punch him in front of a church.*

She shouldn't have even brought him along, but he knew exactly what to say to tag along, putting her right back at square one after she'd sworn Esmedralia would be the last time she'd take him out anywhere again. Not to mention that setting up Malice as his babysitter was already horribly backfiring since she'd passed out on the couch right before Noa had been about to step foot out the door.

Noa checked her phone, and her stomach twisted. She remembered Faraji Kamau to be punctual—annoyingly so when she and Nyx had first sat down with him and his younger sister. He'd carried a sense of positive tranquility about him while she took on anxiety—as if the weight of the world rested on her shoulders, though that could've been due to her encounter with Noa as a still-then member of the Volkov.

Noa scraped a boot against the edge of the stone-slab steps and lifted her head right as Faraji strode toward them, wearing a pinstripe suit and crisp white dress shirt against dark skin, brushing against the locs loosely banded at the nape of his neck. A whole five minutes late, but his face remained that ever-present mask of joyous calm exuding from his dark eyes.

"Zoya," Faraji said, greeting her with a wink that nearly made her knees wobble. "And I see you've brought a friend." His smile was still just as warm when he turned towards Glacier, a hint of curiosity lit in the taller man's gaze.

"This is Morgan," Noa said. "He's my partner's assistant."

"It's nice to meet you, Morgan," he said, extending a hand for Glacier to shake. "Please, call me Faraji. Let's head inside, shall we?"

And the inside was just as well-kept and beautiful as the outside with dark-stone pews radiating out from the center stage like waves. Tapestries hung over the balconies of the circular congregation hall, their gold-thread accents highlighting everything from stars to swords and spears.

Faraji skirted the circumference, leading them down another wide corridor, and Noa tensed at the sight of priests and priestesses heading the opposite direction. They smiled, seeming friendly enough, but there were a couple that looked a little *too* long at her and Glacier. She tried to tell herself it was because they were the two palest people in the building, rather than one of them eyeing her because they were a robed Seer that could see straight into her soul. Perhaps her paranoia was the result of Lazarus's jokes about Seers wanting to be closer to Seraphine. Still, it unnerved her.

When they stopped, it was in front of a set of large double-doors inset with swooping diagonal, gold lines. Faraji pressed a keycard to a panel off to the side, pushed one of them open, and motioned for them to go in ahead of him. Noa led the way, immediately looking around the room in wonder as soon as the automatic lights turned on. It felt like she had been transported back to Lazarus's workshop, lined with shelves and shelves of books.

Except these were uncaged, sitting neatly on display like the much smaller collection housed in a certain office she has broken into months prior.

The door closed softly behind them, and Faraji strode across to the object resting in its glass box. The Sphere of Mharu's jade stone was cut down to a four-pointed star with fragments fanning out from it into the gold, angular branches.

"I believe this is what you're here for, correct?" Faraji asked with a slight smirk as he tapped the top of the glass. She started towards it while Glacier buckled to that luring call of the books from the corner of her eye.

"That I am," she whispered.

So, he unlocked the case, and she held Nyx's thin replica box open to him. His hand hovered over it before plucking it from its foam cushion, turning it over with a smirk. A twinkle of mischief lit his gaze as he moved to swap them out, and Noa tucked the Spear of Mharu in her bag.

"I'm quite impressed," he said. "You'll have to give me the name of your artist the next time we discuss business. I might have an idea for a commission by then."

"I'd be more than happy to once your sister can come home."

"I'd like that very much. Thank you, Noa." Not Zoya, but *Noa*. It made those words mean so much more as a genuine, private thank you.

"No. Thank *you*. I promise to make it up to you."

A chuckle escaped him. "I'm pretty sure you already have, but sure. There's no harm in having someone with quite a bit of power in your back pocket, is there?"

He led them back into the corridor, Noa and Glacier walking side-by-side to the circular auditorium. It wasn't until they hit the final stretch that she caught Glacier fall from view. She spun around to find him standing in the middle of the main aisle of pews, staring up into the domed ceiling.

Faraji must've heard her footsteps trailing away from him against the jade runner, slowing when she caught sight of what Glacier was fixated on: the statue of a woman on a platform suspended from the ceiling. Flowers dripped from the base, and wilted petals teetered along the walkways to get to her through secret passageways.

It reminded her of the statue of the Messenger back in Miralta, yet this wasn't the same woman—the backs of her hands didn't bare those marks. Her hair was also cut shorter, pinned back from a face that didn't so much exude that same serenity, but... mercy?

"Ah," Faraji's voice pulled her from her examination, the sound sending Glacier whipping around with surprise. "It seems you've found our depiction of Seraphine."

"I remember her looking..." Noa began slowly, "a little different."

"Unsurprising. She's been imagined differently by each country throughout the thousands of years we've recorded. No one knows what She truly looks like. We simply guess and pray She's pleased."

"I can't imagine She'd be unhappy," Noa said honestly. "She's lovely."

NYX

Nyx's head jerked up as Noa strode into her room, twirling around the Spear of Mharu with a triumphant smile. "Ten," she said, pulling the cord over her head with a chorus of metal clinking together.

"And here I was wondering where Glacier disappeared to," Nyx mumbled. "Well, until I realized that he tolerates you enough to escape the hotel for an hour." Or more than just tolerate, but she didn't want to alert Noa by pointing out that her line between client and prospective relationship had blurred. Nyx could tell it scared her too, seeing how she'd gone from gravitating toward him every waking minute up until she'd tried avoiding him when they'd stopped in Miralta to wait out the new year.

"He was persistent this morning," Noa said. "I figured I wasn't going anywhere unless he came with me. He was acting a little strange though..."

"Strange how?" Nyx asked, her movements feeling a little stiff as she continued tucking things into her bag.

"He just detoured to the auditorium area on the way out. Ended up admiring a statue of Seraphine."

Nyx's fingers twitched.

"I think he just might be stressed about everything," Noa continued. "He vanished in Razbia too. Wandered off to that lotus fountain in the heart of downtown. It scared the shit out of me trying to find him."

Nyx absently nodded, zipping her bag shut and pulling it over her head. "Yeah. He's probably stressed." Or Adam was right and Glacier's been hiding that he's a Seer from the rest of them—but *why?* She considered Cecilia's reaction when they'd discussed their brief encounter with Adam, but she seemed just as shocked and adamant. She *should* know if he was one. Something didn't add up.

Unless Glacier doesn't know.

She dismissed it almost immediately, but then she thought about his question on the walk to the hotel about why there were so many Miraltans in Mharu. He hadn't known that Miraltans had spread all the way from Amarais, Bellegarde, King's, and Mharu way back when—an oversight of his education that she hadn't anticipated because those answers had been a little too far out of his reach.

Much like the signs associated with Seers.

Nyx tightened her grip on her bag strap, leading the way out of the bedroom with Noa on her heels. Glacier brushed Nyx's shoulder as he rushed to collect his things, and she stiffened just thinking about how to approach that subject. He'd kept quiet about her secret, despite his concern, but this wasn't something he could dismiss forever. She wasn't even that experienced with Seers—not like Noa was...

"Ready to go?" Noa asked, ripping Nyx from her thoughts.

"Yeah," she replied automatically, keeping her eyes dead ahead to avoid looking at Glacier. "Let's go."

GLACIER

Splitting between two train cabins had made Glacier nervous enough, but ending up with Malice had left him on edge. But she'd fallen asleep on the bench across from him right before Noa had ventured out, and then Nyx followed about an hour later.

She shivered, and Glacier abandoned his tablet to pull down a blanket and drape it over her. He'd run out of homework to dig through, leaving him to explore the nooks and crannies of his thoughts like why he'd wandered over to that pool in Razbia and the Seraphine statue in Biana.

His brain itched for answers to questions he didn't have the words for, even after typing in search after search to connect them.

I need you to start asking the right questions.

He sighed, shaking his head. But he *was*, wasn't he? He was questioning everything around him. It was all feeling like a waste of time now, like he had foolishly invested too much in a dream that didn't matter. He absently twisted the black ring on his finger, wishing Kat were really here. Wishing that they weren't two keys away from having to go back home.

After such a rough start that had just about taken everything out of him, he found that he actually *enjoyed* this. There was freedom here that he had never experienced before, and he wanted *more*.

But how fair is that to everyone else still trapped in Amarais?

Glacier's eyes flicked up from his device, focusing on the movement across from him. Malice sat up, blinking drowsily as she tugged on the blanket.

"You looked cold," he said. "So, I got you a blanket."

Her eyes narrowed on him. "Why are you so *nice?*"

He tensed, surprised.

"Kole talked about you like you were evil," she said, her face contorting like she was trying to solve a riddle.

He wasn't even sure what to say to that. She stood with the blanket still wrapped around her, and placed herself next to him, pulling her knees up to her chest. Then her head tilted to the side. "I think Kole's wrong."

Glacier lowered the tablet to his lap. As odd as she was and as odd as her *name* was, Malice didn't exactly seem... *malicious*. "Malice, did... you actually *like* any of the Volkov?"

Her lips pressed into a thin line, and her eyes went to corner of the cabin before she looked at him again and *shrugged*. "Maybe Kole because Noa likes him and told me to leave him alone, but mainly just Noa. I don't think anyone else really liked my anyway. Why?"

That warped mask fell away to a fragment of her he recognized—a piece he found deep within himself of having a select few people to lean on. Noa had likely been to Malice what Kat had been to him. "And do you have any family?"

"Noa is my family. None of the other families matter."

Families?

"Were... you fostered?"

There was a slight roll of her eyes, accompanied by a resigned huff. "They would all say that there was something wrong with me. Too quiet. Too moody. Too *mean*," she mocked. "I was only mean because the other kids they had would start things. They'd pick a fight with me, so I'd fight back. Then *I* was the one to get in trouble. At least Myron let me defend myself, even if he'd stop me sometimes. Noa was the only one to actually care about me. That's why I chose to come with her."

"I'm sorry you went through all that," he said quietly. "I know how it feels to be pushed around too."

A silence settled between them before she scooted closer, wrapping her blanketed arms around one of his. Her hair tickled his neck, waterfalling over his shirt. "If anyone pushes you around again, I'll kill them," she said, closing her eyes with a grin. "Since you're too nice to do it, I'll just do it for you."

23

ASTRAVNY ✧ 2705-01-14

KOLE

Kole flinched at the shattering impact of that resin crescent paperweight into the fire. The flames sputtered, consuming the object that'd appeared when Noa had vanished—a wasted item since Myron hadn't kept any papers.

A growl sounded from Myron, teetering on the edge of feral, as rage contorted his features. Kole swallowed, despite his mouth being dry, and waited as his master pulled at the headrest of his chair like he might tear it off and hurl it into the fire as well. Talon and Lexa hadn't even flinched.

And then there were four.

"I've had just about enough of this," Myron said through clenched teeth.

"I think she's got an informant or a hacker working with her," Lexa said, her tone even, factual, and wholly unapologetic. "There's no way that I should've missed her in Razbia."

"I don't give a *fuck* who's with her, Lexa," he snapped. "Get your things. We're taking the next boat out."

A new sort of anxiety replaced the one that had overwhelmed him moments prior—the anxiety that he would finally face Noa again. He took the dismissal with his fellow underlings, turning to leave with them.

"I'm not done with you, Kole."

Kole stopped at the threshold while the others continued forward, not bothering to spare him a glance. Not like Noa would've—a ghost he bottled again because he still couldn't throw her away.

"Shut the door."

He did as commanded and slowly turned to face him.

"When we corner them, take care of Caelius," Myron said sharply, his anger finally receding back into its metaphorical box. "Make it quick. I want this job completed while I deal with Noa. The other two can deal with whoever else is with her. If you run into Malice, kill her. Do *not* hesitate. We're done playing her games. She's wasted my time and resources for far too long."

24

KING'S REPUBLIC ✧ 2705-01-14

GLACIER

Glacier hadn't realized how much he'd missed their old rhythm when he woke from Kat's reminders to remember—an exercise that always failed. Locking eyes with Noa from across the cabin, quietly slipping on their shoes, and leaving Nyx and Malice behind in favor of an early morning breakfast as they passed through the King's Republic countryside was more than welcomed.

The treetops flitted past, cresting the purple sky. It tinged a shade darker in his haze, the world going eerily still as a thrum of fear pulsed through him. A fear he'd known all too well: familial loss.

"Malice told me that you're her family," Glacier said, pushing around the last of his eggs.

She paled in surprise for a brief moment before relaxing into contentment. "Well, I've always thought of her as my younger sister," she said, tracing the rim of her coffee cup with a finger. "I'll admit that I was a little nervous about how she'd get along with everyone, but I'm glad to see that she's warming up to you."

"What about Kole?"

Her head jerked up, revealing a brief flash of guilt before finding another portion of the table to focus on. "Yes," she said in a near-whisper. "I feel like an idiot, but yes. I miss him. The... the problem with Kole is that I always had to keep secrets from him when it came to anything with magic. He hates it." She looked into Glacier's eyes. He could almost hear the unsaid words, 'he hates *you*.'

She shook her head, sighing. "It's why I couldn't tell him about Lazarus. It's why I didn't tell him about the books he let me borrow. I was being subconsciously trained for all *this*, I guess, but I couldn't tell him about any of it... He might've gotten to Lazarus before Myron, he would've burned the books I hid in my room, and he would've hated *me*. He used to look after me, and I used to look up to him. Now he thinks I've betrayed him."

Glacier chewed on the inside of his cheek. "You're afraid that you'll have to kill him, aren't you?" It was the horrible reality of her saving him that undoubtably continued to haunt her. She'd traded someone she loved for Glacier's life.

"I... I think I might be able to convince him to flip sides, but... I don't know if I'll get the opportunity. I guess I'm just at the mercy of fate, just like I have been since the moment I outlived my parents and Myron took me in."

"I'm sorry I ruined it for you." Glacier twisted his ring, remembering the first time he had encountered Noa in the halls of the palace.

"Glacier, no, you—*You* didn't ruin anything. Kole would've figured everything out eventually, or Myron would've told him I was colluding with a Seer to turn him against me before that. You're just one of his many reasons to be upset with me. I don't regret what I did back in Amarais. I don't regret saving you and Cecilia."

He could've sworn she lingered on that last 'you' a little longer than she should've. "I'm glad I finally got to see places that aren't absolutely buried in snow," he said with a smirk, getting a chuckle out of Noa.

"It's okay if you're stressed about going back, you know. But we're not going to die, okay? And if it turns out that they don't want you, we'll leave and continue to find the Vault."

"You make it sound so easy."

"I'm a rogue assassin, Glacier. I'm pretty sure a bunch of rich brats aren't going to be able to stop me from running in there and getting that last damn key. I'll stab them or blow some shit up."

He stifled a laugh. "At least one of us is confident." He slid out of the booth, hesitating as his eyes landed on the coffee bar. "Does Malice like coffee or tea?"

NOA

Noa watched Glacier nudge Malice awake, an action that was rewarded with a death glare before he held a cup in front of her. Her eyes widened, and she shot up, greedily taking it from him. With the addition of a muffin, she stared up at him in awe. Noa held a hand over her own mouth, hiding a smile at how giddy she was to be delivered breakfast.

"So," Noa said, leaning against the small coat closet in the doorway. "Miralta?"

"I've been working on that," Nyx said, "but I think that it'll be difficult with how Corris is set up."

"Because the city blocks are compartmentalized, right?" Glacier asked.

"Correct," Nyx said. "They're pretty good with security, so even their security systems are split for each block, which means that I can't take over the entire system at once to prevent anything from going sideways."

"It's because they're built for war..." Glacier said.

Noa shifted, eyeing him wearily. He was right. Corris had been built to withstand a possible invasion from Amarais the moment they decided to strike, and the fact that he'd known that told her that at least one member of his family had considered it too.

"That's precisely why getting in and out isn't going to be super easy," Nyx continued. "Not to mention that we're extremely limited in terms of magic. People study magic there, so we're not exactly going to be able to get away with Cecilia creating any illusions without someone noticing."

"Plus, she also killed someone, so..." Noa mumbled.

"Cecilia *killed* someone?" Malice asked, like she had discovered a newfound respect for her.

"Yes, Malice," Noa said begrudgingly. "Anyway, I ran into a Seer while I was there. I think that I could try to convince her to give me the opportunity to slip out with the key. However, I'm...not all that sure if that'll work. I assume she'd help me since I'm, well..."

"You want me to throw out a 'chosen one' for you, or...?" Nyx trailed off.

"Shut the hell up."

Nyx smirked.

"But if Lazarus was right," Glacier said, "and you're the one to open the Vault, then isn't it possible that she'd just give it to you?"

Noa bit the inside of her cheek. "Maybe."

"Let's hope that a 'maybe' is good enough," Nyx said. "In the meantime, Glacier and I will examine some potential alternatives. When we get there, find your Seer and see if she'll help us out. If she refuses, we're on our own."

The only problem was that Noa didn't even know the Seer's name.

ALYVIA

Journal entries had flooded Alyvia's dreams, spilling into every waking thought during her working hours. Not that Shane would realize her work was suffering since he'd kept to his office. His most recent visit with Arrington had kept him quiet, and Jinko had only popped in to tell him she was heading out early for the second day in a row now. So, when the clock hit five, Alyvia packed up and left.

She stood on the commuter train, flipping through the news feeds on her phone as she waited for her stop. Her thumb stopped its scroll as the image of a man appeared on the screen. The caption under it read, 'last seen on 2704-12-31.' She remembered this guy—one of Shane's friends had approached him at the pub right before midnight. Should she contact authorities about it? Did they already know?

She bit her lip, trying to recall the guy's name over the noise, and started composing a message to Shane.

> Does this guy look familiar to you?

After a few moments, she received a reply.

> Should he look familiar? I don't recognize him.

> I think he was at the pub during the New Year's party.

> One of your friends were talking to him during the countdown.

The train slowed. And she jogged off onto the platform, checking the screen as she passed townhouse after townhouse.

> Which one?

> He was the one sitting on the end? Along the wall. Dark hair, plaid shirt.

She reached into her bag for her building keycard.

> Huh. I'll talk to him. He probably was the one to make the report.

She chewed on her cheek as the door shut behind her, the bluish light of her phone followed her as she passed the sconces, re-reading the message until it buzzed again.

> He said that he made the report, so don't worry about it.

Alyvia paused, pressing the device against her chest. But then why wouldn't he have filed the report as the first of the new year? The pendent pushed against her skin, calling on the memory of the boy who'd given it to her.

You dropped this.

Her father's advice about never turning down a gift made her uneasy now. She remembered his stories about how the Shield of Miralta was named for its protection—protection from the creatures that had tried to ravage Avaria thousands of years ago. There hadn't been many Mages around to fend them off then, much like how few there were to protect them now.

It brought her back to the creepy stories she'd endure during sleepovers, listening to her friends describe shadowy figures with silvery eyes hovering in dark corners. They'd always emphasized how they'd stalked Mages to unleash their revenge, which made Alyvia thankful she wasn't a Mage. That is, until she realized once they were all gone, there would be nothing left to stop them from going after her next.

Her phone fell away from her chest, and she stared down at the image of the missing person again. That's when she saw it: he was a Mage.

25

MIRALTA ✧ 2705-01-15

NOA

Noa panic searched the Corris University campus directory until they arrived mid-afternoon. The woman simply didn't exist. It'd left her stomach knotted as they piled into the hotel—its dark green blackout curtains framing her destination off in the distance, taunting her. So, it became her immediate next stop.

"Would it help if you had someone else with you?" Glacier asked. "I could come along—"

"No," she said, trying to keep her tone even. "You should stay here and help Nyx with a back-up plan." She zipped up her jacket, starting for the door with Glacier at her heels. "Malice," she called out, grabbing the handle as Malice shot out from the hall in answer, "make sure that he doesn't leave, *please.*" She pointed at Glacier. His face crumpled to mixture of irritation and disappointment. Noa flashed him a quick smile while Malice wrapped around his arm, ensuring he'd be staying put.

Fifteen minutes later, fresh-cut grass of the campus lawn lightly crunched under her boots fifteen minutes later, taking a shortcut to the concrete pathway to the museum with her hands tucked into her jacket pockets. The keys weighed against her neck, dragging her down with every step. Her eyes swept over each stray, uniformed professor and groundskeeper until another pedestrian slammed into her shoulder. Noa spun around on impact, stunned as a bronzed arm looped through hers and guided her *away* from her destination.

What the hell?

"Shut up and walk with me for a minute," came the older woman's breathy answer—a Miraltan about twice her age, give or take.

"Why?" Noa asked, glancing over her shoulder. "Do you need help? Is someone following you? Look, if you have a creep on your tail—"

"What? You'll kill them for me? How nice of you, *Amelia*."

Noa sputtered, gritting her teeth. "Godsdamned *Seers*. Here I am looking for one and find *another*."

She flinched as a melodious laugh escaped her captor. "I hate to break it to you, but the woman you talked to in the museum wasn't a Seer. I told her you'd be there, and she wanted to meet you. She's a friend of mine."

"What? Then why isn't your *friend* in the university staff directory?"

She shrugged, her mouth tipping up with a hint of mischief. "I think you'll figure that out later, but don't worry about your Seer quota. I'm sure you'll meet at least on more before you're reach your goal."

"Lovely. I'm *so* looking forward to it. Who the hell are you anyway? Do you have a name? Where are we going?"

"So many *questions*." The woman rolled her bright green eyes. "Call me Solaris. I'm here to make your life a little easier, so the least you can do is cooperate with me for a few minutes."

"Easier, *how?*"

She pushed Noa through a door, and they stumbled into a lobby filled with booths and long bar tables stretching along the wrap-around windows of the corner store. A check-in desk sat at the adjoining business wall, breaking up numbered doors. A study parlor.

Solaris brushed past a student, apologizing as she bumped into them and slipped a card into her pocket. Noa's jaw dropped, her mind stuck on the face she was held hostage by a *thieving Seer* while she was shoved into one of the numbered rooms.

The door slid shut. "Don't act so surprised," Solaris chided. "You're a killer and I'm a thief. Let's just get that all out in the open." She dipped her hand into her crossbody bag and held up a thin, small box with a smirk.

Noa blinked in disbelief. There was no way it was going to be *that* easy, right? She hesitated, reaching for it before it was ripped away.

"Ah-ah—Replica first." She held out her palm, and Noa scrambled to sift through her own bag.

"You're kidding," Noa hissed. "You already swiped the Shield of Miralta?"

"Well, since I knew that you were coming and Corris isn't exactly the easier place to steal from, I decided to pull some strings. You're lucky that I have friends in high places to overlook my shenanigans." Solaris gave her a pleased, cat-like grin while she tilted the fake in the dim light. "*Damn.* Lyris never ceases to amaze me."

"You know Lyris?"

"We used to work together once upon a time." She moved the emblems to the opposite boxes, closing them again. "It's been a while since we've seen each other, but I suppose that's because I'm fortunate enough to be able to see danger coming to make myself scarce. That's the only reason why I'm still in Corris." She passed Noa's box back to her.

"So... what I was told is true then?" The eleventh key in her hands might as well have weighed as much as the ten around her neck, combined. Sweat beaded along the taught cord holding them all.

"It... can be scary to be asked to do something that you know nothing about. But as someone who's been told to do things that might not make any sense many, many times, you realize that there are things that we are *made* for. You were made for this, so don't let it scare you."

Noa's face dropped down to the box before she let out a quiet, mirthless chuckle. "You know, I'm pretty sure anyone else handing me a key and knowing what I planned on using it for would call me a crazy bitch. So, thank you for refraining from telling me what I already know."

Solaris laughed, shaking her head as Noa reached for the door. "Oh, Noa—One more thing..." All joking fell away into somberness. "You may have fate on your side, but that doesn't make you invincible. Be careful."

Noa smirked, twisting the box in a wave goodbye. "Don't get myself killed with only two keys left. Got it."

NYX

Nyx pushed up her glasses again, trying to make herself focus on the scribbled plans on the computer mat. Instead, she'd been stuck on thinking about how to bring up Glacier's potential *condition* to Noa. And Glacier not knowing that he has a Miraltan cousin. And how incredibly *fucked* they were if Noa couldn't get this key on her own because this security system could take her anywhere from four-to-five days to force into with all the damn hoops she kept finding to jump through.

She rubbed her forehead, wincing.

"You okay?"

Nyx jerked her hand away, taking in Glacier's concerned frown. "Yeah. Just have a bit of a headache."

"Why don't you take a break? I can take over for a bit and share my ideas with you later, okay?"

Guilt flooded her, but she nodded and pushed herself off the black pleather sofa. Her seat was stolen almost immediately by Malice on her way to her room, only for her stride to be broken by the front door opening and closing. Nyx cringed and turned back, pressing a gloved hand to the wall.

Noa grinned and held up the box. "Got it."

Nyx's knees buckled, leaning her full weight into the wall with a deep breath. "Oh, thank gods," she whispered, catching the box as Noa tossed to her. She popped it open and stared down at the Shield of Miralta, dropping her into the thundering yard outside Lyris's cabin with the ward in Glacier's palm. She snapped the lid back over it, unable to hear the conversation between the others with her pulse thrumming in her ears. Noa pulled the keys free again and Noa slide the box free from Nyx's hands.

"That saves us the hassle of figuring out how to bypass security," Glacier said. "I'm sure Nyx is happier than I am though."

"O-oh, y-yeah." She cleared her throat.

"We should probably schedule tickets to leave in the morning," Noa said, focused on looping her next key onto the cord. "Guess we'll be heading to Jinwon next, seeing how that's our last stop before Amarais."

Nyx nodded automatically, telling herself that she'd have time in Jinwon to finally talk to Noa privately about everything. If not, she'd forcibly delay their trip to Amarais because Glacier *had* to know before then. Going back as a prince with Miraltan blood was one thing, but for him to also be a *Mage* could change everything.

NOA

The clinking of plates sounded up and down the large glass coffee table while Noa showed off her keys during dinner, receiving awestruck, nervous, and excited looks.

"You got it already?" Weather asked, a forkful of fruit part-way to her mouth.

Noa nodded, grabbing her glass of water. "Yep. Eleven down, two to go. We're just missing the Mind of Jinwon and the Soul of Amarais." She gave Glacier a sideways glance.

"So, we'll be going home soon?" Cecilia asked with a hint of hesitation.

"Seems that way," Crow mumbled, his cheek puffing out with a slight shrug.

Noa rocked back, eavesdropping on their ideas of what might come next—of Jinwon, Amarais, and the Vault. Rune bumped Cecilia's shoulder with a smile, and Weather snickered as Crow kept jerking his plate away from Malice. Glacier covered his mouth to suppress a laugh, and Nyx... Noa's smirk faded at the sight of Nyx pushing food around her plate, excusing herself shortly after. She abandoned her plate and vanished down the hall, but barely anyone stopped to acknowledge the void she'd left behind.

Noa gave Glacier a small nudge, nodding to the hall. "Is she okay?"

He hesitated, giving a half-hearted shrug. "She said that she had a headache earlier. I think she planned on laying down for a while before you came back."

Noa frowned, glancing back at the table to lock eyes with Rune. His gaze flicked to Glacier for a brief moment, and Noa gripped her fork tighter. The others erupted into laughter, and Noa reached for Nyx's plate. She left for the kitchen, her blood pounding as footsteps followed behind her.

"Noa—"

She rounded on Rune, her voice dipping to a low whisper. "What part of 'drop it' do you not understand?" She turned to the trash can, scraping off each plate.

"I really think that you should at least mention something to him before we get to Amarais. It could be his last stop if they take him back. I doubt they'd let him leave once they have him either—at least not for a while. Cecilia can leave whenever she wants, but Glacier's going to be a king. I don't want you to regret not saying something." His shoulders fell as she started for the sink. "I'm trying to tell you this as a friend, Noa."

"I've come to terms with the fact that as long as the Volkov are alive that I'd be putting him in even more danger," Noa said under her breath, scrubbing down the dishes and slotting them into the drying rack. "Imagine you're in my shoes for a second and Cecilia was in his. Would you risk *her* life for your own selfishness? Because I'd rather they go after me than aim for him first because they want to hurt me—because *Myron* wants to hurt me. At least if I put on a damn mask, he might actually have a chance to escape." She dried off her hands and turned to him again. "It's out of the question, so drop it."

Noa strode out of the kitchen, down the hall, and into her room, falling against the door. Tears pricked at the backs of her eyes.

Shit.

She rubbed sting away and crawled into bed, letting the keys spill out onto the mattress. She prayed it would all be worth it in the end—prayed that once they made it to the end that she would have the power to finish off the Volkov once and for all. Only then would she be able to sleep well at night, knowing that both she and Glacier would finally be safe, even if it meant they'd be separated.

26

KING'S REPUBLIC ✧ 2705-01-16

ALYVIA

Alyvia tucked her chin into her scarf, shielding her face with her knitted visor cap whenever she ducked her head in the crowd. It was outside her usual winter wear of a headband and peacoat ensemble, hopefully making for a decent disguise as she tailed one of Shane's friends. She imagined herself as one of the Monettes, stalking her next target through the Bellegardian district with frigid rainwater lapping at her boots under the neon streetlights.

Edmund—the one that supposedly filed the missing person's report, who Shane had decided not to name in their messages for some reason—led the way. He strode in and out of shops, tapping through his phone before picking up a small bag and meandering through the rest of the street for close to an hour.

Her feet started to drag, and she started feeling foolish that she was still following this guy until she fished out her own phone and paused. Another blinking dot told her another one of Shane's friends was nearby, and when she looked up, Edmund had his phone to his ear, heading straight for it. She broke into a light jog, grateful for the time she'd spend looking up every single detail about all these once-nameless individuals that piqued her interest.

Edmund turned down an alley, tucking his phone in his pocket while Alyvia peeked around the corner. He lingered with two others—one she recognized as the other tracked friend, and another she didn't recognize. They appeared to exchange introductions and began the rest of their walk to the next street over.

They stepped onto the sidewalk, and she counted to ten before following. She wove through the crowd again, slowing at the edge of the district, where they took the steps up to the entry of a squatty apartment building. Her countdown began once the door closed behind them, and she peered up at each of the windows for a stray stream of light cutting through. She slipped down the side street, her phone in her hands, trying to make out where they were in the building. Bikes leaned up against walls and dumpsters, giving way to the occasional busted TV or dilapidated chair.

The necklace's charm pulsed against her chest, twisting her stomach. Her head jerked up, and she stopped. Two hovering, fluorescent silver dots blocked her path like *eyes* staring back at her. They blinked once, and she spun on her heel, a scream caught in her throat as she ran.

Everything went too fast and too slow, her boots hitting the halo lights under the streetlamps not feeling as safe as she hoped. Her legs kept going, pushed by the necklace's continuing pulse against her skin—a warning not to stop. The world blurred past in her sprint past shop after shop, apartment after apartment, person after person, all while her head spun in her daring need to look back.

Her shoulder collided with another body, and her knees turned to jelly. "I- I'm so sorr—" she began, her mouth drying up.

Shane.

"What's wrong?" he asked, his hands hovering over her shoulders. "Are you okay?"

She shook her head. "I- I'm fine. I just ran into some guy—" She glanced back, her stomach knotting at the thought of the creature in the alley. She wasn't sure if she should burst into laughter or tears, both seeming equally appropriate since she was teetering on the edge of hysteria.

How much did he know? What was going on? Was that a *fucking daemon* in the alley after a *Mage* disappeared?

"Calm down." His hands finally fell into place, and she suppressed a shudder. "Let's get you home, okay?"

"It's fine—" she blurted. No way in hell was he walking her home. Not if he had *anything* to do with what was back there. "I can get home myself. I wouldn't want to trouble you."

"At least let me take you to the commuter station."

Even that sounded like too much, but she forced herself to nod. He let go of her, moving a hand to her back to guide her toward the train. The necklace thrummed in warning, keeping her heart rate higher than she wanted until she boarded the train.

When the train pulled away, the charm quieted. Shane's wave fell away from view. And Alyvia collapsed into a seat, dropping her head into her hands.

27

BELLEGARDE ✧ 2705-01-17

NYX

Nyx woke to the rolling, country hillside of Bellegarde and a manic, rambling message from Alyvia she had to re-read at least twice before replying.

> What's going on? Are you okay?

A reply came about a minute later.

> About to head into work.
>
> Didn't sleep last night.
>
> Think my boss is fucking insane.
>
> Need help.
>
> Not sure what to do.

Nyx rubbed at her eyes and took a deep breath.

> Let's start with 'what happened last night?', okay?

There were a few minutes of typing, stopping, and typing again.

> I don't even know anymore.

> Then start from a point that makes sense.

Finally, a flood of messages.

> I saw a missing notice for a guy I recognized from a New Year's thing. One of my boss's friends was talking to him at midnight, but the notice said that he was last seen on the 31st.

> I asked my boss about it, and he told me that his friend was the one to fill out the report.

> But why the hell would his friend fill out the report for the last day of the year when he'd seen him on the first day of the year?

> So, I did a little digging and followed him back to an apartment last night with another friend and some random guy that I think they just met.

> Now... I know this is going to sound insane, but I saw... something.

Nyx paused, reading through the text chain again.

> What's the name of the missing guy?

After a moment, Alyvia sent it over, allowing her to pull up his information. A registered Mage. She sucked in a sharp breath, remembering Adam's list.

> Which boss?

> Shane Delacroix.

> Just lay low. Keep me updated. I'll see what I can do.

> Just go to work and go home.

> Okay. Okay, I can do that.

The message felt more for Alyvia herself than for Nyx.

> Text me every couple of hours or so to check in.

> Will do.

Nyx clicked off her phone screen, staring at the floral walls of the cabin. She needing to fucking talk to Noa. Her phone tapped against her palm as she wandered down the hallway, finally running into Noa, Glacier, and Malice huddling into a dining car booth. Trying to act casual, she collected a cup of coffee and slid in next to them, unable to really stomach anything on the menu—even dishes that normally would've comforted her with the promise of home.

"You feeling better?" Noa asked with a slight frown.

She paused after blowing on her coffee, refusing to look her in the eyes. "A little."

Glacier's worry rolled off him, sending a tidal wave of uneasy through the others until a plate slid in front of her. She looked up at Malice, her plate sitting between them, and Noa cleared her throat.

"Malice, that's not how this works," she said. "You can't just *steal* half my plate and give it to someone else."

"You didn't say I *couldn't* take anything," Malice shot back. "So now it's mine, and I can share it with whoever I want to."

"*Gods.* Nyx, just slide out of the booth, and I'll get you something if you're hungry."

Nyx plucked up the half-sandwich off the plate, stuffed with a brown-sugar dusted omelet. Even though it had been a spiteful action to take a bite while staring into Noa's eyes, it had threatened to break her. An old familiarity amongst the new, blending so bitter-sweet between past and present.

Noa fake-fumed. "*Wow.*"

Glacier covered his face, stifling a snicker. Nyx couldn't help but smirk. Exasperated, Noa leaned back, her head thumping against the top of her seat, and Malice abandoned them for Weather and Crow when they stepped into the car.

"Where's Cecilia and Rune?" Nyx asked, setting the sandwich back down. "I sort of thought they'd be in here before those two got up."

"We ran into them earlier," Glacier answered. "They were finishing up breakfast, and Cecilia mentioned heading to the observation car."

"They're probably making out," Noa said with a wry smile.

He rolled his eyes. "I think she was a little disappointed that we weren't stopping in Bellegarde, so Rune said he'd point stuff out to her for a mini-tour on our way through before Jinwon."

"There's always the possibility that we'll stop here on our way back," Noa said. "I mean, we kind of have to get back to Amarais somehow."

Nyx squeezed her cup, thinking about Alyvia. The decision to detour before Amarais wasn't one they should take lightly, considering their time crunch, but the fear that Alyvia might end up like Hugo weighed on her conscious. Even if Alyvia didn't have any direct connection to Daxton, Arrington and Delacroix did. And if there really were questionable activities going on that lead back to Arrington, Delacroix, and Matsuoka, then they needed to strike hard and fast soon after the found the Vault. No more hunting Mages. No more Volkov. No more corruption lurking in plain sight, waiting patiently to destroy what everyone cared about.

"Do you need help with anything before we reach our destination, Nyx?" Glacier's words ripped through her throughs.

"No. Don't worry about it. It's already taken care of."

And she refocused her mind on Kingsheart, Amarais, and the Vault.

GLACIER

The lush green hills of southern Bellegarde gave way to mountains by the time the sun poured over the top of the train car, it's light soaking the landscape as Glacier drifted to sleep with a tablet in his hands. He woke to snow, his head spinning while he grappled as the edges of the seat. This wasn't Amarais, was it?

"You okay?" Noa asked, leaning forward in her seat.

He shook his head—no, this was the pass from Bellegarde to Jinwon. A sigh escaped him, interrupted by a loud tone over the speaker system. Snowflakes batted against the window, hitting slower and slower until he realized that *they* were the ones slowing down. Malice stood, bracing herself with a look of bewilderment as Noa rose and put a hand to the window. Instructions sounded for passengers to disembark at the next station.

"We're getting off?" Malice asked, pushing Noa out of the way to press her face to the glass.

Glacier checked the time on his phone. "But there's not another scheduled stop for at least another hour. This isn't on the itinerary..."

"What the hell..." Noa breathed, whipping around as the door slid open.

Nyx stood on the threshold. "With me, *now*." She barely waited, turning to start down the hall when Noa jogged after her. Glacier pushed himself up, and Malice followed on his heels.

"What the hell is going on?" Noa asked, a question directed at Nyx, despite glancing over her shoulder at Glacier with a glimmer of worry in her gaze.

"We're being flushed out."

The words hit Glacier in the chest, numbing him like the cold radiating off the windows. Everything slowed as Noa pushed past her to the next car, the door opening to the rest of their group, huddled in the lounge with varying looks of concern. Nyx lifted her phone, typing something in right before all the window shades of the car snapped on. Crow jumped, stopping him in his tracks from the circle he'd been making along the patch of carpet.

"What's going on?" Cecilia asked, twisting a once-neatly-folded napkin in her hands.

"There are Volkov waiting for us on the platform, isn't there?" Noa said, peering out as the train ground to a halt.

Hesitantly, Nyx nodded.

"What?" Weather asked, shooting up from her seat. "How did they know we're on *this* train? Did they manage to track on of you?"

"That doesn't matter now. What matters is that we're staying on the train once everyone evacuates. It's set to autopilot to the nearest hub for maintenance. That's why no one's throwing up any red flags. I just noticed it about ten minutes ago, which is why I had you gather here."

"So, now what?" Crow demanded. "We take the train to the hub? Can't you redirect it somewhere else for us to hop off?"

"Even if she did that," Noa began, "I can almost guarantee that they're tracking the train. They'll know if she reprograms it, and they'll follow us there. We're trapped. We either get off here and make a run for it, or we stay on."

Rune's hand went to his mouth with a low hum. "And if we try to make a run for it... I can't imagine it'll end well for some of us... They'll pick us off."

"I can glamour us," Cecilia said. "Then we can get off the train—"

"With what IDs?" Nyx asked, and Cecilia flinched. "We'll get detained without anything to match, and we're all out of spares for the moment. After that, they'll have us cornered well enough to kill us."

"So, we're left with Nyx's original plan," Noa said, drawing back from the window, her face darkening.

"You're not actually suggesting that we..." Weather shook her head, letting out a nervous laugh. "Oh, *gods*..."

"We have two Volkov. They have four. Malice and I can each take care of one, and then you four can pair off."

Noa's head swiveled toward Glacier as he took a step forward. "What about me and Nyx? You've been teaching me to fight for a reason, and she's not exactly helpless either—"

"You and Nyx are the two here with *all* of the plans. Not to mention that Kole will go straight for you the moment he steps foot on this train. He's *far* more experienced than you are, and he'll stop at nothing to kill you. I gave you lessons in defense, not how to kill."

"She's right," Nyx said, Glacier's heart pounding in his chest the second the train pushed forward again. "Glacier and I can at least sequester ourselves from the Volkov's line of sight and try to manipulate the train to our advantage from our hiding spot. My tactical guess is that they'll try to use one of the tunnel overpasses to get on board once they realize we didn't get off. From there, they can use the emergency train exists on the roof between some of the cars. Four overhead exits. Four Volkov."

"Right..." Noa mumbled. "Which means that they'll likely either organize themselves to sweep the cars from front to back, highest to lowest, or they'll put the highest ranking on the outside to box us in. Either way, Myron will take the front to manually stop the train to prevent possible escape into a nearby town or something to cause a scene."

"Then I'll take the front," Malice said in a near-growl.

"*No,*" Noa snapped, and Malice shrank back. "*I'll* take the front. He wants *me,* not you. I know how he thinks, which will give me an advantage. And he'll probably do whatever he can to push anyone else to the side for now in favor of strangling me if I pissed him off enough by now."

"What about the rest of us?" Weather glanced from her to Crow, rubbing her arms.

"Pair up however you see fit. Cecilia has the advantage of using magic, but the rest of you have some sort of street fighting experience, right? Use anything and everything you have. Act unpredictably and unfair because they'll do the same."

"Crow, you take Weather," Rune said with a nod in her direction. "I'll stay with Cecilia."

"I- I've never been in a fight. I—" Cecilia choked out.

"Just blind the shit out of them," Crow said with a smirk. "Do whatever you did to me back in Amarais and let Rune take the lead." She nodded hesitantly, bumping shoulders with Rune as he wrapped an arm around her.

"Rune and Cecilia," Nyx said, pointing toward the back of the train. "You two take the last car just after the final emergency exit. Weather and Crow will take the next one up. Malic—"

"I'll take the second." A feral grin spread across her face, her blade at the ready.

Nyx let out a breath, starting again. "Even if we can't predict the order they'll go in, we can still lure them to the back of the train if we end up overwhelmed. Keep communication going, and if we need to get rid of any of them, take them to the back and we ditch the last car with them in it. I can throw on its emergency breaks before it gets too far away from the rest of the train. That should be enough to minimize damage and deal with them as-needed later. Our goal is to survive and get to the Vault."

Everyone nodded, some a little more confidently than others. But Glacier couldn't make his head move. The world deafened around him, and his breathing came in shallower and shallower. This wasn't happening, was it? If it was, he could at least trade places with Cecilia, hell—*anyone*. He couldn't bear the thought of hiding while everyone else stared death in the face.

His stomach churned when Noa turned to him again, her hand plucking at the cord around her neck. *Gods, no. No, no, no—* But the keys were already over her head. He tried to take a step back, but his body wouldn't move, accepting the horrible burden she was about to place on him. She grabbed his hand, looping the black string through his fingers.

Say something. Do *something,* that voice inside his head screamed.

He couldn't make himself reach out and grab her by the shoulders—to tell her this was suicide, and how she promised they wouldn't die. But all he could do was shake his head, angry how his vision blurred while he quietly pleaded her to listen to what was trapped in his mind.

"Hold these for me," she said quietly, nearly nose-to-nose. An intimate goodbye before her hand fell away from his and she left the car.

"Noa, wait—"

She didn't turn around. She didn't look back. The train car elongated, turning into a tunnel, stretching forward as Malice bounced after her. An inappropriate laugh threatened to force its way out with the world tipping sideways—one matching the chuckle he'd heard in the hall of his father's house constructed by his dreams. This had to be another nightmare. He'd wake up any minute now like when he'd felt the bite of cold in the halls of the palace with his mother dead at his back. Or like when he'd pressed against that sheet of ice, trying to call out for Kat in the freezing water. Or like when those red-ringed eyes peered back at him through the glass.

Glacier would wake to Jinwon. He just needed to find... "Kat."

"Glacier." Nyx grabbed his arm. "We need to go."

A phantom overlay of Kat flickered in Cecilia's place until Rune stepped between them. "We'll walk with you."

28

BELLEGARDE ✦ 2705-01-17

CECILIA

Cecilia's arms wrapped around Glacier, holding tight until Nyx touched her shoulder. The desperation in his face—the pleading—ripped into her as he was dragged away. Her arms fell loosely at her sides while she stared after him, even once they were gone, remembering Noa's hint of jealousy when Cecilia had given him a gift for his birthday. The way she'd hovered so close to him when she handed him the keys...

"They like each other, don't they?" Cecilia asked, unsure of whether or not Rune would say anything.

He let out a breath of a sigh. "Noa would probably kill me if I told you, but... seeing how there's a possibility she might not have the chance... Yes. She likes him."

Tears pricked at the backs of her eyes, looking up at him. "I've never seen him look at anyone the way he looks at her." She released a soft, bitter laugh. "And now we're probably all going to die."

"With two keys left too." Rune slid his hand into hers. "But we made a good run of it, and I'd do it all over again if it meant meeting you."

A drop slipped down her cheek as she forced out a helpless, breathy laugh, swiping at her face.

"And here I was just getting used to the sound of Cecilia and Gabriel Angelis."

She paused, meeting his soft, warm gaze. An underlying promise of a future together. She squeezed his hand a little tighter.

"We're going to live," she said, a fierceness ripping through her she hadn't expected, though Rune's surprise was cut short by the thud of boots against the roof of the car.

His hand pulled away as they faced the door, and Cecilia's blood pounded in her ears while she curled and uncurled her fingers at her sides, recalling Rune's instructions to ensure she didn't lock up. And when the door opened, Cecilia prayed she was ready, especially when she caught the sight of snow-dusted blond hair.

Kole.

NOA

Noa leaned against the manual override cabin door in the control car. Deep breath in. Deep breath out. So long as she stood between this and Myron, that's all that mattered. So long as Myron didn't get to Glacier, that's all that mattered. So long as Myron *died*, that's all that mattered.

It was as if she could feel Lazarus standing next to her, his ghostly grip on her shoulder, guiding her toward what could very well be her demise. But even if she died, she wanted everyone else to step off this train—she *needed* Glacier to step off this train.

When the door slid open, she watched Myron pull down his hood. His red-brown graying hair damp from the snow, and his dark eyes gleaming with fresh venom, matching his smirk.

Noa pushed off the control door, jerking a thumb behind her. "I'm guessing you want in here."

He raised a brow, a chuckle slipping into his reply, "And *you're* going to stop me?"

"I'm not going to let you have the advantage here. Not so you can clean up the mess you made for yourself. So *yes*, I'm going to stop you, even if it kills me."

"Step aside Noa. You're wasting time."

"Oh, *please*—" She chortled. "According to you, my time's way past up, or are you forgetting that you had Ezra give me a 'choice?'" She made air-quotes, bitterness tumbling into the words. "Do you honestly think that I would believe that, by the way?"

"I would've at least made it quick as a lesson to the others, but I've clearly underestimated just how godsdamned persistent you are. Out of all the Volkov I trained, I saw *you* as the one who would see things the way I do. But it seems that you diverged from that path as some point—it was because of that damn Seer, wasn't it?"

"You can blame him all you'd like, but I was born to be a pain in your ass." She smirked. "You hate what you can't control. And what you can't control, you kill, don't you? After all, that's what you did will all the other Volkov before you struck out on your own."

Myron's mouth twitched at the accusation, confirming Noa's suspicions.

"Then you decided to put yourself at the top," Noa continued, twisting that metaphorical blade a little more. "You pick up a bunch of kids that were abandoned just like you were. You give them a blade to defend themselves and a new father to praise for saving them from their wretched lives. All of it so they'll worship the ground you walk on with no one left to turn to. A perfectly controlled environment where you're a *god*."

He chuckled, shaking his head. "You would know, wouldn't you? Isn't that exactly what you've done with the rest of the people left on this train? You're just like *me*."

A smile pulled across her face, smooth as silk. "You're right, Myron. I am just like you. The only difference is that I don't need to control my people with fear. They can leave whenever they want, but the *choose* to stay with me. I don't have to resort to manipulation to get what I want."

The words stuck true, wiping that taunting smirk off his face. He was done with the banter with a flick of his wrist, a blade sliding free to teach her a one more lesson.

Final round.

MALICE

Malice pouted as she ran a hand over the bar top of the dining car. Her favorite spot on the train was about to be ruined, though it did give her quite a few things to throw around. She only wished Ezra were still alive to smash his head in with a plate.

The door opened ahead of her, and Malice grinned, a thrill pushing through her at the mere thought of one final battle against Lexa. Once a member of her tormentors, now another person threatening to harm those who treated her with kindness.

"Of course you chose that *bitch* over the rest of us," Lexa hissed, ripping a dagger from her belt. "What did she offer you? A *hug?*"

"A chance to finally kick your ass."

Malice lunged, the blood singing in her veins. The blade in her hand became an extension of her body. It was no longer a weapon because *she* was the weapon.

CROW

"What's up, bitch?" Weather said, earning a growl from Talon the second he stepped into the lounge car. He bolted forward, straight through her and Crow as they split apart.

Talon rounded on him, and Crow ducked, feeling the slight breeze through his hair. "You just *had* to say it, didn't you?"

She kicked Talon square in the ass, sending him forward, and Crow knocked the dagger from his hands. He took the swing this time, a punch Talon whipped away from, sweeping his legs out from under him. Crow grimaced, colliding with the wall, and Weather smacked into Talon, knocking him to the floor.

He sprung to his feet in the same amount of time it'd taken for Crow to regain his balance, another blade flicking out from his sleeve.

Crow's mouth fell open. "Oh, *motherfu—*"

CECILIA

"Out of all the people I'd expect to find protecting that damn Miraltan," Kole said, taking a slow, deliberate step forward while the overhead lights reflected off the blade at his side, "I didn't expect an Amaraian. I'll give you *one* chance to take me to him and *maybe* I'll let you live."

Cecilia stood firm. He was her family—her little brother. She wouldn't let this monster anywhere near him. She was done hiding in plain sight. She was done relying on Glacier or anyone else to protect her. It was her turn to protect *him*.

She drew in a slow, calming breath and closed her eyes, pulling the light from the room and bottling it up in her soul. She plunged the car into darkness, ripping all but pinpricks of light from the windows to turn the observation car into a starry sky—one reminiscent of her first night of freedom.

When she opened her eyes, Kole's face was a mask of horror, quickly slipping into one of fury.

Rune's voice dropped to a deadly calm, sliding a foot back in preparation to fight. "You'll have to go through us to get to him."

NOA

Noa mirrored his steps—back and forth, side to side—like an elaborate dance, pushing up and down the car in a game of gaining and losing ground. She hissed at the sting of the knicks along her arms when she'd thrown them up in retreat. But she'd surprised him at least twice, especially once she'd managed to slice his arm, and his actions turned reserved.

Noa kicked the button next to the door and shoved him through, her body nearly toppling into the next car with him. He staggered back, and she locked it again, staring into the seething, fire gaze of her former mentor. Noa sprinted for the window, hitting the emergency latch so he wouldn't have time to give up on her just yet.

Eyes on me. Forget the others. It's me you want.

Beeping filled the car, screeching as the window fell free and she hoisted herself through. Icy wind whipped against her face, gnawing at her ears and nose. She forced open her eyes and gasped, throwing her body against the side of the car, her legs tensing from her seat in the window frame as the tunnel wall grazed the back of her jacket.

One. Two. Three... Seven... Ten...

Blinding white seared her vision again, and she scrambled upward to the top of the train, prepared to go down the hatch after Myron—except he was already standing over it. The phantom sensation of Lazarus's hands guiding hers reminded her she was the one in control here. Her hands had been used to murder and mend pages, but her mind was the sharpest weapon she had. Noa had always used everything to her advantage.

And she knew exactly what to do.

MALICE

Malice growled, irritated that Lexa continued dodging her every move.

"You stupid little *bitch*," Lexa hissed as she dodged her again.

So, Malice took a step back, recalling Noa's advice of letting the enemy come to you. She puffed out a breath, feigning weakness, and Lexa lunged. She dodged again as Malice thew an arm out, and a blade sunk into Malice's side. The adrenaline pumped through her, feeling her own dagger pushing into Lexa's stomach.

CROW

"Where the *fuck* does he keep getting all these godsdamned knives?" Crow yelled, dodging another swipe from Talon. Sweat trickled down his back, gritting his teeth.

A scream interrupted his sluggish thoughts, combined with the blur of a table leg smashing against Talon's head. The knife fell from his hand, his body swaying before he rounded on her. Weather gasped as she was slammed into the wall, and Crow scooped up the blade, burying it into Talon's lower back. A howl echoed through the car.

CECILIA

Kole went straight for Cecilia, and Rune bodied him. The scenery shifted, her magic folding down the seats to blend into the carpet. Kole cursed as he bumped into one, and she shifted the room again—seafoam lapping at the soles of his boots, warping the entirety of the car.

He blocked another one of Rune's blows, and the blade clattered to the floor, the metal sliding along the tiled walkway her ocean parted for as she victoriously trapped it under her boot. Kole punched him in the stomach, and Cecilia's eyes widened at the sound of a gasp. Rune's head smacked against the door, and he collapsed, slumping over as Kole took a step back.

"*Rune!*" she screamed, fumbling to secure the knife. It shook in her hands, holding it up at the sound of Kole's steps growing closer. He knocked it out of her hand, and she froze, half-expecting him to seize her arm like Astor had.

"I don't even need a weapon to deal with *you*," he seethed, finally releasing her from the spell, and her back hit the car door. "Don't you think it's a *sign* that Mages are disappearing? You're obsolete. The world had moved on, and we're better for it. The only thing that you people are good at is destroying. You hurt everyone else around you—all because you only care about your precious *magic*. Do yourself and everyone else a favor: just *die* already."

Fear and self-loathing were immediately replaced by that slow-stoking spark of anger, fueled by the quiet groan from Rune. She still had one last trick up her sleeve. The car's windows immediately burst into a bright, white light. Kole yelped and threw his arms over his face, giving Cecilia the opportunity to forced open the door and *run*.

Follow me, you bastard. *Leave Rune and follow me.*

"Nyx!"

NOA

Myron dodged, and Noa spun around to follow, losing her balance as he kicked in one of her knees. Her body tried to correct, but instead, Lazarus's voice caressed her thoughts.

Fall.

Her back slammed against the roof of the car, terror gripping her as air pushed from her lungs. Myron dropped down, and a scream ripped from her—her throat burning as hot as the knife digging into her shoulder.

"You should've just done what you were *told*," he shouted over the howling wind. "I made you a killer. You'll never be anything else. You're *nothing*."

Noa spat out a laugh. "I'm the Queen of Avaria, bitch."

His eyes widened, and the world around them went dark, the tunnel barely leaving enough room for the two of them. So, she jerked her arms up between them, and thrust him upward with the last of her strength. Fear reflected in his face a little too late.

NYX

Nyx rapidly tapped each car on her screen, the status of each one popping up over and over again. Glacier paced the width of the cabin, pausing as he stared off at the front of the train through the walls. About fifteen seconds passed before her tablet beeped, indicating a door opening, and Cecilia called her name. A shiver worked through her—he'd *known* what would happen before there'd been any indications.

Shaking it off, she focused on the tablet again. "Ready," she told Cecilia through the comms, listening to the sound of heavy footfalls passing their cabin. It came and went, her fingers hovering just above the final car's commands. The lock's indicator lit up, and Nyx shot up out of her seat, throwing herself into the hall to make sure Cecilia was outside.

Sure enough, she was, and on the other side of the door was Kole. Glacier followed her out, and Kole's blue eyes lit with fury. He slammed his fists against the door's small glass window, and Nyx pushed the button.

The car drifted away, and she pressed the button for the break, sending Kole's smacking against the window as the emergency door sealed the car opening.

"Where's Rune?" Glacier asked, his voice rising with panic just as Cecilia turned to face them.

"I'm here."

Nyx and Glacier spun around, her shoulders falling at the sight of Rune in the doorway. He grimaced, rubbing the back of his head. "He nearly knocked me out cold, though."

She tapped her comm piece. "Status on Weather and Crow."

"Talon's down," Crow answered.

"Malice?" she asked, leading the way to the lounge car.

"She's with us," Weather said. "What happened back there?"

"We had to drop Kole," Nyx said, the doors folding away until they stepped into their car, two covered forms lumped along the carpeting. Weather and Crow leaned against the lounge chairs, blood seeping from a couple gashes in their clothing. Malice looked a little worse with a dark spot spreading at her side, but she stood, undaunted, staring at the other door.

"I was starting to think that you two might be dead," Crow said, crumpling slightly with weary relief.

"Where's Noa?" Nyx demanded. "I don't think she took a comm piece."

"Haven't seen her."

Nyx followed Malice's gaze before her eyes caught the glint of the pile of daggers resting at the corner of one of the sheets. She crouched down, pressing her knee to the soft green carpet.

Noa stumbled inside, and Nyx perked up at Glacier breathing her name like a prayer, starting toward her until Nyx shot to her feet, knife in hand as she grabbed a fistful of his jacket, yanking him back.

"Nobody move," she said sharply. The whole room stilled while Nyx held the knife out, tilting the blood in the light for Noa to see its purple hue.

"What the hell..." Crow's hand went to his cheek, brushing across a thin cut.

"How often do the Volkov use poison?" she asked, glancing between Noa and Malice.

"I..." Noa started, shaking her head.

"Those two play with poison," Malice said, pointing to the bodies and crossing her arms in an X. "The rest of us wanted nothing to do with it."

"It'd be slow-acting," Noa said, her voice sounding distant and numb. "They would sometimes use it on targets if they know that they couldn't get close to them, but they were able to get close to something they consumed. They probably thought that we'd run, so they must've added it to their weapons just in case."

"How *slow*, Noa?"

"I—" She grimaced, shaking her head again. "I don't know. Twelve hours? Eight?"

"Myron's dead, right?" Nyx asked. Noa nodded rapidly before Nyx nudged Glacier forward. "Glacier, get a container and some spare gloves from the dining car. In the meantime, no one touches each other. I'll try to patch us up as the sole exception." She pulled out her phone, and Glacier started past Noa, slowing for a moment before he pushed forward into the next car.

"What are you doing?" Noa asked, her voice wavering.

Nyx only typed as fast as she could.

> We need a doctor. Toxicologist.

"Calling in a favor."

"I thought we already used that favor—"

> ETA?

Nyx let out a breath, her eyes flicking back up to Noa. "Good thing I keep good relationships with our clients, so they stop caring about favors."

Noa's shoulders fell while Nyx retrieved her tablet, rerouting the train to Razbia.

GLACIER

Glacier hovered over the covered form laid out in front of the control car's door. He swallowed, kneeling down and running his finger over the edge of the blanket. He needed to know if Myron was that man from his nightmares, or if maybe he was still very much trapped in one, unable to make himself wake up.

He closed his eyes, pulling the sheet up with a deep breath and slowly opened them again. Myron's lifeless, familiar gaze stared back at him. Glacier let go, shooting to his feet. His head spun as frost clung to the windows. The sound of dripping followed him through the halls, turning from green to white and back again, his breath puffing out in small clouds of smoke.

Wake up. Wake up. Wake up.

He fumbled with a small, plastic container in the dining car, and pushed forward. Everything blurred and blended together until he stood in front of Nyx, holding the box out to her like he was offering one of the storage containers to Kat. Blonde hair shifted to black as she took it from him with a frown.

"Are you okay?" she asked.

"Yeah, I'm fine."

NOA

"Noa, I'm *so* sorry," Cecilia whispered, helping her retrieve her bag from the overhead compartment.

"Why?" Noa frowned. "I should be thanking you for helping my avoid ripping my stitches and getting my ass kicked by Nyx."

Cecilia shook her head. "Rune and I—We—" She her lip. "I panicked in trying to get Kole away from Rune, so Kole's still alive."

Relief washed over Noa—a silver lining to this entire mess. She still had that chance to talk to Kole. "Don't be sorry. I'd hug you right now if I could for sparing him."

She hesitated. "I- um, I wouldn't really call it *sparing* as much as fear that he was going to kill Rune—"

"It doesn't matter, Cecilia. Kole was one of the few people I considered to be my family. I'm... just sorry that you had to deal with him. If anyone should be sorry, it's me."

More sorry than you know.

"We're going to make it in time, aren't we?" she asked.

"Yeah. We will." Noa said it with more confidence than she felt. She would do anything to get them all to Razbia. They had to live because Noa couldn't do this without them.

29
ESMEDRALIA ✧ 2705-01-17

NOA

When the train pulled into the maintenance bay, Nyx led the way outside into the dusky outskirts of Razbia. Two automated taxis idled along the curb, where Rune and Cecilia helped a pale-looking Crow and a winded Weather into one, and Noa strapped Malice into the other, her head lulling against the door with a groan as the others piled in.

Every minute ticking away on the dash made Noa's knee bounce. So, when the cars pulled up in front of the hospital, Noa tore out of the vehicle, storming into the lobby and shouting in a combination of Astravnian and International. The hospital staff hurried around their desks, trying to calm her down while she demanded to see Devi Patel—cuing someone to mash the dial pad to call her down.

Devi profusely apologized when she appeared, bowing slightly as she motioned for the group to follow her, making up some sort of excuse about wealthy patients and accidents. Then the elevator doors closed.

"Do I want to know why you've brought poisoned friends to my hospital, Nyx?" Devi asked with a tight-lipped smile, pressing her badge to the elevator keypad and selecting a specially marked floor.

Noa shot her an uneasy smile. "We fucked up."

Nyx groaned, pushing up her glasses.

"All right then..." Devi whispered. A chime sounded, and the doors fell away to a sterile, white hall sectioned off with neon tape and clear, plastic tarps. "This part of the hospital is under some construction at the moment, but there's a private room with equipment we can use. I'm one of the few allowed on this floor just in case the lab is full."

Their footsteps echoed through the cool, dim corridor, setting Noa's nerves on edge until Devi popped open one of the lab doors and its light clicked on, spilling out from its large hallway observatory window. She held it open as each of them filed in, wandering over to a seat on the padded bed or one of the seats along the wall before they were all taken, leaving Noa, Nyx, and Glacier left standing.

"Do you have a sample of the poison?" Devi asked, prompting Nyx to hand her the box. "Perfect, thank you. Everyone needs to line up. I'll need your names—I don't care if it's real or fake, just have it ready for me in a moment."

Devi typed a few things into the terminal and plucked off the lid, her smile fading slightly as she glanced over her shoulder, almost like she was about to ask, 'what the hell were you doing?' before she returned to her task. She scraped some of the dried blood from the blade into a dish, transferred it to her little white machine, and the computer flashed through database images. Devi hummed as she collected a vile and turned to Weather. "Can I have your name?"

"Weather," she replied, giving her a bright, dashing smile. "You have *beautiful* eyes."

Crow's head swung towards her. "Seriously? You're doing this *now?*"

"Shut the hell up. I'm *dying*. You better believe I'm going to do whatever the hell I want if this is the end."

"You're not going to die." Devi chuckled. "We have the antidote in our system, and you've still got plenty of time if it ended up in your bloodstream around the time that Nyx contacted me."

"Oh, thank the gods." Weather placed a hand to her chest.

"And *your* name?" Devi asked, getting Crow's name before moving onto Malice.

"I'm Mal—"

"Alice," Noa interjected, getting a look of irritation as Devi marked an 'A' on her vile.

She returned with a vile already labeled for Noa, motioning for her to roll up her sleeve. "You don't have to give me your name. If you had to, I think that we'd have bigger problems."

"Like memory loss?"

"Just about." She laughed.

After that, she moved on to Rune and Cecilia before standing in front of Glacier.

"And you are...?" Devi paused, looking him up and down.

"Morgan."

Devi bit her lip, eyeing him suspiciously while she marked down an 'M', stealing a glance over at Nyx. Nyx looked away, rubbing her arm for a moment until her hand stopped and she mumbled a curse.

"What?" Noa asked.

"Son of a bitch. How the hell did he catch up to us?"

Panic surged through Noa, and she pushed past her to the monitors. Kole prowled across the cameras, keycard in hand. "Damnit, Kole..." Noa growled. "Cecilia, I need you to make it look like no one's in here. Glamour the observation window and the glass door. I have to deal with our loose end."

"But what about—" Cecilia started.

"If I'm poisoned, it can wait," Noa said, starting for the door. "I have enough time to deal with one more dumbass before I keel over." She shoved her hand in her pocket, her fingers grazing the memory card before she slipped out of the room and watched Cecilia start marking up the window. The light pouring into the hall disappeared, and Noa pushed up her sleeves.

She slowly made her way to the plastic sheets, each sticky *click* of her rubber soles perking her ears. Noa pushed back the curtain, the blurry shapes coming into sharp focus—a ladder, a couple of plaster buckets, a small stack of leftover tiles. Dim wall sconces reflected off the windows, framing the twinkling city landscape.

She turned to the next tarp and paused, catching the outline of a figure. Golden hair, pale skin, white winter coat. A white glove cut through, pulling it back, his blue eyes locking with her brown. And then she ran.

Noa bolted back down the hallway, turning at an intersection and toward a set of open double doors, straight into the completed part of the floor. Another corner, and she picked up speed, hurtling into her final sprint. She threw a hand against the button on the wall, and a set of doors snapped shut behind her, almost catching the back of her coat.

When she turned around, Kole stood mere centimeters from the doors. "You fucking coward."

"Call me whatever you like."

"He did everything for us, and you *killed* him—"

"He *manipulated* us, Kole!" she screamed, her voice reverberating off the marble walls. He reared back like she'd slapped him. "He did everything to make us believe that he was the best option, but he wasn't. If anyone or anything else tempted us with a better offer, he'd eliminate it. I would know because that's what he did to me."

"You're a fucking lair, Noa."

"Am I?" She held up the memory card. "Because he's done it to you too."

He hesitated, and that's when she knew he'd been lying to himself. He'd been avoiding unmasking that monster for so long because he'd been afraid of what he might find. But now she had all the answers, and it would be up to him to decide if he could accept the truth or not. She dropped to a knee, sliding it under the gap below the door. Kole stared down at it for a moment until he realized she wasn't some trick for her to turn and run, so he scooped it up.

"There's your proof. It's all the proof I needed to put it all together. So, I'm giving you one last chance to walk away from this, Kole. We both know how this will end, and neither of us will like it."

He slowly turned it over in his hand, his face falling to something that Noa could only describe as defeat. She hated seeing him like this. She *missed* him, but they couldn't get back that time they had together. Everything from here on out would be different between them, regardless of his decision.

"Walk away, Kole," she whispered, taking a step back.

His shoulders fell, and she took her leave, vanishing back toward the people that still needed her.

NYX

Nyx breathed a sigh of relief as Kole slipped into the stairwell. She spun back to Devi, who handed out three bottles of pills to Crow, Weather, and Malice.

"Okay," Devi began. "So, the antidote will take a lot out of you over the next few days. These will help with that. Take one in the morning and one at night, preferably with food since it can make you feel queasy without. Outside of that, you're in the clear." She pulled off her gloves with a smile. "Please don't go around getting yourselves poisoned again."

"Trust me," Weather said with a chuckle, "that's the last thing on our lists."

Crow and Malice nodded tiredly in agreement as Noa stepped back inside. "How's everything?"

"All of you are good to go," Devi said. "It was isolated to these three. If you had any trace of it, it's so minimal that your body will be able to handle it. Do you... want the knife back, or...?"

Noa held out a hand, and Devi snapped the lid back on the container.

"I'm... assuming you'll update me later?" Devi asked, her eyes flicking between Noa and Nyx.

"Yeah, just..." Noa said. "Just give me a little time to work a few things out first."

"And we should probably go," Nyx said, "before we cause any more trouble. They probably want Noa as far away from the building as quickly as possible."

Devi's eyes gleamed with amusement as Rune and Cecilia wiped the runes from the glass. Noa pulled open the door again, ushering everyone out.

"Nyx—" Devi spoke up. "Can I have a word?"

Nyx hesitated, motioning for Noa to go on ahead. The door fell shut, and Aiza stepped up next to her.

"It was Volkov, wasn't it?"

"I figured the knife would give that away." Nyx rubbed the side of her face. "I wouldn't say that we're one hundred percent in the clear yet, but..."

"Understood, but... now you have me a little more worried that you *are* going to get yourself killed, Nari." She frowned, tucking her hands into her coat pockets.

"I think I'd be lying if I were to say that the worst of it is over, but I believe that most of the imminent threats have been dealt with, minus *one*. I just... don't want to get your hopes up before we finish what we started, okay?"

Aiza bit her lip, tugging her hands from her pockets and intertwining their fingers. Nyx closed her eyes, biting down on her tongue. "Aiza, when this is all over... If I asked you to follow me to wherever the hell I end up—"

"For someone so smart, you really ask some stupid questions," she said with a giggle, pressing her forehead to Nyx's. "I'm pretty sure you asked me to follow you once when I didn't even know who you were. I did it then, so I don't see why I wouldn't do it now."

A smile tugged at the corners of her mouth, the world fading around them, giving way to that foolish myriad of hopes and dreams on the horizon. Everything was just within reach. All she had to do was live.

NOA

Noa could've collapsed onto the plush ruby mandala rug of the hotel suite the second all eight of them stepped inside. They'd done it. They'd beat the Volkov and *lived*. The only member of the Volkov to remain now was Kole, but there was hope that he might give up the chase and let them finish out the rest of this trial.

But that was it. No more Myron. No more running. No more fear that

Noa needed to keep any of the safe—needing to keep *Glacier* safe. She stole a glance at where he'd collapsed onto the end of the couch, abandoning his bag. The others flooded into the kitchen, pulling out bottles and glasses or poked into the nearby rooms.

She stopped in front of him, listening to the keys *clink* with the jerk of his head. He reached for the cord, and she grabbed his hand, leaning in close. "Can we talk in for a minute?" she whispered. "In private?"

He nodded, and she helped him up, strolling past the framed pictures breaking up the windows. She reached for the handle of the last door, her heart fluttering when it opened to a dark, unclaimed room. She held it for him, her thoughts racing when he turned his gemstone eyes on her.

"What did you want to—"

Noa grabbed his shirt and yanked him inside, pushing him against the wall as the door slammed shut. He tensed until her mouth met his, and he reached for her hand clasped around his neck. She pulled back slightly, listening to his shaky breath. *Gods*, she loved his eyes—rich, dark green and blue like crushed velvet searched hers in the pinpricks of light from the city at her back.

"I changed my mind," she breathed. "I don't want to talk."

The slow way his hand tugged at her shirt collar—ever-so-gently pulling her toward him—lit a fire within her as he initiated a tentative kiss back.

30

BELLEGARDE ✧ 2705-01-19

NOA

Light filtered through the white sheets, rippling above her head as Glacier shifted and rolled out of bed. Noa smiled and closed her eyes, her shoulder throbbing to balance out the euphoria she was riding on. The shower kicked on, and she tangled her fingers in her hair.

No rush to get up. No pressure to pack up and leave. She was *free*, and the only thing better was if it could last forever.

Her eyes flew open. They could stop. They didn't need the keys anymore, did they? She'd avenged Lazarus and the Volkov were dismantled. Wasn't that enough? Noa had everything she ever wanted—ever *needed*. Glacier didn't even have to go back to Amarais because they all assumed he was dead anyway. They could go *wherever* they wanted.

Noa sat up, wincing as she crawled out of bed and tugged on her clothes. She tied back her hair, staring at the keys cascading over the night-stand. Grumbling, she pulled the cord over her head, dropping the relics under her shirt with the promise it would be temporary. A once-anchoring weight now nothing but a burden.

The bathroom door opened to Glacier rolling up his sleeves and a towel resting against his head.

"Why don't we take a morning walk?" she asked, unable to tamp down a smile.

The towel fell around his shoulders, and he smiled back—an expression that warmed her all the way through.

They tip-toed down the hall and through the living room, sneaking past a softly snoring Crow and Weather tangled in each other's arms next to the couch. When the door shut behind them, they broke into a shared giggle, letting it expand into a full-on laugh in the elevator. The bubbly sound of relief and joy filled the air in their walk through the lobby and into the bright morning sun.

Noa slipped her hand into his, relishing the way he bumped against her —side-by-side on a walk through the nearby park. Leaves rustled through the tall, bowing trees shading the path, and Noa inhaled the scent of jasmine.

"We're alive," she whispered, loving how his hand squeezed hers.

She imagined them on a walk somewhere else—outside of a little house or an apartment of their own. They'd venture out every day to try a new restaurant and talk about where they'd like to travel. They could move from place to place until they found a spot that felt like home. As long as they woke up next to each other, anywhere would be home for her.

She pulled on his arm. "We can stop," she said, grabbing his other hand. "We don't have to go back to Amarais, Glacier. We can go wherever we want because there's no one left to stop us."

"Noa..."

"Just pick a place, and we'll go. Anywhere, even Valentia. I don't care, as long as we can finally be together. No more running and hiding. Just... *us*."

He started shaking his head, dropping Noa's heart like a stone. "Noa, I can't—"

"Yes, you *can*. You don't own those people anything." She dropped his hands and threw an arm out to the stretch of land between them and Amarais, blocked by mountains covered in the blood of the man who'd kept her from so much. Her voice waivered somewhere between frustration and choking back a sob. "You're so convinced that they'll kill you, yet you still want to go back?"

"I can't just stop here. I have to at least try or everything my father and Kat have worked so hard for will be for nothing, Noa."

"So you'd rather kill yourself than be selfish? To let yourself finally be happy for once in your godsdamned life? I said that I wouldn't let you die. I won't just stand here and let you throw your life away for a bunch of people who never gave a shit about you." She stormed past him, her vision blurring over.

They weren't godsdamned heroes. They were a mess of thieves or *worse*. They could easily abandon it all and fall into obscurity together. They could put this whole mess behind them. They could be *themselves*. But instead, she walked back through the hotel lobby alone. Rode the elevator alone. Walked into the hotel room alone.

She almost spit at Rune when she passed him in the midst of so many confused looks when she collected her bag. Her damn ears perked up at the sound of the door creaking open again, turning to see Glacier timidly picking up his bag.

Nyx either decided to ignore it or didn't care as she stepped in front of Noa, dropping her voice to a whisper. "Noa, I need to talk to you in private."

"Then book another cabin. Glacier can ride with Cecilia and Rune."

Nyx's brows shot up, and Glacier's head turned away.

Good, she thought. If she was going to be miserable, then he should be too.

Nyx led the way down to the lobby, stealing looks at Noa in the awkward silence shared between her, Nyx, and Malice in the taxi to the station. Weather and Crow quietly complained about their hangovers while they waited for the train, and Malice hunched over next to them like a kicked puppy, guilt tripping Noa in her trail behind Glacier, flanked by Cecilia and Rune. Rune's pissed expression with his hand on Glacier's shoulder left her unfazed since Noa was too busy swallowing back her rage.

Noa shoved her bag into the overhead compartment of the cabin, ignoring the pain radiating out from her stitches and straight into her soul. She turned around, and a hand fell across her face with a hard, stinging slap.

Stunned, Noa stared at her, blinking until all her pent-up rage focused on Nyx as her new target. "What the *fuck*—"

"Shut the hell up. It's my turn to talk," Nyx snapped. "Don't think I'm so stupid that I'm unable to figure out what happened back there."

She choked out a dry laugh. "Excuse me?"

"You asked him to run away with you, right? You got your prince, you killed your Volkov, and now you can ride off into the sunset to live happily ever after. But he told you, 'no,' didn't he?"

"Well look at you. You just have it all figured out, don't you?"

"And what about the rest of us, dumbass? We didn't come all this way to help you just to get dumped the second you decide to throw in the towel."

"Then walk away, Nyx. All of you can. I'm done hunting down damn keys on a fool's mission. I never asked for any of this. I only ever wanted control over my own damn life—"

"And you hoped that Glacier would see it the same way, but he didn't."

"Because he feels the idiotic need to throw his life away!"

"*No*, it's because he's a godsdamned Seer, Noa!"

She rocked back. "That's not funny, Nyx."

"Good, because it's not a joke."

Noa's jaw set. "If he were a Seer, don't you think he would've told us? Don't you think at least Cecilia would've known?"

"That's exactly what I thought before I came to the conclusion that *he* doesn't know."

"Out of all the ridiculous—" Laughter bubbled up. "How would he not know? That's the stupidest—"

"How well could Cecilia control her magic when you first met her? Do you honestly think that an Amaraian would understand what was happening to them if they've never really been exposed to anything like it before? Stop and consider all the weird shit he's been doing or saying since we've been traveling with him."

Noa's amusement melted away, replaced by that sinking, horrible feeling in the pit of her stomach. The statue he'd wandered off to back in Biana, his draw to the lotus fountain back in Razbia, his immediate discovery of the emblem back in Casovecchia... *Amarais*—he'd asked about nearby bodies of water after he woke, and they crossed the border into Miralta.

Her blood ran cold, recalling the pinprick of fear she'd felt at the strange question. She hadn't even considered that she would meet yet *another* Mage in Amarais. Stumbling across a fledgling Seer hadn't even come close to crossing her mind. Especially not one so horribly attracted to Noa's end goal—not one that might've accidently fallen into her memories of breathless, soaking cold.

Nyx folded her arms over her chest in a slow, deliberate motion, gently delivering the final blow. "He told me that he's been having strung together dreams with Kat in them, Noa."

Something in her broke. Her knees buckled, dropping her into her seat. Her head fell into her hands. It wasn't Lazarus after all. That's why he had pushed her away instead of letting her save him. He hadn't been her Messenger. He'd just been her guardian to guide her toward *Glacier*. Glacier, a level-headed, tactical Seer that she would have to keep alive to get to the Vault—that would *guide* her to the Vault. But he didn't even realize it yet.

"I..." Nyx said, sitting down next to her. "I... had my suspicious after running into Adam, but... it wasn't until after we left Talie that he mentioned the dreams. I assumed he might've been hiding the fact that he was a Seer from all of us until after he asked those historical questions back in Mharu..." She cleared her throat. "I thought that it would be best for you to be the one to tell him since you're the closest to... well, him and Seers, in general."

And Noa had just tried to damn him by asking him to run from his calling. How long would it have taken her before she noticed his decline in health? How long before she would've realized that she had coerced him into a horrible, *horrible* mistake?

"I don't think he'll even want to talk to me now," Noa whispered. "I just ripped into him for telling me that he had to keep going. Nyx, I... I thought that Lazarus was my counterpart when we discovered all that shit back in Talie, but..."

Nyx squeezed her shoulder. "I don't think he can stay mad at you."

"I'm sorry. I'm sorry I was so selfish, I just—"

"Noa, I can't say that I wouldn't have tried to do the exact same thing."

She pressed her lips together, gathering the strength to stand. Noa stole one last look at Nyx before she pulled the cabin door free, fighting her way past the Esmedralian grasslands whipping past the windows.

CECILIA

When Cecilia had woken up in Rune's warm embrace that morning, she'd been convinced that nothing could ruin her day.

Cecilia and Gabriel Angelis.

She hadn't stopped thinking about it after they'd dropped their bags in the hotel—after they'd created a trail of clothes from their bedroom door all the way to the mattress. It thrummed through her soul whenever they held hands.

But now, seeing Glacier so miserable, every pleasant, hopeful idea slipped through her fingers. She remembered how he and Noa had snuck away together, but everything had seemed *fine*, especially when he didn't emerge before she and Rune had made their exit. They had to have fought, but he didn't answer her whenever she asked another question.

"I'm fine, Cecilia." His tone was gentle, but firm—a lie that she saw right through.

She bit her lip, locking eyes with Rune in his seat across from them in the confines of the cabin. Glacier turned his face to the window again, and Rune's brows knit together as he stood. "How about I grab us something from the dining car? I'm assuming you'll want some tea, right Cecilia? Glacier, do you want anything?"

"Thanks, but I'm not really in the mood for anything right now."

She and Rune exchanged disappointed looks, disrupted by the cabin door sliding open. Noa hovered in the doorway, and Cecilia went rigid, her fists clenching against her lap.

"I'd like to speak with Glacier," Noa said levelly. "Alone."

Cecilia opened her mouth to tell her no, but Glacier's voice cut through with, "It's fine."

Her head whipped around, shocked as a gentle tap pulled her gaze back to Rune. "We were just heading to the dining car anyway," he said.

So, she stood, taking her time brushing off her leggings for one of them to change their mind before she led the way out. When she turned back to Rune, she spotted him whispering something into Noa's ear, his face a hardened mask that made Noa's crumple as he walked away. But she continued inside anyway, and Rune put his hand on Cecilia's back, pushing her toward the next car.

NOA

"I don't know why you two are fighting but go easy on him." Rune had said—words that twisted the dagger Nyx shoved straight into her heart. Admittedly, she was glad Rune was on his side. She didn't deserve anyone's mercy after what she'd said.

"I didn't tell them about how you want to quit," Glacier said, his eyes fixed on a spot along the kaleidoscope-like patterned red, blue, and gold-flecked carpet. "I figured that you would end up telling them yourself."

Another twist. Of course he hadn't told them.

"I'm sorry," she whispered, her voice pitching. His head jerked up in surprise. "I'm a huge dumbass, and I'm sorry. I waited so long for the possibility of *us* that I—"

"Noa..."

She dropped down next to him on the bench. "You have every right to be pissed at me."

The immediate feel of his arms wrapping around her, pulling her into his comforting embrace was like being welcomed home. She hugged him back, grabbing fistfuls of his jacket's thin fabric.

"Noa, I know you don't want me to do this, but I have to try."

She nodded into his shoulder, trying to find her voice, but the wrong words tumbled out instead, "You said you wouldn't let me drown, so I won't let them kill you."

"We're not going to Jinwon."

"What do you *mean* we're not going to Jinwon?" Noa rounded on Nyx, confused after she'd huddled next to Glacier for the past hour and started to notice fields instead of mountains. East instead of west, back toward Bellegarde. She'd told Glacier to meet her in the dining car before storming off to confront her. "I thought we were going to get the next key?"

"Well, since you threw a fit about wanting to drop this quest altogether, I assumed that you wouldn't mind if I sent us on a bit of a detour."

Noa threw her hands up in the air. "Look, I'm *sorry*. I really am."

"Save it. The Mind of Jinwon can wait. I think I have a lead on our missing people in King's, and I want to see if we can gather evidence. If we *can*, we can out these people and end up in the government's good graces once we crack open the Vault."

Noa guffawed. "You want to hunt down our Mage hunters? Have you lost your godsdamned mind?"

"Clearly a little, or else I wouldn't be here." Nyx leaned back in her seat, holding up her phone. "I have an associate that can give us some additional information, plus we can gain access to the office of that man hunting down our twins."

Noa hesitated, wearily taking in Nyx's smirk. "So, you want to grab a ton of dirt?"

"To put us as allies of the Republic and potentially the rest of Avaria, yes. It would help you appear less of a lunatic if you emerge out of nowhere and start calling yourself the *Queen*." Nyx's eyes flicked to the cabin door. "Which reminds me, where's your Seer?"

Noa's hand went to the back of her neck. "So, about that..."

"Good gods, Noa... You didn't tell him, did you?"

"I *tried*, but I couldn't, okay? We made up, but I couldn't bring myself to say that he's a Seer, let alone possibly *my* Seer. He's going to lose his shit when he finds out, and we just survived dealing with the Volkov—"

"Noa," Nyx said, standing up to meet her eye-to-eye the best she could, despite her shorter stature, "if you don't tell him after we leave King's, I'll tell him myself. He *really* won't want to hear it from me, but he *has* to know."

"I know. Just—" She made a frustrated noise. "Just let me figure out the best way to break it to him. I'll tell him, I promise."

"*Before* we leave King's, Noa."

"I will." She dropped down onto her seat, shoulders falling. "Gods, this would be so much easier if he wasn't Amaraian."

Nyx slid off her glasses, rubbing the bridge of her nose. "I think he'd likely say the same, but in a general sense. It seems that it's done nothing but cause him grief." She pushed them back onto her face again, reclaiming the seat across from her. "We have a few days. I would recommend telling him before we reach the city, so he can be better prepared this time around. It's possible that he might have an inkling of where the Vault is."

Noa's hands cupped around her mouth with a sigh. Slicking her hair back, she stood again. "I'll see what I can do."

She pushed her way out of the cabin, stopping in the middle of the corridor as Glacier appeared in the doorway ahead. Every word caught in her throat the moment his eyes lit up.

"I was just looking for you," he said. "Everything all right?"

Noa pressed forward, groaning as she grabbed his arm and dragged him behind her. "I just want to chug coffee and find a will to live..."

"Noa, I don't think we'll have a whole lot of time for you to do *both* of those things before we make it to Jinwon," Glacier argued, trying to pry her hand off.

"*Hey*, if you make me rip my stitches, Nyx will come down here and kick your ass," she warned, holding back a comment about them apparently not going to Jinwon. Noa froze when they stumbled into the dining car, locking eyes with Rune as he raised a brow, along with his mug to his lips.

Glacier nudged her. "You wanted coffee, didn't you?"

She bit back a curse, pulling him over to the ordering station. Plates clinked against metal trays, and they turned around to where Cecilia waved them over. Noa's knuckles turned white as they sat down, stuck face-to-face with a smug-looking Rune.

"Wipe that smirk off your face, or I'll do it for you," she grumbled.

He shook his head and went back to his plate.

KOLE

Kole stared at the tablet in his hands, backdropped by threadbare carpeting and worn, sheer curtains. He rubbed his eyes and reread the note.

```
Kole,
    I know that what you're about to read won't
be easy for you, and I'm sorry. I never wanted
to hurt you, but you have every right to know
the truth. Myron was a liar and a manipulator.
He took care of us because he wanted to use
us, not because he actually cared about us.
    We've all done horrible things, and I'm no
exception. Knowing what I know now, if I were
to go back and change things, I would. He
tried to make us into monsters, and some of us
let him. I don't want you to let him have that
hold over you anymore. You have a chance to
finally be free. Take it.
    You will always be my brother. I love you.

Noa
```

Kole flipped back to the documents—dated files and pulled names so easily strung together his memories fell back into place like puzzle pieces. He wasn't sure how Noa managed to find it all, but she had. And what he found was what he'd always been afraid of: being wrong.

His former home in the snow-covered Amaraian countryside had been one where the lights were always left on. His parents greeted visitors at odd hours of the night, reassuring Kole they were work colleagues. Including Miraltans—the last of which being a boy not much older than twenty-two when they'd met, who'd been able to manipulate electricity. It'd been a skill that excited an eight-year-old Kole whenever he snapped his fingers and brought his toys to life.

The night Kole met Myron, he'd been upstairs in his room, reading homework on his tablet and trying to block out the argument coming from the main floor. It was always something about numbers and weird words that didn't make sense, but whenever Kole walked in on them, his parents' mouths snapped shut, traded in for smiles. That night, a yell echoed up the steps, and Kole dropped his tablet in his rush to the door.

Blood pooled around the stairs, lapping at the boots of a tall man with reddish-brown hair. His gaze slid up to Kole's wide blue eyes before he sprinted back into his room and shimmied under the bed. Kole's heart pounded in time with the boots pounding against the steps. The bedroom door squealed open as Kole pressed himself up against the wall. A knee dropped to the carpet, then a hand, and finally the man's gray eyes peered back at him.

"Come on out. You're safe now."

Those smooth, easy-to-swallow lies spilled out from Myron's lips about the Mage killing his parents, and how Myron had been a little late for them but just in time for Kole. Eventually, Kole crawled out, and Myron scooped him up, pressing his face into his shoulder as he carried him out into the snow. He never saw the bodies—never saw what remained of his parents. Kole never questioned whether or not Myron had lied to him that night because he couldn't make himself accept anything but the lie he'd been fed. After all, why would some non-Amaraian stranger would rescue him instead of kill him?

But Kole tugged the carefully wrapped ribbon of a lie away from his box of repressed memories, lifting the lid to find what he'd known all along:

the Mage hadn't killed them, Myron had. Myron killed them all because they'd orchestrated a network of Mage hosting in Amarais—the very thing Kole had grown up to despise, feeding on the idea that magic had killed them when it hadn't.

And he'd been a damn fool for buying into it. For buying into Myron's lies and ripping into Noa for taking Glacier's side. For wanting to kill a prince that his parents would've stood behind. What would they think of him? They'd probably stare at him like he was a monster, just like that Amaraian girl on that train after he told her to kill herself because of her magic.

Kole squeezed his eyes shut, wanting to take it all back. He didn't deserve the forgiveness Noa wanted to give him. He didn't have a right to any of it after he had carried out the hate his parents had worked so hard to fight against. He simply wanted to fade from existence, but he was too much of a coward to even get rid of himself. So instead, Kole lay back on the bed and stared at the ceiling while he tried to force himself to accept his mistakes.

31
TABIR ✧ 2704-12-05

NOA

"So let me get this straight..." Weather spoke up, her arms folded over her chest as she leaned against the cabin window. "We're going *back* to Kingsheart."

"Correct," Nyx said.

"And why the hell would we *want* to do that?"

"Because," Noa began, resting her arms against her knees from her spot along one of the benches, "we know that there's someone hunting Mages in Kingsheart, and we might have a lead. So we're going to get as much information as we can and get out."

"I can agree with that part, but I have one *additional* request if we're going back." Weather held up a finger. "I'd like to kick the ass of a certain Giovanni Fontaine."

"*Weather...*" Rune growled.

"Is he connected to your former employer, Rune?" Nyx asked, pulling his attention away from her with a hint of surprise.

"He unfortunately seems to be... Why?"

"If that's the case, then we might be able to use him for some additional information to take down your ex-boss. I don't know *exactly* how much dirt we can get on him, but I figure it's best to get whatever we can find."

"Sounds like you got yourself a deal." Noa smirked. "What flavor of crazy do you want? You got me or Malice." Down the row, Malice's eyes lit up as Glacier bumped into Noa's shoulder. He jumped slightly as she wove her fingers through his, tethering her to his soothing presence. Regret pulsed through her when he shared a brief smirk, calling on that wretched reminder of Nyx's ultimatum.

Her trance broke with Weather tapping a finger against her lips. "Let me think on it. I mainly want to scare the shit out of him, but I'm not exactly *opposed* to killing him."

"Do *not* kill him," Rune said. "He may be a scumbag of a human being, but I think one of us killing him will just make things worse."

"Okay, *fine*." She patted Malice on the head. "Sorry, sweetheart, but I'm going to have to go with Noa." Malice pouted, and Weather crouched down to console her.

Crow bit his lip, scowling. "How, exactly, do you plan on getting anything on Arrington when the man practically *lives* in his office? I think he *sleeps* under his damn desk."

"We have low Mage restrictions, and an Illusionist," Nyx said, shrugging. "They don't have any illusionary magic detection to get into the building because no one's ever been caught pulling anything like walking in as someone else before. So, we have two direct reports to Arrington that no one would bat an eye at if they walked into his office, correct?"

Rune hesitated but nodded. "I don't think Cecilia should—"

"I'm not suggesting for you and Cecilia to go. I'm saying that we go back to the original pair of you and Noa for this. If something *does* go wrong, and Arrington happens to be in his office, Noa can improvise while I work to get you out. As useful as Cecilia would be with you, I've also confirmed that there's someone in the building that would *love* the idea that a Mage simply *walked* right in to greet them."

Cecilia shuddered, and Rune's expression darkened.

"That's what I thought," Nyx said. "We're fortunate that his direct reports are a man and a woman so at least Noa can sneak in with you."

Cecilia tugged on her hair. "What if they need to talk? I can't exactly disguise their voices..."

"I'm fairly good at mimicry," Rune said, "and if Noa's going as who I *think* she's going as, I'll be the one doing most of the talking. Shane and Jinko, right?"

Nyx nodded.

"Good. Shane's a dumbass who puts his foot in his mouth more often than not. Jinko likes to sit back and let it happen."

Noa smirked. "I kind of like this woman."

Crow scoffed. "Yeah, too bad you're about seven centimeters taller and not a *raging bitch*."

Rune hummed, frowning down at Cecilia. "She wears heels to make herself taller, so I don't suppose we can fake that?"

"I can *try*..."

"Regardless," Nyx said, "I'll have eyes on the inside with clearance to get you through the checkpoint you need to gain entry to Arrington's office. You just need to involve her as little as possible in the process in order not to implicate her as an accomplice. Keep the talk to a minimum. She's a direct report to Shane, but she has to defer to Jinko if Shane's absent."

"So we're just using her as a key to get past the doors and into his office?" Rune asked.

"Correct. Take her with you into his office, wait a few minutes, and then dismiss her. That way she'll have plausible deniability when you scan her card at each entry. According to her, *you* will be the one to scan your card to get in, but the scans will claim it was *her* because you swiped it off of her. Just make sure to swing by her office and drop it before you get the hell out. The plan is to spend no longer than twenty-four hours in Kingsheart. Immediately following this data grab, we jump on the train and head straight back to Jinwon for our twelfth key. Then, after that—"

"We head for Amarais to collect our thirteenth key," Noa finished.

32

KING'S REPUBLIC ✧ 2705-01-19

NOA

Noa absently fidgeted with Glacier's jacket zipper while the two of them laid on the pull-out cabin bed. It was surreal laying this close to him, like she'd fallen into a dream she never wanted to wake from. Purple sky tore past the window, casting his eyes in midnight hues. He was hers in so many ways, including ones she never wished for, but now...

"What are you thinking about?" he whispered.

"About... *everything*," she said with a short laugh, relived he was a Seer and not a Reader, or he'd definitely see that she was skirting the truth.

"Amarais?"

"Yeah," she breathed. Not a complete lie since she still wasn't sure if the entire resistance would rally under him. They only had Cecilia's mother and Ariadne to bet on, but they still didn't know who sat in charge of it all or if either of them had any say. She hoped it would be enough, but if it wasn't, they'd find another way—mainly because they had to.

"We still don't know where the Vault is either," he said, concern slipping through. "How are we supposed to open it if we don't know where to find it?"

Kingsheart sprung to the forefront of Noa's thoughts, imagining the possibility that it was sitting somewhere in the heart of the city, waiting for Glacier to find it. "I think maybe it's somewhere in Kingsheart," she said, gently planting that idea in his mind. Her thumb pressed into the zipper, unable to force out the rest of what needed to be said. It felt too cruel to heave all of it onto him, or maybe it was her being selfish since she'd finally been able to enjoy their first pillow talk.

Glacier frowned, chewing on his lip. "I'm... not so sure..."

Noa swallowed back her surprise, telling herself he'd know better than she would. "Then where do *you* think it is?"

Trees flitted past, casting him in eerie shadow while his face contorted in thought.

"I don't know," he breathed. "Maybe it is in Kingsheart? I'm not sure. There's too many possibilities and not enough proof."

Noa sighed, her heart sinking at the realization he'd second-guessed his instincts. "Then let's just sleep on it." She snuggled into his chest, warming at the sound of his chuckle.

"Maybe you can ask one of your many Seers where it is," he joked.

Noa clutched the fabric of his shirt, glad he couldn't see her face. "Yeah... maybe."

His arms encircled her, and she focused on the flickering of shadows until she fell asleep.

GLACIER

Glacier opened his eyes to small cracks in the ceiling, spanning out from the platinum chandelier bathed in an orange glow. Another item to add to his growing list of problems. He forced himself up, running a finger over the layer of dust on the side table as he nudged the rug's corner back into place.

When he started into the hall, he kept his distance from the windows on his way to the entry, where Kat sat in one of the armchairs. One of the books from the office rested in her lap and a glass of liquor sat on the small table beside her.

Typical.

Her blue eyes flicked up to him. "Are you finally ready to stop fooling around, or...?"

He folded his arms over his chest, and she sighed, closing her book and sliding it onto the table. Dust motes swirled upward as she stood and patted her leggings. A smile pulled at her lips when she stopped in front of him. "I *really* want to strangle you in the nicest way possible."

Glacier rolled his eyes, considering the most obnoxious thing he could do in that moment. It came to him with a smirk. "*Why* can't you tell me what I should already know?"

"Glacier."

"Oh, wait. You can't answer that, can you? And yet I'm supposed to ask you questions, but I can't just ask *any question* because that would be too easy—"

"How are you so smart, yet so incredibly stupid?"

"What are you so damn cryptic? It's not like—"

A scratching sound sent a chill through him, and the two of them spun to face the front door.

"Did...you invite someone over?" he whispered, watching her head shake out of the corner of his eye. He swallowed, taking a couple steps forward and jumped as a loud, reverberating pound shook the glass on the table.

Kat grabbed his arm, tugging him back. "Do *not* open that damn door," she hissed.

A slam, and they both ducked. Glacier's heart raced, moving faster and faster to match the increasing speed of the the strikes growing closer and closer together. It cracked and buckled. His legs wobbled, and panic seized his throat as Kat's fingers dug into his jaw, forcing him to face her.

"Glacier, you *need* to listen to me," she ordered. "You need to *wake up*."

33

KING'S REPUBLIC ✧ 2705-01-20

GLACIER

Glacier shot up, gasping for breath. His head spun and the room blurred, twisting and shifting into something unrecognizable. No frost. No blood. No body. And yet... He tried to untangle his legs while shadowy shapes sat up in the dark corners of the room.

Oh gods.

Kat's name stuck in his throat as something grabbed his arm.

"Let *go*—"

He tried to wrench it free, smacking into the padded wall. Trapped. He was trapped. His breathing quickened as a woman's voice cut through the panic of his thoughts, though the words sounded garbled. Her hands cupped his face, her dark eyes searching his with a glimmer of concern.

"Noa," he breathed, finally pulling up a name.

"You're okay," she whispered. "It's okay."

His arm loosed from her grasp, and he rubbed at his eyes. "Just a nightmare..." he mumbled, more to himself than anyone else. Noa's fingers traced his sleeve, her palm pressing into his bicep and guiding him back down to the bed. Her lips found his forehead, steadying his breathing as he wrapped an arm around her to anchor himself to reality. The feel of her fingers combing through his hair allowed him to close his eyes again, but he knew he wouldn't be able to fall back asleep—not after whatever *that* was.

From Noa's movements, he could tell she wouldn't be sleeping again either. So the two of them basked in the silence that remained once Nyx turned over in her bunk, saying nothing until the first signs of morning.

NOA

Noa scrubbed at her face after breakfast, slowly working through sorting her luggage in the cabin while Nyx stared her down.

"You want to talk about the night-terrors, or...?" Nyx asked.

Her hands stopped, refusing to make eye contact with her. Instead, she pictured Glacier's confused, terrified expression—zero recognition of who she was. Her stomach had dropped, afraid that she'd run out of time.

"Honestly? No, I really *don't* want to discuss that."

"Noa, it's going to get *worse*."

"Yes, Nyx. I'm well aware that it can get so much worse."

"When's the first time you can remember him doing something or saying something that screams 'Seer'?"

Noa bit her tongue and mumbled, "Amarais..."

"*Noa—*"

"Godsdamnit, Nyx—I know—*I know*, okay?" Noa exhaled, resting her hands on her head while enduring Nyx's scowl. "I'm going to take care of it."

"Today," Nyx ordered.

"You said *before* we leave King's, so I'll tell him before we leave King's."

"Why wait?" Nyx motioned to the door. "Do you *want* him to start trying to fight you in his sleep?"

"Look, we need to deal with everything in Kingsheart *first*, and if Glacier's a mess, then he might do something incredibly *stupid*. And *then*, not only am I down a boyfriend that I waited a very long time to get, but I'll be down the Seer I'm undoubtedly tied to because that's just my damn luck."

"Fine," Nyx said. "But I'll be keeping an eye on him, and if he starts to lose it while you're working, I won't have a choice but to give it to him straight."

"Fair enough," Noa breathed.

GLACIER

The narrow stairwell to their temporary apartment reeked of spoiled food —the last thing Glacier wanted at 11PM when he was running off of little sleep and barely any food. He covered his nose with his sleeve as he followed Nyx up the steps, swaying while his stomach lurched, threatening to empty out the rest of its contents.

The apartment itself wasn't much better. A two-bedroom for eight people with ice cold or scalding hot water made him long for escape back into the other reality—the one where Kat was still alive, and he'd never left Amarais. But he knew he had to help Nyx. Dream or no, that was his goal. His drive. His reason to keep pressing forward, even though each hazy movement felt like pushing through water.

The mug next to him always managed to stay filled, and the coffee maker's tune kept the living room alive in the midst of glowing screens and dim lamps. Those who refused to sleep traded hushed stories and joined into phone games, telling those who were involved in tomorrow's plans to rest. None did, not that he could blame them when they were all already asleep.

34

KING'S REPUBLIC ✧ 2705-01-21

WEATHER

Weather stood in front of the whirring advertisements on the candy-red cased slot machine, watching her reflection in the monitor shift from a tanned Valentian woman to her pale Corvian-Republican. Her fingers rubbed together with the remnants of Cecilia's travel eyeliner. The idea of being whoever she wanted to be on a whim pulled her soul from her body —detached from the world around her like she was weightless.

Free.

Powerful.

She hoisted up the plush-cushioned stool, flipping it around like the makeshift weapon she'd hit Talon with. Only this time, she was pouring all her rage into a man who'd manipulated her and pushed her around for his own personal gain. She knew the world wasn't fair, but she'd taken enough shit not to fight back. And that made the crunch of glass sound so much sweeter.

Weather moved down the aisle to the next machine, unable to suppress a sinister grin. Another screen sparked and flickered in her wake, pumping adrenaline through her veins before a deep, booming voice ordered her to stop.

Just one more.

A pop, hiss—then tinkling from the casino tokens caressing each other on their way to the carpet. They rolled around her feet, falling flat as they hit her boots.

"What the *fuck* do you think you're doing?"

Weather spun around, staring down a fuming casino owner. She tossed down the stool and brushed her hands together with a lazy grin. "Hello, Giovanni."

"Why the hell are you back here, you stupid bitch?" His face reddened like he was about to burst a blood vessel.

"What? You think I wouldn't have the balls to come back? I'm done running, Gio, *honey.*"

"Don't let this bitch leave," Giovanni ordered his following of sloppy-suited goons.

They all advanced down the aisle toward her, so she waited, her pulse thrumming with every step until she couldn't take it anymore. She bolted, whipping down the next row. The electronic lockpick at her waist clicked and whirred to life—exactly like she'd requested from Nyx—and coins poured out of machine after machine in her wake.

Shouts and cries of surprise followed, feeding her euphoria as she kicked over stools. She skidded to a stop in the middle of the game tables, turning to find two men and Giovanni remaining.

"I think you lost a few." She pointed to the space around him.

"Look here, you stupid little whore—" Giovanni growled, pushing up his sleeves as he stalked toward her.

A thrill shot through Weather as a shadow fell from the second floor, dropping onto one of the men as the other went for his belt with a yelp. He raised it, and it was twisted from his hand. A punch in the throat sent him to his knees, and a kick in the head sent him sprawling. Giovanni whipped around, backing up against one of the tables.

Noa pulled off her mask and let it dangle between her fingers.

"Who the fuck are you?" Giovanni's voice pitched while he slid along the table, working along the edge.

"I wouldn't run if I were you," Noa said, flipping a token in her hand. "I'm honestly pretty damn fast. You might've heard a thing or two about me from your father." She tossed it to him, and his eyes widened before it dropped like it'd burned him. A V jutting out from a triangle gleamed in the light of the chandeliers.

"It's this some kind of fucking joke?" he demanded, his voice still hard with rage but teetering on the edge of panic.

Weather chuckled, moving to stand next to Noa. "Oh, I assure you, Gio, it's *not*. And you have a few questions you're going to answer for me, or my new friend here *will* kill you. So, here's my first question to determine just how painful this is going to be for you: what were you planning on doing with that knife on your desk?"

Giovanni licked his lips, his eyes darting between them.

"Answer her damn question," Noa snapped.

His knees buckled, dropping him to the carpet. Then he started from very beginning, all the way from the phone call he'd received from Wilton Arrington.

ALYVIA

Alyvia fumbled with the phone in her hand, the vibration pulsing through her fingertips as she stared at the caller ID. It read, 'Mom' with a little black heart. She put it to her ear, hunching over her desk. "Mom?" She stole a glance at her coworkers, but all of them chatted and tapped their monitors.

"Walk out into the hallway," came Nyx's instructions. "Keep going for three or four meters and face the wall. Keep talking to me."

Her chair scraped against the tile, her heart thumping at the sound of this woman's voice. It was strange to finally hear her, rather than read her words on a screen. "Yes, Mom—I had that shipped to the house. Give me a second to check the tracking on it..." She slipped out into the hall. The door swung shut behind her and she counted her paces until she faced the wall. "It says it was just delivered."

"Go with them."

Alyvia frown, jumping when someone tapped her shoulder. She spun around, and her mouth went dry. Shane and Jinko. She pointed to the phone before Nyx's instruction clicked.

"Arrington wants us in his office. Let's go," Shane said, jerking a thumb toward the double doors to the next wing. There was something about the movement that didn't strike her as Shane-like. Maybe it was how his other hand half-tucked in his pocket, but his posture was *off*.

"Do what they say. Delete this contact when you get to the office," Nyx finished, and then the line when dead.

Alyvia sucked in a breath and shoved her phone in her pocket. Jinko pressed a badge to the keypad, and they started toward the office again. The necklace didn't pulse in warning, even when Shane started acting less fussy and casual about his appearance—more like Shane. They popped open the door to Arrington's office and filed inside. Shane flicked on the lights, motioning to the table and cushy chairs off to the side, but there was no Arrington in sight.

Shane seated himself with his back to the hall window, forcing her to take the seat opposite him while Jinko prowled to the other side of the office, completely out of view.

"I wanted to talk about your current performance, as an impromptu evaluation," he started.

"I thought my evaluation was—"

"Next month? Well," —he shrugged— "you've clearly been putting in the work lately, so I've managed to get you a raise. It'll kick in after next month since there's only so much I can do with the red tape of bureau-cracy, but it's there."

Alyvia stopped paying attention to his words in favor of the cadence of his voice. It was slightly off—something she wouldn't notice on a phone call, but in person it gave him away as someone other than the Shane she knew.

"Is... that all you wanted to talk to me about?" she asked hesitantly, and Shane smiled. It was a cordial, relaxed smile that blossomed behind his eyes in a way she hadn't noticed from the real one.

"That's all, Alyvia."

She stood. "Thank you—" She cut herself off, unable to say his name because it felt wrong. Instead, she nodded, and he rose to show her out.

Alyvia's footsteps sounded quiet in the bustle of the hallway. She stepped through the double-doors with a small hoard of people on her way back to her desk in a surreal daze. Reclaiming her seat, the necklace tingled against her skin. When she looked up, Jinko's office door shut.

RUNE

A quiet, angry beeping sounded from the hacking tool as Noa forced open one of the desk drawers on Rune's way over to help.

"Remember to put everything back where you found it," he mumbled, running a gloved finger over the shelves. He'd sworn there was something off about this bookcase whenever he and Crow had stood in front of his desk, being forced to wait while he pulled up various documents on his machine. Several of those office visits included Shane, who'd perused Arrington's décor much like Rune was doing now.

It'd also been the reason why it'd taken everything in him not to look Alyvia dead in the eyes with a hand on his chest and say, "I'm a huge asshole."

Noa pulled out her phone snapped a few pictures with her phone, keeping an eye on the disc humming against the desktop. He chewed on his lip, squinting at one book distinctly lacking dust in front of it. Rune tugged it out, and a slip of synthetic paper flitted to the floor. He shoved the book back into place and knelt to retrieve it.

It unfolded to set of coordinates, along with a set of numbers and letters. He held it under his phone for a picture and replaced it. "I think we'll have to make another stop after this," he breathed.

"Fine by me," Noa muttered, tugging open another drawer. The disc blinked rapidly, and she popped it off the desk. "And it looks like Nyx got everything she was looking for... Anything else you want to violate before we leave?" She smirked.

Rune rolled his eyes. "As much as I'd love to leave him a note, I'll pass for now. He'll get what's coming to him later once Nyx decrypts his files. Let's go." He nodded toward the office door.

She shoved Alyvia's badge into his hand on their way down the hall, slipping out with the other employees. He left Noa staring in one of the windows to fret over her glamour while he ducked into the tech lab and grabbed the back of Alyvia's chair. She tensed as he leaned over and tucked her badge under a small stack of synthetic paper.

"Your boss is a dick," he said quietly in his own voice with a smile, and her eyes widened.

He stood up straight, fidgeting with his tie on the way out.

"Shane."

Jinko.

"Shit," he hissed as Noa whipped around. "*Go.*" He nodded towards the elevator, the two of them outpacing the click of Jinko's heels. Noa jammed her finger against the elevator button, and the doors parted like a sign from the gods. He repeatedly pressed the close button once they were inside, watching Jinko's jaw drop at the sight of her very own replica. Noa wiggled her fingers in mock goodbye as the elevator doors shut.

Noa grinned up at him. "That was *too good.*"

He couldn't help but smirk on their sprint out of the building.

35

KING'S REPUBLIC ✧ 2705-01-21

NOA

They took a detour to purchase new clothes and change before plugging in their mystery destination. Noa pulled down the hood of her new jacket to obscure her face without Cecilia's glamour, keeping an eye on Rune to make sure his face was shadowed under his snapback. The graying sky was as good of an excuse as any with more and more umbrellas appearing under arms of residents wearing university-logo sweatshirts, prepared for the slushy mix of rain and snow.

"So you have no idea where we're going?" Noa asked under her breath, peering at the map display.

"If I knew, then I would tell you. I don't even know what the rest of the information is for yet..."

They stopped at a platform for the next commuter train, blending in by busying themselves with their phones. When their ride hissed to a stop, they climbed on, watching the buildings shift from district to district until Rune nudged her. They hopped out as thunder rolled overhead, and Noa urged him to pick up the pace.

"Nyx is going to be *pissed* if we end up running late."

"It's just ahead," he said, nodding toward the boxy apartment building.

"Okay…" Noa frowned, examining the dimmed windows. No way to tell which might be their destination.

Rune swapped from the map to the picture of the note as they strolled up the set of steps. His finger hovered over the keypad before punching in a code. The light flashed green, and Noa pushed it open. A dull, beige hallway greeted them, the doors nearly flush in their frames. Rune crept toward the elevator with her on his heels. Number pads sat above door-knobs with keys worn down from overuse—all dated tech.

"I think it's on the fourth floor…" He tilted his phone for her to see as a ding rippled through the silent intersection.

"44B," Noa whispered. "What the hell would Arrington need a run-down apartment for?"

"Maybe it's filled with drives and drives of blackmail," Rune grumbled before the doors opened again. They started down the next hall, turning to an apartment tucked into one of the far back corners. Noa imagined it must have a lovely view of the alleyway.

"I'm assuming there's a keycode on the note?" Noa asked.

He nodded slowly, pressing in each number until they got another green light. Noa pushed the door open slightly, squinting into the dark recesses of a yellowing kitchen and another beige hallway. No violent reaction to their presence or blaring alarm, so she shoved it the rest of the way open and hit the lights.

Her boots tapped against the linoleum as Rune shut the door. A flimsy, folding table sat in the corner, and a few folding chairs scattered around it in the kitchen and bare living room. The only thing they appeared not to skimp on were the floor-to-ceiling black out curtains.

"All right. I guess it's not a vacation home…" Noa mumbled, making her way down the hall. She popped open the first door, and light flooded the off-white tiles of the bathroom. She frowned and moved on to peek around Rune on his journey to the next door.

An empty room with more light-blocking curtains. Her brows furrowed, and she stalked down the curve of the hall to the final room, pushing it open to one filled with bookcases—bookcases cluttered with filing boxes, lining the walls and covering the closet and windows. Another folding table sat in the middle of the room, but this one had a sheet thrown over it, covering a small bulge in the center.

Noa stared down at it, stepping forward until she pinched the fabric between her fingers. Rune hovered behind her, his breath hot on her neck as she ripped it away, and the world fell out from under her. A grimoire sat on the table, it's dark gray cover pressed with a dented circle like a sun-swallowing eclipse.

"That fucking bastard—" Rune growled.

Noa scooped it off the table, trying not to throw up from the stickiness of the cover.

Rune seized her arm. "Noa, we *can't*, I know you want to—hell, *I* want to—but we can't destroy it because he'll know someone was here, and he might even suspect *us*—"

"Let go."

"*Noa*—"

"If you don't let me destroy this, then I will *never* forgive you."

"Noa, of the two of us, I would love nothing more than to destroy it—"

"It's not just *you* anymore, Rune," she snapped. "Glacier is a *godsdamned Seer*."

His eyes went wide, and she shook off his arm, storming past him to the kitchen. She ripped open drawer after drawer, searching for the right damn tool. The lighter felt heavy in her hands like a proper weapon. Her stomach heaved as she flicked it on, making her way to the bathroom. No smoke alarm, but her head spun with the distorted image of Astor laying in the tub.

The little voice in her head tried to tell her she was no better than the owners of this book, even as the flame climbed up the side, gnawing at the pages. She stood over it, watching it collapse, twist, and fold in on itself with Rune standing next to her.

He followed her when she decided it was destroyed, saying nothing on their train ride back to their own shithole of an apartment. The last student they'd been sharing the car with ducked into the rain, and Rune's gentle voice cut through her empty mind.

"Why didn't you tell me? Who else knows?"

"Just Nyx," Noa clipped, staring at her warped reflection in the aluminum pole.

"Why didn't Glacier tell Cecilia?" he demanded. "They're practically family—"

"Because he doesn't know, Rune."

"*What?* How? How do you and Nyx know but he—"

"Nyx started noticing his weird behavior after we ran into that guy in Talie... He thought Glacier was a Mage, remember?"

Rune nodded, waiting like he expected her to continue.

"So... she started to pay a little more attention, and... he's been having dreams. With Kat in them." Tears welled up in her eyes, hating the uncertainty of whether or not she should blink to clear them away or if they'd fall instead.

"Gods, Noa..." Rune rubbed his face.

"I thought Nyx was lying when she told me, but then I remembered he'd said something strange back in Amarais—I... I think he saw one of my memories and didn't realize it."

"How long have you known?" Rune finally asked.

"Since we left Razbia a few days ago. I kept trying to tell him, but I..." Noa shook her head and let out a bitter laugh. "How do you tell someone that they're a *Mage* when their entire country has done nothing but murder them for *years*? He's already half-Miraltan, and he's just going to look at all of the strikes against him and—"

"I already promised Cecilia that if they try to kill Glacier that he'll come with us. Cecilia refused to leave him behind, and weeks ago, she was afraid that you might, which clearly isn't the case."

"Rune, think about it for a second. Just... think about the story." She let out a breath. "I don't think he's just *any* Seer..." She looked up at him, pleading for him to understand.

"You think that he's *your* Seer..."

"I used to think that it was Lazarus, but I think that son of a bitch knew the whole time, which is why he wouldn't let me save him. I have to

tell him. *Gods*—I don't want to because it's going to kill him to hear it."
She sucked in a sharp breath, feeling Rune squeeze her arm.

"If it'll make it easier, I can tell everyone else," he whispered. "Okay?
It'll be okay. We won't abandon him, even if all of Amarais does, remember
that. He has Cecilia and her family, he has all of us, and he has *you*, Noa."

"Thank you."

Her time was up. Once they got on the train, she would tell him.

SHANE

Shane loosened his tie after his eighth and final meeting of the day—final
only because he refused to go to another. He rummaged through his desk,
collected the bare minimum he needed to take with him, and threw his bag
over his shoulder right as a shadow darkened his doorway.

"Shane," Jinko said, starting to shut the door behind her, "we need to
tal—"

"I don't have time to talk," he ground out, pushing past her. "Whatever
it is, it can wait." She chased after him for a few steps, making a strangled,
frustrated noise as he headed for the elevators.

It *could* wait. It could wait because his quarry was back in the city, and
he'd be damned if he'd let it slip away again.

Past kiosks, pedestrians, and turnstiles, his senses overwhelmed him like
plunging into pool of cold water on a hot day—refreshing but painful on
first impact. People chattering on their phones fluctuated from muffled to
blaring, sending his head spinning while he followed that instinctual path.
He shuffled through droves of people lining up on station platforms, and
his heart threatened to beat out of his chest when he realized he was
drawing closer and closer to one of the platform gates.

Shane cursed and bolted past, scanning terminal after terminal until his
body slowed next to a gate that'd began boarding. His eyes grew wide,
taking in the woman from the cameras—the one from the museum, barely
able to make out her features under her hood. And what he'd been
searching for walked right next to her.

The boy's head turned, his Miraltan-green eyes clouded with confusion before the woman following his gaze and seized him by the arm. Shane scrambled to push through the gate, smacking a fist against screen that demanded his ticket. He sprinted to the kiosk to purchase one and found the option grayed out. The doors closed. The train hissed. It was over.

Shane slumped onto a bench, watching it crawl out of the station. His phone buzzed, and he pulled it out to find Jinko's name scrawled across the display.

"Shane, someone burned the damn book."

The phone's plastic frame cried out in his grip as the final car of the train disappeared. "I think I know exactly who did it."

GLACIER

"What the hell was that?" Glacier demanded, rounding on Noa as she locked the cabin door.

"Someone I'd rather not have following us," she growled, dumping her bag on the floor. "Glacier, we need to talk."

His gaze flicked to the door, then back to her before folding his arms with annoyance. "Noa, I'd rather not have us needing to 'talk' be your go-to for whenever you're feeling like ripping my clothes off."

"Wha—No! No, I actually mean *talk* this time." She pointed to the bench, silently ordering him to sit.

His arms slowly fell back to his sides, and he shuffled over to take his seat, wearily watching her. There'd definitely been something wrong with that guy back there, but she'd ripped him away before he could determine what he found so strange. Her anxiety radiated out from her though, feeding his own until his hands started to sweat.

She exhaled and chewed on her lip while she readjusted her hair tie.

"You're kind of freaking me out," he said. "What's wrong?"

She dropped down next to him, gathering up his hands in her own and giving them a squeeze.

"Glacier, I don't know how to say this..." she mumbled. "Do you remember the story I had you tell back in Miralta?"

He nodded slowly. "I'm pretty sure that's why we're all here right now."
He let out a nervous laugh. "It's a little hard to forget."

"I'm specifically referring to the King and his Messenger. Originally, I
thought that one of them can exist without the other, but I'm now pretty
sure that they *can't*. They're a set. If I exist as the next person to claim
Avaria, there's a Seer specifically for me to make sure I don't back out and
stop what needs to happen."

"Lazarus."

Noa winced, shaking her head. "Not Lazarus. Lazarus wouldn't let me
save him because he knew that it might prevent me from finding *my* Seer."
She squeezed his hands again, and a thrum of unease pulsed through him.
"Glacier, it's *you*."

He stared at her, trying to rationalize that he'd misheard. His brows
furrowed as he pulled his hands away and forced out a nervous laugh.
"Noa, just because you and I are—That doesn't mean that—" He stood,
and she mirrored the movement, his stomach dropping when that serious,
remorseful expression didn't yield.

"Whether or not I like you because you're my Seer or fate decided to
make you my Seer *because* it knew that I would stupidly fall for you doesn't
matter—"

Glacier shook his head more emphatically. "I'm *not* a Seer, Noa. I
can't be—"

She reached for his arm, and his back smacked against the cabin
window. The room tilted and warped as he struggled to breathe. It's a
dream. He was still stuck in a damn dream—nightmare—*whatever*.

"I know you don't like the idea of—"

"That's *enough*, Noa." He tried to push past her, stumbling when she
cut in front of him. Another attempt, but he took a step back, afraid to get
too close because she'd restrain him. "Just let me *out*," he begged.

The regret in her eyes snapped his heart in half. "I know you've been
having dreams. Dreams with Kat. And I can't help but think about when
we were training in Tabir and you managed to surprise me—And in Valentia, where you somehow *knew* where the Vision was... You didn't have to
look for it. Hell, I doubt you could've even seen it through all those parti-

tions. That doesn't even cover all your random disappearances whenever I turn around, and you just happen to end up at something related to the keys—"

"*I said stop!*" His whole body trembled, and his hands clapped over his eyes. He heard Noa's soft step forward against the carpet, and he bumped back against the window. He shook his head, his thoughts spinning with the memories of every single incident he'd written off as a strange compulsion of stress.

"Do you remember after we first met back in Amarais? Back when you fell asleep in the car with the others?" she asked quietly.

His hands pulled away from his face, feeling stricken as he met her eyes.

"When we got out and started walking across the border to Miralta, you asked me if there were any lakes or ponds around because you didn't want to walk across ice. What did you dream about before we got out of the car?"

He swallowed. "I... dreamt that I was trapped beneath the ice, and I couldn't get out. I just remember a shadowy figure walking away above it..." He refused to label the figure as Myron and admit he'd seen the body. He didn't even want to admit any of this to Noa in the first place. "Then I was just pounding as hard as I could on the ice, trying to escape."

Noa's face crumpled, her shoulders falling. "That wasn't a dream, Glacier. It was one of my memories."

Noa—Are you hydrophobic?

His stared past her, his knees buckling and taking him straight to the floor. The world around him might as well have stilled, even as Noa knelt down at his side, grabbing his knee. A Seer. A Mage. A Miraltan. A bastard prince. So many labels that tightened a noose around his neck.

"What am I supposed to do?" he breathed, his vision blurring. "How am I supposed to go back to Amarais like *this?*" He dug the heels of his hands into his eyes, trying to keep the tears at bay. After all this time trying to tell himself he wouldn't die because Noa promised him...

Noa pulled his arms down and cupped his face. Her thumb traced over Cecilia's invisible rune, rubbing it away to reveal his blue eye—the only Amaraian piece of him now. There was no way he could stand in front of a country he was supposed to command with the knowledge they'd call for his head.

Her nose bumped against his. "If they even consider trying to kill you, they'll have to get through *me* first. You're *my* Seer, and if they don't want you, then they don't deserve to have you. But the one thing I won't allow is for them to take you from me. Once we find the Vault, they won't get a say in what either of us do, and if you don't want to take the crown, then I'll find someone else to do it. Then they'll fix that mess of a damn country, and you won't have to step foot in it again unless you want to. You'll be with me, and *no one* will bother you because they'll know that they'll have to deal with my wrath."

She wrapped her arms around him, knotting her fingers into his hair as he buried his face into her neck with a quiet sob. All of his hopes and dreams for taking the place of his father or Kat crumbled in hands. He was nothing they were, someone completely ill-equipped to take on whatever lay ahead of him.

So, Glacier finally let his body give in to the struggle that he had been fighting since the train ride to Kingsheart and slipped into sleep.

Glacier woke to the crackle of the familiar faux fireplace. No dust tickled his nose. No rugs curled up at the corners. No gloominess hung in the air. He pushed himself up, sitting face-to-face with Kat. The numbness gave way to fresh pain—a torrent of emotions ripping through him with the realization the fuzziness was gone.

"You're dead," he whispered.

Sighing, she moved to sit next to him. "Unfortunately, yes. I am, in fact, dead." She put a hand on his shoulder with a sad smirk.

"Is it *really* you, or just... me, wanting you to exist?"

"I think you're pretty spot-on if this is your imagination of me, Glacier. I'd be a little concerned, but extremely impressed." She chuckled. "I'm real."

"Did it hurt?"

She tilted her head, confused before she winced. "Let's... not talk about that. I don't think it's something you really want to hear, and it's not something I'd like to relive either." He picked at a loose thread of his sleeve and moved to hug her, earning a quiet laugh and a pat on the back. "I severely underestimated your stubbornness for accepting you're a Seer. It's why I asked Uncle Cyrus to come talk to you, but clearly you have a problem with listening."

Glacier pulled back, hope replacing grief. "He was—"

"Real. Yes, Glacier, that was really him. He was glad to see you again, even if you didn't realize it was really him." Her small, remorseful smile made his heart crack. "He wanted to impress upon you that you're different. You're *supposed* to be different, Glacier. That's the entire point of why you'll be able to change the things that he and I *couldn't*."

You don't fit the mold of your predecessors, so don't try to fit yourself into it.

"Stop holding yourself back and use what you're given," she continued. "Amarais needs it, and Amarais needs *you*, not me."

"But—"

Kat held up a finger. "I've come to terms that it was never supposed to be me. Now it's your turn. My job was to help and protect you, and when that was over, I was given a decision to continue that role in a different capacity. So here I am." She held out her arms, then dropped them into her lap. "Plus, all of the people that were considering taking the job as your guide endorsed me because they either didn't want to take it from someone else, or they weren't sure that they would have as great of an impact as I would."

Glacier immediately thought of his parents, and Kat nodded, seemingly reading his thoughts.

"You'll see them again. As long as you keep going, they'll show up when the time is right. But first, you need to focus. Focus on the task ahead and help Noa. It's clear that you need her as much as she needs you."

"You know... about Noa?"

She snorted, rolling her eyes. "Glacier, I know a *lot* of things. I'm just limited in what I can and cannot tell you at certain times. However, I am *always* up here." She tapped his temple. "We may not think the same because we're not of the same consciousness, but I know what you know. You can't hide anything from me, so don't bother trying."

He searched her face, taking in the twinkle in those blue eyes. It was her. She was here. But she was *stuck* here—she'd never interact with all the people he'd met or the friends he'd gained.

"I miss you," he whispered.

"I'm still here, stupid. As long as you're here, I'm here with you. All you have to do is close your eyes, and we can talk. It doesn't even have to be about Seer business." A warm smile tugged at her lips. "Now we can *both* finish what Cyrus started."

RUNE

Rune pulled Cecilia into their cabin and locked the door, his stomach clenching when her eyes went wide. But the words came out in a rush, telling her everything Noa had told him before she had a chance to question what was going on.

Her face paled. "*What?* I- I don't understand—"

"Glacier's a Seer," he repeated.

"I- But—He's *not*. He doesn't have magic—"

"He *does*, Cecilia. Nyx found out and realized that Glacier didn't know. She told Noa because she thought it would be better for her to break the news to him, and now Noa is doing that right now."

"Oh *gods*, Rune—" Her hand went to her mouth, making his heart squeeze. "They're going to kill him..."

He wrapped his arms around her. "They won't. If anything, Noa will kill anyone who even thinks about trying to hurt him. They won't hurt *either* of you, not with us around."

She clung to his shirt, pressing her face into his chest. He ran a hand up and down her back until her breathing steadied, hating how he thought about that grimoire. The idea he'd tried to stop Noa from burning that damn book filled him with regret.

Cecilia forced out one last, steadying breath and pushed away, swiping at her eyes. "I... should find their cabin. I should be there in case he needs me."

"Okay." He unlocked the door, stepping aside.

"Thank you," she whispered.

He leaned down to kiss her forehead. "I love you."

"I love you too."

Rune followed her out, watching her vanish from the corridor. Footsteps sounded behind him, and he spun to find Crow.

"Something wrong?" Crow asked, slowing when he neared the cabin door.

"We need to talk. Where's Weather?"

"She's with the small psycho." Crow jerked a thumb back down the hall. "They said they were starving, and then my damn plate got jacked, so I decided that I'll just go back when I can eat in peace." He followed Rune inside, and Rune flipped the lock again.

Crow raised a brow, folded his arms over his chest, and leaned against the door. "All right, who did you kill?"

"A grimoire."

Crow's jaw dropped. "I'm sorry, what the fuck did you just say?"

"We broke into Arrington's office. I found spot coordinates and apartment information printed on a scrap of synthetic paper between a couple of his books. We went there, and we found a grimoire."

"Son of a bitch—Shane and Jinko have *got* to be in on it. There's no way they're not with how much time Arrington spent with them."

"I'm pretty sure you're right. I tried to stop Noa from burning it because it would be a sign that we were there, but..." Rune grimaced, pushing down that sick feeling again.

"But *what*, Rune? I would've expected you'd be the one to burn it—"

"Noa... told me that Glacier is a Seer."

"*What?* How the hell have we not known about this?"

"Because *he* didn't know, and Noa's telling him right now. Nyx figured it out, and we're talking about an *Amaraian* with magic, Crow. Cecilia didn't know how to use her magic until she got to Miralta and started to actually learn about it. But I think I've also realized why Arrington was interested in *us*."

Crow's throat bobbed, waiting for him to continue.

"I think he used us as spies to start to rope us in as comrades, but I think his endgame would be to reinstate us as thieves. That's why he wouldn't take only one of us without the other. I could cover for you as a spy, and you would be able to cover for me as a thief. He knew that."

"And why would he need *thieves*, Rune? That doesn't make any—Holy shit. That son of a bitch..." Crow's hands went to his head. "He was going to have me steal him more damn grimoires..."

"And we'd be in cahoots with his two underlings as well," Rune said tightly.

"We'd be killing Mages right now..." Crow said, a hint of fear lighting his gaze. "If Noa had brought Glacier and Cecilia to Kingsheart, we might've—"

"*Enough*. It doesn't matter now because we escaped. Glacier and Cecilia are with *us*. What *matters* is that we're going to hang this motherfucker out to dry the moment we get the opportunity. He's not going to get away with this shit anymore."

"If I have a chance to go back to Corvia, you better believe I'll take it," Crow breathed. "I'll smash open those cases, snatch that rune blade, and burn that damn grimoire before I hunt him down *myself*."

"And I'll be right behind you if it comes to that," Rune promised.

36

KING'S REPUBLIC ✧ 2705-01-22

NOA

Noa stared at the base of the opposite bench, resting her cheek against the top of Glacier's head from their spot on the floor. She hadn't moved for the past couple hours partly because he needed the sleep and partly because she liked how he rested against her shoulder. She didn't want to move either, mainly because she was too exhausted to bother. In that moment, they weren't the Queen and her Seer—they were the uncertain killer and the abandoned prince.

The door popped open with an angry beep, and Nyx stepped inside, snapping it shut behind her. "Did you kill him, or did he pass out?"

"I think the exhaustion and my little helping of extra stress finally did him in."

"How did he take it?"

"He tried to run," Noa said with a sigh. "I think me managing to keep him in the cabin counts as a win." She forced a tired smirk.

"Cecilia was out there looking for him. Rune told her, so I'm assuming you told Rune..."

"Yeah... I told him. We found more than just data in Arrington's office.

Rune found some coordinates. It was for an apartment. There was a grimoire. I burned it, even though Rune tried to stop me because it would leave behind evidence that we were there."

"That's... what I was afraid of." Nyx pushed up her glasses and rubbed at her face.

"I couldn't stand the thought of him getting a hold of Glacier, and I saw Shane hunting us down before we boarded. I think he was looking for him."

"I doubt he'll follow. He'll be too restricted anywhere outside of Kingsheart if he has a tag-along. I can't imagine he'd be able to hide it easily on a train."

"You think there *is* one attached to him, though?" Noa pried.

Nyx nodded. "My associate saw something, but she wouldn't talk about it. It was the girl you took the badge from."

"And you're not worried that she's in danger because her boss is summoning *daemons?*"

"He won't go for her. His goal is to grab as much magic as possible, right? Is it possible that he'll go for her if she keeps poking around? Yes, but I have some serious doubts it'll be right now. By the time we get the thirteenth key and open the Vault, Arrington, Delacroix, and Matsuoka will be done-for with all the dirt we pulled today. Outing them as Summoners either just before or after the fact will be the final nail in the coffin. Alyvia will be okay as long as she keeps her head down between now and then. She's still considered vital to their department, so she's not going anywhere. Plus, now they're down a grimoire. They can't do anything without it."

Nyx's eyes flicked back to Glacier for a moment, and a weight lifted from Noa's shoulder.

"Nice of you to join us." Nyx leaned back in her seat.

Glacier scowled at her. "You told her about my dreams, didn't you?"

"You caught me, officer."

"Are you okay?" Noa asked, gently nudging him with an elbow.

He shifted, pulling his legs toward him and staring down at the floor. "I... I will be. I just need some time."

"You have everyone here with you. You're not alone."

A nervous, breathy laugh escaped him. "I don't know how I'm supposed to tell anyone."

"You won't have to. Rune took it upon himself to do that. I'm sure everyone knows by now."

Glacier twisted his ring, wringing out her heart with it. "Noa... what would someone need a grimoire for?" he asked, lifting his head to stare her dead in the eyes.

Her throat constricted, so she cleared it before having to force out the inevitable explanation. "As much as I don't want to tell you, I believe that you have a right to know because the moment we open the Vault, it's us versus *them*. So I want you to be sure that you want to know *now*."

"Tell me."

She ran her hands over her pants, her somber mood darkening with the thought that she'd touched one mere hours ago. "A grimoire is used to call daemons," she stated. "From what I've read, if you're strong enough, then you can bind one or maybe multiple to you, and if you bind one to you... You can have it consume raw magic, which would allow you to access it as well. The man in the station was a Summoner. He was there because he was looking for *you*, Glacier."

Glacier's eyes widened.

"And if he got his hands on you and gave you over to that *thing* he summoned, he would have your power, and you would be a shell of a person."

Nyx shifted forward, catching their attention. "It cleaves the soul from the body since the magic is fused with it. People believe that everyone's soul has some sort of predetermined magic, and it's simply dependent on whether or not it's allowed to manifest. So my magic is somewhere coded into my soul, but I don't have access to it or know what it is. *Yours*, on the other hand, took time to manifest, but it would've never led to anything other than you becoming a Seer."

Noa nodded. "Seers are the strange exception since they don't typically show any signs of magic until they're around their very early twenties. At least, that's what Lazarus told me. Once they're independent enough, they're able to carry out what they're supposed to, so that's why it doesn't manifest until later. That's why you didn't start *seeing* anything until—"

"Until we started to leave Amarais," Glacier mumbled. "Is that why Daxton's friends were being picked off? Because every person—every *Mage* they collected would have a signature to them?"

Noa cringed. "Yes, and if that Mage is dead or *believed* to be dead, then it makes it easy to track a Summoner."

"That also goes for the other way around," Nyx said. "If a Summoner was able to obtain something like that, they could better stalk their victims if they don't have a decent sense of detection—at least, that's what I've read during this insane expedition."

Glacier frowned. "But... I thought Mages were created to *stop* them—"

"Initially, yes," Noa said. "And they still have the advantage if they're well-trained, but there's a considerable number of Mages that are just... normal people now. They have no combat training or know-how to defend themselves with their skills. They just have an ability for party tricks or *maybe* some sort of seemingly practical use, but it's hit-or-miss. And that's what we have to change. We'll need a *lot* of people, and it won't be something that happens overnight, but there are already enough Summoners out there that they're clearly starting to build their forces."

"Which means that we're the last line of defense," Nyx said. "We're a skeleton crew of six, plus our Queen and her Seer."

"So we're still on a time-crunch. We either take back Amarais or run after we grab the final key because we need to locate and the Vault. Then we build an army however we can and prepare for war."

GLACIER

Glacier ran his thumb over the handle of his mug while Cecilia turned her own around and blew on the steam escaping her tea. The dim glow of the dining car became a warm calm in a sea of fleeting stars. The last time he'd sat alone with her like this was when their journey had began—a newly freed Mage and a runaway prince. Now they were two Mages hunting keys alongside criminals for a wild story he might be tied to.

He spun the ring around his finger, still absorbing the idea that Kat would always be with him. At least he wouldn't be facing all this alone, even if he'd have to flee with Noa. He leaned back in the booth, lifting his chin to meet Cecilia's eyes. "Do you feel ready to go back?"

"I... don't know," she said. "I don't know if I'll ever be quite ready to go back after all of this. I *love* this. Even though we almost died, and we've turned into criminals, I-" —a bubbly, disbelieving laugh— "I finally feel *alive*."

He smirked. "I think you'll eventually want to settle down, though."

Pink flooded her cheeks. "I don't know how I'll be able to introduce him to my parents. I think they'll think I've snapped once I say: 'Here's my Bellegardian-Republican boyfriend that kidnapped me. Oh, and he goes by Rune.'"

"Maybe skip the kidnapping part? Wait—do you even *know* his real name?"

"*Yes*. He told me his last name in Valentia because I forced it out of him, and then he finally told me his first name before Kole came in and tried to kill us."

"It took you to get to the point of nearly *dying* before he told you"" Glacier asked, holding back a laugh.

"*Hey*—He wanted to take *my* last name, just like *you* did."

"So... where do you think you two will go after this? Valentia?"

"I... don't know. I think it'll depend on what happens in Amarais... What about you and Noa?"

Glacier forced out a breath, turning his mug around. "Well, if we have to leave Amarais... I don't know. I guess wherever Noa decides."

And he realized he liked that answer more than he thought he would. Regardless where they all went, whatever future they had would be one filled with another wild journey to keep him on his toes. Another adventure where he'd wake up with more questions than answers, but at least he'd feel less and less alone.

37

JINWON ✧ 2705-01-24

GLACIER

Neon lights evaporated the stars and wrapped around buildings in large blankets of news feeds and ads. Commuter trains shot over glowing railways, bridging clusters of taxis. Multicolored umbrellas covered the streets below, undulating with pedestrian traffic.

Glacier pressed a hand to the rain-spattered window, his breath fogging the view.

"It's always so damn dreary..." Nyx mumbled.

"I kind of like it," Glacier said.

"That's probably because it's practically the opposite of Amarais—dark, unruly, and loose on restrictions."

"And yet they all manage to survive without a monarch imposing laws against just about everything."

"I'll give you that," she said, leaning back in her seat.

The door burst open to Noa, who grumbled and yanked down her bag from the overhead compartment.

"Someone's excited," Nyx commented.

"You haven't even told me what we're doing. I'm *stressed*."

Nyx rolled her eyes. "And *I* told you not to worry about it yet. We can't do anything until tomorrow. We're certainly not going tonight."

"Are we breaking in somewhere? Do we have a contact? Wait—Are you trying not to *laugh* at me?"

"Calm *down*." Nyx snorted. "I remember when I could tell you to jump and you would ask how high—"

"Well, now I have a lot more things to worry about, and we're at the end of this. The last thing we need is to get road-blocked before we get to Amarais."

"Why don't you ask your boyfriend?" Nyx jabbed a thumb at him as she stood.

Glacier shot her a frown, reaching for his own bag from the rack. "Very funny. I don't think I get to choose what information I get."

"Not with that attitude," Nyx said. "Noa, if you really want to know—"

"*Gods, yes.*"

"*I'm* your contact, dumbass." She yanked down her bag and made her way out of the cabin.

Glacier locked eyes with Noa before the two of them scrambled out the door and bolted after her down the hall.

"Hold up—" Noa demanded, her voice rising with a newfound excitement. "*You're* the contact? Are you just going to go get it for me?" Glacier choked back part of a laugh as Nyx turned to glare over her shoulder.

"If it were that easy, I would've just grabbed it when we met here, you idiot. It's a little more complicated than that—"

"How much more complicated?"

Nyx threw up her hands. "Wait until tomorrow. I'm begging you. You're lucky I'm not stressed to hell since we got rid of the Volkov first. I'd be so unbelievably paranoid that I'd run into someone I know while we're here, and that's the *last* thing I'd want to do."

Glacier braced himself as the train slowed, falling in with the rest of the group. Malice's eyes lit up and pushed past Crow, latching onto his arm. The usual complaints and bemoaning sounded, giving him a sense of peace when the doors opened to the glossy dark interior.

Nyx led the way through security, navigating the bright, pulsing direc-
tional lines of the station. Two darkened town cars idled in the pickup
zone, attended by suited, white-gloved drivers who opened the doors for
them at the wave of Nyx's hand.

He slid inside with Malice, sandwiched in by Nyx while Noa climbed
into the front and the others collapsed into the second car. Nyx's conversation with the driver yielded little to no information with most of the
exchange in one of the many Jinwonese dialects that took over electronic
billboards and station announcements.

Cars other than taxis fought for control of the roads, passing those
pinned up against curbs and letting out passengers in short, shimmering
dresses and jackets over designer tee-shirts. The glint of silvery fingers or
overly-inked arms made him look again, squinting to try to make out if he'd
caught sight of openly-worn mods.

"Kaeyong's always so busy..." Malice mumbled. "I hate it."

"Where did you live before?" he asked.

"A little further north of here. There were a few places I lived, but they
were all smaller cities or suburbs. My siblings from one family would ask to
come here sometimes, and they'd try to lose me..."

"Well, we won't be trying to lose you here," he said, patting her arm,
"so don't worry about that. Just stick with me."

She beamed back at him, dropping her head against his shoulder, and
he turned back to the window just as the car turned onto a quieter street. It
pulled up in front of a white-arched hotel and an attendant rushed to the
curb, opening the door for Noa. He hesitated mid-question when she
stepped out and diverted his attention to Nyx before Noa answered in
Jinwonese, sending the man's eyebrows shooting up. He gave a quick,
apologetic bow and hurried to the next car.

"Don't touch my shit," Noa grumbled, adjusting her bag.

"Relax, he was just offering to help," Nyx said. "They deal with snooty
rich clients who want to be waited on hand and foot."

"I'm well aware, but he talks too damn polite."

"That's because you talk Jinwonese street slang that would have mothers covering their children's ears," Nyx shot back. "Leave the talking to me, please."

Noa huffed, hugging herself while Nyx nabbed their keys from the front desk. Glacier slowly spun around the lobby, taking in the stylized, old wood-block paintings hung in the marble recesses. Fingers laced through his, pulling him back to reality.

"Feeling better? You're not going to wander off, are you?"

His other hand went to the back of his neck. "Hopefully I don't... But I'm not sure I can really control that."

She bumped shoulders with him as the rest of the group flooded in and they pushed into the elevators. He admittedly felt a little less lost walking hand-in-hand with her, glad to be surrounded by so many people propping him up when his mind had enough.

They fell into another line down the hall, Noa half-dragging him through the large, red door at the end and straight onto the crimson rug pooling at their feet. A sleek fireplace warmed the main room from the chilling rain slowly pattering against the windows, drenching the white furniture in an orange glow.

Rooms were called, kitchen cabinets were thrown open, and cries for room service barely overtook the sound of the TV. Glacier didn't have the opportunity to take it all in since Noa pulled him inside one of the rooms and kicked the door shut with a grin.

"I don't like where you're going with this." He eyed her suspiciously.

"Oh, come on." She frowned, shoving his shoulder. "I just want to talk about the Vault. But if you want to start taking your clothes off, I won't stop you."

He dropped his bag and flopped onto the bed with a sigh. The mattress dipped as Noa climbed in next to him.

"I don't know where the hell it is," she admitted.

"Considering that you were telling me you thought it was in Kingsheart a few nights ago, I kind of figured you're out of ideas."

She scowled, slugging him in the arm. "What's that supposed to mean?"

"And here I thought that I would be immune from abuse if we hooked up..."

She threw back her head, loosing a laugh. "And *I* thought you'd dial back the sass, but here we are. So where is it?"

Glacier sputtered. "I don't *know*. Just because I guess I'm a Seer, it doesn't mean I just automatically know everything."

"*Gods*, we're useless..." Noa mumbled, staring up at the little silhouettes of birds painted along the ceiling.

He hummed, twisting his head to take her in. "Well... you're Astravnian, right?"

"Yeah..." She dropped her cheek against the bedding, squinting at him. "Why...?"

"Because I want to make sure we cover everything. If there's any information we're missing that could lead us to it, now's the time to put it out in the open."

"The Volkov were in Astravny too," she mumbled.

"So, you're from Astravny, and you've lived there your whole life. Is it possible that the Vault was hidden away to be close to you, or...? It *is* a large island, like Talie..."

Noa squirmed while he tried to image the Vault being dropped on an island—somewhere not all that easily accessible by most of Avaria, meaning very few would be able to disturb it. Something about it didn't sit right with him though. Then again, even the idea of it being in Kingsheart—a place built in the name of the King—didn't sit right with him either. There was too much foot traffic. Too many eyes everywhere. Too much of *everything...*

He groaned, throwing his arms over his eyes. "I don't know."

"What about Razbia?"

"Too many people. There's no good place to hide it. It runs into the same problems as Kingsheart."

"Then what about the cathedral in Biana? You were drawn to the fountain in Razbia and then you were drawn to the emblem on the floor in the cathedral."

He bit his lip, turning the idea over in his mind. "Maybe..."

"But you don't have a good feeling about it." Noa sighed. "Then let's just go to bed. You'll have time tomorrow to think it over while I go with Nyx to pick up the key, and then we'll have the entire train ride back to Miralta. We're bound to think of something."

"Maybe I'm wrong and it is somewhere in Kingsheart..."

"I think you're overthinking it, Glacier," she said, the bed shifting. She pushed his arms away from his face and stared down at him, lightly brushing away the hair curled over his forehead.

"What if we have to go back to Kingsheart and that guy starts hunting me again?" Glacier whispered, anxiety bubbling up from the pit of his stomach.

"Then I'll kick his ass and set him on fire to match his book. He's not touching you," she said. "Now let's get some rest."

38

JINWON ✦ 2705-01-25

NOA

"I should go with you."

Noa's soul might as well have greedily consumed the words the second they came from Glacier's mouth. At least she knew *why* now, not that it helped her all that much with needing to convince him otherwise. She called Malice over in the midst of Cecilia and Rune collecting breakfast plates from the kitchen bar top, the coffee table, and the actual dining nook —all smiles and hums that filled the hotel suite with the calming energy she needed before the final storm.

"Nyx said she just needs me for this," Noa said, shoving a tablet into his hands as Malice plopped down next to him on the couch. "Stay here with everyone else and think on the Vault, okay?"

His shoulders fell when she stood, but he sunk into the cushions, letting Malice lean into him. "And what if I can't come up with anything?"

"Give yourself some time. You were chosen for a reason." She gave him a quick peck on the cheek, despite his scowl, and followed Nyx to the door. The eerie sensation of Lazarus standing next to her returned and dissipated just as quickly with those words, leaving her breathless as she pulled the door behind her.

Another town car idled outside the lobby, driver and all, which turned the ride into one of disconcerting silence. Tall skyscrapers dropped down to slightly older apartment and business units, spreading out further than she'd originally expected before a sprinkling of suburbs emerged and dropped them straight into farmland. Noa ripped her gaze from the window to frown at Nyx, but she appeared unconcerned, fiddling with her phone.

A few minutes later, the fields gave way to trees, and the car slowed. Its slow, wide turn through parting wrought iron gates took them under weeping willow and dripping, pink cherry as the rumble of the brick drive heralded their destination. Noa reached for the empty seat in front of her, her hand on its shoulder to position herself for a view of the mansion that emerged from the foliage.

It sat a single-story tall like an older, traditional Jinwonese home, but it reminded Noa of a Bellegardian hillside manor with its pillars and narrow windows. All of it intermingled with Jinwonese design like how the frosted entry doors bore an etched, circular design of cranes, or how what would normally be a fountain in the middle of the circular driveway was a small fishpond with a waterfall cascading down large, flat rocks.

The car jerked to a stop, and the driver opened the door for Nyx while Noa hurried to throw off her seatbelt and scoot out after her. Her pulse thrummed through her fingertips as they approached the door, and she glanced back to find the driver standing outside the car, waiting.

"So, uh... are we meeting some Bellegardian businessperson here, or...?" she whispered.

Nyx smirked, a small, amused hum sounding with it. "The previous Bellegardian-Jinwonese resident is no longer with us."

"Oh..."

Nyx pressed the doorbell, and a middle-aged Jinwonese woman dressed in a pressed uniform opened the door.

"I'd like to speak with Song Haneul," Nyx said in Jinwonese—the sound of her native tongue catching on Noa's ears.

The woman nodded once and stepped aside, ushering them into the dipped-down foyer. Glass decorations on small tables and built-in shelves offset the darker stain of what Noa swore might be real wood comprising the coffered ceilings. She'd barely even noticed the woman vanish down a side corridor while Nyx tugged at her gloves and scraped her boots against the large, woven entry mat.

Candles sputtered around tiny white-marble statuettes of Lady Geneviève and Jae-Seong book-ending a color rendering of the cranes on the door—white birds twisting along the edges of a red circle. Noa peered up the rounded view above it to a darkened second floor, shoving her hands into her pockets with a low hum.

"So... who's Haneul to you?" she murmured, half-turning on her heel.

Nyx pushed up her glasses, slow-blinking in reply right before the house attendant wandered back in. "This way."

Noa trailed behind them into the corridor, passing door after door until the woman opened up the one at the far end. Nyx nodded and stepped through to where a large desk sat to the left of a window over-looking another pond. The empty executive chair reminded Noa of the first time she'd faced Nyx, but now the roles had reversed and Noa was at her mercy instead.

She paced the outer edge of the room, skimming over the paintings and charts until she reached a family portrait. Five people, all dressed in hanbok. Two adults in the background: a Jinwonese man radiating a calm, hopefully energy from his toothless smile with an arm wrapped around a nervous-looking woman with lighter skin and darker eyes—the half-Bellegardian resident Nyx mentioned. Three children in the foreground: a taller girl, matching her father's energy with her electric blue attire, though the boy next to her wore a forced smile, and finally the youngest stood with her right side angled away into the folds of her father's clothes. She was decked out in bright pinks, looking weary with her father's other hand cupping the back of her head. They must've ranged somewhere from ten to five.

"I always hated dressing up," Nyx mumbled, stepping next to her with eyes pinned on the little girl in pink. "But my mother would always tell me that I looked cute in whatever she threw on me."

"She was right. You were a cute kid."

"A cute kid missing an arm…"

The sound of footsteps padding onto the carpet make Noa spin around. Sure enough, the older sister from the picture shut the office door. She'd traded the blue hanbok for a fitted suit and a smart bob. She took her seat, folding her hands on the desk.

"Nari," Haneul said. "I'm honestly a little surprised that you've come back to see me."

"I'm here to make a deal," Nyx said. "You have something I want, and I can get you want you want."

"I'm listening."

"Trade me the Mind of Jinwon."

Noa's head whipped toward her, ignoring Haneul in favor of puzzling out how the hell Nyx had access to one of the keys the entire time.

Haneul leaned back, her eyes flicking to Noa with a glimmer of mischief. "She's Volkov, isn't she?"

Noa clenched her jaw to keep it from dropping. Brains ran in the family then…

"Does it matter?" Nyx asked. "I can get you what you want, Haneul. Just promise me the Mind of Jinwon, and it's yours."

Haneul smirked, drumming her fingers against the blotter. "It's a deal."

"You mind explaining what the hell that was?" Noa asked, stalking after Nyx when the driver dropped them outside a graffitied building and a barbed wire chain link fence. She glanced back over her shoulder, frowning at the flickering neon signs missing letters and the shuttered windows.

"My family is in possession of the Mind of Jinwon. My father received it as a recognition for national innovation, and then he willed it to his oldest child. However, there's one thing she'd trade it for, and that's my father's company."

"Wait, what? Isn't she already in charge of it, or is your brother…?"

"Both of them own a portion of the company, but when my father died, he left the majority of the shares to me. I'm the owner. We'd be trading our inheritances." Nyx slowed, turning to face her.

"Oh, this is great!" Noa said, grinning. "So you're going to give her your shares, and then we're good, right?"

"Not quite."

"What do you mean? She'd own the company then..."

Nyx shook her head. "She wants my brother *out* of the company. He's been trying to figure out how to buy us off for the past couple of years because he wants it too."

Noa threw her head back with a groan. "Why fight over it when you can just *share* like normal siblings?"

"Because Seok is a mod *enthusiast*. He takes things to the extreme, and he wants to push into a full-replacement market. It would drag our father's name through the mud. We'd be selling street mods instead of medical prosthetics. Neither Haneul nor I want that. If we push him out of the company, and I let Haneul take control, she'll be happy, and I'll be happy. It's a win-win."

Noa reached for her arm, giving her sleeve a light tug as Nyx started to turn back around. "But... it's *your* company, Nyx."

She sighed. "I never wanted it. I don't have the mind to run this business like Haneul. She knows how to market things. I work with data and information. She liked us working together, but I don't want to be working in what she would imagine me doing. She can take it further if I let her run with it. All I've ever wanted was to solve puzzles, and this is the greatest puzzle you can give me. I've pulled information and pieced so many things together for so many other people before you that I actually felt like I was doing something I *wanted* to do. As much as my father wanted me to take his company as the poster child of his work, I'm not fit for it."

The weight to her voice spoke louder than her words—that weary, tired cadence told Noa she didn't want to go back to that life. Noa's shoulders fell, unsure what to do or say, but Nyx continued for her.

"Noa, I've already decided where I'll end up when this is all over. You either take me as an advisor, or I beat the shit out of you for all the trouble you've caused me." She folded her arms over her chest.

Noa's fist jerked up to her own mouth, holding back her laugh until it bubbled out. "You're serious? You *want* that job?"

Nyx scowled. "Yes."

"You act like I can stop you from taking it—Hell, you asked for Glacier to be your assistant just after you met him, and I didn't know how to stop you from that either."

"Glad we could come to an understanding," Nyx said, lifting her chin.

Noa snickered, shaking her head. "Can... I be honest for a minute?" She rubbed her elbow until Nyx motioned for her to continue. "When we first met, I saw you as an opportunity to escape. You were there when I decided to leave the Volkov. Saying I could go anywhere without you is... insane. The only reason I let you skip out on Amarais was because of an excuse and the fact that you'd left me with dumbass and his brother."

"I figured you needed to know what it was like to live without me for a little while." Nyx smirked and started back down the alley.

"Well, it worked. So how are we going to get the shares from your brother?" Noa asked, jogging to catch up with her as she wrenched open a metal door.

It opened to a chorus of cheers and shouts, crashing into Noa the second the door slammed shut behind them. Harsh hot pinks and violent reds colored the rows and rows of people in bleacher seating converging downward to the floor-to-ceiling plexiglass like a coliseum.

In the ring, fluorescent blue droplets were spattered and smeared against the concrete and white half walls. Blood trickled down the nose of one of the opponents—a guy in a black, over washed tee-shirt. Yells ripped through the crowd as the shirtless guy hammered his fist into his opponent's stomach, sending him flying.

"Time to put your fighting skills to use with a bet." Nyx said over the crowd's noise.

Noa's face went slack. "You have got to be shitting me... You know what? That whole advisor thing? Not really feeling it anymore since you're advising me to fight a *modded man*."

"You want the Mind of Jinwon?"

Noa gritted her teeth. "I *hate* you." She stalked down the steps, grabbing onto the railing and leaning into the plexiglass for a better look.

"It'll clear out after this," Nyx shouted over the audience again. "We'll have a private match."

"*Fantastic...*" Noa grumbled, watching the two opponents slowly circle each other. She could barely make out which was Seok—no longer the scrawny, sullen-looking boy from the portrait, but a tall, ripped, shirtless man with a malicious grin on his face that didn't reach his modded eyes.

Wrath poured off him with each and every punch or kick to drive back his opponent. There was a degree of skill behind every strike, telling her he'd earned his muscle, but at some point, he'd sacrificed his arms and legs for ones made of metal, now partially covered by baggy athletic shorts. Steel casing gleamed under the bright white light of the circular arena, offset by the pulsing blue tubes occasionally flashing into view.

Noa's hands tightened on the railing, feeling her blood boiling at the mere idea that he'd *chosen* to do this to himself while his younger sister stood on the sidelines without having that option. He'd purposely thrown away his humanity while she'd done everything to fit in—begging to be accepted because she was afraid of what people might think of her. And most of it was because of people like *him*. Sure, there were those devote followers of gods that swore up and down that adding machine to flesh was unnatural—that it was something disgraceful or dangerous to buy into, even though there were those who needed the help since the same people didn't care to accommodate others suffering through.

Seok lunged at his opponent, the crunch of metal making Noa flinch. A wail followed, drown out by cheers. The only ones who didn't cheer were those jeering through the glass on the other side. Three others stood, mumbling and snickering while Noa took in their modifications: one with a replaced arm, mirroring his inked one; one with his arms replaced to his elbows; and the last appeared completely untouched, save his eyes that snaped from person to person inhumanly, though she couldn't see any of their lower halves to assess the rest of the damage done.

"This man is going to snap me in half," Noa mumbled in a sing-song voice.

"He has vulnerabilities, Noa. The issue with most mods is that it can't be fully plated for some parts since it restricts movement too much."

Noa pulled her fingers free from the railing, the air caressing her sweat-drenched palms. She recalled Nyx's gloves, the blue liquid dripping all over the apartment tiles, and Glacier's steadying hands to help her replace the cut tube in her arm.

Dead weight.

Her eyes snapped to the inner elbows of Seok's arms. He ducked and spun around at another punch being thrown, and she focused on the backs of his knees. The same bright blue fluid pumped through his modded veins. She chewed her lip, wishing she had a knife.

She jumped as the guy in the black shirt smacked against the floor. The crowd screamed and chanted in mass hysteria when he didn't move to stand again. She swallowed, rubbing her hands on her pants. "Can I have one final request? I'd like to go back to the hotel and lock myself in my room with my boyfriend for, like... an hour."

Nyx's hand went to her temple as the crowd began to rush to bookies holding up tablets. One by one, they cashed in their winnings and shuffled out the door, still riding the high that filled Noa with a sense of impending doom. But she'd killed Ezra. She'd finally put an end to Myron. Her hands curled into fists. She was Volkov, *damnit*—she wasn't someone to be trifled with either. And this modded junkie had spat in the face of his own sister—Noa's best friend. All for the sake of entertainment, not caring that he was dragging his father's legacy through the mud.

Noa's fists shook as she shoved open the gate, fueled by her conjured anger to face him. Nyx said something before footsteps sounded behind her, but it was too late. Noa couldn't hear past the blood pounding in her ears as Seok finally turned away from his friends.

"Hey, *asshole*," she yelled, pointing a finger directly at him.

He barked out a laugh as if he were a god being called out by a child. "Look, if you're here because I kicked your brother's ass or something—" His modded eyes shifted over to Nyx, his entire demeanor changing to something a little more predatory. "Well, well... would you look who came back."

"Shut the fuck up and listen," Nyx snapped.

Those inhuman eyes went wide before he broke into a snicker. "Little Nari thinks she can just walk up and start giving orders after vanishing for —*what*—a year, huh? Who's your boring-looking friend?"

Noa snarled. "I don't give a shit if I don't look appealing to you. I'm here to kick your ass."

"I'd like to see you try, little girl."

Nyx stopped next to her, her voice echoing through the arena. "I want to make a bet. Your company shares—If you win, I'll double them. If you lose, you relinquish them to me." It sounded just as crazy as when she'd offered her services to Noa, minus the slight wavier.

Seok guffawed, throwing his head back and his three minions joined in with clashing cackles and loud expletives in Jinwonese. "You're serious? You think this tiny firecracker can actually best me? Holy shit, you're stupid." He shook his head, his grin returning in full-force while he pretended to crack his mechanical knuckles. "But, if you insist, who am I to deny a challenge like that?"

What an arrogant piece of shit.

"Clear the arena."

Nyx grabbed Noa's arm, dropping her voice to a whisper. "I don't think I need to tell you how to fight him, but don't get your face smashed in."

"No problem. It's not like I still have stitches from the last psychopath I fought or anything..." Noa flashed her a fake smile.

A long, drawn-out sigh escaped her as Seok called out a charming reminder that his friends had made their way back to the stands, and they were delaying the inevitable. Her hand fell away.

"Want a good-luck kiss?" Nyx asked, that dry edge to her tone not nearly as mocking as she expected.

Noa's eyebrows shot up. "Wait, you're serious? Is that actually an option? Okay, but like, what kind of kiss are we talking about here?"

Nyx rolled her eyes, and Noa jolted at the fleeting sensation of her lips on her cheek. "Just... imagine it was from Glacier, and don't die, *please*. I really don't want to have to explain this to him..."

"Awww, would you look at that..." Seok mocked, combatting Nyx's glare as she started for one of the doors. "Nice of you to give your girlfriend one last goodbye, Nari."

Noa rolled her shoulders, feeling the tightness of the stitches baulk at the movement. All she had to do was take it easy—a bit of a feat she reconsidered from her past victories against the Volkov. Her heart picked up speed at the scrape of her boots against the concrete and the lingering scent of body odor.

"Your move, princess," Seok said with a mock bow.

"It's Queen, actually, but I admire that you recognize my superiority." She shot him a grin and lunged.

His fist hurtled past her as fainted to the side. Another dodge, and his other fist collided with the half wall. The loud scrape of steel against painted brick made her skin crawl, but it also yielded a light skittering across the floor. A loose plate spun a few meters away.

Adrenaline pumped through her veins as she shoved off the wall and dipped down to scoop it up with Seok's heavy footfalls pounding after her. She turned and ducked, dropping into a crouch and launching past him again—only this time catching her makeshift weapon against the back of his knee. Blue sprayed outward, staining her hands mid-sprint back to the other side.

"Fight back, you bitch," he growled, stalking after her until his body tipped, catching him by surprise. He bared his teeth in frustration, grabbing at it with a curse.

So, Noa hurtled forward, and bodied him. She ran the plate along the inside one of his elbows before he got a chance to swing again—though not at hard as he probably would've liked—clipping Noa's jaw. She smacked into the floor. Her head spun as she pushed herself up, swaying slightly with a smirk. "Better?"

His leg finally buckled, and the crunch of uneven metal plates rang throughout the arena. A loud, agitated scream escaped him. "What the *fuck*—"

Noa started toward him, dropping the plate at his knees, just out of reach. "I don't need mods to kick your ass. I've been trained to do far worse to people with far less. So, you're going to give your sister your shares, or I'll make sure to come back and finish what I started. But next time there *won't* be an arena, and I'll have much sharper tools with me, got it?" She threw up her fingers in the shape of a V, enjoying how his mouth fell open in horror. "Are we clear?"

Noa and Nyx sat across from Haneul, an ice pack pressed to Noa's aching jaw while each sister took turns signing electronic documents pulled up on her desk. Her vision glazed over from the tedium, catching Haneul's hair swaying with every tilt of her head. Nyx tapped the final signature box, and Haneul's stylus looped across the document field before clicking against the desktop.

"I'll admit, I didn't think you'd do it," Haneul said. "Clearly, I've underestimated you." Her dark eyes slid over to Noa, who dumped the ice pack on the desk.

"Well," Nyx said, "when I put my mind to something, I tend to find a way to achieve it."

"While I have a lot of questions..." Haneul raised a brow at Noa. "Are you sure there's nothing I can do to get you to stay?"

Nyx shook her head. "I've made up my mind before I came back. I decided I wanted to trade, so we've made the trade."

She chuckled. "The Mind of Jinwon comes with some weirdos that like to drop by. You know that, right?"

"I'll file a change of address once things calm down if some old guy wants to come look at it." Nyx waved a hand. "I can handle that."

Haneul smirked—a humorless expression laced with a touch of sadness. "Then I suppose I should give you what you're owed." She pushed off the desk and smoothed out the wrinkles in her blouse on the way to the door.

Nyx stood and followed, leaving Noa flabbergasted as she scrambled to jump up behind them. "Can't you people at least say something when you're entering or exiting a room?" she hissed when she caught up to Nyx. "A 'please follow me,' or 'hey, bitch, let's go.' Anything. Really."

Nyx coughed, covering up a laugh on their way past landscape after landscape of mountains, temple shrines, and the Jinwonese-Bellegardian pass. Haneul opened a door, and started down a set of steps, her dress shoes clicking against the lacquered flooring.

Lights popped on in her wake, illuminating the thatch-mat flooring extending out to another set of shrines on either side of a door. Swords hung from racks alongside shadowboxed prototypes of early mods—ones that Noa imagined could've very well been used to replace Nyx's missing arm with the increasing sizes.

Haneul stopped near one of the shrines, placing her hand in the recess under one of the shelves of candles and incense. A snap of springs cried out before a blue ring spun around once, twice—a green pulse replaced it. A new panel blinked blue in its place, which Haneul dipped down to meet. Another flash of green, and the door split down the middle, folding inward. A biometric vault. It couldn't be all that different from the one that awaited them in Amarais.

She strode inside the dimly lit room, pulling something from a drawer. When she reemerged, she offered it to Nyx. "I don't suppose you'll tell me why you want this?" The Mind of Jinwon rested on a pillow just under the box's glass cover.

"I'll tell you later," Nyx said, pulling it from her grasp.

"It really is a shame that you don't want to stay with the company, Nari. You have a brilliant mind..."

"I know our father would've wanted me to take it, but it's not me. My heart's just not in it like how his was. I know that you'll carry on his legacy better than I ever could. He should've given control to you. He'd be proud of you."

"You'll always be welcomed back, Nari."

Noa watching Nyx's fingers press against the box, her shoulders falling.

"Thank you. But I think I've finally found where I belong."

39
BELLEGARDE ✦ 2705-01-26

NOA

"Still nothing?" Noa asked, resting her cheek against Glacier's shoulder.

He rubbed at his face, his silhouette breaking up the sunlight pouring onto the indigo seat covers of the train cabin. Every minute that passed became another minute closer to them reaching Amarais—something Noa was both wholly unprepared for and ready to infiltrate. She hooked his sleeve with a finger and ran a thumb over his wrist.

The idea that they might willingly accept him left a worse taste in her mouth than the alternative. What if they took him back? What if they tried to lock him away? What if they refused to acknowledge her as Seraphine's little chosen one or *whatever* and decided to villainize her for kidnapping their prince? So many creeping questions thrummed through her, planting doubt after doubt in her mind.

He sighed and laced his fingers through hers. "I don't know what else I'm missing... I don't know where someone would hide something like this."

"*The Origin of Magic* doesn't have anything else to offer?" Noa asked, plucking the tablet off his lap.

"Nothing that I can find..."

Noa skimmed over the familiar words of this open-ended version, chewing on her lip. No mention of specific countries or places, outside of what she assumed would be modern-day Kingsheart. She pulled up the version closest to the one Lazarus had given her. Everything he had told her was here, but she could imagine that he believed she and Glacier would be able to figure out the rest—the *where*.

She clicked off the display and hummed.

"You too?" Glacier asked, sliding further down into the seat and resting his head against hers. "Maybe..." he started, his voice trailing off, "Maybe I could try asking Kat? I don't know if she'll be able to outright tell me since I think she's restricted in some of what she can do, but... I might be able to get some sort of hint."

Noa pulled away, leaning forward. "Has she tried to give you information before?"

"Sort of? I've learned some things from her before, but I thought it was a lot of nonsense... Clearly, it wasn't. I should've asked her about it earlier, but I wasn't really thinking about it."

Noa pushed herself up and tapped the window shades. "Then sleep on it. Hopefully Kat has something to point us in the right direction. I think I'm going to think it over in the dining car with a cup of coffee. It feels like there's something we're missing, but I... can't quite put my finger on it." She grabbed the pillow from the overhead compartment and shoved it into his arms with a smirk. "Sweet dreams."

He gave a breathy laugh. "Here's hoping one of us can figure something out."

She started out into the hall, tugging her hair tie free. Shaking out the loose strands, she stretched and pulled it all back up again. The snap of the band against her fingers brought her back to the story during all those hours holding books with sore hands.

The Messenger and the King. Two nameless forces lost to time.

She closed her eyes and placed herself back in front of the statue of the Messenger. The world around her stilled in that memory, leaving her staring up at the white marble holding the Shield of Miralta. Noa reached out in her mind's eye and touched the glass, unable to see past her own scrappy reflection.

Where would you put it?

Noa opened her eyes and tugged open the door to the next car. Rune hovered by the coffee bar, looking up as she approached. He passed her a mug, and she stared out at the fields of frosted grass.

GLACIER

"Kat?" Glacier stepped into the hall, following the sound of her reply echoing from the office. He nudged open one of the doors and stopped, blinking at the sight of her teetering on a stepladder shoved up against the bookcases. "I... have a question."

Kat's blonde hair fluttered around her shoulders as her head swung toward him. "Yes?" Her eye glittered with hope, matching the hesitant smirk tugging at the corners of her mouth. "Please don't ask me something ridiculous again—"

"Can you tell me where the Vault is? Not the family vault, but—" Glacier tensed at the sound of her crescendoing laugh. She wobbled, hooking an arm through the supports. "What's so funny?"

"Seriously? Why do you need *me* to tell you that when you've already seen it?" She crammed the book back onto the shelf and dropped to the floor, brushing off her hands on her way over to him.

Glacier blinked. "I... have?" He racked his memories. Nothing stood out as anything he could picture being Vault-like, let alone anything that had places for thirteen emblems to unlock it.

Her smile twitched. "You... seriously don't..." She huffed, pushing past him. "Chop, chop. With me. Let's go."

"Wait, where?" He jogged after her. "I don't remember—"

"Think about it for a moment." Kat spun around, walking backward to the front door. "You're the ruler of all of Avaria, you're from a snowy near-wasteland to the north that doesn't have a name yet, and your lover—the woman who gives you the opportunity to choose your most trusted allies—discovers you're dead. Now, let's look at *her*. She's from somewhere in that strip Nyx said the majority of Miraltans spread out between there and Mharu, collecting her people at the base of Amarais and giving the newly appointed Miraltan ruler their emblem. Wouldn't she strategically place them to protect the Vault?"

Glacier nodded. "That... makes sense."

"So... said King from a snowy wasteland was sent home to his people for his final resting place, which is now called Amarais, correct? Naturally, the Messenger doesn't want to leave him, and she escapes there to mourn him. Their people are closer together than ever before, so where better to put a Vault than somewhere surrounded by water *and* guarded by its only bordering neighbor, Miralta."

She smirked again, throwing open the door to the bright lights beyond. His knit long sleeve shirt transformed into a layered suit jacket and pressed dress shirt. He stared down at his hands before his head snapped up to the wide, sparkling ballroom of the palace.

Kat's silvery gown dragged along the white tiles, past phantasmal, twirling couples in black dresses and ties. Each and every one of their faces was obscured by masks—barely curved, shapeless things in blacks and grays, just like the ones he'd seen Noa, Rune, and Crow wearing the first time they'd met. Their images faded in and out under the stars piercing through the glass ceiling.

She stopped in the center of the floor, spinning to face him. "You remember how we roamed the halls as kids, trying to find secret passageways that we were convinced existed somewhere to be able to smuggle out royalty in times of crisis?"

"Yes... What does that have to do with this?"

"You remember how we were told there were none? How they weren't on any of the designs or recorded documents? Because this building is a stronghold. The base is *here*." She held out her arms. "She hid it in the one place she knew it would be kept safe, and, over time, Amarais forgot about it. It caused war and hate between us and Miralta for years upon years until everyone forgot *why*."

"It's *here*?" His eyes went wide. "*Where?*"

Kat pointed at her feet. He stared down at the indent on the floor, sitting just outside the edge of sparkling fabric. The sensation of holding his father's hand while they walked through to the garden took over—back when he'd found meaning in every little mark, like he'd been subconsciously looking for runes before knowing he was a Seer. He'd assumed it'd been some Amaraian emblem, but seeing it now, it didn't match the Soul of Amarais.

Instead, Lyris's mural came to mind, along with the charm Niklaus had given him. The Shield of Miralta would've fit perfectly there. He lifted his head, watching Kat's smile grow.

"We've been standing over it for *years*."

NOA

Noa spun her mug around, tuning into the hum of its scrape against the table. She stared past Rune, fixating on the pattern of the seatback like it was mocking her with its regal Bellegardian design.

"Any luck?" Rune asked, pulling her attention away from one potential clue to another: his dark eyes.

Bellegardians were all over the Republic. Their influence was so far spread, that perhaps that was the answer staring her right in the face. Maybe it'd been in Bellegarde, and they'd walked past it right before making their way to Amarais the first time.

"I'm not sure..." she said, her brows knitting together. Her fingers drummed against the tabletop. Still, something didn't feel quite right. Maybe she was attacking this all wrong.

Noa shook her head. *The Messenger was Miraltan. Start from there.* She glanced out the window. The Shield of Miralta was always in her hands, and everyone had just went with it, but... Why not The Heart of the King? Wouldn't that make more sense for her to hold when it sat at the center of it all? That would be like Noa holding the Sword of Astravny—an all too fitting idea as former Volkov—or Glacier with the Soul of Amarais.

Her fingers halted against the table. The Heart of the King. The Shield of Miralta. The Sword of Astravny. The *Soul* of Amarais.

"Holy shit," she mumbled. "He was Amaraian."

"Who was?" Rune asked, frowning.

Noa slid out of the seat and started back toward the cabin, everything piecing together in sharp clarity. It would explain the tension, the threat of war, the want for Amarais to isolate itself and claim things as petty as former Miraltan names for themselves like they needed to conquer and fortify their borders.

She jogged forward as Glacier threw open the cabin door, his eyes lighting on her. Their voices clashed in unison. "I know where the Vault is."

And they both broke into wide grins.

"So..." Weather began, bumping against Crow along the cabin bench. "You two think the Vault is in Amarais because you think the original *King* was Amaraian?"

"He was," Glacier said, shifting his footing next to Noa against the window.

"But... I guess I'm just confused." Cecilia frowned, shaking her head. "Amarais *hates* magic."

"After protecting it for so long, Miralta tried to access the Vault because they saw magic was starting to diminish. So, when Amarais wouldn't let them because the greed for magic had killed the King to begin with, it started problems between them. It eventually turned into outright prejudice and hate against Miralta and everything that it stood for. Miralta was meant to *shield* Amarais from the rest of the world, and Amarais simply cut itself off over time. Then no one could access the Vault because it was so secluded, and people just... *forgot* about it."

"Until fate finally got the ending it wanted," Nyx said, folding her arms over her chest and eyeing Glacier. "It found a way to bring a Miraltan Mage and an Amaraian King together again, didn't it? The perfect combination for its next Seer: a symbol of unity for two divided forces."

Glacier's hand moved to the back of his neck, a small flush creeping up it. Noa tried to think of something to pull the attention off of him, but Rune did that for her.

"And then it decided to hand the reigns over to the Sword of Astravny," he said, staring at Noa from where he leaned against the small closet door. "To take it all back by force, rather than asking for permission."

Noa slipped her hand into Glacier's, a confident smirk dancing across her face. "It sure does seem that way, doesn't it?"

Crow's brows furrowed. He ran a hand through his hair as he glanced around the car. "O...kay... This is great and all, but *where* in Amarais? We can't just go around blindly searching an entire country for it..."

"It's in the palace ballroom," Glacier said. "We need the Shield of Miralta to get inside. I remembered wondering what it was when I was a kid, but I eventually thought it was another Amaraian emblem since I'd never really seen the Shield of Miralta before. But by the time I looked at it myself, I'd forgotten all about it."

Cecilia's eyes went wide. "You're *sure?*"

Glacier nodded, and Noa jumped in again. "We just need the Soul of Amarais, and then we can open it. I'm assuming that we'll need the rest of them once we unlock the initial seal with the Shield."

"Then I guess our last stop is Amarais," Nyx said, "whether we like it or not."

"Sounds like it," Rune agreed.

Malice shrank down, wearily pulling her knees up to her chest with a sideways look at Noa. "But won't they try to stop us?"

"Yeah, no kidding," Weather mumbled, biting her lip.

Nyx pushed up her glasses. "That's why we need to rally with the rebellion if they'll take us. It's our best bet to use them to get inside. If we can get to the Vault, and Noa manages to take control of whatever's inside, we could actually take back Amarais in one fell swoop without many casualties."

"Will the rebellion even accept foreigners?" Weather asked, scrunching up her nose.

"I'm wearing on one of them, and I think she'll vouch for me, plus a few friends. She doesn't know about Glacier or Cecilia, so it'll be based on us alone. I'd rather none of them expect that we're smuggling a prince and a Mage back into Amarais. I think we'll be able to get in, and I'm confident that we'll at least be relatively safe in their care when we meet them in person. I'm just uncertain about the rest of the rebellion. If they tell us they won't stand behind Glacier, we'll have to wait and use them as a distraction to slip inside. My hope is that we can work with them instead, though."

"I guess there's only one way to find out," Rune said.

Noa squeezed Glacier's hand. "Let's break into Amarais. Again."

40

MIRALTA ✧ 2705-01-28

GLACIER

Puffs of cold smoke curled in front of Glacier's face, his coat weighing him down as much as Noa's anchoring grip. Her gloved hand in his reassured him he wasn't walking into this alone, even as he stared at the Miraltan man walking with Rune around the SUV. Every test of the emergency latches set him on edge—worse than the anxiety that prickled at him just thinking about stepping back into a place that'd once been his prison.

"It'll be okay," Noa said, giving his hand a squeeze. "You're not alone."

His eyes flicked over to Cecilia, watching Rune call her away from Weather's fussing over Cecilia's scarf. Nyx waded through the snowbank in front of the vehicle, stopping next to the Miraltan for what appeared to be one final question before waving over Glacier and Noa.

"Time to go," Noa breathed.

He squeezed her hand a little harder, forcing himself to trudge through the snow drift. Panic bubbled up with the order for him to stop.

"VIPs get the trunk," Nyx said, tugging up on the false bottom. "It'll be a little cramped, but it's better that you two are secured in here to cut down on the risk of being recognized."

Numbness spread through his torso as Rune hoisted himself up into the truck and held his hand down to Cecilia. She took it, and he pulled her into the back with him, easing her into the compartment. Then he held a hand out to Glacier.

Noa wrapped her arms around him. "It won't be for long. I promise." She stepped back and nodded for him to go.

Glacier reached for Rune's hand and tucked the toe of his boot into a recess of the bumper, propelling himself up. He climbed in with Cecilia, nearly nose-to-nose with her as Rune grabbed the compartment cover.

"Try to enjoy the ride," Rune joked. "Just don't get handsy, or else Noa and I are going to be pissed." He pasted on a faux scowl.

Glacier chuckled and Cecilia rolled her eyes. Then it was just the two of them alone in the dark with the muffled noise of the rest of the crew opening and closing doors.

"You ready?" Cecilia whispered, wringing her hands.

"No, but I don't think I'd ever be ready."

"I know my mom will be happy to see you again. I hope she's okay."

"I'll be glad to see her again too. I just hope the rest of Amarais doesn't try to kill me before then."

41

AMARAIS ✧ 2705-01-28

GLACIER

Glacier tensed when the SUV rolled to a stop, holding back a shaky breath. He tried to peer at the set of soft blue eyes across from him, but he didn't really need to since he could feel the anxiety rolling off her in waves.

Cecilia's hand found his in the dark. "We're not alone," she whispered —like a mantra Rune had been telling her too.

The vehicle rocked slightly as people got in and out. Doors opened and shut. Boots crunched in the snow, catching his breath and sending his heart pounding in his chest.

If they don't want me, I'll leave with Noa. If they don't want me, I'll leave with Noa...

It wasn't enough, but it kept him from falling straight into a panic attack. Though, he wasn't sure if that was better or worse since it was slow-building now. Heat spread through him while his lungs worked a little harder. He squeezed his eyes shut and tried to focus on the muffled voices coming from outside.

"I'm looking for V," came Nyx's rumble, followed by a reply too faint for him to hear anything but the stern cadence of what he thought was a woman's voice. Something about it rung familiar to his ears, but he couldn't place it. Nyx moved on to introduce herself anyway, and then footsteps sounded again.

"Why are there a fucking dozen of them?" Noa hissed.

Glacier's head spun, and he gripped Cecilia's hand a little tighter. "Oh, gods."

The trunk popped open, and the back dipped under the weight of one body, then another.

Nyx's voice rang out again. "I didn't want to detail what we had on us, just in case something happened during transport."

Fingers scratched against the felt lining until they found the latch. It pulled free, backdropping two silhouettes in blinding white. Glacier put his arm up with a wince, feeling a hand fumble past him for Cecilia. His heart thumped harder.

Like surfacing from water, the other woman's voice broke free of the barrier. "What do you have that's so confidential?" Hard. Tense. Still oh-so-familiar.

Cecilia was pulled upward, her frame steadied for a mere moment before he heard another woman's voice. "Cecilia!" Soft around the edges, warm to the core, and a deeper imitation of her daughter's. Mrs. Angelis.

Cecilia dropped into the snow. "Mom!"

Rune grabbed his arm next, ripping him up into the harsh white landscape. Noa helped him down into the snow, despite everything seemingly moving in slow motion. His eyes fell on the small crowd of Amaraians several meters away, where Mrs. Angelis stood bleary-eyed and arms wide.

Not wanting to let himself have the opportunity to lock up in fear, Glacier ran behind Cecilia, taking in the blurred faces until he changed course. He slowed as Cecilia fell into her mother's arms, all attention falling on them.

A sob escaped Mrs. Angelis. "Gods, you're alive—"

Those same words stuck in Glacier's own throat as he stood in front of the source of that familiar voice. Her blonde hair was cut shorter than his now, aside from the fact that he'd managed to catch up to her in height.

"Ari?"

Her head whipped toward him, her eyes wide. The last time he'd seen this woman was in the palace all those years ago, back when Mrs. Angelis nudged him into her arms for what he always thought was a final goodbye. No more books read to him while Glacier's father consulted her brother, North. No more adventures of make-believe through the palace halls like they were on some thrilling quest. No more Ari to hold his hand when he was scared of a strange noise, a new place, or a weird shadow in the dark.

She paled like she'd seen a ghost. Her hand raised as she took a staggering step forward.

"Hey..." he said, welcoming the warm embrace that followed.

"You're alive," Ari breathed, her voice shaking while she grabbed fistfuls of his coat.

"It seems that way, huh?" He forced out a short, quiet laugh. Her arms felt just as safe as they had all those years ago—like nothing could touch him when she was there to protect him. It'd been something he'd taken for granted until he'd met Kat. At least she didn't have to crouch or scoop him up this time as her little charge. A child prince, now newly twenty.

"Glacier!"

Ari released him, and Mrs. Angelis grabbed for his arm, pulling him against her for another welcoming hug.

"Oh, gods," she whispered in his ear, running a hand through his hair. "I can't believe both my children are alive."

Glacier's face dropped into her shoulder and close his eyes to drive back the tears. Those simple words told him he was home. He was safe. Noa had been right: he wasn't alone. Everyone he loved and cared about was here, surrounding him.

You can do this, he thought. *You can face this.*

"H-how?" came Ari's confused question. "How did you...?"

"Let's not worry about the details for now," Nyx said while Mrs. Angelis coaxed him to take a step back.

The rest of her speech fell to the background when Mrs. Angelis spoke, "Look at you... Always managing to surprise us..."

He swiped at his eyes, unable to suppress a smile. "I had a lot of help to get me back here. I'm just sorry it took me so long."

Mrs. Angelis opened her mouth to add more, but Ari's hardened tone overtook it. "What do you all have to gain from this? Why bring them back here?"

"Because Glacier and I made a deal."

Glacier spun around, catching Noa step forward. His stomach dropped the second Ari replied, "A *deal?*" It might as well have been a growl through clenched teeth.

He turned back to Ari. "Yes. I made a deal with her."

"What did you promise her, Glacier?"

He flinched, the words pelting him like whenever Mrs. Angelis has pulled him aside and scolded him, though everything she'd ever said had been out of concern. Ari's was all fire and fury. But he wasn't a child anymore. He wasn't the scared little boy she remembered. He'd escaped his prison and found a brighter world than he could've imagined.

And he'd been brave enough to return.

Glacier started for her, feeling that bottled-up anger spill out into a controlled blaze with a hand to his chest. "I promised her something that's *mine*, Ari. It's mine to give her, and I'm willingly trading it for us being here."

Her face slackened slightly with shock, eyeing him with slow realization that things weren't the same as what they had been back when his father was alive, let alone back when Louis had been alive.

"Trust me," Glacier whispered. "We can trust them. *I* trust them."

Ari gave begrudging nod, folding her arms over her chest as Mrs. Angelis gripped his shoulder. "All right," she called out, as if answering for Ari. "All of you can come back with us."

"One condition," Nyx said. "Glacier and Cecilia stay with us until we reach our destination."

Ari hesitated, glancing at Mrs. Angelis. "I'll go with—"

"No," Mrs. Angelis said. "I'll go. You take the others back. I have things to discuss with them before we get there."

"But—"

Mrs. Angelis's firm grip made Glacier glance back at her stern expression. He turned back to Ari. "I'll see you again once we stop, okay?"

Ari's face crumpled, and Mrs. Angelis let go of him long enough for her to pull him into another hug. "I missed you so much."

"I missed you too, Ari."

Her arms fell away, signaling for the crew behind her to round back up into their SUVs. Some lingered and frowned before adjusting the machetes and swords at their backs and belts as they took their leave. About half couldn't be much older than he or Noa, while the rest varied ranged somewhere between Ari's mid-thirties to Mrs. Angelis's forties. With a familiar, comforting smile and a steady hand on his back, she guided him back toward the others.

"Please don't tell me I have to get back in the trunk," Glacier said Nyx was in earshot.

Mrs. Angelis chuckled, patting him on the back. "There shouldn't be anyone around to see us between here and our base. You two should be fine as long as we keep you relatively out of view."

"Sounds like you're off the hook, Your Highness." Nyx said with a mock bow as she pulled open the back door. Crow, Weather, and Malice climbed in, shuffling to the back row of seats.

Rune tossed the key to Noa. "You should probably drive. Just in case."

A giddy, child-like smile broke out on her face.

"Maybe I *should* ride back with Ari," Glacier muttered, turning Noa's expression sour.

"No," Nyx said. "If we have to suffer, you have to suffer with us." She climbed into one of the two remaining middle seats, and Glacier climbed in after her, dropping to the floor by her feet and cramming himself up against the front passenger's seat. Rune followed suit with Cecilia, and Mrs. Angelis climbed in front with Noa.

Cecilia smiled as a hand came into view, their fingers intertwining. "You have no idea how happy your father will be to see you again."

Glacier's eyes followed the tops of the other SUVs skimming past, leading the way into the thicket. Noa pulled out after them.

Nyx leaned forward, her knees moving around Glacier. "I do apologize for not being able to tell you sooner. We didn't want anyone to know the Glacier could be alive since it would put you in danger."

Noa's head jerked up, her eyes narrowing at what had to be the rearview mirror. "*Hey*. Don't play with that." The clacking sound stopped, and Glacier shrank down a little further upon the realization Malice had been playing with her violin case.

"She's threatening me, *again*," Crow shouted. "Keep your damn minion under control, Noa."

"Oh, don't act like you didn't deserve that one," Weather snapped.

"I *will* turn this car around, *Alice*," Noa growled. An unhappy hum sounded as her worn boots slid forward into the center aisle.

"At least we weren't bored?" Cecilia said with a nervous smile up at Mrs. Angelis.

"At least two are safe."

Cecilia's smile spread from Glacier to Rune, who stared down at her with that loving, protective gaze. Glacier quietly prayed Mrs. Angelis wouldn't notice just yet, and that she'd give him a chance. For Glacier's sake, he also hoped that she'd give Noa a chance, but he didn't think that would be as big of a hurtle.

"So," Mrs. Angelis started, "all of you are here to help because Glacier made a deal with you? How do I know that you won't turn on us?"

"Mom—" Cecilia piped up, and Mrs. Angelis hushed her.

"*I* made the deal with Glacier, not Nyx," Noa said.

Never mind. The horrible silence that followed definitely told him it'd be a *bigger* hurtle.

"Noa, was it?"

Glacier pushed himself up, elbowing the back of Mrs. Angelis's seat. "I asked her to take Cecilia and I to Kat in Miralta before we found out she..." He couldn't force the words out.

"I see," Mrs. Angelis clipped response saved him the trouble, but there was a thin layer of hostility there. "I suppose you'll leave the moment you get want you requested then?"

"If the future King of Amarais asks us to leave, we'll leave," Noa said. "I personally have no intention of leaving. I don't think they rest of us plan to turn and run the second we're done either. We're invested just as much as you are."

A faint tapping sounded against pleather before Mrs. Angelis spoke again. "If we step out of this car and he orders me to have all of you killed, I'll have it done without question. I doubt he would say that he feels threatened by any of you while we're at your mercy."

"It's a good thing he won't do that then," Noa said.

Glacier bit down on his tongue, willing her not to preemptively spill any of her solid reasoning. "She's right. I won't. I'm alive because of them, and we trust each other. You can trust them too."

"That's all I needed to hear," Mrs. Angelis said, though her tone indicated otherwise.

The car rolled to a stop, and Cecilia's door opened. She fell back against Ari, who helped her out as Rune hopped out after. The chattering chaos outside made him tense up, sending him flailing as the door opened behind him. Mrs. Angelis steadied him as he turned around to face a sea of varying shades of blond. Blue eyes from pale to navy stared back at him, pausing mid-task at saw tables and hunting stations cluttered with weapons and skins.

His breath caught, and the world around him spun. Mrs. Angelis grabbed his arm, pulling him forward when his legs locked up—straight toward the front door of his father's vacation home. Ari called for some of the rebels to move out of the way, weaving through to grab the handle.

The entry was crammed with metal cabinets shoved up against the wall and work lights strung up along the ceiling. Rugs were rolled up and leaned into corners. Every table held some sort of electronic equipment. It was no longer the same house he remembered from his past, let alone where Kat dwelled.

"Dad!" Cecilia's cry cut through his thoughts, her boots squeaking against the entry tiles.

Glacier glanced back to see the others stopped near the door—one of the younger men that'd gone with Ari ordered them to stay put while he called over a few others. Panic surged through him, despite being unable to force out an order to stop or ask for Noa to come with him. Instead, he caught his own reflection in the windows, his stomach twisting with the thought red-ringed eyes might peer back at him.

What he found was far worse: his own. "*Shit—*" he hissed, feeling Mrs. Angelis jump as his hand smacked to his right eye. "I forgot to ask Cecilia to glamour it."

Ari clutched his arm. "If anyone here says *anything* about you being half-Miraltan, they'll have to deal with *me*."

"Don't worry about it," Mrs. Angelis said, her voice soothing. "No one here is against Miralta. You're safe." She shoved opened one of the office doors, the three of them filing in as Ari latched them shut. Mrs. Angelis rounded the desk, and Glacier's heart sank at the display of clutter and stacks of books packed away in plastic tubs.

He had to remind himself Kat wouldn't show up here. This wasn't the same domain.

"There's something I should tell you," Glacier said quietly, twisting the ring through his gloves.

"What?" Ari asked. She stepped closer, her brows furrowing with concern.

"I... I'm a Seer."

Mrs. Angelis's mouth parted in surprise, and Ari grabbed his shoulder. "You're a Seer?" Ari breathed "You're sure?"

Mrs. Angelis's palms hit the desk, rattling the metal racks of old synthetic paper documents. "That information doesn't leave this room, Ari." The ferocity of it took Glacier by surprise before she pinned her eyes on him. "Who else knows?"

"Everyone that came here with me."

"And will they tell anyone? If this were to spread, even around camp—"

"They won't." He shook his head. "They understand what might happen if the wrong people were to find out."

The way her lips formed a thin line told him she was contemplating whether or not they'd use it for blackmail, but she rocked back. "We keep it secret for now. No one else needs to know that you're a Mage. You're already at risk if we run into anyone that might've infiltrated our ranks. I'm fairly sure that everyone here won't let any harm come to you, but I can't say the same for any of our other scattered factions." She grimaced. "We clearly made that mistake before when they used us to kill Louis and Katerina. The fact that you're still alive is a miracle."

"I wouldn't say that." Glacier forced out a quiet laugh, feeling Ari squeeze his shoulders.

"No, she's right. It is," Ari said. "For you to be alive and discover you've had magic... I don't think you realize just how happy your mother would be right now."

He pressed harder on the ring through his glove. "Who, exactly, is running all of this?"

Ari's hands dropped to her sides, turning to Mrs. Angelis.

"I am," Mrs. Angelis said. "If you're looking for the rebellion's leader, you're speaking to her."

His brows furrowed at the idea that all of those commanding posts he'd combed through months ago had been from *her*. They hadn't sounded like anything she'd say, let alone for any of this to be something she would go out of her way to *do*.

"I... don't understand. Why would you..." He shook his head. "What about Cecilia? What if Louis had found out?" His stomach dropped at one of the last memories Glacier had sitting across from his uncle. A rebel recording had been snuck into his desk—one he'd accused Glacier of putting there before Kat had stepped in. "Did *you* send those threats to Louis?"

She exhaled, motioning to one of the chairs. "You should sit down." Ari pulled out the closest one for him, and he shifted his footing before following their orders. "You're right to question the idea that I'd decide to do this on my own. When the enemy faction took Amarais that night, they killed our former leader, and I was the next in line." She cupped a hand over her mouth, closing her eyes. "Glacier... it was Kat."

The chair might as well have been ripped out from under him then. Hurt blossomed in his chest, lancing through his soul. She'd *lied* to him when he'd confronted her about covering for him that night, saying she'd been in his room because it'd been her alibi for planting that video. Every time Kat brushed him off with an excuse or he caught her roaming the halls at odd hours of the day or night, it'd been because she was ramping up for her final act: facing her father.

It'd been *her* rebellion. And she still hadn't told him, even after death. Did she not trust him?

"What?" he breathed, unable to keep the crushing disappointment from his voice.

"She told me she'd had enough of her father's tyranny, and she cornered me to say that she was starting a resistance. It would either be with or without me, but if wanted to see you and Cecilia to live past your twentieth birthday, then I should help her to overthrow Louis." She sank into her seat. "So, I agreed. I never expected his own daughter to turn on him, but she did, and I helped her. I enlisted old friends that'd flown under the radar —even my brother and his family joined without knowing that I was behind part of it until I thought I had lost you both. I'm *so sorry* that I kept it from you, but we couldn't risk either of you knowing and getting caught. *Hell*, I didn't even know I was talking to Ari until a few weeks ago when she showed up with a car full of supplies. We've been operating in the shadows for so long that we can't tell who's who anymore..."

Glacier's fingers dug into the seat cushion as he leaned forward. "Let us help. Let me help you finish what Kat started. All of the people I brought with me are incredibly crafty individuals, some of which specialize in strategy. If we can infiltrate the palace while you have the rebels take the outside, we can seize it all at once."

Mrs. Angelis sat back, blinking before she covered her mouth to stifle a laugh. "You sound like your father when he used to take charge. If you're sure that those six will be useful, then I can't go against you. I'm here to follow *your* orders, Glacier. I'm in *your* service, not the other way around. Not to mention that you being a Seer is a rather large advantage."

Glacier cringed. "I'm... still not completely familiar with it, so I don't know how much use I'll be."

"It'll be more than we currently have," Ari said, gripping the back of his seat. "The more Mages, the better, in my opinion."

"Then you'll be glad to know that Cecilia's learned a trick or two while we've been away," Glacier said. "I think you'll be proud to see what she can do now."

42

AMARAIS ✦ 2705-01-28

CECILIA

Cecilia tugged Rune over to her father, nervously smiling in the face of those curious, deep blue eyes narrowed on him. She squeezed his hand like she was reassuring Rune everything would be fine, when it was actually more for herself. Her father's gaze dipped to their hands before he raised an eyebrow. He folded his arms over his chest when Rune didn't let go.

"Dad, this is Gabriel, but he goes by Rune," Cecilia said, "Rune, this is my dad."

A nearby Amaraian boy looked up from his workstation, adjusting his glasses as he stole a glance at the two of them. His tablet's display winked out, and his head whipped around to it again.

Her father smirked, holding out a hand.

"It's nice to meet you," Rune said, shaking it. "Cecilia speaks highly of you and Mrs. Angelis, it's nice to finally be able put faces to you both."

Her father paused, cutting another glance over to Cecilia. "It's a pleasure to meet you as well, Gabriel. Or would you prefer I call you Rune?"

"Rune was the name my stepmother gave me. She was more of a

mother to me than my birth mother, so that's what I prefer—if that's all right."

"Rune it is, then." He released Rune's hand with a warm smile, turning to the other boy with the bottom of his metal leg brace scratching against the planks. "Jovian—"

Cecilia's mouth popped open in an 'o', staring as the boy scrambled up from his seat. Pink spread over his cheeks while his feet caught on cables, and he smacked against his chair. Jovian—she knew that name from her childhood. It'd been nearly fifteen years since she'd seen any of her cousins.

"Y-yes?" Jovian forced out.

"Why don't you help Seneca with getting our new arrivals situated?" he suggested. "I can imagine if all of you came from Miralta, it was a long trip today."

"It... definitely was, sir," Rune said, releasing a breathy chuckle.

Her father clapped him on the shoulder, peering back at the rest of their group until his face slackened. Both of them followed his gaze as Jovian jogged over to who had to be Seneca—his older brother, despite Jovian's slightly taller stature. Right in the middle of Noa, Weather, Malice, and Nyx stood Crow, hunched in on himself with an uneasy scowl.

"Are you...?" her father started.

"Ah—yes, I'm a twin. *Unfortunately.*" Rune said with an uncomfortable chuckle.

"Oh, good. I thought I might've hit my head a little too hard earlier when I was assisting with some repairs."

Jovian returned with Seneca leading the pack, still decked out in his fur-lined coat in contrast to Jovian's buttoned flannel. "Sorry to interrupt, but Jovian and I are going to take them to the sunroom. It's just being used for storage, and I think they'll want to get away from all the gawkers. You two are welcome to join—especially you, Cecilia. I can imagine you're exhausted after the cramped smuggling ride."

"Thank you, Seneca," her father said, pulling his hand off of Rune's shoulder to nudge her arm with brows knitted together. "Cecilia, you should rest. If you want somewhere a little quiet, I can talk with your mother, and she can find somewhere else for you."

Cecilia shook her head. "Wherever they go is fine. I'd like to stick with them if that's all right." Guilt would probably follow her around if she left Rune alone, considering he was partly here because of her.

"Follow me then," Seneca said, waving them to follow with Jovian anxiously ringing his hands until they all passed to bring up the rear. "So," he continued, walking backward, "where have you been for the past three months if you weren't—you know—*dead?*"

"Well... I've been here and there, I guess," Cecilia said.

"Picking up strange men, it seems," Seneca said with a wry smile and a twinkle in his cerulean eyes as he spun around to throw open the double doors.

The sunroom was in as bad of shape as he'd implied. Crates stacked up against the walls, blocking the direct view of the woods. Faint, bleached light filtered through the ceiling, passing over dust motes and spilling over the matte gray tiles.

Weather strode in past them, running a gloved hand along one of the crates with her neck craned to take in the treetops. "They may be strange, but I can work with it."

Seneca snorted. "At least all of you are colorful, to say the least."

"Was that a jab at her hair, or...?" Crow said, grinning until Weather punched him in the shoulder. He hissed, clapping a hand over what must've been a leftover wound from their encounter with the Volkov. "*Why?*"

Rune's mouth tipped up at the corner, and Crow gave him the middle finger. Seneca chuckled, leaning back against a crate.

Noa stopped in front of him while the others continued milling about the room. "How long do they plan on interrogating Glacier, exactly?"

Seneca's grin faltered like the question had taken him by surprise. He dropped his hands to his thighs, pushing himself to stand a little straighter. "Well, I can check... but they might want to keep him secluded for a while, considering all of the shit we're dealing with. Mariana and Ari will probably hover a little more since he's the only one left to officially take over without any dispute..."

"Make an exception," she said sharply, a dark edge to her tone that made Cecilia spin on her heel.

"Noa, hold on. Seneca, can I talk to you outside for a minute?" she asked, starting toward them.

"I don't think I really care for your attitude," Seneca said with a humorless smile.

"I don't really care what you think." Noa folded her arms over her chest. "I just know that you've separated him from us immediately, and he doesn't get a say in it."

Jovian's eyes nervously darted from Seneca to Noa as he took a shuffling step back. Cecilia grabbed Seneca's arm, feeling a sense of déjà vu—then again, perhaps it was from a distant memory of when he'd pick fights with his brothers and Cecilia would beg him to stop.

He didn't budge, so she squeezed his bicep. "Outside. Now. *Please*," Cecilia said, barely holding onto a tight smile.

Seneca's muscles pulled taught under her grip, but he finally relented, following her into the hall. Jovian jogged out after them, pulling the doors shut.

Cecilia dragged him past several windows before rounding on him, dropping her voice to a low, threatening whisper. "If you won't talk to Mom, I *will*. You can't lock Glacier up and keep him from the rest of us."

"Cecilia, he's *our* prince, not theirs. If Aunt Mariana decides he needs to be quarantined from everyone, then that's what we're doing."

"*No.* They're not just here because Glacier made a deal. That's how it started, but there's more to it now, and if you piss off Noa, she'll snap and find him herself."

Seneca scoffed. "Excuse me?"

"You can't tell anyone if I tell you, Seneca," she hissed.

"Tell me *what?*"

"They're *together.*"

Seneca rocked back, blinking. "*She's* with—" He shook his head and let out a laugh. "You're kidding."

"No, I'm not, and she'll beat you to a pulp you if you keep him from her. Glacier won't be happy about it either. Ask him if he wants to see Noa and see what he says."

"Did you ever stop to think about the possibility that she might just want a *title*, Cecilia?"

Jovian slowed, stopping next to Seneca with a tilt of his head. "Who?"

"Cecilia just told me that girl is Glacier's *girlfriend*."

Jovian's eyes nearly bulged out of his head. "W-what?"

"*Seneca*—" Cecilia's jaw dropped. Of course he couldn't keep his mouth shut for more than two seconds.

"He's my brother. I'm going to tell him if he asks."

Cecilia grimaced. "No, Seneca, she *doesn't* want a title. In fact, I think she'd prefer it if he *wasn't* a prince because of situations just like *this*." She huffed. "Please just go get Glacier. If my mom won't let you, then come get me."

"What's going on?"

Cecilia spun around, her shoulders falling at the sight of Glacier started down the hall wearing a quizzical look.

"I was worried they were going to lock you up somewhere," she said. "What happened? What did they talk to you abou—" She cut herself off, when his expression turned confused. His eyes slid from Cecilia to Seneca and Jovian with a frown. Both of their mouths were agape, staring straight at Glacier's green eye. Fuming, she snapped in front of Seneca's face. He coughed into his fist, and Jovian's head dipped, sheepishly looking down at the floor instead.

"Sorry, I-I—Ari told me that you were half-Miraltan, but I didn't know that your eyes..." Seneca trailed off, pointing to one of his own before Glacier's hand flew up to cover his.

"*Seneca*," Cecilia growled.

"It-it's okay," Glacier said, his hand sliding down his face with a hint of unease. "I honestly just got so used to Cecilia not glamouring it that I forget now. It catches me off-guard, especially *here*..." He glanced back toward the shadows dancing along the wall from the lobby. "I was told that everyone is in the sunroom. Are they still back there?"

Cecilia nodded. "Yes, I was just talking to Seneca to make sure you could find us." She glared at Seneca and grabbed Glacier's wrist, pulling him down the hall.

"Cecilia, you might want to speak to your mom," Glacier said, forcing them to slow before they reached the doors. "There are... some things I think you should hear from her before you hear them from anyone else."

"Is it bad?" she asked nervously.

"It's..." He sighed. "It's just something you need to know."

GLACIER

Noa pulled him into a hug the second Glacier stepped inside. "Gods, I was worried when Cecilia had to drag that little shit outside. He said they might keep you somewhere else."

"What?" he breathed, slipping from her arms with furrowed brows. "Mrs. Angelis pretty much told me the exact opposite, especially once I said all of you could help."

"Then... where's Cecilia? Wasn't she out in the hall when you came in?"

He tugged off his gloves. "Yeah, I said she should go see her mom while I tell the rest of you."

"Something happen?" Nyx asked, wandering forward.

He sighed. "It's... Kat. She was the original leader of the resistance. Mrs. Angelis was her second in command, so she's taken over in her place."

Nyx closed her eyes, slowly nodding. "I'm honestly not that surprised by that. It makes sense, no matter how unfortunate the circumstances, but it can work to our advantage..."

"I also convinced her to let us take the inside of the palace if she directs the rest of them to deal with the outside."

Nyx huffed out a chuckle. "That's my assistant. Perfect—let's start planning, shall we?" She dropped to a knee, rummaging through her bag for her electronic mat. Weather and Crow started tugging over a crate, and Malice skipped over to help, giving Nyx a makeshift table on the edge of the room.

"Let's take a look at our resident dumbasses..." Nyx tapped the corner of the screen, and palace feeds popped up one by one, brightening the dark corners of the mat. "I've been checking in on them occasionally. They still have no clue I'm still messing around in their system."

"I don't suppose you can check to make sure no one else is doing this once we take it back, right?" Glacier asked.

"Of course. *I'm* the only one allow to spy on my friends. Now, onto our players..." She pointed to the profiles cascading down the side of the screen. "We have Lucian Scevola. He's the ringleader. He *looks* full-blooded Amaraian, but his father is from Roth. His legal father, who was on the council, planned to skip him entirely to pass his position down to his younger brother."

"Oh, come on. Don't tell me he killed a kid." Weather grimaced.

"He didn't. Fortunately, getting rid of dear old stand-in dad seemed to satisfy him, and he's got thugs watching his mother and younger brother. We also have his right-hand woman, Chryssa Tatianus. Her father had a thing for Bellegardians, and she's Lucian's polar opposite in appearance," Nyx pointed to a woman with long, black hair and dark eyes against pale skin.

"She looks full Bellegardian," Rune said.

"Pretty much like us." Crow snorted. "Man, that sucks for her."

"Then we have his other three go-tos. The other part-Roth cohort, known as Iason Gratianus, who has the blond hair, but Roth's gray eyes— so he only *almost* passes. Daniil Naevius, who's the dirty blond with purple eyes—"

"Corvian," Weather mumbled, biting her thumbnail.

"And Kostas Omiros. His brown hair is Astravnian, so at least he's got the eyes to show he's Amaraian." Nyx tapped his image while her eyes flicked up to Noa's frown.

"So we have five bastard kids to deal with..." Noa said.

"And all of their troops that think that their Amaraian blood is better than Glacier's rumored Miraltan blood. None of them are from countries that emphatically endorse or praise magic. They're either restrictive of it or have absolutely no leaning on it for one reason or another."

Rune pressed his palms against the edge of the plastic crate. "They believed they'd all be better alternatives than Glacier, so they decided to take it for themselves."

"They're clearly doing a piss-poor job of it, considering all the rebels still banning together," Weather grumbled.

Malice grabbed Glacier's coat sleeve, sending a jolt through him at the sudden movement "I want them dead," she whispered.

"Easy there, killer," Noa said.

"They tried to kill Glacier, didn't they?" she snapped.

"She's got you there," Crow said.

Glacier cupped a hand around hers, ignoring Noa's eye roll. "You don't have to avenge me or anything, Malice. It's okay. Really."

Her arm slackened, and her face fell.

"Well," Noa said, rubbing at her temple. "I'm not going to say '*no*' to killing these assholes if they try to go for Glacier. If they try it—by all means, eliminate them."

Malice's eyes lit up again, accompanied by a feral grin. Glacier brought a hand to his head.

Nyx tapped a few more windows. "I hate to burst your bubble, but we don't need to fight them when we get inside. We just need to distract and confuse them long enough while panic ensues *outside*—long enough for Noa and Glacier to collect the Soul of Amarais and open the Vault. Once that's done, Noa can put an end to the chaos and shut down Lucian and his crew."

"What kind of distraction are we talking about?" Weather asked.

Nyx paused, tilting her head and rubbing a thumb against her chin. The sunroom doors popped open again, and the room turned to Cecilia making her way across the floor to join room.

"Sorry... What did I miss?"

Nyx raised a brow and slowly turned to Malice last.

Noa narrowed her eyes at Nyx. "Um... what's that look for?"

"I think I have a really stupid idea that just might hold them off long enough for you to open the Vault," Nyx mused.

43
AMARAIS ✧ 2705-01-29

NOA

Noa's body complained against the thin mattress, feeling her shoulder dig into the hard floor. But, pressed against Glacier, she was too tired to move and too warm to care. Admittedly, it was sort of romantic sleeping under the stars like this, despite the groans from the rest of their crew scattered nearby. At least they didn't have the rest of the rebels in here with them since they were either busy patrolling or sleeping elsewhere in this makeshift base.

"What are you thinking about?" Glacier whispered.

She stopped fidgeting with his coat button, just visible outside the layers of thin blankets. "Well... when all this is over, I was wondering if I could stay with you, seeing how I'm homeless."

"You sure all of Kingsheart isn't going to unearth some fancy castle for you?" he teased. "Everyone's going be offering you a place to stay. Who wouldn't want to host the Queen?"

She rolled her eyes, unable to hold back a smirk. "But none of them would have *you*."

He puffed out a quiet laugh, resting his forehead against hers. "Of course you can stay, Noa. You're always welcomed, assuming I'm actually given the title of king." He shifted, rolling away slightly to stare up into the dark. "If not, we'll both be homeless together. Again."

"To be fair, it doesn't sound all that bad with you."

He snickered quietly, and she brushed some of his hair away from his eyes. When her arm passed over him, his smile receded. He swallowed. "I told Ari and Mrs. Angelis about me being a Seer."

Her body stiffened.

"Mrs. Angelis wants to keep it a secret. I didn't tell them about... well... whatever I am to you. I figure that's something to discuss after the Vault."

"And did they say anything else?" Noa asked cautiously, Ari's magic floating to the forefront of her thoughts.

"No, not really, but..." He worried his lip. "I'm a little concerned about how they might want me to conceal it. I can't help but think about everyone out here that's bought into my family's endless lies, and all the lies that came before ours... How many years will it take to earn enough trust and stability before I can be open about my magic, along with my blood? Gods, that still sounds so weird to hear—*my magic*."

"Well..." Noa hummed as his head rolled toward her again. "If I walk out of the Vault as the Queen, I think it's possible people would be open to the idea of my counterpart, right? They won't see you as just *some Mage*."

"Maybe..." he whispered. "I guess I'm sort of hoping that people would accept me for me, and not because I may or may not possibly be predestined for something."

"Trust me," she said, smirking as she tugged at his coat collar, "there's only so much you can do to make people like you, and I'd say you're far more likeable than me. But... and this is just a thought—but what if we..." She bit down on her tongue, shaking her head. "Never mind, I don't know what I'm saying. I think the sleep deprivation is getting to me—"

"What?"

She choked out a nervous laugh. "I was going to suggest that maybe we —I mean, assuming you and I are—um... We're sort of stuck together anyway, right?"

His face scrunched like he was trying to decipher what she was saying, and then his eyes went wide. "Are... you *proposing?*" he asked with a chortle. "Noa, we've been officially together for *maybe* two weeks—"

She shoved him. "And that's exactly why I said never mind, but you asked. So, I answered, and there's my counter question—take it or leave it." She grumbled, throwing an arm over the side of her face.

He nudged her elbow away and bumped his nose against hers. "I think I'd like that," he breathed.

She raised a brow. "So, is that a yes?"

He chewed on his lip. "Let's say if you leave the Vault with magic, and I get... whatever title you think I'm going to get, then we'll talk about it."

Noa narrowed her eyes at him. "That sounds suspiciously like you're backing out now."

He snorted, breaking into smile. "I'm saying it's a tentative yes." The expression ebbed away into something a little calmer, despite retaining its wistful edge. "But joking aside, I don't think I've met anyone I'd rather spend my life with."

Her heart melted from the way he said it. "Then we'll talk."

He nodded, covering a yawn. "We should probably sleep on it."

She smirked, tucking her head under his chin. The thrum of his snicker soothed her as she wrapped her arms around him, and she succumbed to sleep.

"Well, shit. She wasn't kidding."

Noa cracked an eye open to the blond halo of hair breaking through the dark navy sky. "What the hell did you just say to me?" Noa snapped, lifting her head slightly with a scowl.

The sound of rustling echoed on the other side of the room before Cecilia's voice rang out in a warning Noa hadn't expected. "Seneca, what are you doing?"

Glacier's arms tightened around her. "Ignore him," he mumbled into her hair.

"Let go—I got to beat the shit out of this guy."

"You're not going to fight him," he mumbled.

"Like *hell* I'm not."

"Seneca, I would leave," Cecilia said, followed by the sound of boots dropping against the tile.

"No, *stay*, Seneca. I want to teach you a thing or two." Noa grinned up at him.

"*Noa.*" Glacier warned. "No."

"You're not the boss of me," she hissed.

"You sure about that?"

She paused, squeezing his arm while she squinted at nothing in particular. *Oh, son of a bitch he is.* She gritted her teeth and pointed a finger up at him. "You are so damn lucky he's the one thing that can stop me from beating you to death right now."

Seneca smirked. She had to refrain from shoving Glacier off of her. Instead, she buried herself a little further into his coat.

"I hate to break it to you," Seneca said, rocking back on his heels and surveying the rest of the group, "but Aunt Mariana wanted me to come get all of you, so don't go back to sleep."

A small, defeated groan escaped Glacier.

"Let me end him," she hissed.

"Tempting..."

"Imagine uninterrupted naps."

"Then I'd have to get rid of *you*, Noa."

"You little—" She bolted up when Seneca threw his head back and laughed. "All right, that's it. You want to take this outside so I don't get your blood on the floor, or should I just go ahead and get it over with?"

The sound of the mattress crinkling behind her alerted her to Glacier sitting up—the last thing she wanted when they were so damn exhausted. She was ready to wipe that smirk off Seneca's face.

"I think you're all bark and no bite," Seneca said.

"Seneca," Glacier said, Seneca's eyes flicking down to him. "She's *not*."

His smile faltered as his eyes met Noa's again.

"No fighting in the sunroom," Nyx called out with a huff. "If we have to sleep here, then I don't want a mess. Leave him alone, Noa. If you're not going to listen to Glacier, then listen to *me*." She grabbed her glasses off a crate, scrubbing at her face.

"But—" Noa started, earning a glare from Nyx before she turned back to her original opponent. "I hope you sleep well tonight." She flashed him a bright, fake smile and turned on her heel to find her bag, stewing on each one of his words. One sharply stuck out in her mind, and she slowed, glancing over her shoulder. "Wait... did you say *Aunt* Mariana?"

He puffed up his chest a little. "Yes, I did. So maybe you should consider talking to me with a little more respect."

Noa hesitated, narrowing her eyes at him before she dropped down to a knee and rummaged through her bag. Seneca's arms fell to his sides when she didn't snap back in answer, and he shifted slightly, quietly answering a couple more questions before he left. The banter left a strange taste in her mouth now—something that she hadn't been able to place until that moment.

Crow stretched, letting out a moan as Weather dragged her bag across the floor and plopped back down on the mattress. "Do you think she wants to talk about any plans that we have for infiltrating the palace or something?" he asked.

"Plan to keep it purposely vague if she tries to ask," Nyx said. "I'd rather not spill anything about Noa and Glacier just yet. We just need to say that we have a plan to get inside and distract them from giving any orders to their people on the outside."

"Well, *how* are we going to get in? I don't think we established that," Weather asked, pushing her hair back.

Nyx tugged out a balled-up sweater from her black duffel. "There are a couple of side entrances. Noa and Glacier will take one, and we'll take the other."

Noa pulled off her coat, shivering as she traded it for a clean sweater and slid it back on. Glacier zipped up his own bag and stood, the two of them side-by-side.

"Come on." He nodded toward the door, where everyone surged into the hall, peeking out into the rest of the makeshift base.

Her hand brushed against Glacier's on their way out, making her shove it into her pocket before they emerged into the entry. She skidded to a stop at the sea of people clustered in the main foyer, all staring up at Cecilia's mother standing on a crate while she scrolled through her phone and rattled off orders like a check list. A mix of daily tasks and preparations for the infiltration of Synos left Noa's head spinning. The crowd appeared mostly tense or determined, despite a few of their weary glances shared with their fellow rebels once they caught sight of Noa and Glacier. She wondered if it was because she was standing next to him, or if it was because she clearly wasn't one of them.

Finally, Mariana dismissed them all and jumped down from the container. "All of you," she said, motioning for them to follow, "with me."

A chorus of boots sounded in her wake, along with a few whispers and frowns. Seneca and another, slightly shorter boy fell in behind them, all the way to an office at the end of another hall. They filtered inside, Noa catching Ari's narrowed gaze from her seat at the window.

Mariana stepped aside and started folding the doors shut behind them, cutting off the two intruders. "Seneca, Linus—wait out in the foyer. I'll send them out when I'm done."

Seneca's shoulders drooped, and Noa smirked, taking the opportunity to flip him her middle finger. Glacier smacked her hand down with a reprimanding glare that triggered Seneca's amusement. Fortunately, his face vanished with the *click* of the doors, and Mariana rounded the desk.

"What's going on?" Cecilia asked quietly.

"I want to make sure that we're all on the same page. The plan is to mobilize in a couple of days once I get ahold of the other camps. Glacier, you said you would work with your little team to form a plan of infiltration. Do have that in place? I'd like us to have everything prepared as soon as possible, in case we need to move up our timeline."

"We do," he said. "We were working on that last night, but Nyx has some requests."

Nyx stepped forward, pulling Ari's attention away from Noa long enough for her to relax.

"I'd like to get in touch with whoever's in charge of your digital surveillance team here. My hope is to take a look at your system and patch you into palace security so you can help control the outside. They'll be able to lock down entrances and exits, as well as disable cameras and lights."

"*You* have access to palace security?" Mariana's brows knit together, exchanging a hesitant, nervous look with Ari, who appeared just as disturbed.

"I'm good at what I do, and what I do is get into things I shouldn't be able to. I've been in their system for the past few months to monitor them. That's how we were able to formulate a plan overnight."

"Do you care to share with the rest of us?" Ari demanded.

"Considering what happened last time," Nyx said, folding her arms over her chest. "I'd rather not tell anyone else our plan because it could be compromised. I know you trust your people, but I don't know them well enough to assume they won't fuck this up for us."

"Understood," Mariana said simply.

"Mariana, I—" Ari started.

"She's right, Ari. If we keep it to as little people as possible, then we have a better chance at success," —she turned back to Nyx— "assuming that your plan is a good one."

"I have a habit of over-analyzing things. It's a double-edged sword," Nyx reassured her.

"You can trust her on this," Glacier said. "She knows what she's doing."

Mariana nodded, taking in a deep breath. "Then I'll direct you to my husband, Livius, and my nephew, Jovian. They're the primary caretakers of our technical resources. They can get you the information you need. They're usually sitting out near the nook on the way to the sunroom."

Cecilia tugged at Nyx's sleeve. "You met Jovian yesterday. He was the one with Seneca."

"Now," Mariana continued, "I'm not sure where the rest of your talents lie, but I'd like for you to at least integrate a little in with everyone else for the next day or so. I have my camp split into groups, based on task, and everyone has to pull their weight to get everything prepared in time. *However*, I want to make one thing *very clear* before I assign you to a job for the day." Mariana gave them a stern look that made Noa tense. "Absolutely *no one* outside of this room is to know that Glacier is a Mage, understood?"

"Of course," Nyx said, cuing a series of nods throughout the rest of the group out of the corner of Noa's eye.

Noa's hands absently tucked into her pockets, lost in thought over Glacier's mother, Ari, and Cecilia—the three Mages Mariana had watched suffer at the hands of her country's former rule. Was she worried someone might harm Glacier as a Seer, or—

Mariana scowled, pointedly staring down Noa when she didn't indicate the same agreement as the rest of the group. *You're no longer the obvious exception here, Noa. They don't get why you'd protect him.*

"Understood," Noa forced out.

Mariana's sharp blue eyes lingered on her for another moment before she turned on a tablet resting on the desktop. "We need a few people for weapons check and assignment."

Malice's hand shot up, and nearly inaudible, panicked whispers followed before Weather and Crow's arms shot up as well. A nervous chuckle spilled out from Weather. "The three of us can handle that. It's probably best we keep an eye on this one." She nodded her head toward Malice with a tight smile.

"Your names?" Mariana asked. Weather—thankfully—called her Alice, despite Malice's head whipping around with a pout. "Done." Mariana nodded and moved on to the next item. "We also need support for patrol."

Rune raised his hand, and Cecilia threw her hand up in turn. Mariana's expression faltered at the seemingly odd choice.

"Cecilia, I'd like for you to assist me in organizing and playing messenger for today," she said. Cecilia's arm dropped back down to pick at her fingernails. Mariana homed in on her now-sole volunteer. "I don't believe I caught your name either."

"Rune." He dropped his hand.

Her mouth opened with a slight nod of recognition. "Ah—my husband mentioned you last night. It's good to put a face with a name." She put on a tight smile. "You'll go with Seneca and Linus—the two that tried to follow us in a little while ago."

"Understood."

"Nyx is with Liv and Jovian..." Mariana muttered before she took in a breath and looked up. "Glacier, I'd like for you to work with me today as well. I'd rather not send you out with anyone else because of the risk," she advised. Glacier gave a somewhat-reluctant nod before Mariana's gaze fixed on Noa again. "So that just leaves you."

So much for tagging along with whatever Glacier planned to do. Noa inwardly cringed, trying not to sweat under Mariana's scrutiny.

Ari's voice broke through the tension. "She can patrol with me."

Noa nearly got whiplash from how fast she turned to stare at Ari with wide eyes. Her hard expression made Noa's stomach twist into knots at the mere idea of trekking outside *alone* with a Mage that clearly wasn't thrilled with any of them tagging along with Glacier.

She's certain you want something from him. Well, that was true, but she wanted *him.*

"Then we're sorted." Mariana gave Ari a satisfied smirk before returning to Noa and her own strained smile. Glacier shifted next to her, as if to say to play nice. "Glacier and Cecilia, stay here and we'll discuss the plan for today. The rest of you are dismissed."

Ari prowled over from her window seat, and Noa bit down on her tongue to refrain from saying anything else that might drop her straight into more hot water.

"Come on. Let's go."

RUNE

The armory wasn't much more than a once-posh winter garden shed strung with the same harsh work lights among tools. Linus pointed out a few tables to Malice, who began pestering him with questions until they detoured inside. The other workers huffed out unsettled laughs with puffs of cold smoke and shook their heads as they waved Crow and Weather over to show them what they were making.

"Alice is rather... excitable, huh?" Seneca asked, folding his arms over his chest with a quiet chuckle.

"A little," Rune said, matching his amusement with a breathy laugh.

"So..." Seneca dug his boots into the snow. "I saw Cecilia introduced you to Uncle Liv yesterday. I'm surprised she didn't come with you. Looks like you two are pretty serious."

Rune tucked his hands into his coat pockets, keeping his eyes fixed on Weather and Crow. They carefully watched their young instructor, elbowing each other in the side whenever the other spoke like they were sharing inappropriate jokes. Rune smirked, lost in old memories blending with new ones. "Yeah, she tried to come along, but Mrs. Angelis kept her back to help with things. Cecilia should be with her now anyway."

He raised an eyebrow. "And here I thought you'd be a little jealous with everyone else pulling her in so many different directions—you two are *together*, right? Or am I being delusional?"

"Yes, we are together, but her family's important to her. She hasn't seen them in months, so I'd rather she'd catch up on lost time. You never know how much time you have left with them."

Snow crunched under Seneca's slight shift, his voice hitting an edge of suspicion. "And what's that supposed to mean?"

"I know what It's like to lose a parent. Or, at least, someone who's as close to a parent I've ever had."

"I'm... sorry to hear that," Seneca said quietly. "I'm glad you value Cecilia's time with her parents. We all lost an uncle and his family, but we never got to meet them. I remember how gutted my dad was when it happened. I don't think I can imagine losing Linus or Jovian—I'd feel like a failure of an older brother."

Linus stretched on his toes, pulling a box down from the shed shelf and popping it open for Malice. Such a simple action that reminded him of when he'd give Crow boosts in their old kitchen when their dad was away.

"My brother is a bit of an asshole, but I would probably lose my shit if something happened to him," Rune said. The thought of Corrine pierced his mind—a woman who Crow didn't have the same relationship with as Rune had, but who he had so much in common with. Every job after her death had left Rune at least a little worried about if Crow got caught or injured.

Seneca's breath curled out with a laugh. "That's what family's for. I can see why Cecilia likes you. You seem like a nice guy—a little rough around the edges, but you got a good heart."

"She makes it that much easier to be a good person. Her kindness has definitely rubbed off on me."

"And what about the others in your group? Is Noa always like that?"

Rune flashed back to the seat he'd taken across from her in the dining car back in Bellegarde all those months ago. He'd thought he fell victim to some joke until she told him to get lost, underestimating a plain-faced girl reading through her phone with a cup of coffee. The memory gave way to them holding hands for the first time for a job as playing make-believe partners. And finally, her tear-stained face on their ride back to the dirty Kingsheart apartment after burning the grimoire.

"Noa's... *difficult* when you first meet her. She doesn't play well with others, but if you gain her trust, you can trust her with your life."

"Did the same go for Glacier, or...?"

Rune gave a hesitant nod before he smirked and shook his head. "They actually hated each other for a while. Glacier was nervous around Noa because she seemed unpredictable, and Noa would get angry with Glacier because he just let himself get pushed around."

"Then what the hell changed for those two to actually *like* each other?" Seneca snorted.

"I think they realized that they've both lived in similar situations growing up, but they had drastically different ways of coping to survive. Noa learned to fight back, and Glacier learned to shut up. They've helped balance each other out a little during the time we've all been together. It's funny to think how protective she is of him after feeling so frustrated for not acting how she would."

"Do you think she'd be a good queen?"

Surprise rippled through Rune, turning to stare at Seneca's watch over the other rebels jogging through their makeshift camp, past haphazardly parked SUVs. The thought that these could be her people—*this* could be her home...

"I don't think she'd be conventional by any stretch of the imagination," Rune began, "but she knows how to take charge, and she listens to the people she trusts. She may seem reckless and stubborn, but she knows her faults. I think Glacier and Nyx are the two who keep her in line the most, but I've been able to talk her down on occasion. And if she does something that you don't think is a good idea, she has a good reason. She cares about the people close to her, and she wouldn't let anything happen to them. She'd do the same if this was her country. She'd fight for them until the end."

Seneca closed his eyes, biting his lip. "I want to believe you, but I have a hard time imagining it..."

"Give her a chance," Rune said. "You won't regret it."

NOA

Snow consumed Noa's boots as she trudged behind Ari, ducking through prickly sprigs of pine needles. The biting chill that filled her lungs with every breath reminded her of home but in all the wrong ways. She shoved down the rising nausea whenever she lost sight of Ari for more than a second, buying into her mind's lie that she'd fallen back in time—back to where she was following Myron to the pond.

"I think you and I should have a chat," Ari finally said, slowing down as they crested the ridge and the gate around the slanted mansion roof came into view. "I don't know what kind of shit you're trying to pull, but I'm not thrilled with your attitude. Frankly, I can't imagine *why* Glacier is even bothering with your damn deal." She turned halfway, shoving her hands in her pockets near the brush of a tree, narrowing her eyes at Noa.

Noa gritted her teeth, her frustration hitting its limit from the sheer lack of control. Any other time, she'd happily play the villain, but here—*now*—not anymore. "How about *you* cut the shit, Ari. I get that you don't like me, okay? But I'm not going anywhere. I'm not just here because I made a damn deal with Glacier. Sure, that's how this whole thing started, but I do actually give a shit about him. And *yes*, I get you're suspicious of all of us because we're not Amaraian, so what the hell are we doing here, right? Well, I, for one, don't want him to fucking *die*." Noa held out her arms at her sides.

Ari reeled back in surprise before her face darkened. "And why would *you* care about what happens to him? He's not *your* prince."

"Funny since I would ask you the same question as a fugitive, except I already *know* why you're hovering around him. You were in love with his mother," Noa said, almost regretting Ari's flinch. "I don't plan on telling anyone else, but Nyx and I did our research before we came here to make sure we weren't marching Glacier into certain death. He was utterly terrified to come back here, but he insisted that he had to try—at *least* for Kat and his father. So *you* were the only insurance we had that he wouldn't be killed on sight. It also wasn't hard to put together that you're a Mage too, Ari."

Ari's mouth worked until her hand ran over it. Her eyes searched Noa's like she was trying to puzzle out how she'd figured it all out. "H-how—" Ari shook her head and grimaced. "Never mind, I can assume that Nyx dug things up, but I—who else knows? You've just listed at least a few Amaraian laws I've broken, and I'd rather keep those a secret."

"Just me and Nyx," Noa sighed, nudging the toe of her boot further into the snow. "I didn't even tell Glacier because I didn't know if he knew, and it's not my secret to tell. You also shouldn't be punished for being who you are. You should be proud that you're a Mage." A mirthless laugh bubbled up as she shook her head. "And I don't think Glacier should be punished because he has a green eye and black hair—that his mother was Miraltan... Cyrus loved her. You loved her. Glacier never had the chance to love her, and he never got the chance to be loved by her. It's horrible and sad and *wrong*. Amarais can't continue like this."

She stared out at the winding trail leading up to the house, her shoulders falling as she took in all the fortifications. Generators, crates of supplies, a scrapyard of materials. Her heart crumbled, thinking of Astravny and all the harm that'd come to it because of the very country she stood in now. And here it was, just as destroyed because of selfishness and greed.

Glacier's home he'd begged to come back to, even if it was a hopeless case.

"I love him, Ari," Noa whispered, unable to meet her eyes out of fear that she'd use whatever magic she had on her for having the audacity to say it.

Instead, the soft crunch of snow sounded, and Noa turned just as Ari stopped in front of her. Her features softened, and sympathy rolled off her in waves, threatening to knock Noa over.

"How does he feel about you?" Ari asked.

Noa let out a tired laugh. "I would hope he feels the same way since he finds every stupid excuse to follow me around. I'm surprised he still puts up with my shit. That's why I'd throw myself in front of a train if I knew it would save him from harm."

Ari ruffled her own blonde hair. "I may have jumped to conclusions about you too soon. Either that, or you're a *really* good actress." She broke into a tired smile, mirroring Noa. "Come on, let's actually try to patrol while we talk. Just—no more Mage talk out in the open, okay?"

Noa nodded and followed her back into the trees.

"You're back!" Cecilia chirped from the office doorway. Mariana's eyes flicked up from her tablet, her lips drawn into a thin line.

"Cecilia's mom hates me, doesn't she?" Noa mumbled out of the corner of her mouth as she and Ari trekked down the hall.

She snorted. "Well, she doesn't know you're interested in a boy she's fondly referred to as her son, and she thinks you're not being cooperative. I'm pretty sure she's less than thrilled with you."

The slosh of melting snow against the floor gave way to chatter in the living room, and finally to the thump of a stack of synthetic paper being dropped onto a metal filing cabinet. Glacier brightened, smiling when they came into view. "Welcome back."

"Easy now," Ari whispered into Noa's ear.

Noa folded her arms over her chest, trying to play off her embarrassment. She rubbed her arms a little, hoping the heat in her cheeks would be mistaken as a result of her patrol. Mariana, however, narrowed her eyes at them, thanks to Ari's smug expression.

"What are you two colluding about?" Mariana asked slowly, the corner of her mouth dipping down.

"We had a good walk." Ari shrugged. "Got to know each other a little."

Glacier gently patted the edges of another stack of papers, shuffling them into place with a quizzical look in her direction. She flashed him an innocent smile and unzipped her coat. "Do you need help?" she asked.

He held out a stack of papers to her. "There's a lot of printed data we need to sort if you're up for it."

Mariana's jaw flexed. "Perhaps Noa should join the others in the armory instead if she'd like to help?"

Noa paused mid-reach, holding her tongue.

Ari waved a hand as she tugged off her gloves and tossed them onto the window seat. "Let her help, Mariana."

Despite Glacier's surprised blinking and Mariana's furrowed brows, Noa plucked the stack from his hands. She took a seat on the floor, and Glacier hesitantly sat down next to her.

"Cecilia, dear," Mariana said, clearing her throat, "would you please take this out to your father?" She grabbed something from the desk and held it out to Cecilia. The gleam of an old hard drive came into view as Cecilia hopped over, took it with a cheery, "Sure!", and left. Mariana motioned to Ari, and she pushed the doors shut.

"They're together, Mariana."

Noa's jaw dropped. "Ari!"

Glacier cringed, shielding his face with a hand.

"It's like ripping off a bandage," Ari said.

Mariana's tablet clattered against the desktop. "I-I'm sorry, Ari, I think I misheard you..."

Ari shook her head. Glacier groaned, staring Noa down. "*Why* do you go and say things that you don't want people to know?"

"Would you rather Ari kick my ass in the woods and bury my body where no one will find it?"

"Good gods..." he breathed.

She lightly smacked him with her paper stack.

"I'm going to shove you in this bin and bury you myself," he threatened.

Noa scoffed. "Oh, please. I'd like to see you try."

He ripped the stack out of her hand smacked her back.

"*All right*—that's it!" She lunged forward, grabbing at the papers again. He fell backward, trying to keep them out of reach and shoving her shoulder away. A melodic laugh broke their squabble, the two of them pausing to stare at the source of the sound.

Mariana covered her mouth, unable to stifle her amusement. Noa sat back again, brushing off her coat as Glacier pushed himself up.

"I'm sorry—" Mariana said, shaking her head. "I didn't expect..." That's when Noa saw it: that deep sadness barely covered by the twinkle of joy in her eyes.

Noa stood. "I-I'll go to the armory."

Mariana's eyes widened in surprise, but Ari snapped her fingers and pointed back to the floor. "Sit." Noa paused, staring at her until she reiterated the silent command. Her knees hit the damp rug.

"I apologize," Mariana said, running her fingertips under the cuffs of her coat sleeves. "I assumed that you were being difficult out of spite, rather than unease. All of the people you came with appear to hold you in high regard, including my daughter. I just... wasn't sure why since I felt like you were simply here for yourself."

"I didn't mean to—" Noa started.

"It's fine, Noa. You're in a place that doesn't act kindly to anyone that doesn't fit their standard of 'normal'. I've seen Glacier go through it for years, but he didn't have the option of acting uncooperative without consequences."

He quietly tapped the papers against the carpet, unable to meet their eyes.

"I know," Noa said. "Which is why I'll beat the shit out of anyone who even considers exploiting Glacier. And I didn't cut a deal with him because I was trying to exploit him either—I made him a deal because it was beneficial for both of us at the time, and then…" —she tore her gaze away, catching Glacier's eyes— "we got to know each other." He held out his hand, and she took it, curling her fingers into his. "I realized we bring out the best in each other, and that's worth so much more than whatever deal we made. So, I'm here to see this rebellion through to the end, for Glacier."

44

AMARAIS ✧ 2705-01-30

NOA

Noa lifted herself up on her toes in the midst of the foyer, bumping shoulders with Glacier. Mariana stood on her crate against the wall with a somber expression and a hand to her heart.

"Tomorrow night we'll be in Synos," she began, her and curling into a fist. "We sent a couple of runners out last night to pick up some additional vehicles, and they'll be back in about an hour. When we arrive, we'll control the situation on the outside of the palace and take back the city while a small group infiltrates the palace. We need to be efficient in our communications and coordination. Our tech team will be monitoring our systems around the city thanks to one of our new arrivals. Each team will have a technical advisor monitoring their division. Stay alert and play it safe but hold your ground. There's enough of us when we're all together that we'll be a force to be reckoned with. Remember that. It's time to take our country back." Mariana held her fist in the air. "For freedom!"

The rest of the room threw their own fists up, sending a chill through Noa. "For Amarais!" they shouted back in unison. They dispersed, falling into their assigned groups and splitting off into the mansion or wandering outside for their final preparations.

Mariana jumped down and strode over to her remaining eight subjects. "If you need time for any additional preparations for tomorrow, do it now. We'll be traveling through some backroads to keep our distance, so we can converge on Synos with the rest of the rebels. It'll be a long day, but we need to make sure we're undetected until it's too late for any of them to realize what's happened."

Nyx tapped a knuckle against Glacier's arm. "I'd like to double-check a few things with Glacier today, if that's alright. After that, I think we should be ready."

Mariana nodded. "Of course."

Nyx waved him to follow, and they started toward the sunroom, already quietly chatting once they were out of earshot.

"If there are any concerns," Noa said, "they'll come and get us. Just point us where you need us in the meantime, and we'll help finish up everything else."

It'd been worth earning Mariana's proud smile. Noa couldn't help but liken it to Lazarus's whenever he'd given her a task she'd gone above and beyond with.

"Cecilia," Mariana said, "why don't you and Rune assist me today while Noa goes with Seneca and Linus?"

Noa fought back a cringe, catching sight of Seneca leaning against the entryway. He wiggled his fingers at her with a smirk.

Shit.

Seneca jogged up the path, sliding in the snow and sending chunks skittering over Noa's boots. Linus sighed behind her. "Sorry about my brother, he's a little... *excitable* sometimes. Are you okay with deep snow?"

"I'm from Astravny," Noa said. "I was practically born in snow." The admission of her homeland tasted strange on her tongue after twisting her narrative for so long. But there was no Volkov left there to give her a reason to hide it and no real motive to cover up that little fact.

"What's it like there?" Linus asked.

She thought of Kole when she stared at the longer waves of blond hair poking out from under his gray knit cap. He'd grown his hair out a little when he was eighteen until Myron ordered him to cut it off.

"Um... it's pretty shitty there, honestly," Noa said with an awkward laugh.

"Worse than here?"

She hummed, staring out at the faint lights far past the protection of the tree line. "Maybe a bit, though right now you guys are giving them a run for their money."

He sighed. "Yeah. I hope it'll give better after tomorrow, but I can tell Aunt Mariana's worried."

"Just do your part, and everything will be fine, okay?" Noa nudged him with her elbow. "You'll be able to relax when Glacier gets his throne back, and everything will start to fall into place."

"You sound so confident," he said with a chuckle.

"I always like to think I have some sort of trick up my sleeve." Noa winked.

He grinned. "Malice was saying the same thing yesterday about you."

"Yeah, well Mal—" Noa stopped and her head whipped back around. "*Malice?* Gods, I told her not to ask people to call her that..." She rubbed her forehead and trudged forward.

"I think it's a cool name," Linus said, beaming—that relation to Cecilia spilling out and making Noa cringe. "And she showed me her violin."

"Sweet Seraphine, strike me down."

"What?"

"I said, maybe we should catch up to Seneca." She forced out a puff of smoke as she jogged after him.

His smirk filled her with dread when he glanced back. "Rune put in a good word for you yesterday."

"Did he now?" Noa grumbled.

"What, you don't trust he'd say anything nice?"

She rolled her eyes. "I trust Rune, but he's also had a track record of attempting to throw me under a train when the opportunity strikes."

"I think I like him even more now," Seneca said with a chortle.

"Yeah, well you can have him. You can take him out on long walks when Cecilia finally gets sick of him."

"Is that what you do with Prince Glacier? Or do you just get cozy with him at night?" Seneca shot her a teasing grin, tugging his coat collar up further around his chin.

"If you *must* know, they're mutual walks and mutual cuddles for emotional support."

"So... you really like him," he said, all joking gone now as he slowed.

"Yes," she said, feeling Linus's eyes on her.

"I told Cecilia you might be in it for the title—"

A laugh spilled out of Noa. "Hell no. I'd prefer he didn't have one. It'd make my life a hell of a lot easier."

"And that's what Cecilia said." He snorted, shaking his head. "But you're willing to take it on? Even the responsibilities that come with it?"

Noa groaned. "Honestly? Yes and no. Yes, because I think I might be able to help. No, because it's a pain in the ass, and I don't really know the first thing about ruling a country. I can be a leader, but... I don't know. I'd rather support Glacier. He's got the mind for it with all the tactics and planning, which I tend to lack. But I can enforce his rulings."

"That's actually really reassuring to hear," Seneca breathed, plucking at a sprig of pine needles and sending a dusting of snow into the air. "Rune was right about you. You're a fighter, and I think that's something we could use right about now, Your Highness." He smirked.

45
AMARAIS ✧ 2705-01-31

NOA

Noa woke to Nyx shaking her shoulder and mumbling to Glacier about Mariana stopping by. Bags were left once they were dressed—a stark reminder that they'd either be able to return victorious to reclaim their things, or they wouldn't come back at all. It left a phantom weight at her back, feeling the incessant need to reach for it when they started down the hall and she caught the glint of light off Malice's metal weapons case.

Cecilia broke off from Rune as they reached the end of the corridor, falling into her father's arms. The quiet request for her to come back safe nearly cut Noa's heart clean in half. Cecilia would come back, even if Noa couldn't.

Seneca gave Jovian one last pat on the shoulder before Linus gave him a hug. Noa's vision swam, superimposing the images of her, Ezra, and Kole. *You can't go back now,* she reminded herself. *You can only go forward. Make what time you have count.*

"You ready?" Seneca's voice cut through her thoughts, snapping her back to reality.

"Rarely," she said with a bolstered smirk. "But that doesn't stop me getting knee-deep in tough situations."

"I guess no one's truly ready to stand face-to-face with an enemy."

The gentle mumble of well-wishes from Linus to Malice next to them was broken by Ari's commanding order for their group to follow her outside. This time Seneca and Linus didn't trail behind, despite Malice lingering like she wanted to walk with them. The trample of boots sounded in time with Noa's heart on their way through the mansion's door into the snow. Pink licked past the trees as car lights flicked on and engines turned.

Ari brushed alongside her, nodding to their SUV. "Mariana told me to ride with you."

"Where's—" Noa spun around, finding Mariana at the side of the door, wrapping her arms around Cecilia and Rune before grabbing Glacier's hand.

"They act like we're walking to our deaths," Crow mumbled as he stepped up next to her, his tone laced with unease.

"If we slip up, we could be," Nyx said.

"Don't hesitate to send us a signal if things start to go south," Ari said.

"Believe me, I'll be keeping that in mind," Nyx breathed.

Glacier finally nodded and stepped away from Mariana, swiping his wrist over his eyes on his way over to Noa. The same sky-pink brightened his nose. "You ready?" he asked.

Rarely, but for you?

"Always."

GLACIER

Noa's fingers twisted around Glacier's as the sun rose, jostled by the SUV's crawl over the snow-blanketed pavement onto rocky side trails. He closed his eyes and focused on the thrum of the vehicle, taken back to the swipe of blades against the windshield. The world fell in and out of focus the longer they drove. Time became measured by idle chatter, musings, and grand ideas about parties to throw once it was all over.

At least the optimism fueled his spirit when the sky bled into darkness again. Piercing city lights broke through the sky ahead, haloing the deep purple sunset. They closer they got, the further forward Glacier leaned in his seat, grabbing onto the shoulders of the driver's seat to peer past Rune.

Windows were boarded over or covered up with tarps, iron fences were warped or snapped, the glass ceiling of the palace—the once large, domed epicenter of Synos—was caved in from its platform on the hill of its sector namesake. His heart ached at the scene of destruction he'd escaped from, further evidenced by the flashing signs with curfew times. People dressed in heavy, faux-fur coats and protective vests with swords at their backs stood in a cluster on a street corner, throwing back their heads in raucous laughter—makeshift guards near an idling security car with its logo partially stripped away.

His hand squeezed Noa's as the SUV slowed to a crawl, letting pedestrians hurry past with small children and light bags of food. All of them kept their heads down as if they thought it was another patrol car.

Go home. Stay safe, he willed, adding a silent prayer to Seraphine that she'd call upon the other gods to shield them from what might happen next.

Rune revved the SUV up the winding hill, passing small mansions and snow-dusted gardens with knocked over statues. Shattered lightbulb cables swayed and tapped against hollow, plastic pergola beams. His stomach turned as the car passed through the palace sector walls and its busted gate.

"Holy shit..." Ari whispered, ducking slightly to stare up at the buildings from the front seat.

"It wasn't like this before, was it?" Weather asked. "What the hell did they do to the place?"

"They turned the whole thing into a hell-hole," Crow murmured, "even the damn palace sector. You'd think they wouldn't shit where they eat..."

"Well, it's a good sign since it proves they're disorganized," Nyx said.

Ari pointed out the windshield. "Stop it right there, by the open gate."

The car rolled to a stop, and Ari threw open her door. Noa followed suit, and Glacier climbed out after her. Cecilia jumped into the next row, grabbing at the door handle.

"Be careful," she said.

"I will," he breathed, and jogged off after them as the SUV rolled down the street.

A shiver rippled through him as the gate clanged in its frame, and they ran through the palace side yard. He felt like he'd been plucked out of his body and dropped here from all the times he'd stared out the windows.

He jumped at the sudden clamor of shouts and hum of ads launching on street displays, making his heart race as he pressed up against the concrete wall's marble façade.

"Nyx," Noa hissed, pressing a thumb into her comm. "Door's locked."

"Move," Ari said, nudging her to the side. She placed her hand on the door, right over the lock, and a faint, orange glow darkened to red. Glacier's jaw slackened when she pulled her hand away and kicked the door free. She'd *melted* it.

"Never mind," Noa said.

"You're a—" Glacier breathed.

"You're not alone, Glacier," Ari said. "Now finish what your parents started and make your cousin proud." She smirked an stepped back, letting Noa shove the door open the rest of the way to check the corners.

His hands curled into firsts. "We'll fix this."

She put her hand to her heart in respect. "Good luck."

Noa snorted. "Who needs luck when you have skills and a Mage?"

Ari's grin grew devilish as she gave one last wave and dashed across the yard. So, Glacier ducked inside, and the door closed behind them.

NYX

Nyx threw herself through the western door, cringing at the sound of the blaring alarm. Her boots squeaked against the dusty white tiles as she swiped through her phone to see the security feeds. Malice's violin case smacked against her side, flailing with her small bag of electronics in her hurtle toward the first set of locked doors.

The thud of a body slamming against another door somewhere down the hall at her back made her smirk, especially when it was followed by the jiggling of a handle and confused yelling. She tapped the control for the doors dead ahead, and hurtled through, locking them behind her making a sharp turn down another corridor.

Control room, control room... She mapped out the path based off the blueprints she'd studied every night since she first stepped foot in Amarais. Every camera dimmed before she came into view, and she silently thanked Jovian.

She skidded to a stop right outside frosted glass sliding doors, panting as she tapped the panel with a finger. It lit green, and she waved to Jovian on the camera behind her before stumbling inside. Motion-activated lights poured over the panels as her hands grazed their frames.

"Here we are," she whispered to the small army of blinking lights and feeds. She dropped her bags into a rolling chair and dug out her hacking tools. The disc stuck to the panel top, whirring to life and reverse-switching everything from entrance and exit door access, reinforced shutters, and disabling all out-bound communications.

No one was leaving until Noa opened the Vault and they'd dealt with everyone inside.

WEATHER

Weather brushed back jet-black hair as she strode down the hall. She was riding on hope that this new glamour was as convincing as Cecilia said it was after she and the others scrubbed off their Amaraian masks. But it wasn't like she had many other options. She pushed open the doors to the grand hall, stepping into the light of the grand chandelier with its half-burnt out bulbs and prismatic glass shards.

The rugs cascading down the parting, double staircases looked gray and muddied from overuse, torn and ripped in places. The cracks and dents along the walls reminded her of the apartment she'd once shared with her father—back when fixing those things had been a luxury just out of reach. Instead, these monsters were sitting on everything they'd stolen and left the rest in ruins. And, to top it all off, they'd obscured the view of the balcony with a banner made of poorly-stitched sheets and paint in ancient Amaraian script she couldn't read.

Her blood boiled, despite the confident smirk that climbed across her face.

Lucian Scevola looked up from his makeshift desk—comprised of a former entry table frame and a door pulled from its hinges—and his blue eyes sparkled, matching a devilish smile that made her skin crawl. "Chryssa, there you are. I was wondering where you got off to."

They still had no idea what was happening, even with their clutter of laptops and projections strewn about their pathetic setup for a nerve center. There was still a whole other breezeway between them and the palace steps —no entries or exits, plus the soundproofing meant they likely hadn't heard any of the rioting outside. Everyone at the west entrance was likely still scrambling after briefly abandoning their posts with Nyx's earlier destruction. Too few of them had real military training.

She forced her voice lower to a deep, soothing tone, remembering the hours of practice the night before with Rune. "I was—"

"What the *hell?*"

Weather whirled around, her heart stopping at the wide, dark eyes of the *real* Chryssa. She mirrored her uncomprehending stare. "Who the *hell* are *you?*" Weather demanded in Chryssa's mimicked, sultry cadence, feeling giddy when she paled in horror.

Lucian took a step back, his brows furrowing as he slid his gaze from one to the other. Daniil, Iason, and Kostas got up one by one, reaching for their daggers with hesitation.

"This *bitch* is an imposter!" Chryssa said, pointing at Weather with a navy-painted nail.

Weather gritted her teeth, shaking her head. "*I'm* the imposter? Lucian, didn't you say that you wanted me to check into the supplies? That's what I was coming back from."

Chryssa's jaw dropped. Weather had to push down a giggle, knowing full-well that the real Chryssa had been fumbling around, poorly counting everything out from the view on Nyx's phone. Chryssa sputtered, running out of validation. So, her face twisted into rage as she marched up to

Weather, making Lucian tense. But Weather stood her ground, curling her hands into fists to combat the fury pouring off of her.

"You listen here, bitch. I don't know who the fu—"

A series of sharp clicks rang out through the room, and their crew spun around, pulling out blades in panic. Chryssa stiffened.

Checkmate.

"Did *you* just lock us in here?" Lucian demanded waving his dagger at the real Chryssa.

She gaped at him. "And *how* would I have done that? Wouldn't that mean that I'm locked in here with you, too?"

"What if she was in the control room while I was checking supplies?" Weather said, taking a panicked step back and reaching for the blade at her hip.

Lucian, the ever-vigilant white knight, started toward the real Chryssa to defend who he thought was his actual girlfriend.

Good boy, Weather thought.

"*What?*" Chryssa sputtered, her eyes darting around, putting her hands up and shaking her head.. "I—How—There's no way that I would know—"

"One of them *has* to be a Mage..." Iason said, closing in on them.

"*Clearly,* but how to we prove which one?" Kostas snapped.

Chryssa's lips pursed, and she whipped a knife from her belt, lunging toward Weather. Weather gasped and jerked away, but not before feeling the sting of a scratch across her cheek. She staggered back, slapping her hand to the shallow wound and pulling it away to find a thin line of blood. The spell was broken. The rune was useless.

Weather rubbed the rest of the way and lifted her head to take in the audience of wide-eyed stares. "All right, *all right.*" She held up her hands in a half-hearted surrender. "You caught me." A sly smile broke across her face in response to their rapidly increasing anger, barely masking their panic.

"I'll give you *one* chance to tell me who you are before I kill you," Lucian growled.

She let a single word roll off her tongue, excited to see how quickly they might beg for forgiveness like Giovanni had. "Volkov."

GLACIER

"This way." Glacier shoved open the door to the stairwell on shaky legs, winded from their starts and stops through the corridors. They raced down to the parking level, and he shivered at the dwindling number of cars left. He swallowed back the fear that a hoard of rebels would pour out after them and turned on his heel to run off in the opposite direction.

Staggered steel doors mirrored his movements with their warped reflections, all labeled for servers, cleaning supplies, and storage. He made another turn, hearing Noa skid to a stop behind him while he fiddled with a keypad to the side of a set of locked doors. She pushed on the handles and took a step back, checking behind them. He pressed his thumb to the pad, it flashed green, and she jumped at the doors again, shoving them open.

The clang of the lock set him on edge, but there it was: the family vault. Its circular entrance sat undisturbed at the end of the harsh white hall. Their footsteps echoed through the wide corridor as it sloped downward to the menacing, red-lit machine off to the left. He rolled up his sleeve, steadying his breathing as he mentally replayed the instructions to open it.

You just have to put your arm in and follow the prompts. That's it.

He'd been fifteen when he was finally given access, along with Kat, while Louis glowered behind them. The technical assistant had been a kind woman though, walking him through the necessary steps that popped up on the screen in blurry succession.

Glacier tucked his left hand into the recess and pressed his palm to the smooth glass scanner inside. The instruction display flashed red, and he looked back to see Noa right behind him.

"You have to back up. Behind the line on the floor." He pointed with his free hand toward the discolored marble strip. She begrudgingly shuffled over to it, signaling to the machine that he wasn't being coerced into opening it for someone else—something his grandfather had likely requested.

Noa bounced on the balls of her feet, and he returned to the scanner, laying his hand flat again. This time, the screen flashed green, and he jumped at a vice clamping down on his arm. His head swam as he tried to read the next prompt and leaned forward to have it scan his blue eye—a process that dragged on for an eternity, trapping him in a nightmarish prison.

Finally, the pressure on his arm fell away, and the layers of doors slid into the walls. Glacier tugged his sleeve back down and motioned for Noa to join him at the threshold, watching it part to a dim, dusty room lined with glass cases and shelves. After all he'd seen, he found it to be somewhere between a museum and a storage closet, though it had a few other chambers with cots and an office. This was his grandfather's bunker. Louis's bunker. Never his father's bunker because he refused to back down from a challenge.

Glacier stepped forward, striding toward the case in the center of it all, placed under a painting of the late King Elias as if it were mocking him with its presence. He stared up into his cold, blue eyes. The hate may have not started with his reign, but Glacier wanted to ensure it ended with it.

"We did it..." Noa breathed, calling his attention to the glass case again. "Holy shit, we got them all."

He put his thumb to the small scanner at its base, and the lid hissed free. Glacier lifted it and gently dropped it to the marble floor, plucking out Noa's prize. He held the Soul of Amarais out to her, and she slid it from his grasp.

Then they ran, barely closing the vault behind them on their way to the ballroom.

WEATHER

Lucian threw back his head, letting out a cackle and clutching his stomach.

"What? You don't believe me?" Weather asked.

"I *hired* the Volkov. Why the hell would they come after *me?*"

Weather pasted on a cat-like grin, watching his composure waver. "It's called a counter-offer. Turns out we could get a better deal if we dealt with *you*, instead."

"You're lying" he snarled. "If you're really Volkov, prove it."

Weather snapped her fingers, and the sheet-banner obscuring the balcony fell away. A large, fiery V jutting out of a triangle took over the wall behind three figures dressed in black. Malice took center stage with the twins at her sides, hoisting herself onto the balcony railing with a feral grin. The glint of a dagger spinning in her hands made the entire room surge back in surprise.

"I am the Queen of the Volkov," Malice said, her voice dripping with excitement as the color leeched from her face and black spread through her eyes—Cecilia's illusion taking full effect. "And I've come to fetch your souls."

The manifestation of every rumor—every fear people would whisper in the nooks of Kingsheart came to life right before their very eyes: a vivid image of the Volkov being nothing more than soulless, ethereal monsters that people nearly depicted as daemons.

Chryssa gasped, stumbling back from her, and Lucian whipped around, his mouth agape. Weather held up her own chalk-white hand, examining her jet-black nails with a smirk.

"So, you still think I'm lying?" she asked.

Then the room fell into darkness and a chorus of screams.

46

AMARAIS ✧ 2705-01-31

GLACIER

Glacier shoved through the side doors, stumbling into the ballroom to the sound of popping glass under the soft blanket of snow and froze. He swallowed, staring down phantasmal images of all the gray and white suits and dresses he'd seen mere minutes before he and Cecilia slipped away that night to change from the traitorous blacks they'd been provided. But no bodies littered the floor, no music played, and no grand announcement from his uncle projected from the balcony to serve as his distraction. Instead, the faint whir of car alarms carried with the wind over the dismantled ceiling.

He pressed forward, fearing every step might uncover dried blood spattered over the tile—blood that could've been his own. His stomach churned, even as Noa gently prodded him to move a little faster.

Glacier dropped to a knee in the center of all the ripped, sapphire and platinum banners and pushed aside small mounds of snow. Noa joined him, uncovering the curve he'd been looking for. He followed the circle's edge and crawled closer to the middle, where he dusted away that now-familiar emblem. Just as he'd remembered it, minus the snow embedded in the key's place.

The jingle of keys took over the eerie silence as Noa sorted through each of them. The Heart of the King, the Blood of Esmedralia, the Spear of Mharu—

The Shield of Miralta fell into the snow, and she scooped it up while Glacier carved out as much of the snow as he could. She placed it into the recess. A *click* sounded, and they met each other's eyes in a mixture of giddy disbelief and awe. Snow shifted around them, and they hurried to their feet, huddling close to the key as the ring in the middle of the floor dropped downward.

Misty white wisps mixed with glass fell into the cavernous depths, backlit by a faint glow at the center pillar—the one he and Noa were standing on. The pillar holding the key. *Magic* flowed through it, along with the runes glowing at the inner base of each floating step.

"It's *real*," Noa breathed, staring down at the spiral staircase.

A shuttering groan finally echoed from the bottom, and Glacier picked up the Shield of Miralta. Then Noa took his hand, and they began their decent.

CECILIA

When the lights went out, Cecilia bolted for the manual switches.

Keep them blind. Keep them scared.

So far, it was working, but she tripped at the bottom of the steps, sprawling outward into the panicked council heirs who were also running for the same thing. She gritted her teeth, pushing herself up, and throwing herself into another dead sprint. Her heart raced as she hit the wall, fumbling around the faint glow of the panel with Nyx's tool to short it in her hand.

A shove, and Cecilia fell backward, the device crying out in a horrible screech against the tile as light flooded the room again. She felt the flaming V vanish from the wall, along with what had been added without runes to all of there glamours. Her body screamed at the sudden snap of energy, and she winced in trying to pick herself back up with Iason standing over her with a snarl.

Nyx's breathless voice came over the comms, "Plan B."

NOA

Noa's hand traced along the faint white glow of the pillar until they reached the bottom.

It was *real*. So very, *very* damn real.

Every doubt she'd had up until this point faded at the edges and amplified in the center—just like the glow of light focused on the room below. This *existed*, but it felt like when she'd plunged beneath the ice years ago, unable to comprehend death until she'd recovered from it. The fear this might be the same made her squeeze Glacier's hand as he carefully took each step behind her.

The stairs spat them out in front of a circular pattern of what looked like hand-drawn stars on the floor. But as they drew close, Noa's heart raced.

Thirteen indents. Twelve on the outside, a single, final indent on the inside.

They fell to the floor, the two of them ignoring the eerie vastness beyond the light. The keys clattered against the sparkling black slab, sliding free of their old cord shackle. She and Glacier each grabbed one, then another, and another, filling in each slot until he scraped the Soul of Amarais into place. Noa stared down at The Heart of the King and nudged it into the center. Her palm fell over it, pushing it into its slot before she and Glacier stood again and waited.

And waited.

Noa's heart dropped each passing second there was no answering call that she'd completed her task. She took a step back and tapped the Heart with her boot, praying that would do the trick and shoving down the rising panic in the pit of her stomach. Her breathing came out more and more ragged as tears stung her eyes. "Oh, gods. Oh, no—"

"Noa—" Glacier grabbed her arm, but she took another step back.

"Was I wrong? Did I just lead everyone here on a godsdamned thought that—" She gritted her teeth. "I'm so *stupid*. Out of all the people in the godsdamned world, I don't know why I believed it could possibly be *me*."

Glacier cupped her face in his hands. "It doesn't matter," he said calmly.

But it *did* matter.

"If you're wrong, that doesn't change what we've done," he continued. "It doesn't change that we can still finish freeing Amarais. It doesn't matter. We'll find a way."

Tears spilled over her cheeks, her words coming out in heaving breaths. "I *lied* to everyone, Glacier. I let them all down because I'm just a fool who listens to Seers without really understanding. I'm a killer, and a liar, and a thief. Lazarus told me I was good, deep down, but he was *wrong*. I'm just the monster Myron made me, and that's all I'll ever be."

"You're not, Noa." He pressed his forehead to hers.

She squeezed her eyes shut. "I *am*."

"You're smart, strong, and help those who can't help themselves. You protect people, and you're not afraid to stand up and face the evil that takes the shape of those who wield their power to push everyone down around them. You're the type of person the worst monsters fear," he said, and she choked out a bitter laugh. "You don't need some gift to fight back for what's right. You're *you*, and that's enough."

Noa forced open her eyes to stare into his. Emerald green and sapphire blue. She refused to believe that he wasn't just *some* ordinary Seer, but she broke at the thought that he wouldn't be *hers*. She'd spent so long just trying to accept that this was who she was supposed to be, only to discover that it was all a lie. That she had gathered all those keys for nothing. She had led them all on a fool's errand and wanted to tell him to leave her here.

A quiet *click* rang out in the dark, the two of them stiffening at the faint noise behind the edge of light. Their heads turned toward the source of the sound, Glacier's hands falling away as she moved past the circle of keys. Soft, melodic tones lulled her closer as she strained to listen to what they were saying, like whispers holding a secret only she could hear.

Come closer—

So Noa did, allowing herself to be enveloped by the dark.

NYX

Nyx sprinted down the hall, scrolling through the contacts on her phone with a metal case digging into her side. She sucked in a deep breath and pressed the phone to her ear just as the line picked up.

"Hello?"

"Please tell me you worked late tonight like I asked," Nyx said in a rush, trying to suppress her panic.

"I—*yes*. Why are you calling me?" Alyvia asked. "What's going on?"

"I need you to be ready. If I don't text you in the next ten minutes, I need you schedule the data to send and leave the office *immediately*, understood?"

"What? *Why?* What about—"

"If I don't text you, that won't matter anymore. You'll need to leave before the data sends because Delacroix, Matsuoka, and Arrington are *all* Summoners. If you stay, they'll figure out *you* sent it, and they'll be pissed," Nyx said, waiting for a reply that didn't come after five seconds. "Alyvia, I need a confirmation that you understand."

"I-I un-understand. I—"

"Good. Ten minutes," Nyx repeated, ending the call and pulling up her text messages. Aiza's name sat at the top of her list, pinned there with her most recent reminder to be careful.

Sorry.

Her thumbs ran across the digital keys.

> I love you.

Sent.

Nyx shoved the phone back in her pocket, blinking back the threat of tears because she knew if she called, she'd cry. Instead, she funneled that energy into her shoulder with the *click* of a door unlocking. The strap flew over her head, and the case slid across the floor, straight toward Rune. He sidestepped, elbowing Lucian and knocking the dagger from his hand. The case hurtled past, finding its intended target.

Malice grabbed up the handle in one smooth motion, ramming it into Iason with a crack of bone and a snap of metal latches falling open. He collapsed to the floor and a grin spread across her face as she pulled a metallic-blue blade from the violin like a sheath. "Who's next?"

NOA

Noa swallowed a gasp as the world fell out from under her feet. She dropped into a sea of stars, plunging into icy cold. Air ripped from her lungs and panic spread through her as she squeezed her eyes shut. A hundred familiar voices called out her name—all echoey and distant, even as the firm grasp of hands pulled her free of the water.

"Remember your greatest weakness is another's greatest strength, Noa. No one should ever have to shoulder a burden alone."

Fingers pressed into her shoulders, and she swiped at her eyes, cracking them open. The blurred image of a man outlined in a soft, golden glow knelt in front of her. Her hands dropped into the water lapping at her thighs as she stared into the face of Lazarus.

Hot tears burned her eyes as she forced out a whispered, "Damnit." *Did I die?*

The feel of him patting her cheek lingered as he dissolved into a tiny spark. She waded a couple steps through the frigid water and cupped it. It brightened, and she reared back, shielding her eyes as it burst into a blinding white.

"Noa."

Noa flinched at the sound of that soothing, feminine voice and cautiously opened an eye again. Sure enough, a woman stood in front of her, adorned in a long, black dress—its layers and layers of sheer fabric cascading around her. Noa's arms fell to her sides as she took in the woman's own dazzling green eyes. Soft lights winked in and out along her black hair like it'd been woven through with stars.

"Y-yes?" Noa forced out.

CARA NOX

"I've been waiting for you for quite some time. You've done well."

Noa half-turned, staring off at the white abyss behind her, then pivoted back, pointing at her own chest. Noa the killer—the fool who'd used this errand as an excuse to seek revenge—did *well?*

The woman chuckled, and the white void fell away to the lush green of a forest. Trees closed in and saplings rose up at her feet. Noa jumped, her heart doing double-time because there was no escape. She was a mouse stuck in a cage with a cat—something far more powerful than she was, which left a sense of unease in the pit of her stomach.

"Who are you?" Noa asked weakly, stepping around the blooming flowers that licked at her heels.

"I believe you know me by my title, rather than my name. Very few seem to remember me by anything else. Such is your fate as well, to be known simply as the Queen." Her eyes twinkled as she placed a hand to her chest, her dark skin mapped with a midnight-inked crescent cradling a star. "The Messenger."

GLACIER

Glacier rubbed his gloved hands together, peering into the dark. Should he keep waiting? Should he go in after her? He took a step forward and stopped, hugging himself when his gut told him to stay put. This wasn't for him. This was for her. This had been Noa's task, and his was to accompany her to take her here. He'd done it. He fought it, but he'd seen it through.

The only question now was what his next task would be.

He tensed at the scrape of boots against stone and spun around to Daniil taking the last few steps down to the bottom. His violet eyes flashed with disgust, his face twisting into a snarl. Glacier's arms fell to his sides, his hands curling into fists.

"So it *is* true," Daniil scoffed. "A half-Miraltan prince tucked away in the palace, hidden by the filthy little Mage that I'm sure Lucian's killing right now—along with the rest of your foreign *friends*. And here we are, trying to prove our worth while you get everything *handed* to you because your father was a spineless fool that buckled to some Miraltan bitch. He broke the rules because he thought he was above them, and he deserved whatever he got." A contorted smirk danced onto his lips as he jumped off the last step, seemingly satisfied by Glacier's glower. "Just like your bitch of a cousin. You should've listened to her scream through that car's microphones when it burst into flames."

Glacier lunged at him, course-correcting as Daniil fainted right. Images flashed through his mind of what might happen next, and his body adjusted to Daniil's boot hooking behind his ankle. The heel of Glacier's palm met Daniil's nose, and he staggered backward, unable to steady himself before Glacier shoved his shoulder into his side. Daniil rolled to his feet, flicking the blood from his hand onto the floor. A blade slid from his sleeve while he grinned through blood-stained teeth.

You're not that helpless little prince anymore.

He charged at Glacier, who side-stepped Daniil's swing. Glacier fell back, ready to elbow the knife from his hand, but the blade spun around in his grasp. Glacier gritted his teeth and staggered to the side, his palm smacking against a sticky warmth at his abdomen. Adrenaline-laced pain shot through him as Daniil hurtled forward, and Glacier jabbed him in the throat, pulling his hand away from the wound and seizing his wrist.

Daniil tackled him to the floor, dripping blood onto Glacier's face while they struggled with the knife. And with a single shove, the blade pierced through Daniil's throat. He gagged as Glacier rolled him away and panted as he struggled to his feet, wincing with every gush of warm blood spilling over his gloves.

When he turned back to Daniil, vacant eyes stared up at the moonlight trickling down from the ballroom. The floor tilted with every step back to the stairs, worsened by the drip of blood following him. He fell against the pillar, sliding down it with his eyes pinned on Daniil.

Don't get up. Don't get up before Noa comes back. Don't get—

He shook, the world spun, and then everything slipped into black.

NOA

"Like your predecessor, you must be prepared to take on the responsibility to distribute power to those you can trust to wield it. It is not a job to be taken lightly," the Messenger said. "You've already proven yourself to be worthy of the task. You have the strength to carry this burden if you chose to accept it. If you decide you cannot, then I will choose another."

"I can take it," Noa said without a beat of hesitation, watching the Messenger break into a warm smile. "I'm ready to do whatever it takes, as long as I can save whoever I can from what's coming."

"It won't be easy."

"I know." Noa took a step forward, blocking out the ever-changing scene around her. "But I can handle whatever's thrown at me."

The Messenger nodded, gently taking Noa's face in her hands. "Then I entrust you with the power of Seraphine to protect Avaria from the growing dark, my *Queen*."

Noa's eyes drifted shut, the sound of birds chirping and leaves rustling cut short. Her eyes flew open to the dark again, and she spun around to two figures: one prone to the right of the steps, and the other slumped at its base.

Glacier.

She sprinted toward the stairs, her stomach lurching as she fell to her knees in front of him. "Oh no—*no, no, no*—" Something took over her in a way she couldn't describe, feeling the need to cup his face in her hands. She pressed her forehead to his, just like the Messenger had, and found a brilliant mark on his soul, growing brighter at her touch.

He gasped, sputtering as she rocked back.

"I'm sorry, I—" She panted, staring down at her hands.

He cringed and shook his head. "I- I killed Daniil," he said weakly, half-nodding to the body.

"And you got yourself stabbed, you dumbass," she hissed. "We said we weren't going to get ourselves *killed*." She forced him up, hearing a whine as she put pressure on the wound and pulled him against her. She tugged one of his arms around the back of her neck. "If you die on me, I will find a way to bring you back, and then I'll kick your ass."

A weak chuckle escaped him in their journey up the stairs. Every wince and groan left her on edge until they made it to the top. *Almost there,* she thought on their way to the doors, biting down on her tongue when his feet began to drag. *I'm not losing you.*

She just had to get him to Nyx—right? Would she be able to fix him up in this state? The drip of blood made her eyes sting as she threw her body against the ballroom doors, emptying them out into the pretend-rebel's lair. Chryssa and Kostas laid on the floor, unconscious or dead—it didn't really matter to Noa—Iason was backed into a corner by Weather and Crow, panting at his last stand, and finally Lucian was pinned to the tiles with Rune's knee in his back.

"Glacier!" Cecilia sprinted toward them, dropping the dagger in her hand as Noa lowered him to the tile. She grabbed Cecilia's hands and pressed them to the wound with a silent order not to let go.

Noa's eyes locked on Lucian, feeling a fiery rage burning in the pit of her stomach as she stood, but instead of calling his name, another tumbled out, "Malice."

Something moved out of the corner of Noa's eye, her head turning toward the limping gate of her younger sister—bruised and bloodied with a wistful smile, even as she collapsed at Noa's feet. Blood smeared over her face as Noa dropped back down to a knee and ran her thumb along her cheek. Their foreheads touched, and Noa found exactly what she'd been looking for: an unlit rune carved into her soul. The dim little glowing ball pulsed as Noa traced it with her mind, turning bright, though not nearly as bright as Glacier's had been. When Noa drew back, the cut on Malice's chin knitted together again, and bit by bit, the rest of her broken body righted itself.

"Fix him," Noa breathed.

Malice nodded and crawled across from Cecilia while Noa stalked toward Lucian.

"Are you *happy* with what you've done?" Her words boomed out with a deadly calm.

Lucian snarled. "Who the fuck are you?"

Rune stood up, and Noa jerked their prisoner to his feet by his shirt collar. "*I* am your *judge*, and I'm prepared to sentence you for the grave crimes you've committed against your fellow people."

Lucian's stark, harsh laugh echoed through the hall, but Glacier's sharp gasp overshadowed it. The air fell still, and everyone looked around like something had changed—though none of them could tell *what*. The energy had shifted. The world had quieted.

Noa dragged him through the doors at the other end, hearing the *click* of the locks free before hauling him out onto the front steps of the palace. She shoved him to his knees, facing a sea of rebels all staring back at him.

"Look at them," she shouted, not even allowing herself to gape in wonderment at the snowflakes suspended in the air.

She did this somehow, but it didn't even feel confusing or powerful—it was as if she was *whole*. It'd been like she'd been missing a piece of herself that'd finally been reclaimed. And now she could finally carry out what she'd been meant to do.

He pushed himself up, rounding on her. "What about them?" he shouted, throwing an arm out.

"*These people* are the ones you betrayed," she yelled, pointing out at the crowd, and feeding off the restless murmurs rippling through them. "You *used* them for you own selfish gain, when they wanted to make Amarais *better* than it's ever been. But you decided to kill their oppressors and take their place. You're no better than they were."

"I should've had the right to take my seat, and I was denied it because of my blood," he sneered as Glacier stepped up to her side. "Yet this little Miraltan brat would be allowed to have his damned crown."

"If you honestly think it would be that easy for him, you're dead wrong," Noa said evenly.

"At least I *look* Amaraian." Lucian jabbed a finger to his own chest. "I look just like everyone else. No one would guess that I'm not. You think you people can just walk in here and act like the heroes when this is something for Amarais to sort out, not *you*."

"You made it my business when you continued to hunt down the people I care about," Noa growled. "So you have a choice to make. You can either submit to your punishment before your new king, or you'll automatically end up with *me* as the one to choose the appropriate reward for your actions. You should be aware that Glacier is far more forgiving than I am."

He looked from her to Glacier, disgusted. "Go fuck yourse—"

A shadow pushed past Noa, and he crumpled to the ground. Malice stood over him with a half-smashed violin in her hand. "Bitch."

Noa pressed her lips together. "I guess we'll deal with that later then..." she mumbled, stepping around his prone form while Malice dragged him away. The others flanked her, fanning out on the front steps up of the palace and staring up at the screens. Their faces were plastered all over the displays, framed by twinkling snow, mid-fall.

The world's watching.

Noa pulled in a breath, steadying her fast-beating heart. "You don't know me because I'm no one," she started, her eyes skimming over the blue ones staring back at her. "Like all of you, I was told that I didn't matter, but that wasn't true. *All* of us matter. There are some of you listening that know me by many names, and how I've asked some of you for favors in return for giving you a second chance. I ask for you to help me now. There's corruption among us, seeking to destroy what we care about to gain power they have no right to take. It's our time to finally stand up for ourselves. It's our time to push back at those who want us silenced and controlled. Which is why we're starting *here*. Amarais has suffered long enough. There are people here who can't be who they are because it's seen as a *threat* to the people who have controlled this country for so long. They cared more about keeping their power than letting their people *live*. No more. No more suffering or hate. It's time for freedom." Noa put a fist in the air, and the crowd turned into a wave of fists, shooting up in answer.

Noa glanced over to Glacier, watching his eyes go wide in awe. She slipped her free hand into his, intertwining their fingers and raising their hands in solidarity. The rest of their group followed suit in raising their fists with heads held high.

"For Amarais!" the crowd cheered.

"For Avaria," Noa breathed.

47

KING'S REPUBLIC ✧ 2705-01-31

SHANE

Shane shot up from his desk with a curse, covering his mouth as his eyes flicked over the data and images popping up onto his holographic screen. Reports including the Monettes, details of the grimoire, a laundry-list of missing persons in connection with their illicit activities. The entire agency would be alerted in a matter of minutes if they hadn't been informed already.

Grab Alyvia and run. Take whatever the hell you can and leave.

He scooped up his jacket, rushing out into the empty department office. Alyvia was *gone*. Shane spun around, finding Jinko's office door ajar with the light still on. She wasn't inside either. He bit back a frustrated growl and rounded Alyvia's desk, finding a note on her screen.

Had to duck out early. See you tomorrow.

His fist slammed on the desktop before running his hands through his hair. Great. First, he'd lost the Seer, then the grimoire, and now *this*. Shane pulled on his jacket, zipping it and flicking up his hood on his way out to the stairwell.

He took the steps down two at a time, pushing his way out into the back alley. Blue light drenched the brick he jogged along, his shadow doubling behind him.

ARRINGTON

Arrington collapsed into his chair as officers flooded the hallway. His head lulled back in surrender, waiting for them to burst into the room. He numbly stared at the image of Gabriel and Michael Monette standing alongside that woman on the steps of the Amaraian palace, rubbing his thumb over his jaw.

How?

How had he lost this game after staying five steps ahead for so long? Where had he messed up? Had it been with the twins? So many questions spun around his head while his door was forced open and officers drew their swords.

It was laughable, really. Did they really think he was stupid enough to bring the damn grimoire to work with him? He stood slowly, straightening his suit jacket, and holding out his wrists for his cuffs.

He didn't bother hiding his face as they escorted him out to the black town car with its flashing blue lights. He glowered at the Bellegardian kid who slowed to gawk at him before breaking into a smirk and jogging toward the local line with a couple officers breaking off to chase after him.

Today was the day for catching criminals, it seemed.

They forced his head down, shoving him into the backseat with Jinko.

It was over.

ALYVIA

Alyvia stopped in the middle of downtown, staring up at the one of the large screens on the side of a building usually riddled with swaths of advertisements. The worlds fell out from under her at the sight of the Monettes, the woman they'd been caught with, and finally, the boy she'd run into on the street weeks ago.

You dropped this.

But his eyes weren't both green—one was *blue*. She'd stood face-to-face with Glacier Caelius—a boy she thought she'd never meet. A *ghost*. Her *cousin*. A *Seer*.

Alyvia rummaged through her bag, pulling out her phone and shaking as she scrolled through her contact list. She pressed the phone to her ear, listening to the hum of its ring until it suddenly stopped.

"Hey, Dad," she breathed, staring up at the display. "I want you to know I'm coming home. I'll be there in the morning. There are some things I think you'll want to hear, but I think I should tell you in person." A grin spread over her face. "I'll see you soon."

48

AMARAIS ✧ 2705-02-05

GLACIER

King Glacier Caelius ran his hand along the balcony railing overlooking the ballroom, surveying Mr. Angelis's coordination of ceiling repairs. He dropped a bundle of metal ties into Crow's arms, and he grumbled before taking a step back. Crow's body flitted away to shadow and reappeared with an arm hooked around one of the ladders, where he called up to one of the workers.

He couldn't help but recall Nyx's baffled question of, "What the fuck are you?" that had left the group fairly amused until Noa beckoned for Seneca to join them. When it was followed by a grumbled, "Oh, fuck. Now there's *two* of them," laughter broke out while Nyx typed question after question into her phone.

Shadowwalker.

Glacier smirked as a door fell shut behind him.

"Ugh," Weather grumbled. "Aren't you cold?" She rubbed at her sleeves, elbowing him.

"A little, but I was just dropping in to see how things were coming along."

She waved to Crow as he dropped off the bottom rung of the ladder, and his shadowy form snapped over the gap of the curving balcony. He swayed slightly, half-falling against the railing with a groan. "I'm probably going to need a recovery day after this."

Weather chuckled, patting him on the cheek. "Well, if it's any consolation. The roof's looking much better than it did yesterday. I'll have to have someone melt down more platinum for Linus. Those runed ties should keep it pretty well-enforced once it's all done." She stared up at the glass panes with a smile and clapped her hands together. "Then we can finish redecorating the rest of the suites!"

Glacier shook his head, unable to hold back a grin. "I think that's going to take a while, so get used to the staff quarters for a bit."

Crow huffed. "The entire Kassandros family is probably going to need to move in at this rate, considering how many you've employed..."

"We'll see about that," Weather said. "Linus mentioned their parents might move back up north once everything's finished up around here. He sounded a little unsure about whether or not to go with them, but when I talked to Jovian, he said he'd stay. I think he likes working with Nyx."

"Crow!"

They peered over the side to Mr. Angelis holding up another bundle of ties, and Crow groaned. Weather leaned over the railing, pointing a finger at him. "Hey! You're supposed to be *sitting*, Livius!"

Mr. Angelis laughed as Crow reappeared in front of him, mumbling something that sent the older man into a coughing fit.

"Crow!" Weather yelled, growling. "Tell him to take a seat, or I'll come down there and order him to." She sighed as he coaxed Mr. Angelis back into his chair, dropping his crutch alongside it. "Good gods," she muttered. "Men never change. Always feeling the need to push themselves, even when they need to rest."

"So I take it Malice couldn't fix his leg when she tried yesterday?" Glacier asked, turning to shove open the door to the stairs.

Weather shook her head. "Nyx thinks it might be too old of an injury to revert. She can alleviate the pain he still gets from it, but it's sort of wound that's healed too twisted to fix. Cecilia said he's had it for at least a decade, so..." She shrugged. "Nyx ordered some modification braces to help support it. Hopefully that does the trick."

Glacier's brows knit together as they strode across the landing, passing uniformed and un-uniformed workers with tablets and bins. "Where is Seneca anyway? I thought he was supposed to be helping them."

"I think he and Linus had to run over to their parents' rental on the other side of the sector. Something about helping them divvy up their supplies and donating things to the palace before they go. I told Linus to talk them down from it if they need it. We have *plenty* of shit in those storage rooms." She threw her head back with a pout. "It's going to take an *eternity*."

Glacier laughed, patting her on the shoulder. "I appreciate the help, though. Really."

"I think I'll feel better once Crow can help me appraise a lot of it. It should go much faster once I'm not bottlenecking what's worth keeping to sell or scraping since most everyone else is stuck with more important things." She waved a hand off to the people below, all walking and jogging to their next destination in weaving lines.

He slowed at the edge of one of the propped-open doors, grabbing onto the frame. "We'll get there. I'm just glad all of you stuck around."

Weather cooed and wrapped her arms around him. "You act like we have somewhere better to be."

He chuckled, and she pulled away, slapping her hand to her chest in mock salute with a smirk. She spun on her heel and wandered past the windows, vanishing into one of the east halls.

The door pushed open a little more as Glacier rapped his knuckles against it, and the room's occupant looked up from his temporary desk. Fuzzy, far-off memories washed over him—ones of sitting next to his father on a plush sofa while this very man paced back and forth through his office, saying things his father shrugged off and Glacier couldn't yet comprehend.

"How are you settling in?" Glacier asked, running his gaze along the beat-up frame of the desk and the bright squares on the wall where paintings had once been.

North Valeria ran a hand through his sandy blond hair—the same color as Ari's, though his was peppered with streaks of gray. He sighed, putting on a tired smile. "Slowly, but surely. I'll eventually remember how to be a proper advisor again. It's been... well, a few years, to say the least."

"We'll start getting the offices fixed up soon. We'll need them as long as Noa's slinking around."

North's chuckle warmed Glacier's heart. It was like being welcomed home after a long time away, not that it was all that far off from reality.

"She's not quite what I expected for the next ruler of Avaria," North said. "But there's something about her that reminds me of dear late King Cyrus... I think it's that stubborn determination."

Glacier twisted his ring, reminded of the twinkle in Kat's eye a few nights ago. He nudged the door shut and rubbed his palms against his pants.

"Is something wrong?" North asked, rising from his seat with a concerned frown.

"There's... something I want to talk to you about, mainly because I need your advice, but I also don't think I can keep it a secret between just Noa, Nyx, and I." Glacier pulled back the folding chair across from him and took a seat, biting his lip until North hesitantly sat.

"Your father trusted me with countless secrets I'll take to my grave," he whispered, resting his arms on the desk with a soft, gentle gleam to his worried blue eyes. "You can trust me to at least listen, even if I don't have all the answers."

He swallowed, twisting the ring again. "Well... you know I'm a Seer."

North nodded, humming in confirmation as if to encourage him to continue.

"And... um... the night we liberated Amarais, I saw the Messenger in my dream." Glacier looked up from the edge of the desk, daring to meet North's gaze.

His face slowly fell slack, followed by, "Oh."

"It's... exactly what you think," Glacier mumbled. "Noa and I specu-lated it, but... I'm not sure who to tell or if I should tell anyone. Noa thinks we should keep it secret, and so does Nyx—" He saw North's brow arch, and Glacier shook his head, holding up a hand. "But they're the only two that know about the dream. Them and you now."

"Did she—the Messenger—say anything important I should hear?"

Glacier started to shake his head and paused. "She called me her brother, the Oracle."

Glacier stepped outside North's office, forcing out a long, deep breath. The click of a tongue made him jump, and he smacked against the doorframe with a wince. Noa's chuckle sounded next to him as she pushed off the wall.

"You okay?" she asked, tugging at his sleeve. "I didn't mean to scare you that bad. You must've been discussing something pretty heavy if you're that wound tight..."

His eyes darted up and down the balcony before he grabbed her hand and dragged her into the west hall. "I told him," he mumbled over his shoulder.

Noa's eyes went wide. "Oh. And?"

Glacier's feet dragged when he hit the suite labeled for construction in crude, brushed paint strokes. He pushed one of the doors open to plastic tarps and gutted carpet. She pushed the door shut behind her.

"He agreed with you and Nyx about me keeping the whole *Oracle* thing a secret, okay?"

"Good man. I knew I liked him." She brushed off his shoulders and ran her hands down his sleeves, slowing when her eyes met his. "You're still unsure, aren't you?"

Glacier tilted his head from side to side and rubbed his face. "I guess I was hoping he'd say something different... I've spent so much time hiding myself away, that I don't want to keep pretending I'm not something I am." His hand fell back to his side, bouncing against his leg, every piece of him weighed down by disappointment.

Noa slid her arms over his shoulders, encircling him as she took a step closer. Her voice dropped to that familiar, comforting whisper that warmed his soul. "It's just for a little while—to protect you, not hide you away like a dirty little secret. Let me test the waters, and you can help keep me afloat, all right?" Her fingers grazed his shirt collar, tickling his skin.

"It's not exactly fair to have you go it alone—"

"I can take it." She smirked. "Plus, I won't be alone."

He leaned into her, bumping his forehead against hers with a small smile of his own.

"*But…*" she said with a slight roll of her eyes and a mischievous grin. "If you're really worried about me tackling this alone, we could always circle back to our conversation from last week."

A huff of a laugh slipped from him. "Yeah?"

"So what do you say, Your Majesty? You, me—co-rulers of Avaria and Amarais?"

He snorted. "You act like I get something out of this. I'm only seeing you get a little more from Amarais."

"Well, you get *me.* I think that's a pretty damn good deal."

Glacier rocked on his heels, humming. "I don't know…" he teased.

Noa threw her head back and groaned. Her mouth opened to argue her point, and he pulled her in close, shutting her up with a kiss. When he drew back, her eyes searched his for an answer.

An answer he'd already thought about every night they curled up side-by-side in the staff quarters, too exhausted to do anything but harass each other with mumbled jabs and jokes. Every moment they'd been awake and stepped into meeting after meeting of deliberations on how to divvy up tasks and who to send out to assist the other districts' repairs. Every time she'd snuck up on him and held his hand or brought him a cup of tea— every minor gesture—he'd thought about how nice it was to have someone to lean on. And how he'd love nothing more than to support and stand with her through whatever might come next.

"Yes."

She threw herself against him, bouncing up and down.

"Calm down, calm down—" he said through fits of laughter.

The bouncing stopped, and she sighed into his shirt. "I'm just glad to finally be home."

"*We're* home," he whispered into her hair.

"I like the way that sounds..." Noa pulled away slightly, surveying the room. "Do you have a preference on where you want your new room? You said you didn't really want to go back to your old one."

"I haven't really thought about it yet. I assumed the offices would be first, so I've been putting it off."

"Then how about this one?"

He glanced around at the dented walls and broken glass spilling out of a ruined picture frame resting against warped baseboard. Glacier raised a brow. "This one?"

Noa grabbed his hand and pulled him toward the set of double doors at the end, pushing them open to a window overlooking the garden, though its panes were cracked. "So this could be the bedroom." She pointed to the dingy rug, slowly turning back around. "And the room we were in can be the main room... Then we can add a closet here and—"

Glacier put a hand over his mouth to muffle a chuckle.

"What?" she asked with a hesitant grin, her hands falling.

"Nothing. I'm just happy to see you make this place your own."

"So that's a yes to the room?"

He nodded, and she jogged up, sliding her hand into his again.

"Then let's go tell Mariana this suite is reserved for us. I'm not letting some other dumbass come snag it."

He shook his head, fighting back a grin as she dragged him back down the hall. "I think Mrs. Angelis is still in another meeting—"

"That won't stop me from popping in to tell her we need to talk after."

Their boots clattered down the marble steps and down a hall past the ballroom, where Noa lightly knocked on a closed door. Glacier's attention fell on the one across from it, letting his fingers unhook from hers to peer inside.

Cecilia stood in front of an orange-haired student. Freckles dotted his pale face, framing his hazel eyes. He spun around while she took a step back, looking him up and down.

"Now try Amaraian," she said.

His eyes closed and opened again, transitioning to a deep navy. The orange hair shifted under the light, its frizzy texture turning a silky gold. He waited patiently as she bit her thumbnail.

"Well?" he asked with a breathy chuckle.

"You're much faster at this than I was."

The glamour faded away, revealing Rune in her student's place. "I had a really good teacher."

Cecilia blushed as he pushed back a lock of her hair, and a shadow appeared at Glacier's side again.

"Disgusting," Noa mumbled, grabbing his arm and yanking him away from the door.

He chortled as she started into a stroll. "I'm sorry, what? Shouldn't you be happy?"

"It's sickening how cute they are. Now they're *both* Illusionists."

"You remember that *you're* the one that did this, right? You don't really have anyone else to blame—"

Noa half-slumped against the wall, dragging herself along it with a fake pout. She pushed off of it with a sigh once they hit the hallway intersection. "You're right, of course. And he'll be an amazing Illusionist. I'm still a little frustrated Mariana keeps turning me away whenever I offer her magic too. I don't want to hand it out to just *anyone*—not yet. But I trust her, and she's being so damn stubborn. Livius is just as bad, using his leg as an excuse."

"I think they might be a little afraid of diving into all this, or maybe they're trying to keep a sense of normalcy to show we can all co-exist in Amarais first. I do think you made the right call by including Cecilia's cousins—"

She turned on him, bringing them to a stop. "Do you North would accept?"

Glacier looked back toward the main hall and started to shake his head. "No. Not yet, at least."

"Then I'll be honest, I'm not sure how we're going to find the other Mages we need." Noa shoved her free hand in her pocket, blowing her hair out of her eyes. "We got *really* lucky with Linus being a Metallurgist for weaponry, but he can barely keep up helping Weather right now. Another would be a godsend—that, and we need a Weaver for armor…"

"We'll manage for now. I think you might be rushing into a war with an enemy we haven't seen yet." He gave her hand a reassuring squeeze. "We have a little bit of time, so let's start with what we have first. We'll figure out the rest as it comes."

Her head dropped, barely hiding a smirk as she rolled her neck. "Thanks. I think I'm super wound tight with everything going on. Too many questions about what's next, versus dealing with, 'oh, just get another key'."

They shared a soft, breathy laugh between them, giving Glacier the chance to freeze that moment. A finish line and a starting mark beyond a point he'd thought he might not make it to. He stared down at their intertwined hands, memorizing every rough and smooth facet of scars.

"I was thinking about going back for Lazarus's books," Noa said quietly. "Would you want to come with me?"

"You act like you have to ask," he said. "I promised I wouldn't let you drown, right?"

She hooked an arm around his neck and kissed his cheek. "Thank you."

A disgusted noise came from the other end of the hall, and they looked over to Nyx waving a hand for them to follow. "Would you two stop running off to make out? Come on. You have visitors."

Noa frowned, staring back at him, and his brows knit together.

"Did *you* invite someone?" she asked, pulling away.

"Not that I can remember..."

They jogged after her, Glacier picking up on the warm laughter behind closed doors they passed. It filled him with a renewed vigor as they hit the steps, hurrying down them toward Louis's old, dismantled office. Nyx shoved open the door, holding it open for the two of them to file inside, where a woman spun around at the edge of the desk.

Her familiar, dark eyes lit up as she charged forward, throwing her arms around them. "It's so wonderful to finally see you both not bruised, battered, and potentially poisoned."

"Devi—" Glacier's hand flew up to her arm. "What are you doing here?"

She giggled, slipping from his grasp with a step back. "Well, I asked

Nari if it was safe to visit after your little stunt show, and she said I was in the clear. So…" She held out her hand. "*Morgan*, I'm Aiza Quinn."

He took it, rubbing the back of his neck. "Glacier Caelius. It's nice to meet you."

"And it's an honor to finally meet you, Your Majesty." Aiza dipped into a slight bow.

"Hey—" Noa said with a mock scowl. "And what about me?"

Aiza laughed and dipped into a lower bow. "My gracious, life-saving Queen, it's an honor to reunite with you."

Nyx gagged. "Gods, don't feed her ego."

"Shut up, *Nari*," Noa teased. "I'm surprised you let her use your real name. It's like you're together or something."

Aiza bit her lip, her dark eyes dancing as they slid over to Nyx, who shielded her face with a sigh.

Noa's jaw dropped. "Oh, holy shit. You two are together? Since when? Why the hell didn't you say any—"

Nyx waved it away. "We'll talk about it later, but I thought you should see Aiza before I bring in your *actual* guest." She stepped into the doorway, motioning to a girl by the stairs who jogged off. "You remember the associate I mentioned from Kingsheart?"

Glacier nodded, turning around with Noa as Aiza slid past, hovering behind Nyx at the girl reappeared in the doorway. A second set of footsteps echoed behind her, and a bundled-up Miraltan woman came into view. He recognized those green eyes from when he'd peered into them in the midst of a busy Bellegardian district—back when he'd pressed a Shield of Miralta charm into her palm.

"I discovered you two might have a little in common," Nyx said, ushering her forward with a gentle hand on her back. "We'll give you three some privacy." She led Aiza out and they shut the doors behind them.

Noa subtle nudged Glacier, shooting him a confused glance.

"S-sorry," the woman began with a nervous smile. "I'm not exactly sure how to introduce myself to royalty—"

He chuckled and took her hand. "I'm sure you already know me, but I'm Glacier Caelius."

"Alyvia Watson. I... believe you know my aunt. Her name was Juniper Everett."

A quiet, "Oh," escaped Noa—filled with as much surprise as he felt with chills running up and down his arms.

Tears pressed against the backs of his eyes, but he forced them back while his shoulders drooped. "I didn't think I had any family left."

"Surprise," Alyvia whispered as he cupped her hand in his. "And my dad—Juniper's brother said he'd love to meet you. No pressure, of course! I'm sure you're very busy and—"

"We're actually heading to Astravny in a couple days to conclude some personal business," Noa said, stepping up next to him again. "I'm sure we can afford to make a detour before things get too hectic around here. I'm Noa, by the way."

Glacier let go of her hand for Noa to shake, and Alyvia stiffened as if starstruck. "Y-you two don't have to go to all that trouble—"

"Oh, please, as long as they're okay hosting a prin—sorry, *king*—I'm still getting used to that new title. He can stay out of trouble for an afternoon with your family, and I can entertain my sister in a hotel somewhere. Trekking up here is a pain, we're a little low on rooms, and they'll freeze their asses off, so I humbly apologize for you coming all this way to deal with that nightmare in itself."

Alyvia covered her mouth to stifle a snort. "I'm sure they'd love to meet you and your sister too if you'd like to join for a bit."

"I'd be happy to."

KOLE

Kole walked around the block for the fifth time, slowing down across from the row of townhouses. His fist swung at his sides while he glanced up and down the street, taking in the construction workers and pedestrians carrying around small boxes and bags.

And you had the audacity to call Noa a coward. Look at you.

He reached for his phone and jogged across the street, checking the address on file again. The loose shingles above the window threatened to

fall free and smack against the sidewalk to alert the occupants of his presence before he even raised a fist to knock. He sucked in the chilly air and
dug his boots into the dusting of snow at the base of the front steps.

Just knock, damnit.

He made it quick—though it sounded far too light for someone
upstairs to hear—and cringed. His heart pounded as he strained to listen
for movement within, but it was drowned out by the excited shouts of children running down the sidewalk. He spun around, watching them run
toward the screen haphazardly set up in the shop window. On it, Noa and
Glacier sat on full display, re-running their victory of liberating Synos.

His arms slackened at his sides while the little voice in his head told him
he should leave. He'd screwed up too much. He'd caused too many problems. He'd—

The door creaked open and Kole whipped back around to face a boy
his age, his blond hair a shade lighter than Kole's and sticking up at odd
angles above a softer face. "Can I help you?" he asked with a confused
frown.

"I'm looking for Mr. and Mrs. Kassandros," Kole forced out before he
had the chance to lie and bolt.

"Oh, um, they're actually out right now, but if you give me your name,
I can let them know you're looking for them. I'm Seneca, their oldest."

Kole let the name roll off his tongue, sounding strange to his ears after
so many years of burying it. "Felix Kassandros."

"I- I'm sorry, did you say *Felix?*"

Kole nodded, feeling his heart catch in his throat.

Seneca half-turned, calling into the house. "Linus! Get down here!" He
grinned back at Kole, waving him inside. "Come in, come in—Holy shit, I
can't believe you're here. We thought you were dead."

Kole stepped inside on uncertain legs, surveying the cramped front
room. It was better than some of the motels he'd been staying in, but worse
than the mansion he couldn't bear to go back to—not yet at least. Dingy-
looking, mismatched upholstered chairs sat in the slim trickle of light
peeking through the front curtains, blocking its trail to the tiny adjoining
kitchen.

"Sorry it's not in the best shape," Seneca said, pushing the door shut. "My brothers and I have been spending a lot of time helping out at the palace, and our parents are in and out because they're planning on helping check in on other cities soon."

A younger boy with hair covering his ears hopped off the bottom step dead-ending into the hallway and wandered inside, enduring Seneca's exclamation of finding their cousin alive. "You should sit down, Felix." Seneca started toward the chairs, patting the arm of one for him. "Our parents should be back in about an hour, and we can ask Jovian to stop by for dinner—Or wait, maybe we should find somewhere else and invite—"

"I don't really go by Felix anymore," he mumbled, gripping the edge of the chair. "I go by Kole. And you don't have to go out of your way to—"

Seneca nodded, lost somewhere in thought in the midst of his explanation. "Kole... It suits you."

Kole tensed as the door popped open again, and all three of them stared at the woman spinning around on her way inside, juggling a couple boxes in her arms. Linus jogged over to her during her small announcement of, "I brought some supplies for your parents' trip. Sorry it took so long, I was finishing up a lesson with—" She froze when her eyes caught on Kole, the two of them face-to-face like they'd been on a train hurtling through Belle-garde weeks ago.

And he'd told her she was better off dead.

"Perfect, you're here!" Seneca said, putting a hand on Kole's shoulder. "Cecilia, you remember hearing about Felix? Turns out he's alive, but he's been going by—"

"Kole," she finished, her voice sounding hallow. Seneca and Linus exchanged confused looks before she continued. "We met briefly. When I was traveling with Noa and Glacier."

His stomach twisted as he tried to find his voice again. "Um, I know we got off on the wrong foot, so if you'd rather I leave—"

"Could I talk to Kole for a minute? Privately?"

Seneca shifted, pulling his hand from Kole. "Yeah, sure. Um, come on, Linus. Let's finish sorting through everything upstairs. Take Cecilia's new supplies too." Linus hoisted up boxes from the floor, and they vanished around the corner. The creak of every step signaled their distance until a door shut and silence enveloped the townhouse.

Kole swallowed. "I'm sorry for everything I said to you." He watched Cecilia's eyes go wide with surprise. "And I'm sorry for everything I said about Glacier. I can explain, but it all just feels like horrible excuses that it wasn't my fault. But... I'm honestly to blame because I let myself believe the lies I was told, rather than looking for the truth myself. I understand if you can't find it in yourself to forgive me because I don't think I can forgive myself for what I've done."

She rubbed her arms, stepping forward. He hated the pity taking over her features, twisting that knife of guilt stabbed into his gut. How could he let Myron manipulate him into thinking they'd been taken advantage of by monsters when he'd been so transparent about being one himself? How had he not ever stopped to think for himself? None of these people should forgive him. He didn't deserve it now.

"I should leave."

"Sit," Cecilia said, nodding to the chair at his back. His knees buckled, and he dropped into it as she unwrapped her scarf and tugged off her coat. She took a seat next to him, draping everything over the small, round end table. "Kole, Noa told me about Myron—about how he was manipulative and controlling. And I can imagine he did everything in his power to make you believe what he wanted you to believe—"

"It doesn't make it right. I was wrong, and you should've killed me on the train."

"No. I don't even believe Talon and Lexa deserved to die—or even Ezra. But it was us or them, and Noa made it clear that we had to fight for ourselves because we wouldn't be shown mercy. I also don't think she would've forgiven herself if one of us had to kill you, Kole. She loves you like family, and I think it hurt her that she couldn't convince you to stop for so long. But she never blamed you for it—just herself and Myron."

"It wasn't Noa's fault," Kole said defensively. "I was—"

Cecilia shook her head. "I can't make her believe otherwise. Maybe you can, but I think she'll always blame herself for not convincing the rest of them to follow her instead. I know you regret your actions now, and I'm sorry that you had to live through all of that. I'd rather have you as a friend than an enemy, especially since we're family. I forgive you, Kole."

Kole's throat restricted at her soft, sad smile. The door opened again, pulling Kole out of that pit just long enough for him to tumble back in. The Bellegardian that'd been with her on the train stood in the entry, staring down at him with his hand squeezing the handle.

"Rune, this is my cousin," Cecilia said, her voice ticking up to something a little brighter, though it was still tainted with remorse. "We thought he didn't survive whatever happened to his parents, but he's finally come home. He goes by Kole now." The door slowly closed, and Rune took a step toward them. "Kole," she said, putting a hand on his arm, "this is my fiancé, Rune."

Kole stood, bracing himself for a punch that never came. Instead, he was offered a hand.

"It's nice to meet you, Kole."

49

KING'S REPUBLIC ✧ 2705-02-11

NOA

Noa stretched on her way down the hall and popped open the buttons of her coat. She answered every warm welcome back home with a tired smile and a thank you, quietly wishing she wasn't roaming the half-renovated staff quarter hall. Glacier telling her to go on ahead just made it worse, knowing she wouldn't have anyone to lean against on the way to Nyx's room after the long ride back.

She covered a yawn and tapped on the door, waiting a couple seconds for a reply before she slid it open. "I'm back," she sang, stumbling over to the bed and throwing herself overtop of the gray, perfectly tucked comforter. She breathed in the scent of iris and vanilla while Nyx rolled her eyes from her seat at the desk built into the wall. "Damn, Aiza's perfume is amazing."

"Yeah, yeah," Nyx said. "How was the trip?"

Noa propped herself up on her elbows, kicking her legs in the air. "Well, Glacier's making sure all of Lazarus's books make it to the Caelius family vault for safekeeping right now, and he'd promised to set me up as a new key so that's exciting."

Nyx snorted, shaking her head.

"Other than that, I got my copy of *The Origin of Magic* back. Kole, Malice, and I demolished the Volkov mansion. And I briefly joined Glacier to meet his mother's side of the family, who are all very lovely people that nearly made me cry. Twice."

She picked at the edge of the blanket, thinking of Ryland's firm, gentle hug that made her heart ache. Myra's made her blink it all back while the ideas pressed in on her that *this* had been what she'd been missing. And the warm, welcoming return from the Angelis's make her fake-grumble about being cranky as Mariana continued the hugging trend. There wasn't any need to waste her tears on happiness. Not when she'd saved them all for the one person she'd wanted a proud, congratulating hug from after all she endured.

Myron clearly hadn't gone back to Lazarus's shop after it was all said and done—or if he had, he hadn't touched anything. The sole missing piece had been that damn paperweight she'd nearly glossed over the last time she stood at his desk, unable to crouch at the bloodstain in the hall. This time, she did, hugging her knees like he was still hunched over there, waiting for her return while Astravnians gawked at the movers hauling crates of damaged, repaired, and preserved books in and out.

"Hey," she whispered. "I'm back. Bitches asked for the Sword of Astravny back though, so I don't know how the hell you got it. But you're a crafty old bastard, so it doesn't surprise me." She glanced over her shoulder, down to where Glacier's shadow passed through the hall from the office door and sighed. "I wish you were here. I think you really would've liked him more in person, rather than whatever way you'd seen him before..." She swiped away the first tear, and the next, unable to stop them all. "I guess this is goodbye. I hope you're at rest, but if you're not, you're welcome to join us. I'd hate to leave you here all alone. Though, part of me feels like you've been following me around this whole time, so I doubt I could make you stay put, even if I tried." She sucked in a breath, scrubbing at her face as she stood. "Love you. Stay out of trouble. One of us has to."

The blanket fell from her fingertips, and Noa sighed along with Nyx's soft hum. "Since everything seemed to go so well," Nyx started, shifting in her seat to pull her legs down from the rung under the desk, "how would you feel about Alyvia coming to work up here?"

"Like...?"

"With Jovian. Under me. For palace security and related endeavors. Livius said he's hoping to rest for a while, and since he's being fitted for his brace, he's hoping to involve himself in some work that's a little more physical than sitting in front of a screen all day. Not to mention Alyvia quit her job about a week ago, even after they begged her to come back. She's been giving a lot of statements to the King's Republic government about the shady dealings that went on, but since they still haven't found Delacroix..."

Noa chewed on her lip and chuckled. "I can't imagine someone *wanting* to move somewhere colder, but if it'd help her feel a little safer with a bunch of Mages and a change of scenery, go for it. It's not like I can stop you, remember?"

Nyx smirked, pushing up her glasses. "Glad we're in agreement. How were Kole and Malice during everything? Is Kole still—"

"Deathly quiet? Yes." Noa dropped her cheek into her palm. "He maybe spoke a handful of times, but it was mostly when he was alone with Malice and I. At least he's managing to *look* at Glacier now. Even with apologies and forgiveness, I think he just needs some more time to work through things... He did help us come up with a family name, though. So that's one less thing you can yell at me about." She pointed a finger at her with a grin.

Nyx raised a brow. "I'm waiting."

"Noa, Kole, and Alice *Alexeev.*" Noa waved her hands in front of her in an arch like it was some grand reveal, but Nyx only blinked. "Oh, come on —I like it!"

"You realize you'll maybe keep that family name for less than a year at this rate, right?"

Noa's arms dropped against the edge of the bed. "Yeah, but *they* get to keep it. I think it fits."

"They're not Astravnian."

"They're Amaraian- and Jinwonese-Astravnian. Get over it."

Nyx rolled her eyes. "Fine. I'll get it all buttoned up in the morning, so we can stop dodging all the news outlets. They're getting more and more antsy the longer we stay silent anyway. I should probably schedule a press release or something..."

"Now, onto *your* assignment," Noa said, rubbing her hands together with a grin. "You have any idea what I'm supposed to be doing next—" She held up a finger as Nyx opened her mouth. "*Besides* making public statements, because if you tell me that again, I'll punch you."

Nyx's broke into a sly smirk and reached for her phone. "Okay, fine. You remember how Haneul and I were talking about a guy that usually checked in on the Mind of Jinwon?"

Noa nodded.

"He messaged and friended me on social media."

Noa narrowed her eyes. "I'm... not sure I see where this is going..."

"Just bear with me. Apparently, the last time I saw a guy check in on it, he was... I don't know, forties? Fifties? This guy—" She turned her phone around, holding it out for Noa to see. "Is twenty-seven. Said he was put in charge a couple years ago."

Noa's eyes flicked to his age under the selfie of a guy with styled, black hair decked out in a suit jacket over a large-lettered logo shirt and an earring dangling off one ear. He was winking, posed outside a shrine with a couple girls. "What the fuck is..." Her brows knit together, reading off his name written in both International and a subset of Jinwonese characters, "Chi Eun-Seong in 'charge of'? He looks like a damn womanizing pop star. Isn't what he's doing a little disrespectful?"

"Funny how I was thinking the same thing." Nyx pulled the phone back. "It seems he works for a special division of the Jinwonese government that's undisclosed in public databases, but he has one place listed on his profile..." She scrolled down and tilted the phone to Noa again.

She narrowed her eyes at the words next to the little office icon. "United Council Hall of Avaria... Isn't that in Kingsheart?"

"Yep. Sounds a lot like all those keys we mailed back went straight to some people who've been keeping King's Republic running without a leader for so long. So, if we want you to be officially recognized as the Queen, I'd say we send them a petition and let them make the next move.

Considering our involvement with the liberation of Amarais and the outing of Summoners within Republic's Intelligence Agency, I think we have a pretty good shot of them handing over the metaphorical keys to drive any future threats out of Avaria with King's Republic as your ruling country."

A smirk tugged at the corner of Noa's mouth.

"What do you say, Your Majesty?" Nyx asked with a mischievous glint to her eyes.

"Let's get started."

50

KING'S REPUBLIC ✧ 2705-02-11

HAYDRIEN

Haydrien Chevalier stared past the desk lamp reflected in his office window to the twinkling city lights below, mocking the sky with their multicolored neon hues drowning out the stars. The United Council Hall of Avaria sat among those offenders, it's large letters backlit by LEDs as a single soul unlocked its doors and vanished inside the dim warm glow.

"What a fucking mess," he mumbled, drumming pale fingers against the pleather chair while he leaned into the edge of his desktop.

He kept his back to the room mainly because he couldn't bear to look at the photos there—his parents staring at him from the shelf in the corner and his siblings propped out next to it. A picture-perfect Bellegardian family with those matching black hair and Chevalier-signature gray eyes, save his mother's toffee hue. All dressed and posed in black suits and black dresses—dressed for greatness.

Greatness that Haydrien was told wouldn't happen in his lifetime.

His eyes narrowed on the blue-hued holographic screen obscured by his suited frame in the window. He twisted slightly, casting his sights down to the woman standing on the steps of the Amaraian palace with her hand

intertwined with Glacier Caelius's, both held high. The eerie frame of snow
suspended in the air had left him speechless when he'd seen her on the live
feeds nearly two weeks ago.

And that's when he'd started his tireless search for her name. A week
went by of him weeding out entry after entry of look-alikes left him baffled,
rubbing his temples in his office every night until frustration set in with the
realization that she didn't exist—not legally, anyways. Then he finally came
to the foolishly obvious conclusion that she'd stolen the emblems, further
adding insult to injury with the fact that no one had even realized they'd
been missing. She hadn't sought him out—or been led to him—or *whatever else* would've been a better alternative.

He'd been circumvented, outsmarted, and *played* by those who
should've known. That's what fueled his slow-burning, all-consuming rage
—that and everything else that'd transpired over the past few weeks.

"Who are you?" he whispered, staring into the woman's focused, determined eyes. "What is your game?" His gaze flicked over to Glacier, who
appeared breathless and awestruck on the world's center stage, bringing
Haydrien's final question: "And what's a king doing allowing thieves into
his home?"

Something didn't add up, but he kept running into more questions
than answers.

The muffled chime that rang out through the hallway made him
straighten his tie and sucked in a deep, grounding breath. Even if he didn't
feel like he'd be in control of this interrogation, he could at least pretend
like he was. A light knock at the door signaled his opponent's arrival.
Haydrien pressed his fingertips against the desktop's glass membrane and
pushed down his nerves.

"Come in."

The office door glided open, revealing a tall man with coal hair and
green-hazel eyes behind black-framed, rectangular glasses. Rather than a
suit like Haydrien's, he wore a loose hoodie over a V-neck tee and jeans. His
sworn rival for the past eight years, ever since they met when they were both
twenty-one. Forever locked in a battle of wits that his father and uncle
called him paranoid for.

Tonight would prove that he wasn't.

"Sheamus." The cold greeting didn't appear to faze him with his consistently neutral expression.

"You called for me?"

"Have a seat. You have some explaining to do." Haydrien motioned to the studded pleather barrel chairs, and Sheamus claimed one, leaning back with one knee over the other and his hands in his lap. Haydrien narrowed his eyes at him, tugging at his shirt cuffs under his suit sleeves. "Imagine my surprise when I discovered you've been lying to me, which is a breach of contract, in case you've forgotten—"

"So, would you like for me to pack my things? Send me out to the slaughter after all the trouble we've gone to secure your new weapon? A weapon that you wouldn't have if it weren't for me, I might add."

Every bitter word left a sour taste in Haydrien's mouth. He gritted his teeth, biting back his initial reaction to snap at him. "Did you convince the others to lie too? Because you believe you're untouchable?"

Sheamus actually *smirked*. "Funny how you choose to blame me without considering that we might've come to the decision as a group, but I think a better consideration would be the simple answer of we were *told* not to say anything."

"I don't believe that for a second."

"Then how else would you care to explain none of your fellow council members breathing a single word of it during your festivities a month ago?"

Haydrien stared him down, refusing to admit that he'd been backed into a corner. But Sheamus's glint of amusement had faded away to a fizzle of irritation while he waited for Haydrien's next move.

"Let me make this clear: you are not leaving, and you are going to answer every single one of my questions before I call in your next accomplice." He pointed to the holographic image of the woman. "So, for my first question: who is *she?*"

Sheamus choked back a breath of a laugh. "The Queen."

MORE BY CARA NOX

For an up-to-date list of all of Cara Nox's books visit their website:

caranox.com/books

ACKNOWLEDGMENTS

This book was the reason I decided to join the community of indie authors, so I want to thank each and every one of you who influenced me to dive head-first into this adventure. I almost shelved this first story arc because I knew the odds of getting two book accepted by a traditional publisher were slim. The freedom you all introduced me to was the greatest gift I could've ever imagined.

Melli, Cybil, Katya, and Dominique—thank you for being such wonderful early readers and supporters of these books. I love you all and your feedback means the world.

Phil, Amanda, John, and my sister—thank you all for your little brain children and references that got a chance to appear in this story. I know not all of them got a huge chance to shine, but I'm very grateful for how they helped along my dumb little children.

Of course, I also have to thank you, the reader of this book, for joining me on this adventure. This was originally supposed to be the end of the tale I had planned, but after a couple months away from it, it evolved into something more. I hope you stick around for the rest of Noa and Glacier's journey and fall in love with the rest of the characters that cross their path.

ABOUT THE AUTHOR

Cara Nox is an urban and science fantasy writer, combining their love of magically-inclined chaotic idiots and modern/futuristic tech. They also love mysteries, thrillers, and anything that draws inspiration from stars. Cara works as a web developer by day, holds BA in Japanese Language and Literature they occasionally use to read video game announcements, and resides in Ohio with their younger sister and two black cats.

For more information on all of their books, visit caranox.com.

You can check out some of their newest works-in-progress, bonus content, and serialized stories on Patreon.

instagram.com/_caranox
goodreads.com/_caranox
bookbub.com/authors/cara-nox
patreon.com/caranox

Printed in the USA
CPSIA information can be obtained
at www.ICGtesting.com
LVHW041818170324
774603LV00016B/49/J

9 781960 379108